Fiona McCallum has enjoyed a life of contrasts. She was raised on a cereal and wool farm in rural South Australia and then moved to inner-city Melbourne to study at university as a mature age student. Accidentally starting a writing and editing consultancy saw her mixing in corporate circles in Melbourne and then Sydney. She returned to Adelaide for a slower paced life and to chase her dream of becoming an author – which took nearly a decade full of rejections from agents and publishers to achieve. Fiona now works as a full-time novelist and really is proof dreams can come true. Fiona's stories are heartwarming journeys of self-discovery that draw on her life experiences, love of animals and fascination with the power and support that comes from strong friendships. She is the author of nine Australian bestsellers: *Paycheque*, *Nowhere Else*, *Wattle Creek*, *Saving Grace*, *Time Will Tell*, *Meant To Be*, *Leap of Faith*, *Standing Strong*, and *Finding Hannah*. *Making Peace* is Fiona's tenth novel.

More information about Fiona and her books can be found on her website, www.fionamccallum.com. Fiona can also be followed on Facebook at www.facebook.com/fionamccallum.author.

T0359837

Also by Fiona McCallum

Paycheque
Nowhere Else
Leap of Faith

The Wattle Creek series
Wattle Creek
Standing Strong

The Button Jar series
Saving Grace
Time Will Tell
Meant To Be

Finding Hannah

FIONA McCALLUM

Making Peace

FICTION

First Published 2018
Second Australian Paperback Edition 2019
ISBN 9781489263513

Making Peace
© 2018 by Fiona McCallum
Australian Copyright 2018
New Zealand Copyright 2018

Published by
HQ Fiction
An imprint of Harlequin Enterprises (Australia) Pty Limited (ABN 47 001 180 918), a subsidiary of HarperCollins Publishers Australia Pty Limited (ABN 36 009 913 517)
Level 13, 201 Elizabeth St
SYDNEY NSW 2000
AUSTRALIA

® and TM (apart from those relating to FSC®) are trademarks of Harlequin Enterprises (Australia) Pty Limited or its corporate affiliates. Trademarks indicated with ® are registered in Australia, New Zealand and in other countries.

A catalogue record for this book is available from the National Library of Australia
www.librariesaustralia.nla.gov.au

Printed and bound in Australia by McPherson's Printing Group

Chapter One

From her driveway, Hannah gave her house a last glance and put the car into reverse before she almost chickened out of going to her colleague and friend Caitlin's New Year's Eve fancy-dress party.

Tristan had been gone just over a year and still she hated turning up to places on her own. She also wasn't sure about partying with a group of twenty-somethings, the age of Caitlin and most of her friends. At thirty-two, the age difference wasn't huge, but Hannah wondered if she felt considerably older than her years because of all she'd had to deal with recently.

She'd briefly considered using the newly rescued mother cat, Holly, and her kittens, Lucky and Squeak, as an excuse to cancel. She could tell Caitlin that she had to stay home to look after them. Now they'd found each other, Hannah didn't like being apart from the cats. She knew it was silly, but it was how she felt – they were her little Christmas miracles. Even so, they were not quite precious enough to make her cancel on Caitlin.

Hannah had been pleased when her dear old family friend and neighbour, her 'Auntie' Beth, had turned up and practically insisted on babysitting the cats. Hannah suspected it was more about their cute cuddliness than Beth thinking they needed watching. Once Hannah would have scoffed at the idea. Once, not so long ago, Hannah had scoffed at the idea of pets full stop! But she'd completely underestimated the joy these creatures could bring and the wonderful distraction from one's sadness and pain they offered. In the six days since their surprise arrival the cats had well and truly made themselves at home in Hannah's house and heart. Now it was as if they'd always been there with her fussing over them, nurturing them. If only Tristan was there as well for her to love. She longed to share this with him. While she grieved for him, Hannah also grieved for the lost opportunity of having his child. Their child. She couldn't imagine being with any other man, ever even wanting anyone else. She still missed Tristan and them as a couple so much that the physical pain in her chest sometimes pulled her up short and caused her to gasp – it was as if a jagged ball of sadness was lodged just below her throat. In the beginning it had been there demanding all of her attention. Now she tried to focus on dragging herself back from the tugging melancholy rather than smarting at the pain. Far too often she had found herself wondering if one could die from a broken heart and how long it took. If not, would the pain ever completely leave her?

Hannah bit her lower lip then told herself firmly, 'No tears, or Beth's wonderful makeup will run.' She'd be a complete mess given that Beth had carefully drawn black lines across her cheeks to resemble cat whiskers. Hannah blinked furiously while telling herself it was okay, she could do it; she was stronger than she thought. That was what her friends had been telling her for one year and six days since The Accident on Christmas Day – the day the rug, which was her entire life, had been pulled out from under her. She'd loved Christmas and everything that came with it. Until the police had knocked on her door. Hannah shook the thought aside and wondered about the night ahead.

Thankfully her best friends Sam and her husband Rob were going too, so she could talk to them as Caitlin would no doubt be too busy racing around being the hostess with the mostest to spend much time with her.

While stopped at a set of red traffic lights Hannah heard a honk and looked to her right. In the passenger's side of the car beside her was someone dressed as a lion – she couldn't tell whether they were male or female as their face was covered with a lion mask. Through the open window the lion gave a loud roar, lifted up the end of a tail and swung it around in a circle. Hannah found herself grinning. She wound down her window and said, 'Meow,' and then 'Purrrrr,' as she held up her own black tail, which was on the passenger's seat beside her and still to be attached to her backside. The other four people in the car let out squeals, whoops and cheers. She couldn't see what they were dressed as or if they were in costumes at all.

'See you there, Hannah!' the lion shouted as the lights turned green and the driver, clearly less distracted than Hannah, sped off. She recognised the voice as that of Caitlin's friend Chloe. The three of them worked at the same company, but in different areas. Caitlin and Chloe were very entertaining when they got together, especially on the dance floor and while doing karaoke duets. Hannah changed lanes and pulled in behind the silver hatchback, now feeling much better about turning up alone.

Despite having to park in the next street over, Hannah arrived at Caitlin's apartment at the same time as Chloe and her boyfriend, who was dressed as a hunter on safari.

'Isn't this fun? I love dressing up!' Chloe said, flicking the tail she held.

'Yes, it is fun,' Hannah said.

Hannah didn't know the other three people with them – a couple dressed as the king and queen of hearts and a young court jester. They nodded and said hello, then Chloe and her friends skipped up the path ahead of her without further ado.

'Yay, you came!' Caitlin pulled Hannah into a tight hug.

'I said I would.'

'I know, but it's New Year's Eve, so you never know what's going to happen. I'm so excited you made the effort to dress up, too. You look really cute as a cat.'

'Thanks. You look great.'

'I'm a bee.'

'I can tell.'

Caitlin had had a few drinks or perhaps she was just high on all the excitement. 'I invited Jasmine, because she's so lovely and so much fun, but I didn't think they'd come. It would have been weird to have one of the partners from work here – one of the big bosses. It's a pity Craig's her husband. Not that he isn't lovely too. But …'

'I know what you mean. It's okay. It's nice that you thought to invite them and I'm sure they would have really appreciated it, especially Jasmine. But you're right, it might have been a little weird for you and Chloe and me. They're actually in Sydney with Jasmine's family.'

Hannah smiled as she thought about what a dear and treasured friend Jasmine, her boss's wife, had become this past year. Craig too, but to a lesser extent – no, different, Hannah corrected herself. She thought the world of him, it was just that their relationship was different, having been forged on a professional standing.

'Okay. Hey, let me introduce you to a few people. Hey, Nate,' Caitlin said, grabbing the arm of a guy walking past. Hannah guessed he was dressed as a surfer – Hawaiian shirt, board shorts, zinc cream across his nose, sunglasses on his head. 'Nate, this is Hannah. Hannah and I work together – well, sort of. Nate's an old friend from high-school days.'

'Good to meet you, Hannah,' Nate said, holding his hand out. 'Hey, you're familiar, have we met before?'

'Maybe with Caitlin sometime? But no, I don't think so.'

'Chloe's around here somewhere,' Caitlin said, looking about.

'Yes, I saw her. We sort of arrived together,' Hannah said.

'I'm going to get a drink. Can I get you something?' Nate asked. 'Saucer of milk perhaps?'

'Very funny,' Hannah said and grinned. 'Thanks, but I'm fine. Anyway, I'm driving.'

'There is plenty of water and non-alcoholic stuff,' Caitlin said.

'Have you heard from Sam?' Hannah asked Caitlin when Nate had wandered off.

'I haven't seen her yet, but as far as I know she and Rob are still coming. So, how's the jetlag?' Caitlin asked, having to raise her voice as someone suddenly cranked up the music.

'Horrible.' Hannah had to practically shout for Caitlin to hear her. 'How long does it last?'

'As long as it lasts,' Caitlin said with a shrug. 'Sorry, I'm no help,' she added, and laughed. 'I still can't believe it was your first flight ever and that you went all the way to New York. All by yourself, too.' Suddenly there was a loud crashing sound. 'Oh god, here we go. I'd better see that they're not trashing the place,' Caitlin said. 'Mingle,' she commanded with a wave of her hand as she rushed away.

Hannah checked her phone and shot off a text to Sam:

At Caitlin's, where are you guys? Xx

She was pleased to get an immediate response, but her heart sank when she read the message:

Sorry, not going to make it. Have a good night. Xx

Hannah texted back:

Are you okay? Xx
Yeah. Just too tired and have a headache. Xx

Hannah replied in an effort at cheerfulness:

Okay. Take good care of yourself. See you next year! ☺ *Xx*

She put her phone away and took a deep breath. She was here now and to leave before midnight struck would be too rude. She may as well attempt to make the best of it and enjoy herself. Starting with seeing what other fabulous costumes people were wearing. At least fancy dress made for easy conversation starters with total strangers.

Before too long Hannah found herself dragged by Caitlin and Chloe into a small corner by the window reserved for karaoke and dancing. After belting out a few songs and enjoying some dancing, made awkward by the tight space, Hannah stood back and waited for midnight while watching all the drunkenness and shenanigans going on around her. Standing there she felt a little old and out of place, but at least she wouldn't have a hangover to deal with later.

Finally the countdown had been shouted and everyone was hugging and kissing their significant other or the person standing beside them. It was a free-for-all that tugged painfully at Hannah's heart as she allowed herself to be man-handled by a perfect stranger dressed as a corn on the cob. She'd only just managed to turn her head in time to avoid the young man's ardent kiss.

'Thank you. Happy New Year,' she said to him politely as she gently extracted herself from his drunken clutches.

When the cheering, whistling, popping of party poppers and squealing of horns had finally ended, Hannah felt decidedly weary. She went to find Caitlin to say goodbye.

'Are you heading off?'

'Yes. Thanks, it's been lovely, but I'm exhausted,' she said, hugging her friend.

'Thanks so much for coming. I know it's not easy to … you know …'

At that moment the young man dressed as a surfer appeared beside them. *What was his name?* He put his face close to Hannah's – too close for her comfort. He reeked of alcohol and a sourness she detected as the aftermath of vomit. *Urgh*. She concentrated on swallowing and trying not to dry retch, and got ready to put her hands up in case his swaying sent him falling against her chest.

'I know,' he said, loudly and pointed at her.

'Yes, I'm a cat,' Hannah said, trying to sound light and cheerful. 'And you're a cool surfer dude. Great costume.'

'Not what, who,' he said.

'Sorry?' she said.

'You're Hannah Ainsley.'

Yes, that's my name, don't wear it out, Hannah thought, but stayed silent while wondering where this was going.

'Yes, Nate, you met Hannah earlier,' Caitlin said, 'I introduced you, silly. Remember?'

Hannah wanted to finish saying goodbye and walk away. This person was clearly drunk and drunk people had a tendency to be argumentative and talk nonsense. But she didn't want to antagonise him.

'You're *the* Hannah Ainsley,' Nate continued.

'Yes, she's one of a kind,' Caitlin said with a slightly nervous laugh. 'And she is leaving now. Excuse us.'

But the young man blocked their way, and what he said next froze the smile on Hannah's lips.

'How do you feel about the man who killed your family getting off scot-free?' he slurred. 'At least the truck company has to answer for their dodgy maintenance practices. Someone should pay, shouldn't they?'

Suddenly, despite the loud music, the only sound Hannah could hear was the whooshing in her ears. She felt trapped. She looked at Caitlin who had her mouth open but also seemed frozen.

'I don't know anything about it,' Hannah finally managed to stammer.

'Are you going to the court case? Can I …?'

'I don't know anything about any court case.'

'I find that hard to believe. Surely …'

'Nate, what would be the bloody point of Hannah knowing?' Caitlin said, clearly gathering her senses. 'Proving the brakes were faulty and laying blame isn't going to bring anyone back. Nothing is, is it, you arsehole! And the driver was badly injured, so he didn't exactly get off scot-free, did he? You want to be a journalist, how 'bout you get all the information and your facts straight. And have some compassion while you're at it,' she added, practically spitting on the startled young man. 'Come on, Hannah,' she said, grabbing her friend's hand and all but dragging her outside.

'God, I'm so sorry about that. Bloody wannabe parasite. I'm fuming,' Caitlin said when they were standing on the pathway.

'Let it go. Don't worry about it. I'm fine. Really. You go back to your guests.'

'Are you sure? Again, I am so, so sorry.'

'You have nothing to apologise for, Caitlin. Thanks for a fun night,' Hannah said, forcing herself to smile.

'Well, happy New Year,' Caitlin said with a slightly helpless shrug. 'And you do look really cute as a cat.'

'Thanks. And you look really cute as a bee.'

'Even if I have lost my wings ...' Caitlin said, and pouted.

Hannah hurried back to her car while wondering if it was normal that she hadn't followed the case surrounding the car crash that had claimed her entire family. Many people probably thought it was strange. But she didn't care about anyone else's opinion, hers was the only one that mattered in this. This was her life and she could make her own decisions. She'd had to deal with her grief as best she could. Shutting it all out had made sense at the time. It still did, one year and one week on, didn't it? Yes. Hannah walked forward with a lighter tread. Just like Caitlin said, knowing all the details wouldn't bring them back.

Chapter Two

As Hannah unlocked the door she wondered if Auntie Beth was still there keeping an eye on the cats, or if she'd gone back across the road to her own house. She took care to be quiet, just in case, and tiptoed into the lounge room, which was lit gently by the lamp in the corner. Beth wasn't in here. Hannah thought about taking a seat on the couch. She was weary, but didn't feel ready to sleep. She tried to tell herself it was the lingering jetlag and not the conversation with Nate – which had churned through her mind the whole way home – that had her so on edge. She knew the words or opinion of someone who was drunk and didn't know her at all shouldn't bother her, but she still felt unsettled from the encounter. She paused with a hand on the back of the couch and firmly told herself she was going to put it aside and not let it start the New Year off on a sour note. *It will be a good year.* Last year had been one largely of treading water and trying not to drown. This year she'd start properly swimming again. Again! She almost laughed. Hannah had always enjoyed her life, her job, but it couldn't be said she was actually striving. She didn't have an ambitious bone in her body, well, perhaps except to be content and be a good wife and friend – and, she'd hoped one day, mother. Until the hope of that had been snatched away.

Poor, darling Tristan. *Damn*, she thought, *don't go there.*

She straightened up, turned and made her way down the hall. Peering into the spare room, she smiled at seeing Beth on the bed, curled on her side, and Holly pressed into a ball against her stomach. Sensing Hannah's presence, the cat opened her eyes, yawned, stood and stretched. Hannah thought she looked a little sheepish.

'*Yes, sprung, you little minx,*' she said to herself, smiling. Seeing Holly made her feel warm and happy. The cat jumped off the bed and came over and rubbed against her leg. 'Yes, darling little thing, I missed you too,' she whispered, picking her up and hugging the cat to her chest as Holly nuzzled her chin and began purring loudly.

'Ah, there you are,' Beth said, looking up at Hannah with sleepy eyes. She sat up. 'Did you have fun?'

'I thought you might have gone home.'

'Miss Holly here wouldn't let me. I think I may have been converted into a cat person.'

'You and me both,' Hannah said and kissed the cat gently on the head. Holly responded by giving Hannah's nose a quick lick.

'Do you want to head straight home or would you like a cuppa, Auntie Beth? I'm not tired enough to go to bed yet. And you had better go and check on your kittens, missy,' she said as she put Holly down on the floor.

'A cuppa would be lovely, dear, thank you,' Beth said, getting up and giving the bed covers a quick smoothing down. 'Oh, and happy New Year,' she said, wrapping an arm around Hannah as they made their way to the kitchen.

'And you,' Hannah said. 'I wonder what's in store for us this time around.'

'Good things,' Beth said sagely.

'Yes. Only good things.' Hannah hoped she hadn't just jinxed the year – or that annoying Nate person, for that matter, had – not that she was all that superstitious. Though, she couldn't say she didn't believe in serendipity and kismet – look how she'd rushed home from New York and was there in time to save Holly and her kittens. And she really did have the feeling that Holly had saved her as much as the other way around.

Hannah thrived on being helpful, it's what made her so good at her job as executive personal assistant. But after a year of feeling consumed by her grief, being constantly asked how she was and scrutinised by well-meaning friends and colleagues all the time, Hannah loved her life suddenly being consumed by Holly and her kittens. She often shook her head with wonder at how, literally overnight, she'd gone from someone who would never have entertained the thought of having a pet, let alone in the house, to welcoming a cat sleeping on her bed. Not to mention digging the poo out of the litter tray using the little scooper without batting an eye. Once she probably would have gagged.

'I still can't believe you're suddenly a cat person,' Beth said, settling on a stool at the kitchen bench.

'Spooky. I was just having that exact thought.'

'She certainly is a lovely cat. And those two kittens, well … just scrummy,' said Beth. 'I'm actually erring towards not getting another dog and becoming a cat lady instead.'

'Really? Do you think you'll go to the RSPCA to start looking tomorrow – er today, later?'

'No, I'll wait a bit longer on account of the heat – they're forecasting a few scorchers. But I've definitely decided it's time to have some furry company again.'

'That's great.' Hannah thought she probably should offer Beth one of the kittens, but couldn't make herself say the words. They were tiny now, but how would it be having three full-sized cats, two boisterous toddlers to keep track of? Cats were untrainable, weren't they? *Oh well, it'll be entertaining, if nothing else*, she silently conceded.

'I'm leaning towards a cat or two at the moment – kittens or adult, I don't mind. They say animals should choose you, not the other way around, so I think it best to go and see what cats and dogs are on offer at the shelter. Maybe I'll get one of each. Ah, thank you,' Beth said as Hannah placed a mug of tea in front of her. 'So, tell me about this party. I have to say it again, you do look very cute dressed as a cat,' Beth said, grinning.

Hannah looked down herself. 'Oh, I'd forgotten about that. Thanks.'

'The party …?' Beth prompted after a few moments.

'Well, Sam wasn't there. She sent a text to say she wouldn't make it after all.'

'Oh, that's disappointing. I hope she's okay?'

'She said she had a headache. I'm a little worried about her. I think she's worrying too much about the market next week. When we were at uni she'd get stressed about assignments, but nothing like this. I keep telling her how good the things she's made are – and she's managed to put together a great variety. She really is very talented. I'm not just saying that.'

'I can't wait to see her work.'

'She's suddenly desperate to make a career out of her art and I'm afraid she's hoping for too much from the market stall and putting too much pressure on herself. It's a good quality event and well known, but I think the shoppers will be mainly tourists having a wander rather than serious art collectors. She's always been quite laidback and not so focussed on the money side, but suddenly … Oh, I don't know …'

'You're really worried about her, aren't you? Do you think something's happened?'

'It's just a feeling. She hasn't said anything, but something seems different. Not quite right.'

'Perhaps she's anxious about the twins starting school this year?'

'Who knows? I just wish she'd talk to me. Once upon a time she would have and we'd have analysed it until the cows came home.'

'If something's up, she'll confide in you when she's ready.'

'Hmm. I can't help thinking that burying herself in her work is an avoidance tactic, though I know she's working to get as much stock done for the stall as she can. Oh, I don't know, Auntie Beth,' Hannah said with a sigh, 'I just can't shake the feeling that something is wrong and I want to help.'

'There are so many stories right throughout history of how complex creative people are and how they're often plagued with self-doubt. They can suffer exhilarating highs one moment and excruciating lows the next. I guess that's why you hear of so many talented, clever people turning to drugs and alcohol or becoming reclusive,' Beth said. 'Without a creative bone in my body, I really don't know. At least Sam knows she can rely on you. I am very keen to visit her stall since she's been so coy about it all.'

'Yes. I'd have been worried she might not have anything to sell if I hadn't seen for myself. She's been very productive.'

'Good. I can't wait. But right now I'd better go and get some sleep,' Beth said, putting a hand over her mouth as she yawned.

'God, it's nearly three,' Hannah said, peering at her watch and beginning to yawn herself. 'I'm so sorry to keep you up so late.'

'I'm not here against my will, dear. Anyway, I never sleep for more than a few hours at a time these days.'

'What do you have planned for the first day of the year?'

'Edna mentioned a movie or two – it sounds like it's going to be good weather for sitting in an air-conditioned cinema. How about you?'

'I'm not sure. If I don't get an invitation to go to the beach with Sam and Rob and the boys I think I'll try to invite myself over and check if she's really okay. And see what else needs doing for next weekend.'

'Good idea. Let me know if there's anything I can help with.'

'Thanks. And thanks again for staying over with the kitties,' Hannah said, as they made their way to the front door.

'No problem. Any time. I can see why you find them so hard to leave.'

'Yes, well, we're all going to have to toughen up – I'm back at work in a fortnight. The kittens will probably be climbing the curtains and driving me nuts by then and I'll be happy to go to the office.'

'Oh yes, fun times ahead. Good night. Sleep well,' Beth said, drawing Hannah into a hug.

'And you.'

Beth waved as she crossed the street and made her way up the path. Hannah went inside and closed the door on the balmy early morning and sounds of the shrieking crickets and cicadas.

Chapter Three

Hannah was surprised to find Sam still in her pyjamas when she opened the door to Hannah at around noon.

'Hi, happy New Year,' Hannah said.

'And you.'

Hannah was further surprised when Sam just stood there. Normally they would be enjoying a warm, generous hug.

'Are you okay?' Hannah asked.

'Yeah, just having a quiet day while Rob and the boys are out.'

'Oh. Would you rather I left you to it?'

'No. God, sorry. Here I am standing here all vacant. Come in,' Sam said, stepping aside.

Hannah wrapped her arms around her friend as she entered and was again a little surprised at Sam's brief, half-hearted hug in return.

'I missed you last night at Caitlin's,' Hannah said as she followed Sam down to the kitchen.

'Yeah, sorry about that. I'm just so tired at the moment. Coffee?'

'Yes, please. Have you been burning the midnight oil in a creative frenzy?'

'Sort of. I've got a few more things done.'

'Are you feeling okay about it all?'

'Well, thanks to you we'll be organised on the day. So, how are the cats, newly crowned cat lady?'

'Good. Oh, Sammy, I love them so much. It's like there was a big piece of my life missing before and I didn't even realise it.' Hannah felt herself grinning widely. She found she smiled whenever she talked about Holly and the kittens.

'That's great. I'm so pleased for you. Here you go,' Sam said, putting two mugs on the table before returning to the kitchen and retrieving a plastic container from the bench.

'The boys insisted we make cupcakes yesterday. Don't worry, it's a packet mix, so completely edible. But you'll have to excuse the overzealous use of icing and sprinkles.'

'Very cute.'

Hannah looked at her friend and tried to stop herself from frowning. Something really was not quite right with Sam. Usually they would have had a barrage of back and forth banter and jokes about the brightly coloured cupcakes until they were in fits of laughter. Instead, Sam was quiet, morose. There were dark circles under her eyes too.

'Yum,' Hannah said, after unwrapping a cake and taking a bite. 'Mmm.'

'Is everything okay, Sam?' Hannah asked, when she'd finished her mouthful and Sam was still just staring at the cakes with her hands wrapped around her mug.

''Course. Just tired.'

'Why? What's going on? Anything I can help with?'

'Not really. You know, just the usual – on top of the market stall.'

'Don't worry too much about it. I know it'll work out. As you said, we've got the logistics sorted. Just as long as you've got plenty of pieces to sell, and you had quite a few the other day. Unless you've had a creative meltdown and smashed everything?' She smiled at Sam, hoping she'd take the cue and say something funny. Anything to lighten the awkward mood.

'No, but I am starting to think everything I've done is crap.'

'Well, stop it. Right now. What I've seen is great. And, no, I'm not just saying that.'

'Tell me about last night. What did you end up going as?'

'A black cat. Remember, I told you? I looked very cute according to Auntie Beth – and Caitlin and everyone else.'

'Did Beth go?'

'No. She stayed at my place and babysat the kitty-pies.'

'Oh. Right.'

It was clear Sam's mind was elsewhere, so Hannah stayed silent and concentrated on her cake and coffee. She didn't want to talk about the party, anyway, because if she did she'd invariably mention the incident as she was leaving. She was trying to forget it had happened at all. Besides, she was here because she was concerned about Sam.

Oh, Sammy, what's wrong?' Hannah asked silently. *I'm your best friend. I might not be able to help, but it couldn't hurt to tell me. After all you've done for me this past year.* She was almost on the verge of tears and thought Sam might be too. But she knew Sam; if she didn't want to talk about something there was no getting it out of her. Sam could be stubborn and proud to a fault, but Hannah was often awed by her discipline and strength.

'So, the boys are off at the beach?'

'Yes. Can you believe Olly and Ethan start school in a few weeks? Where does the time go?' Sam said.

'No idea. It's nuts. How are you feeling about it – sad?' *Perhaps that's it.* Hannah felt bad that she didn't already know how her friend was feeling about this milestone. They'd talked about Hannah's trip and the upcoming market stall since Hannah had come back from New York, but not this.

'I don't know, to be honest. I think I'm too busy and tired to really think about it. It might be nice to have some more quiet time to focus on my art, but I'll probably miss them like crazy and not be able to concentrate – sit here pining and stuffing my face, watching the clock until it's time to go and collect the little monsters,' Sam said with a hint of a smile.

There you are. There's my friend. 'I'm sure that feeling will soon wear off and you'll be able to settle into work.'

'Yeah. God, remember that time I left them sitting in their capsules in the supermarket trolley?'

'You were a new mum, sleep deprived.'

'Exactly. It could easily happen again – I'll leave the little darlings standing there until I realise there are two less mouths to feed at dinner time.'

'Aren't you sleeping? Is there something going on?' Hannah persisted, knowing full well Sam might just snap at her to stop fishing and leave her alone. It was a risk she was prepared to take.

'No, I'm fine,' Sam said, waving a hand dismissively. 'Though, I'm not sure I know what a good night's sleep is any more.'

'Well, maybe you'll feel better once the market is over and done with and has been a huge success.'

'It's only a market, Hann, imagine what a basket case I'd be if it was a real opportunity.'

'It is a *real* opportunity, Sam. You never know who'll wander past. That's the point.'

'Come on, Hann, it isn't really. I know it as well as you do. I haven't completely lost my mind.'

'You still want to do it, don't you?'

'I've committed, Hann, if I don't do it Tabatha will lose her stall. I couldn't let her down like that.'

'Maybe we could find someone else to do it.'

'At this late notice? Yeah, right. I'm fine. Sorry I'm being a sad sack. I'm a bit all over the place. It'll be fine. *I'll* be fine.'

'Okay. But it's only a market stall. It's not worth putting your health at risk.'

'I know. And thanks. But, seriously, Hann, if I can't handle that, what hope do I have of carving out a career as an artist?'

'Please don't doubt yourself. You're very talented. You just need a gallery to take you on and look after the business side of things.'

'Look, Hann, thanks for coming over, but I'm really tired. I'm going to try and have a nap before the boys get back,' Sam suddenly said, pushing her mug aside and getting up.

'Oh. Okay. Yes, good idea. I'll leave you to it,' Hannah said, shocked, leaping to her feet.

They hugged at the door, but again it was stilted and a little awkward. Hannah got into her car feeling hurt, frustrated and sad.

On the drive home Hannah fought back tears and ran through worst-case scenarios of what could be wrong with her friend. *Get a grip, Hannah. Whatever it is, it's Sam's story. It's not about me until she chooses to share,* she told herself firmly as she waited at the red traffic lights. *Please don't be sick, Sammy,* she was saying over and over as she pulled into her driveway.

Inside she plonked herself on the lounge, and then smiled when Holly hopped up onto her lap and began rubbing against her chest.

'Oh, you're a sight for sore eyes, as my dear mum would say, Holly girl,' she said and let the tears flow.

After she'd stopped crying and sat stroking Holly's fur for a few moments, it struck Hannah that, really, if Sam was seriously ill – with cancer or something – Rob would have told her if Sam couldn't. *Yes, so whatever is going on, it's not that serious*, she concluded. And with that thought she felt much better.

Chapter Four

'There. It looks great,' Hannah said, standing back to survey their stall at the Sunday Arts Centre Market at Southbank.

'Yes, it does,' Jasmine agreed.

'Thank you so much,' Sam said, putting one arm around Hannah and the other around Jasmine. 'I couldn't have done this without you both. Fingers crossed these things sell.'

'If they don't, it won't be because of the quality,' Jasmine said. 'You really are very talented, Sam, and in so many different media. It's incredible.'

'Yes. And it won't be because the prices are too high, either,' Hannah said. 'I still think you're selling yourself short.'

'I agree, but Sam is the one who has to be comfortable with the prices,' Jasmine said.

'Thanks, Jasmine. Hannah's been giving me a hard time. I just don't want to seem too full of myself.'

'I don't think you could ever seem like that, but I do understand where you're coming from,' Jasmine said.

Lined up were some gorgeous whimsical ceramic female figurines, all white but with one brightly coloured accessory – a hat, scarf, pair of gloves, an umbrella or parasol. Hannah had been stunned to see the little figures when Sam unpacked them and carefully placed them on the table.

'You didn't show me these! They're incredible!' she cried.

'Really? Do you think so?' Sam said, blushing.

'Breathtaking,' Jasmine said, and promptly put a red dot on the one wearing a bright pink, broad-brimmed hat at an angle. 'If someone comes along and desperately wants it I'll reluctantly give it up,' she said.

'Then I'll make you another one,' Sam said.

'Where do you get them fired? Do you own your own kiln?' Jasmine asked.

'I wish,' Sam said. 'Maybe one day. No, I just use a kiln-hiring service. There are plenty of places around that do it – they charge by the piece or you can hire a whole kiln.'

'How interesting. I had no idea.'

'The main problem is getting the pieces there and back again without them breaking. That's why I'd love to have my own kiln, but at the moment I'm not sure how much I'm going to do with ceramics. And, of course, there is the cost involved. Anyway, it's no problem to get them done.'

Hannah wanted to buy a collection of the figurines. They'd make a wonderful display to signify their friendship group. She could see tiny similarities to each of her friends in the pieces. The one with the glasses with thick multi-coloured frames could be Caitlin, the one with the walking stick Beth, et cetera. But Hannah didn't want Sam thinking it was a pity purchase. Although she hadn't said anything to Jasmine when she bought one, so hopefully she was on the up. Hannah also loved every one of the small,

framed linocuts – a series of well-known Melbourne landmarks
Sam said she'd done especially for the tourists who would hopefully be stopping by.

Sam had brought along plenty of wrapping paper and cardboard
and sticky tape – things Hannah hadn't even considered. She'd
been too busy taking care of their personal comfort – bringing
fold-up chairs, a large umbrella to protect them from the summer
sun, thermoses of tea and coffee, sandwiches, buttered date loaf
and plenty of water and sunscreen. She was determined to make
it a day to enjoy as well as hopefully a profitable one for Sam.
Thankfully the weather was going to be kind.

They had just settled back in their deck chairs with mugs
of coffee when their first potential customer appeared. Jasmine
immediately stood up.

'Let me know if I can help with anything,' she said.

'Thanks. I quite like this,' the woman said, pointing to a
small abstract painting. 'But I'm looking for something larger – I
have an enormous blank wall just begging for something big and
bright.'

'Oh, well, I'm sure Sam could do a piece for you on commission,' she said, looking back at Sam with raised, eyebrows.

'Of course,' Sam said, taking the cue to get up and join Jasmine.

'This is the artist, Sam Barrow,' Jasmine said proudly. Sam put
her hand out to the lady who shook it.

'It's very nice to meet you. You have a lot of lovely pieces.'

'Thank you. I'd be very happy to do something especially for
you and your space.'

'Do you have a business card?'

'Oh no. I don't, but I'll be here next week.'

Hannah made a mental note to remind Sam to organise cards
during the week.

'Here, put your details on the back of one of mine, Sam,' Jasmine said, producing a card and a pen from her bag.

'Thanks,' the woman said, accepting the card. 'Ooh, you're an interior designer. Good to know. Thanks again, I'll think about it,' she said to Sam before moving away.

'Damn, I didn't even think about business cards,' Sam said. 'Thanks for that, Jas. You should have told her more about what you do while you were at it.'

'Sam, today is about you, not me. Why don't we quickly do up some handwritten cards – you can sacrifice a few pages from your sketchbook, can't you?'

'You could also add some colour and details to each one, like swirls maybe,' Hannah suggested. 'Oh, what would I know? You're the artist,' she added with a smile.

'Okay,' Sam said, and set to work.

'You know what we should do?' Jasmine said an hour later when Sam had produced a dozen handmade business cards and they'd watched plenty of people wander up, pause to check out their wares, and then keep walking.

'What?' Sam and Hannah said at once.

'Set Sam up as a working visual display.'

'A what?' Hannah asked.

'You know, artist at work – an exhibit – sketching, painting, carving her lino. It would create interest and draw people in.'

'Oh, now that's a good idea,' Hannah said. 'What do you think, Sam?'

'It's a bit gimmicky, isn't it? And I'm not sure I want people watching me while I work.'

'It's okay, it was only a suggestion,' Jasmine said. 'But you do realise we were looking over your shoulder and commenting on your business cards the whole time you were drawing them, don't you?'

'Oh. You're right, you were. But strangers would be different.'

'As I said, it's up to you. Maybe think about it for next week.'

'You could do one of your clever cartoon sketches,' Hannah said. 'They're awesome. Keep you from getting bored, too.'

Now they were all set up, there wasn't much to do but sit. Hannah was starting to feel that it was going to be a long day. Especially if everyone kept wandering past without making a purchase or even asking questions. She wondered if it was because they were at the start of the line of stalls and she hoped that people would come back after seeing what else was on offer at the other end.

They tried to look eager and attentive, but it was becoming harder as time went on. So they settled back in their chairs and watched the flow of tourists.

'Do you have any of these with black accessories?' a woman asked, pointing to the ceramic figures.

'No, sorry,' Sam said. 'But I could make you one – here, take one of my cards.'

'Okay. Thanks.' She pocketed the card with little interest and moved on.

'They're fun, that's the point, that's why they're colourful!' Sam hissed at Hannah and Jasmine as she sat back down. 'I know we live in Melbourne where black is practically compulsory, but still!'

'You can't please everyone all of the time,' Jasmine said kindly.

'I know, it's frustrating,' Hannah said, offering her a sympathetic grimace. Hannah wondered how she'd feel in the same position. She wasn't creative, so didn't really know what it was like to put your heart and soul into making something. Though she did cook. And she'd be hurt if someone openly criticised her food.

Unfortunately, a big part of being an artist seemed to be holding an already fragile soul out for all to tear apart. Poor Sam. Hannah knew that being an artist wasn't a choice – according to Sam, creativity forced itself into you and you could never escape it for too long. You could try, but it was fruitless, so you may as well accept it. As melodramatic as it sounded, Hannah knew not to laugh – she'd known Sam for a long time, watched the ups and downs, the self-doubt.

She opened up the newspaper she'd brought in case there wasn't enough action.

'Are you making Pikachu? Cool.' Hannah looked up. A little boy was practically standing over a slightly startled Sam who, she now noticed, had created some sort of creature out of yellow putty.

'Sorry?' Sam asked.

'That,' the kid said, pointing. 'It's Pikachu, isn't it?'

'What or who is Pikachu?' Sam asked.

'A Pokémon. Duh,' he added quietly. 'This,' the kid said, thrusting out a smartphone towards Sam.

Since when do children under ten have smartphones? Hannah thought.

'Oh. Well, I see it does look a little like it. Hang on a second.' Sam quickly fashioned a jagged tail, added two little patches of red to the cheeks, made a mouth, added some black to the ears and eyes, and then held it out to the little boy. 'How's that?'

'Oh, wow. Look, Mum, I found one. A *real* real one.'

A woman walked up to them. 'Oh dear, you're not bothering these ladies are you, Jacob?'

'But, Muuum, she's got Pikachu. Look.'

The woman looked at Sam. 'How much is it?'

'Oh, it's not for sale. I was just fiddling about.'

The little boy was crestfallen. His chin wobbled.

'I tell you what. If you promise to be very careful with it, I'll let you take it home,' Sam said. 'But it's delicate, so you'll have to be very gentle. Do you think you can do that?'

'Oh, yes. I promise.'

'It's putty,' Sam said to the boy's mother. 'Pop it in the oven at one-ten for thirty minutes and then it'll be fine. Until then it can still be worked so will be a bit fragile.'

'Okay. Thanks very much. Are you sure you don't want anything for it?'

'No, that's fine. I was just playing around, really.'

'Well, thank you. You've made him very happy. God, this Pokémon Go craze!' she said, shaking her head. 'I thought it had stopped, but apparently not in our house. Honestly, it's doing my head in. And I warn you, you might have a tribe of little boys and girls next week all wanting them once they see what Jacob has. Do you mind if I take your card? I really love some of your pieces, but money's a little tight at the moment. Though your prices are very reasonable,' she added, looking embarrassed.

'It's okay, I completely understand,' Sam said, offering her a warm smile. 'Let's just put Pikachu in this paper bag to stay safe. Here you are, Jacob,' Sam said, holding out the handles of the bag to the child.

'What do you say?' Jacob's mother said.

'Thank you,' Jacob said, beaming. He then held out a hand to Sam.

'You're very welcome, young man,' Sam said, returning his handshake.

The day dragged on with only a few sales.

'I can't believe the most excited customer was a little boy and a freebie blob of putty. If it wasn't so depressing it would be funny,' Sam said. 'I'm really sorry it's been a wasted day for you both.'

'It wasn't a wasted day,' Jasmine said. 'It's been a lovely day relaxing with friends and people-watching, which is never boring.'

'What about all the people who took your cards and showed an interest? They might buy next week or get in touch,' Hannah said.

'And you kept Tabatha's stall secure for her, remember,' Jasmine said. 'So you've done a good deed too.'

'I guess I just expected more,' Sam said.

'Well, there's your problem,' Jasmine said gently. 'Expectations lead to disappointment. Next week come along just to have a day out with us and nothing more.'

'Are you coming back again next week? Really?' Sam asked.

'Of course. This is a reconnaissance mission for my business down the track, too. It's good for me to see what approach might work for me.'

*

'See what I mean about Sam?' Hannah said after they'd dropped Sam off at her house and unloaded all of her things into the garage.

'Yes, she doesn't seem like the happy-go-lucky person who was at your birthday party just last month,' Jasmine said.

'I've tried to get her to talk to me, but she uses the markets as an excuse.'

'Perhaps that's all it really is about. It's a bit of pressure to create on demand and put your babies out on display for the first time. And then only to have people criticise – not openly today, but when someone says they'd rather it was a different colour or a little more like this and a little less like that, it is being critical of her work.'

'I hope you're right.'

'Unfortunately, if Sam wants to be a career artist she'll have to find a way to deal with it.'

'Hmm. In some ways I sort of hope there's something else going on because, like you say, it doesn't bode well for a budding professional artist.'

'You'll have to let it go, too, Hannah. Just leave her be. She knows where you are if she needs you. But you have to be careful not to make it about you and your need to solve someone else's problems. Sorry, that sounds a little harsh.'

'No, you're absolutely right. I've been telling myself the same thing – it's not about me.'

'But it's hard to turn it off, right?'

'Yes.'

'That's why we love you, Hannah – because you care so much. So, changing the subject completely, are you looking forward to going back to work soon? Craig's missing you like crazy.'

'That's nice. Yes and no, actually. I'll miss the cats, but I am starting to get a little bored. There's not a weed in sight in the garden!'

'Ha-ha, says the girl who hates gardening.'

'Exactly. See what I mean? Organising the market has been good. If there's anything I can do to help you, let me know.'

'Careful what you offer – I'll have you setting up the books and filing system for my non-existent business in no time!'

'I'd be happy to. Seriously. I love that sort of thing – crazy, I know,' Hannah said.

'Horses for courses and all that.'

'Okay. So, I'll see you on Wednesday for lunch?'

'Absolutely.'

'Thanks again so much for coming along today.'

'The pleasure was all mine,' Jasmine said. 'I really did enjoy it.'

They hugged in the car and then Jasmine waved as she made her way to her door and Hannah backed out of the driveway. Jasmine was right, she had to leave Sam be. She knew Hannah was there and could be counted on for anything – they'd been best friends for over ten years. Whatever was up with Sam, she wasn't ready to share and might never be. Hannah had to respect that.

Chapter Five

On Monday morning Hannah's doorbell rang. She briefly considered ignoring it; she was sitting cross-legged on the lounge-room floor playing with Holly and the kittens, who were starting to get more mobile and adventurous.

'Back in a sec. Stay here,' she told the cats as she got up with a sigh.

'Rob. Hi.' Hannah peered around him to see if Sam and the boys were waiting in the car.

'It's just me,' he said, running a hand through his sandy hair. 'Do you have a minute? Can I come in?' The formality of his words and the flat tone in his voice caused Hannah to study him carefully. He looked terrible – drawn and pasty, dark shadows under his eyes, like he hadn't slept properly in ages. A bit like Sam, really. And there again was the hand through his hair – a clear sign he was troubled about something and out of his depth. The last time she'd seen that was Christmas Day before last – the day of The Accident.

'Of course. Come in,' she said, snapping back to the present and standing aside to let him in.

She was surprised and disappointed when he went straight through to the lounge room. Whatever was going on was clearly too serious for sitting at the informal kitchen bench. Holly and the kittens were nowhere in sight – probably hiding behind the curtains that went almost to the carpet.

'Can I get you anything?' Hannah asked, hovering as Rob settled himself on one of the couches. *Something stronger, brandy perhaps?*

'No, thanks. Please, Hann, I really just need to talk to you.'

Hannah felt the blood drain from her face as she sat down on the couch opposite with the coffee table between them. *Oh god, this is serious. He's sick. Or Sam is. Oh god.*

'What's going on?' she prompted when he sat silent, running his hand through his hair.

'Sam hasn't told you, has she?'

'Told me what? We've been talking about her art a lot, but nothing personal – if that's what you mean – no.' *Of course that's what he means!* They were both stalling.

Rob's shoulders slumped and he let out a sigh, along with the words, 'We've split up.'

'What? You've what?' Hannah felt her mouth drop open and whatever blood was still in her face drained away. 'When? Today, just now? How?' *How! Come on, Hannah pull yourself together.*

'I've left her. It's a bit of a long story.'

'I've got all day, Rob. You'd better start from the start.' *Oh god, poor Sam.*

'Okay. But I want to say from the outset that I will completely understand if you end up hating me and never want to speak to me again. You're Sam's friend, you've known her for years, so naturally you're going to side with her and ...'

'Rob,' Hannah interrupted. *Just bloody tell me.*

'I'm just saying,' he said, holding up his palms as if in surrender. 'There will be no hard feelings. I'm here because I'm worried about Sam.'

'Just tell me, Rob.'

'I'm gay, Hannah. I've been ...'

'You're what?' Hannah was so shocked she almost laughed. A montage of images of him with his arm around Sam, nuzzling her neck, snogging under the fake mistletoe over the doorframe, being the perfect attentive husband flashed through her mind. 'Don't be ridiculous! Oh god, where did that come from. Sorry I didn't mean ... Are you sure? I mean ...' *Shut up Hannah!* Hannah closed her mouth.

'I know it's a shock. Yes, I'm sure it's hard to believe. And, yes, I'm sure. I think I've known all along, but I've wrestled with it for a long time – pushed it aside, tried to pretend I'm not. I love Sam and the boys so much. The last thing I'd want to do is hurt them and turn their lives upside down. And despite all the progress towards acceptance of homosexuality, coming out is not a great career move in the world of finance.'

Yet you have. Or have you? Hannah blinked. Her head whirled. 'But you've got two children, and a wife,' she blurted. She knew she was sounding like an ignorant, naïve child, but she couldn't help it. 'So, hang on, if you've always known and pretended to be ...?'

'Normal?' he prompted, with slightly raised eyebrows.

'Heterosexual,' she corrected. 'Why now? What happened? Have you met someone?'

'No. Yes. Not really. But that's not really it. Last year losing Tris was devastating to me – he was one of my best friends, Hannah. It served as a pretty serious wakeup call and made me start to question everything.'

Hannah felt terrible. Rob had always been rock solid, right through everything. Had his feelings been ignored because he'd been so stoic and hadn't been in floods of tears publicly? Because he was a man and they were expected to keep it together, at least on the outside?

'It's been so hard, Hannah, seeing his life end in an instant and … Oh god, I'm sorry. I know it's nothing like what you went through, what you're still going through.'

'Rob, what you're feeling, your suffering is no less relevant than mine.'

'Thanks for saying that. You're incredible.'

'Well, I don't know about that, but I do know you've had a big chunk taken out of your heart and your life too. I'm just so sorry I clearly haven't been there enough for you.'

'Jesus, Hann, I think you've had enough on your own plate. Please don't …'

God, everything really is connected, isn't it? Everything, Hannah thought.

'I just can't live a lie anymore. In some ways I owe it to Tris to make the most of my life.'

Oh god, Sammy, my darling Sammy. Hannah felt the sudden urge to grab her keys and run from the house, get in her car and go to Sam. But she had to hear Rob out if she was to help her friend through what was going to be a major upheaval and trauma.

'I'm moving to Singapore tomorrow. To set up the office there for the company.'

'Singapore? Tomorrow?'

'Yes. Permanently. It'll be easier for Sam to deal with all this and move on if I'm not living in the next suburb.'

'But what about the boys?'

'Yes, well, they're the hardest part of all of this. I adore them.'

Hannah felt the anger rise up in her. *You'll miss the boys more than Sam – my best friend? God, Sammy, why didn't you tell me any of this?*

'So, how long has Sam known you're leaving?'

'Christmas morning was the anniversary, as you know only too well, and I woke up realising I just couldn't do it for another day. She knew I was going to be splitting my time between Melbourne and Singapore. I think until Christmas Day I thought I could just carry on. But as I watched the boys opening their presents, I knew I wasn't doing the right thing by them if I continued to live a lie.'

So, instead you'd rather implode their lives, you selfish arse. Sam was just starting to get enough confidence to put herself out there and make a serious go of being an artist and you have to pull the rug out from under her? You bastard. But Hannah wouldn't say any of this because while she felt devastated for her best friend, she couldn't help but be in awe of a person who had denied himself all these years. She couldn't understand what it was to be different and face up to a society that didn't want to accept you, but she could imagine it took a lot of courage.

A thought suddenly struck her. Christmas Day. The day she'd unexpectedly come back from New York, the day of the flood when Sam had turned up to check that Hannah's house and Beth's were okay. But, actually, had she really? Hannah remembered the strange look of surprise on Sam's face – like she'd been sprung doing something she shouldn't have been doing. Now she wouldn't mind betting Sam had been hoping to escape to Hannah's empty house and process Rob's news, have a good cry out of sight, especially away from the twins. Oh, poor, poor Sammy. God, she was so strong. She didn't break down and tell Hannah everything that day. Instead she had feigned her happiness at seeing her and focussed on Hannah and her trip.

'I'll still pay the mortgage and everything. Nothing will change there,' Rob said.

Hannah looked up, his words again jolting her from her thoughts.

Nothing will change? Are you serious? You stupid, stupid man. But still she couldn't be angry. She could be frustrated and disappointed, yes, but she couldn't be truly angry with Rob. Dear, sweet Rob whom she loved very much. Why shouldn't he follow his heart and be true to himself? Why should he be tied to a life that was a lie?

'I'm so sorry, Hann. I love her, I really do, but …' He put his face in his hands as the tears began to flow.

Hannah leapt up and went to him. She gathered him in her arms and held him as he sobbed, big shoulder-shuddering, heart-wrenching sobs.

'Oh, Rob,' she said, as the tears slowly began to subside.

'Hannah, I didn't want to hurt anyone.'

'I know.' And she did know. After her Tristan, Rob was one of the kindest, sweetest souls she'd ever known.

'Oh!' Rob said as Holly hopped up beside him and wormed her way under his arms and into his lap where, after a bit of kneading, she curled up. Rob looked up with surprise at Hannah.

Hannah smiled and shrugged. 'She's a sweetie. She's trying to help. Holly, you look after Rob while I get us something to drink,' she said, grateful for the distraction and opportunity to escape. They both needed to calm down.

When Hannah came back into the lounge room with two mugs of sweet milky tea she saw Holly and the kittens in Rob's lap enjoying his attention. He must have lifted the little ones up as they were too small to get up on their own. He looked up and smiled faintly. It brought a tear to Hannah's eye to think how perceptive of human emotions Holly was and how she came to be in Hannah's home in the first place.

'Here you are,' she said, passing Rob one of the mugs.

'Thanks.'

They sat in silence for a few moments. Hannah took comfort in the warmth of the tea in her mouth and through her hands around the mug.

'I'm really worried about Sam,' Rob said, and put his mug down on the coffee table. He stroked Holly and the kittens as they clambered all over him. Hannah stayed silent in the hope he'd continue. 'She's in complete denial that our marriage is over. I think she's telling herself that I'll be back and forth on weekends.'

'But what about the boys?'

'Of course I'll be back to see them. I'm not sure how often. But Sam doesn't seem to be grasping the full situation – the fact I'm gay.'

'Maybe she's just processing it more slowly. She has been very focussed on her art.'

'And that won't change, I hope. My support won't change.' He looked up at Hannah. 'I don't know what to do.'

'Me neither,' Hannah said. 'I knew there was something going on, something wrong with Sam – she just hasn't been herself since I got back. I guess I'm relieved she doesn't have cancer or something serious like that. Or you. Or the boys.' *Though, a broken heart and a broken marriage are still pretty serious.*

'I'm worried that when I go and she can't pretend any more she'll fall apart. She's going to need you, Hann.'

Of course she's going to fall apart. And, yes, I will be there, as she was for me.

'I just wish she wasn't so damned independent,' Hannah said.

'You're going to have to make her confide in you, Hann.' Hannah could see that ending badly. But she'd have to do something.

'Here are my details in Singapore, if you need me. And, Hann, I hope you and I will still be friends. But if not, I will understand. Your duty is to Sam now,' he said sadly. 'I'd better go. I still have some things to organise.' He picked Holly up and deposited her gently on the couch and then did the same with the kittens before standing up.

Hannah stood and walked out with him feeling shocked, dazed and confused. At the door she opened her arms and they hugged each other tightly. As she waved to Rob when he drove off her tears began to fall. She'd probably just lost one of her best friends. She knew that. He was right, her loyalty and duty were to Sam.

Hannah closed the door on the world and went and sat back into the lounge room. She picked the gorgeous little kittens up from the couch, held them to her and nuzzled them as she sat down. She felt bereft and helpless, the likes of which she hadn't felt since the police had left after delivering the news that she'd lost her husband and both parents in a crash with a truck. Holly peered up at her, with seemingly a look of concern etched on her little face.

'Oh, Holly,' Hannah cried, and began sobbing. 'What a mess. Thank goodness I have you.'

Chapter Six

Hannah felt nervous as she drove to Sam's house. Rob would be on a plane by now. Would Sam crave some company, finally confide in her best friend, or would she be angry at the intrusion? But despite her fear, Hannah would not talk herself out of this and go back home.

Her finger trembled as she reached out to push the doorbell. She heard the chime echo in the hall and then the scrambling of dog claws and little footsteps on the floorboards. Hannah took a deep breath. The door opened a crack and two faces appeared in the gap.

'Hello, Olly and Ethan.'

'Hello, Auntie Hannah,' the six-year-old twins said in unison.

'How are you?'

Before they had a chance to answer, she heard Sam's voice boom, 'Don't you dare let the dogs out!'

At that moment two pale chestnut cocker spaniels pushed into the gap. Hannah reached down and just managed to grab their collars in time.

'No you don't,' she said, as she held the wriggling dogs.

'Phew,' said Ethan.

'Thanks, Auntie Hann,' Oliver said, and opened the door wide. Hannah dragged the dogs inside and made sure the front door was closed before letting go of the collars. 'You're a lifesaver,' Oliver said in what Hannah liked to call his old-man voice. From early on both boys had seemed to have very old souls, Oliver a little more so. 'Mum's a bit grumpy.'

'Dad's gone to swing a paw. We'll visit sometime,' Ethan said nonchalantly as Hannah silently corrected, *Singapore.*

'Would you like a hot drink?' Oliver asked with big wide eyes.

'Yes, please, that would be lovely,' Hannah said, and followed the boys and the dogs down to the kitchen as she wondered where Sam was and if she was happy about the boys opening the front door. Oh well, too late now. At least she wasn't a stranger.

'Sorry, but you'll have to do it yourself, we're not allowed to touch the kettle,' Oliver said, settling himself on a stool at the bench.

'Could you make me a Milo too, please? Mummy said she would but then she forgot,' Ethan said, settling at the bench beside his brother.

'I certainly can,' Hannah said, smiling at their cute innocence. She might have laughed at their precociousness if she were there under different circumstances.

She noticed two bowls with a spoon in each on the bench beside the sink. There were no tell-tale signs of milk or cereal. 'Have you guys had breakfast?' she asked.

'Not yet,' Ethan said.

'Mum's a bit all over the place,' Oliver explained sagely. Hannah really nearly did laugh then.

'And busy,' Ethan added.

'Are you hungry?'

'A little,' Oliver said.

'I'm okay,' Ethan said. 'But I really would like a Milo.'

'Right. Got it.' *Yes, get on with it, Hannah!* 'Oliver, would you like a Milo too?'

'Yes, please.'

'Hang on, you'd really better start with breakfast.' Hannah grabbed a box of cereal from the pantry and tipped some into each bowl. She poured in the milk and handed a bowl to each of the boys.

'Oh, hi,' Sam said, wandering in. 'I thought I heard you. Thanks for sorting out breakfast, and making sure the dogs didn't get out.' Hannah was pleased to see Sam was not in her dressing gown – she took it as a good sign. Although, for all she knew, Sam could be in the same clothes as yesterday.

'No worries. They want Milos – if you're okay with that?'

'Yeah, whatever,' Sam said, waving a hand. 'Sorry, I'm a bit ...'

'All over the place,' both boys chimed in together.

'Yes, I am. So don't test me,' Sam warned.

Hannah smiled to herself at the scene before her. She loved being a part of it. If only the little family had stayed intact. How much did the boys know? Hannah wondered. Sam might seem laidback on some fronts, but she was very protective of her darling boys when it came to subjecting them to deep and meaningful adult conversation.

'Tea or coffee?' Sam asked, joining Hannah at the bench where she was making the boys' drinks.

'Tea, thanks. Still one large scoop of Milo and half milk and half water?' Hannah asked.

'Yep. And then zap for thirty seconds in the microwave.'

'Here you are,' Hannah said, a minute later when she put the plastic mugs down in front of the boys.

'Now, boys, put your empty bowls in the sink,' Sam said, 'and have a big sip of your drinks, then take them carefully out into the back garden and play with Oofy and Inky. Mummy needs to talk to Auntie Hannah.'

'Okay.' Hannah and Sam watched as the boys, followed by the dogs, made their way outside.

'And please close the door behind you.'

Hannah smiled at the well-trained children as they stacked their bowls, then Oliver handed Ethan his cup to hold and proceeded to carefully close the glass bi-fold door behind them. Oliver sat down on the step outside and Ethan handed him both mugs before sitting down beside his brother and accepting one of the cups. *Priceless.*

'Thank god it's a good day in the behaviour department,' Sam said.

'How is everything otherwise?' Hannah asked, taking the opportunity.

'Fine. I'm trying to get as much done as I can for the next market.'

'Sam, I know about Rob leaving.' Hannah could hold it in no longer.

'I know. He told me he called in to see you.'

'And …?'

'And what? He's gone to Singapore, and I'm here with the kids.'

'Sam, it's me, your best friend who you can talk to about anything. Talk to me.'

'There's not a lot to say, Hann. It is what it is,' Sam said with a shrug.

Hannah was wide-eyed. 'How can you be so calm? I'd probably be throwing things.'

'Well, I guess I kind of am — I've done some pretty wild abstracts. Do you want to see?'

'Sure.'

Hannah got up and followed Sam out to the garage off the kitchen, part of which served as her studio. As she went, she reminded herself for the umpteenth time that this was about Sam and not her. Sam was free to react how she wished – or not. But Hannah was worried. This wasn't normal, was it? Sam turned on the light.

'Gosh, you *have* been busy,' Hannah said, looking at several small colourful abstracts placed along the benchtop, leaning against the walls. Far from looking like the work of an angry or depressed artist, they were the epitome of joy in their pinks, purples, oranges and greens. 'They're lovely.'

'Hey, look at these,' Sam said, lifting a sheet and revealing a baking tray with around a dozen colourful cartoon-looking figures on it. 'I thought I might as well try and cash in on the silly Pokémon Go craze if it's still going. So very post-modern of me. Anyway, making them has kept me sane,' she added quietly.

Hannah didn't know what post-modern meant, but was relieved to hear some reality lurking below the surface. 'Whatever it takes, huh?' she said gently.

'Thirty bucks a pop. What do you think?'

'I think they're great. Perhaps a bit cheap, though, with all the work you've put in. Hopefully the boy from last week will bring all his classmates along.'

'Yeah. Fingers crossed. You want to know what the scary thing about them is?'

'What's that?'

'Apparently it's our age group who are really into it – the kids who played with the original Pokémons all grown up.'

'Golly, you *have* been doing your research. I never knew anything about them.'

'No, me neither. Oh, look. I've even made the explanatory cards as Jasmine suggested. So clever of her. No more answering the same dumb questions over and over. I'll just pretend I'm mute and point to a card,' Sam said with an attempt at a grin.

Hannah read the one for the old lady figurines with the bright accessories:

'Ageing gracefully.'
A timeless keepsake to add a touch of elegance and a splash of colour
  to any contemporary or traditional space.
Handmade glazed ceramic
By Samantha Barrow
Commissions available.

'Perfect,' she said. 'You've been very busy. I just hope you're not overdoing it.'

'Hann, I'm okay. Really.'

'Great, because I'd be a basket case.'

'No you wouldn't. You weren't all last year. Anyway, I have to keep it together for the boys. I don't have a choice,' she said with a weary sigh.

'You're allowed to be sad, cry, and talk it over.'

'Honestly, Hann, if I start I might never stop – crying or talking about it. And it's not going to stop Rob being gay or my marriage being over. Right now I'm just so grateful for having the market and my art to focus on. Otherwise, I might fall apart.'

'That would be okay, you know.'

'My first priority is the boys. It's traumatic enough their dad leaving.'

'So what have you told them?'

'That Daddy has gone to work overseas and we won't see him for a long time. What else could I say? They're fine. At the moment their worlds revolve around Milo and fart jokes.'

'Hmm.' Sam was right. Hannah wouldn't have a clue how she'd do it differently. Sam was their mother. Only she could know exactly how to handle it.

'I just have to tackle each step that comes up, as it does. It's all I can think to do. And keep the kids' home life and routine as normal as I can. Thankfully, having a creative mother means normal is a pretty fluid concept.'

'There's my clever, witty friend,' Hannah said, putting an arm around Sam's shoulder.

'I know Rob thinks I'm in denial. That's what he told you, right?' Hannah nodded.

'I'm not. I'm in shock and disbelief. But I'm fully aware it's over and I'm now alone to raise the boys. He'll occasionally swan in laden with gifts and appear the best dad on the planet for a few hours until he leaves again and life resumes. I know how it works and it's not something I ever wanted. But as I said, it is what it is. I think that's becoming my mantra.'

'Aren't you angry at all?'

'Not really. Sad, disappointed, frustrated. But I love him and I always will. I don't blame him for wanting, needing, to see what else is out there – be true to himself.'

'Did you ever realise he was gay? Surely there were signs.'

'Probably, but I'm still not seeing them. Maybe it's too soon.'

'Hmm. Like you said, you're probably in shock. I'm so impressed with how calm you are.'

'Well, I've got a focus. That's a huge help. In a few weeks I could well crumble.'

'If you do, I will be there to help pick up the pieces.'

'Thanks.'

They stood in silence and stared at the bold abstracts.

'I'm hoping he'll realise he's wrong and come back to us,' Sam whispered. 'Maybe I *am* in denial.'

'You be whatever you want or need to be and I'll be whatever and wherever you want and need me to be, Sammy,' Hannah whispered back.

They slipped back into silence for a few more moments before Sam spoke again.

'Oh, I need to show you the artwork for the business cards I've ordered online – they should be here Thursday. Come on.'

Chapter Seven

Hannah had just fed Holly her tuna and chicken neck and was about to open a tin of tomato soup for an easy early Saturday dinner for herself when her mobile phone rang.

'Hi, Sam, how's things?'

'Hann, can you come over?'

'Are you or the boys hurt – do I need to phone an ambulance?'

'No, it's nothing like that. Oh, Hann,' Sam said, and began to cry.

'I'll be right there.'

'Thanks,' Sam said with a sniff.

'Sorry, Holly girl, change of plans,' Hannah said, squatting down and patting the cat. She glanced at the cats' bowls to make sure there was plenty of water and dry food and then popped the can of soup into her handbag and grabbed another from the pantry. Taking her car and house keys from the bowl on the bench, she headed out – careful to not step on any lurking kittens. They'd recently taken to leaping out from under things and jumping in front of passing feet. But at the front door she paused. Tomorrow was an early start. She might still be at Sam's, depending how things went. She raced through to her bedroom and stuffed a clean set of underwear, a pair of jeans, a top and her electric toothbrush into a bag.

As Hannah drove off she wondered what state she'd find her friend in.

She didn't have a chance to ring the bell before the door opened and Ethan's little face appeared.

'Hello darling, Ethan,' she said, ruffling his hair.

'Hello, Auntie Hann. I need a big cuddle.'

'Of course you do,' she said, putting down her bags and picking him up, trying to ignore how heavy he had become. 'Where's your mum and Olly?' Hann asked against the slightly choking grip the small boy had around her neck.

'In the kitchen. We're having soup for dinner.'

'Goodie. That's what I was going to have,' she said, nuzzling Ethan's neck before kissing it. 'Come on, then, let's go see.'

'I'm so glad you're here, Auntie Hann.'

'Me too, Ethan.'

'I can get down now. Mum says I'm getting too heavy to carry. And I don't feel so well. We're all sick.'

'Oh, that's no good,' she said, gently putting the child down and noticing for the first time just how hot he was. 'You're a big, strong boy now,' she said, squatting down and taking hold of the boy's two hands and looking deep into his eyes. 'Ethan?'

'Yes, Auntie Hann?'

'You know how to use Mummy's phone, don't you?'

'Yes. And the house phone,' he said proudly. 'Olly does too. We've practised calling triple zero – well, not for real, because Mum says that would be very naughty. But we know how to do it.'

'That's great. You're so clever. And you know you can call me if ever you need me, don't you? Whenever. Okay?'

Ethan nodded. And his chin wobbled. And then big fat tears started to roll down his cheeks.

'Oh, darling, what's wrong?' *I know, everything.*

'I miss my daddy. And Mummy's really sad too.'

'I know, darling. I'm sure it will get easier, but for now we all have to be very brave.'

'Like when Uncle Tris and Granny Daph and Grandad Dan died?'

'Yes. Just like that. You were so strong. Can you be strong like that again now, do you think?'

'I can try.'

'Good boy,' Hannah said, hugging him tight while she blinked back the tears gathering in her eyes.

'Now, tell me what sort of soup you're having for dinner,' she said brightly when she released him a few moments later.

'Tomato. But it's out of a can.'

'My favourite,' Hannah said, taking hold of Ethan's hand and walking down the hall. 'Hello, Olly,' she said.

'Hello, Auntie Hannah. I've got bugs.'

'That's no good. Are you too sick for a hug?'

'I don't think so,' he said, holding his arms out wide. Hannah held him tightly for a moment before letting him go.

'Thanks so much for coming,' Sam said, gathering Hannah to her.

'Always.'

'So, what's going on?' Hannah asked gently, holding her friend at arm's length and looking at her. 'Is it more than you all being sick?'

'I can't do it.'

'What?'

'Anything. Take care of the boys, create, do the market, survive without Rob. I can't do it,' she whispered, clearly on the verge of tears. 'I'm trying to be tough for them, but I can't. I'm falling apart, Hannah. I was barely coping before, but now I'm sick and so are the boys. And ...'

'Boys, how would you like soup and toast in bed?'

'Yes, please.'

'Well, off you go and hop into bed. I'll be up soon.'

'There's only one tin – not enough for all of us,' Oliver said.

'I brought two more. I was about to have tomato soup too. Snap. So, go on, off you go. Mummy, have the dogs been fed?' Hannah asked Sam as she noticed the two furry faces up against the glass doors, looking in from outside.

'God. I completely forgot them. They need a scoop each of dry food – it's in the bin in the pantry.'

'I've got it. Go and hop into bed.'

*

Later, with everyone fed including the dogs, the plates collected and stacked in the dishwasher, the kitchen tidy, and a story read to the boys, Hannah joined Sam on her bed.

'God, you're a lifesaver,' Sam said.

'How are you feeling?'

'I'm okay.'

'You can drop the act now. You don't look okay to me.' Sam looked terrible, even worse than when Hannah had arrived. Her cheeks were now inflamed.

'Thanks.'

'What are friends for?'

'Oh, Hann, I'm miserable. I miss him so much.'

Hannah leaned over and wrapped herself around her friend. 'Of course you do.'

'He's never coming back to me as my husband, is he?'

'No, darling, I don't think he is.'

'What am I going to do?'

Hannah stroked Sam's hair as Sam sobbed and Hannah tried not to give into the lump in her throat.

'You're strong, Sam, you'll get through this.'

'I don't know how you did it.'

'I had you. Now you have me. You're not alone, Sammy. You don't need to shoulder all of this yourself.'

Slowly the tears subsided and Sam sat up a little. 'I feel so inadequate.'

'Why? What do you mean?'

'Being so upset. Falling apart.'

'What you're going through is huge.'

'But nothing compared to what you had to deal with.'

'It's not a competition, Sammy,' Hannah said. 'I was a complete basket case for pretty much a whole year. Remember?'

'You were not. Look at me. And you lost your entire family. Rob didn't die, he just left.'

'Which is a really big thing to deal with,' Hannah said thoughtfully.

'Oh god, I'm forever going to be wondering, hoping, aren't I? Oh, Hannah, I still love him so much it hurts.'

'Of course you do. You probably always will.'

'And he loves me too. He rang earlier. Can you believe he still says, *"I love you"*? I couldn't tell him how much it hurt to hear him say that. I'm sure this is all just as hard for him, but in a different way.'

'I'm sure it is.'

'Well, why isn't he here then?'

'You know why, Sammy.'

'God, I so badly want to hate him, but I can't.'

'How is his family taking it?' Rob's family didn't strike Hannah as the most liberal or open-minded of thinkers.

'He hasn't said and I don't want to open that particular can of worms.'

'Hmm.'

'And, no, I haven't told my mother. I'm far from ready to have my failings pointed out to me. God, Hann.'

'Just one step at a time, remember, sweetie. Bite-sized pieces.'

'I can't do the market tomorrow.'

'Of course you can't. Anyway, you're sick – you can't go and breathe germs on people. Jas and I will be fine doing it. Your labels will be a great help, not that it wouldn't be better to have you there in person. But right now you need to look after yourself and the boys. Remember what you told me – concentrate on getting through an hour at a time.'

'Hmm.'

'Maybe getting sick is a sign you're meant to focus on yourselves and not art for a bit.'

'I don't think I believe in signs or the protection of the universe or any of that stuff anymore,' Sam said sadly.

'You're just on shaky ground. Look at how the market stall became available right when you wanted to start getting your name out there.'

'It's not going to help.'

'You don't know that. It's an opportunity. You've always said to look out for opportunities and to take them – that everything happens for a reason. Come on, Sammy, you have to stay positive.'

'Hann, what possible reason could there be for you losing Tristan and your parents and suffering like that?'

'I don't know, Sam.' Hannah had wondered this herself so many times. She'd never shared Sam's conviction of the ways of the universe, but she'd nonetheless wondered if there was anything in it. She'd racked her brain for something bad she'd done to warrant such a karmic response, and come up empty.

'Maybe,' Hannah continued after a few moments of silence, 'sometimes what happens to us is collateral damage. Like our loved ones getting in the way of a lesson or something happening to someone else. Maybe the accident was about the truck driver and his family rather than a lesson for me.'

'God, Hann, how can you be so philosophical? I'm meant to be the airy-fairy one.'

'I don't know. My heart still aches so badly for Tris that I think I might die, and I might feel like that for years. But some good things have come out of it. I can see that now. I know it sounds silly, but I'm so grateful for some of the things I've done that I wouldn't have before – like travelling to New York and especially finding Holly and her kittens. It's made such a difference for me to have someone else to live for, to take care of. I'm just looking for the good. Otherwise my grief might drown me. You taught me that.'

'Did I?'

'Yes. Oh, Sammy, you're so wise and such a wonderful, positive influence. It makes me sad to see you like this. I'm not saying I'm glad that what happened to me happened – never – but if I let myself wallow in it I might be sucked under ...'

'Wallow. Like me, you mean?'

'No, Sammy, I'm not saying that at all. You've been badly let down. The life you thought you were going to live forever has

been shattered. You're allowed to be upset, disappointed, angry –
everything in between. Yes, wallow for a bit. Just don't let it drag
you so deep it consumes you. You have to have faith that it will
get better, easier – that there is still a life out there for you.'

'Promise me you'll tell me when enough's enough?' Sam said.

'Well, I can't know that, only you can. You'll be okay, Sammy,
you just have to believe that.'

'It could be worse.'

'It can always be worse.'

'Maybe the boys will get a second dad and I'll get a stylist,' Sam
said with a wry smile.

'That's the spirit.'

'There's no such thing as a normal family, is there?'

'No. You and the boys and Rob can be whatever you want
to be.'

'I'll be okay, won't I?'

'Yes, you will. And so will the boys.'

'Rob can damn well explain homosexuality to them when the
time comes, though, because I'm not.'

'Okay. Noted. That's probably best.'

They lapsed into silence for a few moments before Sam spoke
again. 'Do you think this has all happened to stop me being an
artist? That's what I'm scared of, Hann.'

'No, I don't. But it might be a sign it's not quite the right time.'

'Everything's connected, isn't it?'

'Well, that's what you've always said. And I'm starting to see it.'

Hannah tried to push the guilt aside. No, not guilt, exactly,
Tristan's death wasn't her fault. Burden. That was what she was
feeling – an overwhelming sense of burden at being at the centre
of suffering. Of course her life had changed significantly and irre-
vocably with such a loss, but it seemed The Accident was proving

life changing for many other people too. It was the butterfly theory or whatever it was called, wasn't it?

These thoughts made her very uneasy. But they also made her a little curious to know now how the truck driver and his network of family and friends had fared.

'Can you stay the night with me?' Sam asked.

'Of course. I brought clothes. I can leave from here in the morning.'

'Good. Thanks for everything.'

'You're welcome. Try and get some sleep.'

As Hannah lay in the darkness unable to sleep, she thought of how similar this night was to that Christmas night a little over a year ago. Thank goodness she'd had Sam with her then. Hannah doubted she was as capable, but she'd do her best to look after Sam.

Chapter Eight

'Now, are you absolutely sure you're going to be okay on your own taking care of the boys?' Hannah said as she and Sam finished loading the car with pieces to sell at the market.

Thankfully Sam said she had got some sleep and was feeling much better, as were the boys who were already up and running around the backyard in their pyjamas, chasing the dogs. Nonetheless, Hannah felt uneasy about leaving them.

'Yes, we'll be fine. Thanks. I'm okay. And as you can see, the boys being sick may have been more about missing their dad and being clingy and not wanting me out of their sight than any actual illness.'

'Okay. Fair enough. But I can always call Caitlin or Joanne to come around. I'm sure they wouldn't mind.'

'I know. Thanks, but I think what we need is a quiet day in, just the three of us. Thanks again for dropping everything and coming around. It really helped.'

'Any time. I'm glad it helped. Remember to keep up with the vitamin C – all of you.'

'Yes, Mum,' Sam said, hugging Hannah. 'Good luck for today, and thanks again.'

'Sammy, you need to stop thanking me. It's my pleasure. You have done the same for me, don't forget.'

'Well, it's just that I really appreciate everything you're doing.'

'I know you do. Now, I'd better get going.'

★

Hannah picked up Jasmine and then Auntie Beth, where she longed to race into her own house and give Holly and Lucky and Squeak a cuddle. She hoped they weren't feeling abandoned.

'Don't worry, dear, they'll be fine,' Beth said as she climbed in with her picnic basket, clearly catching Hannah wistfully gazing across the road. 'I popped in again just before to check on them. They had plenty of food and water. And they can wait until this afternoon for another cuddle.'

'Oh thank you. God, I missed them.'

'Hi, Beth,' said Jasmine.

'Good morning, Jasmine, dear.'

'I love your basket,' Jasmine said.

'Why, thank you. It was a wedding present from my dear Elliott. We have tea, coffee and sandwiches, as ordered. And a jubilee cake for good measure.'

'You're wonderful,' Jasmine said.

'Yes, thank goodness you don't sleep and I can call you any time of the night and you're prepared to get up and cook,' Hannah said.

'It's nice to feel useful. Now, do tell what's going on that means the star of the show can't be with us.'

'Yes, you've been very mysterious, Hannah,' Jasmine said.

'I didn't want to say anything until it was okay with Sam for me to tell you. So, here's what's going on …'

★

'Oh dear, poor Sam,' Beth said when Hannah had finished telling them all about Sam's upheaval.

'Yes, that's huge,' Jasmine said.

'We're not to say anything against Rob – that would really upset her – she still loves him,' Hannah said.

'Of course she does,' Beth said. 'He's a very lovely man who can't be blamed for finally being unable to carry on living a lie. Unfortunately tragedy can shine a light on things that need to change.'

'You're so wise and open-minded,' Jasmine said with awe.

'For an old duck, you mean, dear?' Beth quipped. 'Don't worry,' she added, turning from the front seat to look at Jasmine to reassure her. 'I *am* an old duck. I live under no illusions. You know, there's so much pain in the world these days. I look at you kids and it all seems so serious for you. I'm sure at your age we were all having a lot more fun. Your generation seems to have so many more worries.'

'Hmm. I think you're right,' Jasmine said.

'Anyway, we're going to have fun today,' Beth said.

'Hopefully we'll also make heaps of money and get plenty of recognition for Sam,' Hannah said.

'I vote we put up her prices since we're in charge,' Jasmine said.

'Okay,' said Hannah. 'Well, at least have a good look at them. There's a roll of blank stickers in one of the boxes.'

'I'll be the umpire,' Beth said. 'I can't wait to see what she's done.'

'And I can't wait to see what's new this week,' Jasmine said.

'She's been busy – there's a fantastic variety and plenty to keep us busy. I just hope we won't be lugging it all back home again,' Hannah said.

*

'Oh, Daph,' Beth said, pausing after unwrapping one of the figurines and staring at it.

'Sorry, what was that, Auntie Beth?'

'Doesn't this look just like that hat and wrap your mum wore to Sam's wedding?' Beth said, holding the object up for Hannah to see. 'If I'm not mistaken, it's the exact shade.'

'Oh yes, you're right,' Hannah said, her breath catching.

'Fuchsia – one of her absolute favourite colours,' Beth said. 'Oh my.'

'I remember when she came home after shopping with you for it. She'd had the best day and was so pleased with her outfit,' Hannah said wistfully.

'Can I buy this for you, Hannah, to have as a keepsake?' Beth asked.

'That's lovely of you, Auntie Beth, but I think you should have it. I can see how moved you are. It's clearly a very special memory for you of her.'

'Are you sure?'

'Absolutely.'

'Thank you. I have to admit it has got me by the heartstrings. I remember how Daph traipsed all over the city for weeks looking for the perfect outfit. When she saw the fuchsia, it was love at first sight. She was quite beside herself with excitement.

'I will treasure this,' she said, hugging it to her before re-wrapping it in the bubble wrap, placing it in her handbag and extracting her wallet.

'It's lovely,' Jasmine said, taking Beth's card.

'Yes. It's going to go on my mantelpiece.'

'Sam would give it to you as a gift, you know,' Hannah said.

'I know she would. But she's got to stop doing that sort of thing and start behaving like a proper entrepreneurial artist.'

'Hear, hear,' Hannah said.

'Oh, look, she's done more. How awesome are these?' Jasmine said, holding up one of the Pokémon characters.

'Yes, they're brilliant,' Hannah agreed.

'What are they?' Beth asked. 'Oh, hang on, are they those things on mobile phones that people were chasing in the park? Pokémon Go, isn't it called? Thankfully I think they've calmed down a bit lately.'

'Yes, wow, you're up with the latest,' Jasmine said.

'It's been all over the news and my friend Mavis's granddaughter was showing us over lunch the other day. Clever of Sam to cash in. It's funny how every generation has its fad. In our day it was marbles and knucklebones. Of course everything old is eventually new again, like these Pokémon thing-a-ma-jigs, back from the nineties.'

'See, I told you.' Hannah looked up at hearing the familiar voice and saw the boy from last week standing in front of the collection of Pokémon characters at the front of the table. Five children had crowded around, with their parents standing back a little.

'Cool. Can I look at Nidoran please?' a girl asked.

'Sorry?' Hannah said.

'The one at the back – the purple one,' the boy from last week said with undisguised exasperation, and pointed.

'Sure,' Hannah said, handing it to the girl.

'Be careful, Gem,' a voice called from behind them.

'Mum, can I have it?' the girl asked, holding it up for the woman to see. 'Pleeeease.'

'How much is it?'

'Thirty dollars.' They were the only things Jasmine, Hannah and Beth had thought Sam had priced correctly and not too cheap.

'Oh. Well …'

'I've got that much pocket money at home.'

'Have you now?'

'Pleeeease, Mum.'

'Okay. We'll take it, thank you,' the woman said. 'And I'll take Squirtle – that one,' she said, pointing out the blue and white character and smiling at Hannah.

'Sorry, I'm not the artist, just the hired help, so I'm not up with which one is which,' Hannah said.

'How do you know its name, Mum?' the girl said.

'I just do. I'll give you a history lesson when we get home,' she said with a wink at Hannah and Jasmine.

'Oh. Okay.'

'Isn't it funny how a crowd draws a larger crowd,' Beth said after all twelve of the Pokémon figures had been snapped up and the space around their stall was empty again.

'Isn't it just? No one wants to miss out if something looks interesting to someone else,' Jasmine said.

★

Several times during the day they remarked on how instead of a trickle, shoppers came in bursts.

'At least this week people are actually buying,' Jasmine said. 'And I'm so glad we've got printed business cards to put into the bags with their purchases.'

'I hope you're adding your cards too,' Beth said.

'Only to those who I think might be interested. It's really Sam's day.'

'Fair enough. Though I'm sure she wouldn't mind.'

'I know. Anyway, I'm not really set up yet.'

'Um, ladies, we're nearly out of stock,' Hannah said behind them, checking the storage boxes Sam had packed.

'God, what a contrast to last week,' Jasmine said. 'I hope Sam's able to get more done for our final stall next Sunday.'

'I think we'd better come up with a plan B,' Hannah said.

'Yes, I can't imagine Sam's going to be able to focus on her art. Though some people thrive on chaos and need it in order to create. That's not quite Sam, though, is it?' Beth said.

'No, I'm pretty sure she's better when she's not under pressure,' Hannah said.

'Could you perhaps put together a display of a room in miniature, Jasmine?' Beth said. 'You could show what paint colour on the walls goes with what curtains, wallpaper, cushions, et cetera. To promote your business.'

'I suppose I could. Though, it's a little soon for me to be seriously looking to take on work.'

'Why? What's stopping you?' Beth said.

'I just don't feel quite ready.'

'Ah, maybe you'll never feel quite ready if left to your own devices. Maybe you need to be forced into the deep end,' Beth said.

'Oh, well. I … I'll think about it.'

'Sorry, dear, I didn't mean to sound pushy, it's just that you seem very capable to me. And you have finished your course, haven't you? Speaking of not procrastinating, and changing the subject completely, guess what I did yesterday?'

'What?' Jasmine and Hannah said at the same time.

'Drove out to the RSPCA and adopted two cats,' Beth said proudly.

'How lovely,' Jasmine said.

'Oh, wow,' Hannah said. 'Do you have pictures?'

'Of course I have pictures. What do you take me for – an old lady without any technology?' Beth said, laughing as she took her phone out of her handbag. She scrolled through and then handed it over for Hannah and Jasmine to see the tabby cats.

'Gorgeous kitties,' Hannah said. 'Good on you for taking on adults.'

'Yes. They're beautiful,' Jasmine said.

'I'm not sure about that, Jasmine,' Beth said. 'But it's okay, I know they're plain Janes. That was sort of the point.'

'Sorry?' Hannah said.

'I asked to see the cat who had been there the longest and they took me to this bonded pair – they're brother and sister.'

'Oh, Auntie Beth, bless you. I think I'm going to cry.'

'Well I think they look really sweet. And a little regal, sitting there like that,' Jasmine said.

'So, was it an instant bond?' Hannah asked.

'Not really. They're pretty aloof. It's no wonder they've been there for months and months – they actually turned their backs to me, cheeky devils. I have to admit I love their attitudes – we take no nonsense and play by no one's rules. Silly, but they reminded me of myself a little when I was young.'

'Ooh, there are stories lurking in there that I'd love to hear, Auntie Beth,' Hannah teased. 'But seriously, good for you. I can't believe you agreed to come out with us instead of being at home with them. What are their names?'

'Joseph and Jemima. I thought it best they have the day to themselves to explore and settle in,' Beth said. 'They're four years old, so I'm not going to bother choosing other names for them, not that cats come when they're called, like dogs do, anyway, I'm guessing.'

'Well, I think they're lovely,' Hannah said.

'I agree,' said Jasmine.

'I'm sure they will be once they realise they don't need an attitude with me and I'm not expecting them to be grateful. I don't mind if they're not cuddly, just as long as they're not nasty, and they wouldn't be up for adoption if they were. The staff and volunteers said they can be real sweeties.'

'Oh, I'm so happy for you,' Hannah said, giving Beth a quick hug. 'I can't wait to meet them.'

'Well, dear, it's thanks to your encouragement. I'll be forever grateful for the push.'

'What are you doing?' Hannah asked Jasmine who had her tablet computer out and was positioning it up on a box on the trestle table, with another box behind to prop it up. Hannah had got used to seeing Jasmine on it and thought she was just killing time. Now she seemed to be on a mission of some sort.

'Well, since we've run out of wares to sell, and we've still got an hour or so before we leave, I thought we could do a rolling presentation of what has sold for those walking past. If they see something they like we can write its name or description on the back of a card and they can contact Sam about it.'

'That's clever,' Beth said. 'Thank goodness for all this wonderful technology.'

'Yes, and someone with the foresight to actually use it,' Hannah said. She'd taken a couple of photos with her phone so Sam had a record, but nothing like the careful recording of individual pieces that Jasmine had done.

'No worries,' Jasmine said with a shrug. 'I hope Sam takes decent photos of everything she does and keeps an up-to-date portfolio, too. But if not, she can have these. I'm always taking photos of ideas – which I seem to find everywhere – so it's become a bit of an obsession.'

Hannah made a mental note to ask Sam about her portfolio.

'They are very good photos,' Beth said, now standing in front of the table and watching the screen. 'Sorry, I should get out of the way of potential customers,' she said when she realised people were standing either side of her.

*

'What a great day,' Beth said later when they were back in the car and heading home. 'Thanks very much for including me. I had a ball.'

'Thanks for your company and all the yummy food,' Hannah said.

'Yes, thanks, Beth. Sam should be thrilled with how we've done.'

'I don't think Sam's in the right head space to be thrilled about anything at the moment,' Hannah said.

'No, but at least the huge success today might go some way towards Sam starting to believe in her abilities,' Beth said. 'Those little ladies with their bright accessories were a hit. I'm so glad I bought one early and hid it. I really hope she makes more – they're fantastic.'

'I wonder where her true artistic passion lies?' Jasmine said. 'She seems to be good at everything she turns her hand to.'

'Yes, if only she would believe it,' Hannah said. 'I love Sam, but I can't help thinking not having her there helped.'

They pulled up in front of Jasmine's house and she yawned as she got out. 'Oh, I'm actually quite weary.'

'Well, rest up for next week,' Hannah said cheerily. 'Just one more.'

'We'll meet and discuss it during the week,' Jasmine said.

Hannah knew she should be heading straight to Sam's but after the exhausting day she couldn't deal with the boys and the exuberant dogs just yet. She'd phoned a couple of times and Sam had assured her they were all fine. She'd go over later – or even tomorrow – and drop off everything and tell her the good news. But she was dying to see Holly and her kittens. She felt terrible leaving them for so long, despite Beth assuring her that cats really didn't mind being left to their own devices. But first she was going to meet Joseph and Jemima.

'Right, goodness knows what we're going to find,' Beth said as she unlocked the door. 'They were hiding under the bed when I left,' she explained. 'Just pop the basket down anywhere there, dear,' she instructed Hannah and made her way down the hall.

'Oh, well, don't mind you. Just make yourselves at home,' Beth said from the doorway to her bedroom. She shot Hannah a bemused look and stood aside. The cats were on the bed. Seeing they had company they stretched and then curled back up around each other and closed their eyes again.

'They're lovely,' Hannah said.

'I think we'll leave cuddles for another day and let them be, okay?'

'Yes, they do look very content and settled.'

Chapter Nine

Early Wednesday morning Hannah got ready for work in a daze. She was still a little shocked at how quickly her six weeks of annual leave had come to an end. She hadn't wanted to take time off in the first place and didn't know what she'd do with herself. Now she wondered where the time had gone, especially the weeks since she'd come back from her trip overseas. She'd played with the cats, lunched with friends, helped Sam with the market stalls and read lots of novels. Now she wasn't sure she was ready to go back to her job.

She hadn't missed it as much as she'd initially feared. She'd missed the camaraderie of her workmates, using her brain for more than deciding what meals to cook, and the routine and orderliness. But other than that, there wasn't a whole lot she'd craved. Though what else was there to miss? She was an executive personal assistant in a large, busy firm – it wasn't exactly lifesaving or particularly meaningful when you looked at it like that. But she did love it. Didn't she? *Of course I do*, Hannah thought.

'I'll be fine when I get back into the swing of things, huh, Holly?' she said to the cat curled up on the bed watching her. 'But oh how I'm going to miss you,' she said, bending down and kissing Holly on the top of her head.

Hannah had come a long way in her grief. Of course she still had really down days when she could quite easily have drawn the blinds and spent the day weeping. But she always seemed able to keep herself moving. Her good friends helped her when she might otherwise have collapsed and been consumed by her sorrow. And the best tonic of all was Holly and the kittens. Now she had to leave them – be a grown-up and go back to work.

When she got on the tram and nodded hello in friendly recognition to the regulars she travelled with Hannah started to feel better. She thrived on routine and belonging, and after a little over six weeks it felt great to once again join the masses of worker ants that scurried in and out of the city each day.

As the tram made its way, stopping and starting, rattling and grinding along its tracks, Hannah felt a strong sense of time being all mucked up. It could easily have only been last week she was heading into work, but it also felt a lifetime ago.

'Don't think about it,' Sam had said when Hannah had tried to explain this confusing phenomenon to her. 'All it's going to do is mess with your head. What's the point?'

Fair enough, Hannah had thought, and tried to banish it from her mind. But it had kept creeping back in. Time. It seemed to shift at will. Some things seemed like eons ago one moment and to have just happened the next. And time didn't discriminate between good and bad. Sometimes loving Tristan seemed just last week and sometimes she could barely remember him being present in her life at all.

Work, she thought. *It's good to be back.* She got off the tram by Flinders Street Station and was propelled along as part of the group into the middle of the CBD. It was a beautiful bright cool Melbourne summer morning, except between the grey buildings in the shade, where it became a wind tunnel and the breeze was practically arctic.

It's too nice a day to feel anything but happy, Hannah decided as she left a patch of bright sunshine and stepped into the lift just inside the glossy marble foyer.

'Hey, welcome back,' Caitlin cried, leaping into the lift as the doors were starting to close.

'Hey there. Thanks,' Hannah replied as she was pulled into a hug. They lapsed into silence. There was no need for a hurried catch-up on the latest gossip on their way up to the twenty-sixth floor – they'd seen each other plenty of times recently.

Starting back on a Wednesday felt strange to the routine-obsessed Hannah. Monday mornings had a slower vibe. And here she was feeling that vibe on Wednesday, which was usually more energetic.

'How amazing was Sam's stuff at the market? She's so clever. I love my little abstract – it's in my bedroom,' Caitlin said.

'That's great. She was really chuffed to hear everyone stopped by, and that they bought something.'

'It's a pity she wasn't able to be there to see her success for herself. I hope she's feeling better.'

'She'll be okay. Well, here we are.'

'See you for lunch in the kitchen – 12.30?'

'Yep. Sounds good.'

'Enjoy your morning,' Caitlin said as they left the lift and headed for their respective sides of the office.

'You too.'

'Hannah, you're a sight for sore eyes,' Craig said when she'd put her handbag away in the cupboard and appeared at the glass door to his office.

'Good morning.' While Hannah had been regularly having lunch and catching up with Jasmine, she hadn't seen Craig at all in six weeks. It was good to see his warm, friendly face. He had become a treasured, trusted friend during the past year – more than merely being her supportive boss. She really was blessed to have so many wonderful, caring people in her life.

'Anything I need to know, boss?' she asked him.

'There should be a hand-over note on your desk or in your inbox. Though I wouldn't be surprised if there isn't one. Other than that, no, I don't think so. Just a normal day as far as I can tell. Welcome back,' he added.

'Thanks,' Hannah said, returning his beaming smile.

She sat down at her desk and took an inventory of how she was feeling. Good. Okay. She logged into her computer and got to work.

An hour later she'd consumed the first of her two daily coffees and gone through her inbox, deleting most of what she found. She was just about to begin a more enjoyable task – correcting and formatting a large document – when she paused to look at the items strategically placed around her desk. She didn't suffer OCD, but she did like everything in its place. Everything looked just as it had always been. And suddenly it all felt wrong. She felt restless. She moved each object around and sat back to consider the changes. Yes, better. Her restlessness eased and she got back to work.

★

On the tram home that evening, Hannah pondered her day. She'd reached the end of her to-do list – a feat that usually made her practically skip out the door. Today she felt good about it, but not to the extent she usually did. Something was different. *It's your first day back. You're just not quite in the groove yet. That's all.*

Hannah forgot all about it when she opened her front door to find Holly and the kittens sitting upright in a little group as if waiting for her.

'My own little welcoming committee. What could be better than that?' she said, kneeling down to cuddle them. She smiled when she spotted the toys strewn along the hallway. They'd clearly occupied themselves during the day.

Hannah's phone began ringing and she fished it out of her handbag. 'Hi, Jas, how are you?'

'Hi, how was your first day? Craig is very pleased to have you back in charge. And I'm pleased not to have to listen to all his complaints about the latest temp and how she is not as good as you.'

'You never said he didn't like the temp.'

'Temps, darling, plural. He went through at least three. I certainly wasn't going to have you feeling guilty, especially when it wasn't even your choice to take time off. So, how was it?'

'Good.'

'Personally, I couldn't think of anything worse, but each to their own.'

'What, working for your husband or being cooped up in an office all day?' Hannah asked with a laugh.

'Both. But don't you dare tell him that. So it really was okay? I can be the soul of discretion if necessary, remember?'

'It was fine. I missed the cats, but it was great to feel needed at a more intellectual level. And you know how I crave my routine.'

'That's good to hear. I was a little concerned you might be feeling differently about it after being away so long. A fish out of water, maybe.'

'Hmm. I'm fine.' Hannah couldn't tell Jasmine the whole truth because she hadn't worked it out for herself yet. 'Restless' was the best word she'd come up with. She envied Sam and Jasmine their passions, their callings. She'd discovered a whole new love of reading the past year and could while away hours – sometimes a whole day – with a book. It was the same with sitting and playing with the cats. But they weren't exactly things to occupy her week after week, year after year, or a means of making money. While she'd ended up very well off financially from the inheritances, she still needed to work at least part-time. She'd conceded plenty of times that to enjoy your job was enough, and not everyone can have a great passion to pursue. She made a difference to Craig and the company as a whole. Also, she had needed the normality and stability that came with her job when everything around her was shifting, imploding. She didn't like how she was starting to question if she needed more, if she was really being fulfilled. She could do her job practically with her eyes closed. And she enjoyed feeling so highly valued. So why didn't that feel like enough now when she'd always been so grateful for everything about her job? *You just haven't settled back in yet. That's all,* she told herself again.

'So, how are you? What's going on?' Hannah said, forcing her attention back to the phone call.

'Good news. We're off the hook.'

'Sorry?'

'The market this Sunday. My friend Tabatha rang. Her mother is doing better than expected so she's coming back a week early.'

'Oh. That's great. I think.' Hannah felt the slightest wave of disappointment. She'd enjoyed being a part of it and helping Sam. 'Probably best.'

'I think so. I'm not sure if I should be telling you this, but Sam rang me this morning. She was freaking out because she hasn't been able to coerce the creative juices to flow.'

'Oh.'

'Hannah, don't feel left out. She just didn't want to distract you on your first day back. She was in a bit of a state. I checked on her just before and she's feeling a little better. Still not creating, but at least not worrying about it quite so much.'

Oh, Jasmine could read her so well. Hannah did feel left out. *It's not about you*, she reminded herself yet again. Sam needed to do what was right for Sam. Deciding not to contact Hannah was out of consideration, not spitefulness. *You're being over-sensitive, get a grip.*

'I'm glad she felt she could call you.'

'Me too. She's going through a big thing. It will take her ages and she'll need all of her friends.'

'Hmm,' Hannah said, as she remembered her own situation. It had been important to have different friends to call on for support at different times and for different things, and not wear out the welcome or risk breaking a friendship. She'd thought she and Sam were strong enough to survive anything – especially after last year – but Hannah wasn't creative and Jasmine was. Perhaps there were some things she couldn't understand and help Sam with that Jasmine could. She was just being a little insecure because she was feeling so unsettled herself.

'Do you want to do anything together on Sunday, then? I have to drop the eftpos machine off to Tabatha first thing, but I'll be free after that. Perhaps a movie or two?'

'Can I let you know on Saturday? I'm still trying to get my head around being back at work.'

'Sure. No problem. I completely understand. Give the cats some cuddles from me. See you soon.'

'Will do. Yes, see you soon. And, thanks so much for the call.'

Chapter Ten

Hannah felt sluggish on Monday morning. She'd had a quiet, restful weekend catching up with Sam on Saturday and Jasmine on Sunday. It wasn't as if there was something else she craved to do – well, except perhaps curling up with the cats and a book – and it wasn't that there was anything particular at work that was putting her off. She tried to tell herself that perhaps she was coming down with something. The simple truth, she thought sadly, was that after all these years she'd finally succumbed to Monday-itis. Her feet were heavy as she stepped up into the tram. *One foot in front of the other*, she encouraged herself.

As it headed up Richmond Road with the city looming large in front of her, Hannah started to feel so low that she wondered if she really had caught something. She briefly considered getting off and going home. But she knew deep down she wasn't sick – well, not in that way. There was something wrong with her, but she didn't know what it was. Monday-itis was not a condition worthy of a sick day – thought plenty had tried through the ages.

At her desk, Hannah wondered if she should start looking for another job. Doing what, though? She'd always liked this one, she was good at it, and she liked Craig. She doubted there would be many bosses like him out there. And, anyway, she couldn't let him down.

She'd followed the advice her friends had given her, which was to not make any major life changes in the first year after The Accident. But now what? She didn't think carrying on as normal was what she wanted. That was the problem. She felt like a race-horse in a barrier just wanting to be set free.

From that day on, Hannah took her lunch to the park. A couple of times Caitlin and some other workmates had asked if she wanted them to join her, but she'd put them off with a white lie – that she had things to do so she would eat on the run. She didn't like doing that, but she needed air. And solitude, she realised one lunchtime when she was sitting on a park bench. Hannah almost cried out loud at the irony – she'd spent a year learning to be okay with being alone! She still wasn't sure she liked it, but she'd come to terms with it. And she wasn't alone at home now – she had the cats. In the eyes of many, they might not count as worthy company, but it was enough to satisfy Hannah for the time being. She wasn't even scared of the house in the dark anymore, having convinced herself that Holly would find a way to let her know if something was amiss.

Hannah was staring at some tourists checking their map when a new thought struck her. *Am I suffering from wanderlust? Have I been bitten by the travel bug and not realised until now?* Though where else did she want to go? Nowhere really. She'd loved her trip away, but she didn't feel the urge to do another long-haul flight or leave Holly and the kittens. She supposed she could go and visit Tristan's parents, Raelene and Adrian. They were currently in

Broome on their grey nomad caravan trip anti-clockwise around Australia.

You just need more time to adjust to being back at work, she thought as she gathered up her things and set off on a brisk walk around the park before going back to the office. Exercise had become another tonic, and she especially turned to it when she felt a little out of kilter. Like she did now.

*

On her second Friday back, Hannah grabbed her lunchbox from the fridge and headed out, as had become her habit. At reception she saw an out-of-order sign on one of the two lifts. A noisy group of workers hovered, waiting for the other lift so she joined the queue, turning to idly watch the television on the far wall. She smiled at seeing her favourite ad playing – the one with the meerkats going on about insurance. *So cute*, she thought. *I wouldn't mind seeing their antics in real life. Perhaps I could take Olly and Ethan to see them.* Like Sam, Hannah didn't particularly like the idea of animals caged in zoos, but perhaps the Werribee Open Range Zoo would be worth considering. Hannah would mention it to Sam sometime.

'Hannah, you coming?' She half turned. The lift was tightly packed. She hated crowded lifts, especially during the heat of summer.

'Thanks, but I'll take the next one.'

'Suit yourself,' someone said and began pressing a button furiously. She waited until the lift had well and truly gone before pressing the button to call it back, and then turned around again to watch the television while she waited. The news was starting.

'It's only ever bad, you know.' She looked up and smiled at finding Craig standing beside her. He nodded at the TV as if in explanation.

'I'm sure you're right,' Hannah said.

'Going out for some fresh air? I hear it's a nice day. Not too warm yet.'

'Yes. You?'

'I've been tasked with sorting out the ingredients for dinner. Let's hope I remember everything on the list,' he said, waving a pink sticky note. 'God these lifts are slow today,' he said, prodding at the button several times.

'I'm not sure that helps,' Hannah said. 'A watched kettle and all that …'

'Hmm. But it makes me feel better. I know, I know, patience is a virtue.'

But Hannah wasn't listening. Her eyes were wide as she watched the TV that was now showing footage of barristers in wigs and gowns flanking people in suits as they walked into court. The sound was too low to hear the details. A part of her wanted to ask Briony, the receptionist, to turn the volume up. But the captioning really told her all she needed to know – that it was indirectly to do with The Accident. It seemed the trucking company was back in court trying to dodge responsibility. She felt Craig move closer, his large frame now touching her arm.

'Are you going along to court?' he asked.

'Sorry? Oh. Um …' Right from the start Hannah had not been at all interested in following the story on the grounds that there was no point knowing the details – nothing would bring her family back. But suddenly, standing here, she felt differently. She'd tamped down any curiosity she'd felt. Or so she'd thought. And the coincidence of being here, now, the broken lift … It was a sign, wasn't it? Perhaps this was what was at the heart of the restlessness she was feeling. She didn't know how going along to court would help, but right then, like never before, she felt it couldn't actually hurt – that perhaps she needed to.

'I know you're thinking about it, it's written all over your face.'

She looked at him, frowning slightly.

'Hannah, I've known you for what, eight years? And you and I both know you were not cut out for poker. So …' he prompted.

'I think I would like to go, actually,' she said. 'But they're probably on a lunch break.'

'That'll most likely only be an hour. Take an extra-long lunch. Or take the afternoon off if you want.'

Hannah looked at him.

'Seriously. It's fine. Come on, our lift is finally here,' Craig said, nudging her arm gently. Hannah hadn't noticed it arrive as her head was spinning. Did she really want to go to the court? After all this time when she'd been adamant she didn't want to know anything about the case? She stepped in beside Craig.

They rode silently, the only noise the sound of the lift as it made its way swiftly to the ground floor.

'Would you like me to come with you?' Craig said as the doors were opening.

'Thanks, but I need to go on my own.'

'Okay, but remember I'm only a call or a text and a few blocks walk away if you need me.'

'Thanks.'

'Seriously, take the afternoon if you need to – just let me know so I won't worry.'

'You really are the best, you know that?' Hannah said, looking into his eyes. 'But don't forget to buy all the ingredients for dinner or you'll be in the doghouse at home,' she added in an attempt to stop the awkwardness creeping in.

'Go on, then,' he said, giving her shoulder a gentle prod.

As Hannah walked away she was thankful Craig hadn't hugged her. Not that he did at work. But still …

Oh crap, she thought as she turned the corner and approached the imposing court building and saw a mass of TV cameras and reporters. She hadn't thought about that. She considered turning around and going back to the office, but didn't want to draw attention to herself. Best she just get inside. At least they were milling a little way down from the main doors and most of them had their backs to her.

Hannah was nervous as she joined the line to go through security. She'd never been in a court building before. Thank goodness she hadn't been called as a witness or required to do anything else. She had given a statement to the police about when she'd last seen her parents and Tristan – what they'd been wearing, their movements that Christmas morning, et cetera. Then Raelene and Adrian had taken over liaising with the police and most likely they had shielded her from a lot more than she'd ever know. She vaguely remembered them asking if she wanted to do a Victim Impact Statement, and declining. The whole year was a bit of a blur.

Unsure what to expect or do, she followed those in front of her. Just like at the airport, bags were put on trays, pockets were emptied and people were scanned.

Once she was inside she didn't know where to go as people rushed all around her. She spied a board announcing what cases were going on in which court and noticed the name of the trucking company she'd seen on the news report at the office. The case was being heard in the court nearest to where she was standing. Though now she was here, Hannah didn't think she wanted to be. She saw a bench along the wall so went over and sat down to think.

'Hi,' the man sitting at the other end of the bench said.

'Hi,' she replied, though as she spoke wasn't sure if the man had actually spoken. He might have simply looked up at her, acknowledged her presence. Or not. He was fidgeting and seemed quite agitated.

God, I might have just sat down next to a criminal, she thought. And then she almost laughed out loud. *If that were the case, don't you think he'd be in handcuffs and with a police escort, not up here in the public area mixing with the general populace? Derr.* She found herself smiling at her foolishness. She leaned her back against the wall, but couldn't relax. It was cold and hard. She linked her hands in her lap. She must have looked as if she were waiting for something because the man beside her said, 'Nothing will happen in this court until one-thirty – they're on a lunch break.'

'Right. Okay. Thanks.' She toyed with getting her lunch out of her handbag but it seemed rude to eat in front of him. Anyway, she'd lost her appetite. She really should just leave. But then she reminded herself of the signs – she felt sure she was meant to be here, now. Though, why, she had no idea.

'Are you here for the, um, trucking company case?' she asked the man, suddenly feeling the need to make conversation.

'Yes.'

'I've never been in a court before, let alone a court room.'

'Unfortunately, I've been a few times.'

'Oh.' Hannah didn't want to pry.

'It's okay. I'm not dangerous or anything. I was acquitted. Found blameless, not that it's really helped.'

'Oh?'

'It's the truck company – I'm sure you've heard of the accident Christmas Day before last? That's why you're here, right?'

Hannah nodded. 'Yes. I …' She twisted her hands in her lap. 'A very sad business.' She swallowed hard. 'Are you part of the company involved?' Her voice was shaky.

'I was. I got fired. Well, sort of …'

'Oh. I'm sorry.'

'Thanks. Probably for the best, though. I've lost my nerve. I was the …' He caught Hannah staring at him. 'Oh. My. God. You're Hannah Ainsley, aren't you? I've seen your picture in the paper and on TV. Good on you for not commenting. I am so sorry. Honestly, you have every right not to believe me, but it wasn't my fault.'

Hannah couldn't speak, or close her mouth, or tear her eyes away from this man. Oh god. Her heart began to race. She put a hand to it and took a deep breath to try to steady herself. She wanted to get up and leave but she was too stunned to move. Her legs began to shake. She probably couldn't stand up now if she tried. She took a couple of deep breaths. Realising her hand was still at her chest, she noticed that it was shaking too and forced herself to place it in her lap.

'I've clearly upset you, which is completely understandable. I'm so sorry. I'll go.'

As he got up, Hannah noticed there were tears in his eyes. She felt her hammering heart stretch towards him a little. She felt light-headed, headachy, and slightly nauseous. She swallowed and bit her lip against the gathering tears.

'No. It's okay. Don't go on my account. Please.' She found herself reaching up and touching his arm.

'Are you sure?' She saw pain and heartache, but she also detected warmth in his eyes. Her heart slowed and Hannah felt herself calming.

'Yes. I'm sure. Please sit down,' she said, patting the bench and attempting to offer a warm smile that she suspected was more along the lines of a grimace.

'If you're sure. Because you would have every reason to hate me.'

'But it wasn't your fault, was it? And even if it was, hating you wouldn't bring anyone back.'

'You're very understanding,' the man said as he sat back down.

'No, just realistic,' Hannah said with a sigh. 'You seem to be a decent person, so I'm sure you've relived that day often enough and beaten yourself up for it. You were injured too, weren't you?' she asked, remembering what Caitlin had said at the party. 'How are you doing?'

'Yes, I have. And, yes. It's been a long, slow process, but I'm getting there, thanks,' he said, looking down at the floor.

'Please don't feel guilty for being alive,' Hannah found herself saying in little more than a whisper. And then she said a bit louder, 'I'm sorry, but I don't know your name. You see, I haven't been following the story in the papers or anything. I figured what would be ... Well, anyway ...'

'I think in hindsight I should have taken that approach too. I've done the opposite – attending court has become a bit of an obsession, I'm afraid. Henry Peace,' he said, offering his hand.

'Hannah Ainsley, which you already know,' she said, gripping his hand firmly. She didn't know what else to say and had only just managed to stop herself in time from using her automatic greeting. Saying, 'Nice to meet you,' would have been far too glib given the circumstances.

'Thank you for not recoiling in horror, Hannah.'

'I don't think you're a bad man, Henry, and others must agree with that too because you've been cleared.'

'That's very good of you to say.'

'So why are you here? I wouldn't have thought you'd want a bar of any of the legalities after fighting to clear your name. I'm guessing you had your fair share of official proceedings.'

'Part of it is making the company's big bosses look me in the eye.'

'Oh, right.'

'And, well, to be honest, I don't really have anywhere else to be. I'm pretty much unemployed and unemployable.'

'Just because you can't drive trucks anymore – or don't want to – doesn't make you unemployable, does it? Surely you have plenty of transferrable skills you can put to use in other jobs.'

'I'm a little lost, to be perfectly honest.'

You and me both. But Hannah kept these words to herself.

'I'm a bit of a basket case, too. I suffer from anxiety, depression, PTSD now. I've lost everything, including my marriage.'

'I'm so sorry to hear that. I wish there was something I could do or say to help.'

'Hannah you have no idea how much you just sitting here and not hating me means,' he said, choking up. Tears filled his eyes again and Hannah's heart lurched.

'Oh, Henry,' she said, and was surprised to find herself gathering him to her. *Damn the butterfly or ripple effect, or whatever it's called,* she thought as she held him and felt tears of her own run down her cheeks.

'We're a fine pair, aren't we?' Hannah said, wiping her eyes a moment later when an embarrassed Henry had eased himself away and accepted the clean tissue she held out.

'You know, you might just be the loveliest woman in the whole of Melbourne. Sorry, I didn't mean that to sound sleazy. I've pictured meeting you over and over in daydreams and nightmares.

And every time it's been horrible. You've spat in my face, clawed at my eyes.'

'How awful. I can assure you, I am not at all prone to violence.'

'Thank goodness for that,' Henry said, returning her gentle smile.

'Have you had any lunch, Henry?'

'No. I'm not very hungry.'

'Me neither. But would you help me make sure mine doesn't go to waste? There's plenty for two not-very-hungry people,' she said, taking out her lunchbox from her tote bag.

'Ham, cheese and hot English mustard on grain bread,' she said, unwrapping the sandwich and offering him half. 'And an orange.'

'Oh, this is good,' Henry said after his first bite. 'Maybe I was hungrier than I thought I was. Thank you so much.'

'You're welcome.'

'How have you been able to put it all behind you so well, Hannah?' he asked after they'd been silently eating for a minute or two.

'I'm not sure I have, actually. I still have very sad days. But I've got a group of really good friends who always seem able to pull me up.'

'That's great. I did have some good friends. Well, I thought I did. Mainly workmates. But when I was arrested they seemed to stop wanting to know me.'

'Oh, Henry, I'm so sorry. Sadly, during tough times we see the true measure of people. Did your wife leave too? Oh, sorry, that's a bit personal. I take that back. Don't answer,' she said, blushing.

'It's okay. And, no, she was wonderful. She *is* wonderful. Louise. I left her.'

'Why?'

'I couldn't look her or my darling son, Felix, in the eye – I'm a failure as a man and a husband. They're better off without me. I was too gutless to ... you know ... I've thought about it but ... I can't support them.'

Hannah was shocked and didn't know how to respond, so said nothing and nodded to indicate she was listening.

'I've got to pull myself back together somehow before I can try and get them back. There's no point if I still don't feel worthy. That's what my counsellor says. It's a long, slow process.'

'I'm glad you're getting help.' Hannah had never got around to seeing a counsellor herself – she'd found a catch-up with a dear, wise friend tended to do the trick for her.

'That's one good thing about being so badly injured – counselling was part of rehab. A silver lining, I guess you could say. Though, between you and me, the physical side of things is a damned sight easier to deal with than this other stuff,' he said, tapping his head with his finger.

Having finished her half of the sandwich, Hannah proceeded to peel the orange, break it open and hand him half.

'Thanks,' he said.

'So, what have you been doing with yourself while you're not doing rehab and not at court – the case has just started back up, hasn't it?'

'Yes. I've got a small lawn-mowing round. I'd like to expand it, but it's hard. It would be good if I could get it to full-time – I quite enjoy it – but I'm not sure it's possible. The problem is I really don't have much of a clue about running a business and I can't afford to buy into one of those franchises.'

'Well, as long as you enjoy it. That's a start. And you seem personable enough. I'm sure it will build organically as word gets around. Actually, I have a couple of fruit trees that need pruning.

I'm not keen on climbing a ladder and wouldn't know the right place to cut. Do you do that sort of thing?'

'I certainly can. Here's my card,' he said, bringing out a business card from his suit pocket and handing it over. 'It would be my pleasure to sort it out for you.'

'I don't mean as a freebie, Henry, so please don't think that. I'm happy to pay the going rate. You're running a business, don't forget,' Hannah said.

Suddenly there was movement around them. Henry checked his watch. 'One-thirty. They're heading back in,' he said, but made no move to get up. 'It's been too nice talking to you, Hannah. I don't fancy ruining it by going in there and listening to more of their waffle. It makes me so angry. And I'm not sure they have enough scruples to care about looking me in the eye. I think I've been kidding myself.'

'Hmm. I've avoided it this long, I think I should continue to stay away from the case,' Hannah said. 'Perhaps I was meant to meet you, but not actually to go inside.'

'I'm so glad you came and we got to meet,' Henry said, gripping both of Hannah's hands with his. More tears were gathering in his eyes.

'Me too, Henry, but I'd better get back to work,' she said, getting up.

'Goodbye, Hannah.'

'Goodbye, Henry. I'll call you about coming to look at my fruit trees,' she said, holding up his card.

'And I look forward to being of assistance,' he said. Hannah smiled as he nodded and pinched his fingers to the brim of a pretend hat.

Chapter Eleven

Hannah made her way back to work feeling distracted, so much so that a couple of times she almost lost her footing stepping on and off the footpaths. She got quite a fright when a turning car almost hit her and the driver had to quickly sound her horn. She waved in apology to the woman shouting at her to watch where she was going.

Sitting down at her desk Hannah stared at the note from Craig stuck on the top of a stack of folders. She was to update some client files. Looking at the pile, she felt weighed down, as if he'd asked her to write a five-thousand word essay on a subject she'd never studied rather than an easy task she did regularly. She should have been pleased to have something mundane to do that required little processing while she gathered her thoughts.

An hour later she'd got as far as opening the first file and then was distracted by the flashing cursor on her screen. She just couldn't make herself concentrate, let alone go any further.

'Hannah?'

She was startled to look up and find Craig peering over the wall of her cubicle. She opened her mouth but no words came out.

'Hannah, can you please come into my office for a sec?'

She pushed her chair back, got up, grabbed the notebook and pencil that always sat ready on the side of her desk, and made her way around to his glass-walled office.

'Have a seat.' She did and then sat looking expectantly at him, notebook open and pen poised for instructions.

'Did something happen at the court? The media weren't there, were they?'

'Sorry? What? Oh. Well they were, but they didn't take any notice of me.'

'So, what's going on? You look like you've seen a ghost and you've done nothing but stare at your computer screen for practically the last hour.'

'I'm so sorry. I'm a bit distracted.'

'Yes, I can see that. And I'm not fussed about the lost hour of work, Hannah. I'm worried about you. What's up?'

'I met Henry Peace. At the court.'

'I see.'

'He was the truck driver that …'

'Yes, I know who Henry Peace is.'

'Oh. Right.'

'What happened? Did he upset you?'

'No, not at all. We shared my lunch.'

'Oh. Okay. I wasn't expecting that.'

'He's lost everything, Craig.'

'So have you.'

'But I'm okay. He isn't. He's lost his job, his marriage. It wasn't his fault.'

'What are you saying, Hannah?'

'I don't know. I just feel weird about having met him.'

'Because you thought he'd be a monster or …'

'No. I've never actually thought about him at all. I didn't even know the driver's name.'

'Do you think you should take some time off?'

'I just got back!' *Yes, I want to take time off, but I might never return.* 'Do you ever just wonder what the point is?' she said, before sighing loudly.

'Wow. Um, about what exactly? That's a pretty big question, Hannah,' Craig said, smiling sympathetically.

'So much has changed, yet so much is still the same. It feels wrong. And weird,' she said.

'Yes, it's all very unsettling. You're not about to quit on me, are you? Because if you are, I'd rather you took some time out to think it through first. Not for me, for you. Though, ultimately, you have to do what's right for you, Hannah. We all do. You've had a confronting experience today – whether it was good, bad or otherwise doesn't matter. It was clearly unsettling. It's going to take you time to process. It might be best if you at least went home now and sat quietly with the cats and let the dust settle.'

Hannah nodded.

'And, remember, Hannah, you're not responsible for Henry Peace. He needs to do whatever he needs to do for himself.'

'He just seemed so sad, so lost.'

'I bet he's feeling a whole lot better since meeting you, Hannah. You've probably made a huge difference to his life by simply being you. Now go on home before I go getting all soppy.'

'You know, I think I will. I'm not being much use here, anyway.' She got up. 'Thanks, Craig.'

'No worries. Hey, you're welcome to come to dinner – we're having beef stroganoff and I've even remembered to get all the ingredients,' he said, grinning.

'Thanks, but I think you're right about me needing some quiet alone time,' she said. *Actually, there's something else I need to do.* Hannah had just that moment realised it.

'Well, if you change your mind, we won't be eating until seven. Oh, and Hannah?' he said when she was at the door.

'Yes.'

'Don't take it on. We all have to get our own shit together.'

Hannah nodded and left, closing the glass door carefully behind her.

★

When Hannah walked up her street from the tram stop, she could barely recall the twenty-minute trip. Instead of going inside, she took her car keys out of her bag. If she went inside now, she might chicken out.

Hannah drove carefully towards the cemetery where the funeral home had interred her parents' ashes for her. She hadn't been able to bring herself to visit before. She didn't really know why she felt able to now, but she was determined to. She just hoped she could find their location okay. She kept saying the address over and over, having memorised the details included in the letter she'd received from Graeme at the funeral company along with a photo.

Suddenly she found herself indicating and turning the car left instead of right. And then she was turning into the retire-ment village where her parents had lived. She hadn't been here since the day Joanne had been so kind to her and they'd become instant, firm friends. Joanne had made the task of going through her parents' villa manageable. Clearly the universe meant her to visit Joanne now. Hannah almost laughed at the thought. *Sam's the one who looks for signs and believes in the workings of the universe, not me!* Some moral support would be good, Hannah thought, feeling her conviction to go to the cemetery wavering. She should have thought this through and asked Beth to come along.

'Hannah, hi,' Joanne said, clearly surprised, as Hannah walked into the reception area of the retirement village. Joanne put down the pile of manila folders she was carrying and rushed over to hug Hannah. 'Are you okay?' she said, peering at Hannah while holding her hands.

'Honestly, I'm not sure,' Hannah said, trying to sound light.

'Come in and have a seat.'

'Are you sure you have time?' Hannah asked as Joanne ushered her through to her office.

'Of course. I have all the time in the world.'

Bless you, Hannah thought. *I bet you'd say that even when under the greatest of time pressures.* Joanne's calmness was catching. Already Hannah felt better.

'So, what's up?' Joanne asked.

'I didn't mean to come here. I was actually on my way to the cemetery to see Mum and Dad's plaques. I haven't seen them yet.'

'Oh, well, you probably shouldn't do that alone – not the first time. You should have said.'

'It wasn't planned. I've been avoiding it, as you know ...'

'Yes. So, why now? What's up, Hannah?'

'I went to the court today – the truck company's case is back on.'

'Oh. How was it?'

'They were on a lunch break.'

'Well, good on you for at least having the courage to go. That's a big step, Hannah.'

'I met Henry Peace. The driver,' she said.

'Really? And …?'

'He seemed nice enough, though he's pretty messed up.'

'What did he say?'

'Sorry. And that it wasn't his fault.'

'Well, we know that. The poor man.'

'Yes. Oh, Jo, it's got me all out of kilter.'

'Of course it has. It's a huge thing you've done, Hannah.'

'In some ways it was such an ordinary interaction, but something has changed. *I've* changed. Well, I don't know, actually. I must have changed a bit otherwise why would I have finally gone to the courthouse after a year of avoiding it?'

'Why did you go?'

'I'm not entirely sure.'

'Okay. Perhaps the better question is, what made you suddenly decide to go? How did you discover the case was back on? You've always been very clear about not following it. Which I think is fine, by the way. It's entirely up to you.'

'One of the lifts at work was out of order, the other was being extra slow. I was watching the TV in reception while I waited and there it was on the news. I guess it was closer to my mind than before because someone had mentioned at the New Year's Eve party I was at. Anyway, suddenly there I was, sitting beside Henry sharing my lunch with him.'

'Well, you were clearly meant to meet him.'

'I see that. But why? All it's done is unsettle me.'

'You said you felt changed. Is there something else as well as meeting the driver?'

'You know how important my job has been and how upset I was about being forced to take time off?'

'Yes, you've always said it's been your anchor. Now you're back, are you finding it doesn't have the same appeal, the same comfort for you that it did before?'

'That's exactly it. Oh, Joanne, you're so wise. So, what do I do? I don't know what else I'd do for work. I thought I loved my job.'

'I'm sure deep down the love will still be there when you've dealt with whatever else seems to be going on in your mind and distracting you. Or maybe it's served its purpose and it's time to move on. That could be it too.'

'That's no help,' Hannah said with a laugh.

'I'm afraid some of these things only you can decide on.'

'I feel so … Oh, I don't know. Not let down, but …'

'Let down?'

'Sort of. I gave it a year – didn't make any major changes. I'd hoped … Oh, I don't know.'

'Perhaps you'd hoped everything would be magically better? That you'd served your time?'

'I think so, yes,' Hannah said a little sheepishly.

'It doesn't quite work like that.'

'So I'm beginning to see. So much is different, but so much is the same, frustratingly so. I'm sorry, I'm not making any sense.'

'You are to me. It's the futility, the frustration that after tragedy life, generally, simply carries on. You've gone through this incredible upheaval, had your foundations, your beliefs, your *everything* shaken to the core. You've done your best to navigate, survive the horror, only to find that a lot around you is unchanged, that beyond your inner-circle nobody knows or cares what you've been through. It's as if the world has simply shrugged and said, yeah, whatever, it's all happened for eons before and will continue to.'

Hannah stared at the slightly breathless Joanne, and blinked a couple of times.

'Wow,' she said.

'Yes, I know exactly what you might be feeling. And what's more, you want what you've been through to somehow mean something but have no idea how to go about it. But, take it from me, nothing will do this for you, Hannah – no amount of charitable donations, changing jobs, moving house, et cetera, will relieve it. It's inside you. You have to find your reason for living and making peace with it all. And to have met the truck driver, Henry … Oh, I've just realised. How ironic that his surname is Peace. Now there's a sign if you ever needed one! So, how do you feel about him – other than unsettled? What did you think of him?'

'I feel sad for him. I pity him. I'm disappointed for him. And, you know what? I'm disappointed *in* him. Angry too – but not because he was the driver. I'm annoyed that he's dropped the bundle. He's left his wife because he's ashamed. But he hasn't done anything wrong.' Hannah was getting more and more exasperated and animated. 'So, he might not have the nerve to drive a truck anymore, but that's no reason to give up on life. Jesus! I don't get it.'

'Some people don't have the inner-strength to draw on, Hannah.'

'I know I should be more sympathetic. I just can't imagine giving up. I didn't.'

'Unfortunately, men are good at solving things in a practical sense, but when it comes to not having a black and white answer or several clear options, often they struggle. Women are more used to analysing things at an emotional level and nutting out solutions, sometimes obscure ones. That makes us better equipped to deal with emotional upheavals. And that's what feelings are. Henry is feeling let down by his company, feeling guilty about the accident, feeling inadequate as a man for no longer being able to provide for his family as he thinks a man should. Sorry, I'm going on. And I'm generalising. This is all just my opinion.'

'But it makes sense. So, what do I do?'

'About what?'

'Henry.'

'Oh, darling, it's not your place to make him whole again. That's up to him, just as you've had to find your own strength and put yourself back together. I don't mean to sound harsh, but I care about you, Hannah. So, so much.'

'But I had you and my other dear friends. I wouldn't have got through it without you all.'

'I'm sure Henry has his friends too.'

'But he doesn't.'

'Well, that should tell you something, Hannah. Please don't let him drag you down by taking him on as a cause.'

'That's pretty much what my boss, Craig, said,' Hannah said quietly.

'By all means if you know of someone who can give him a job, pass on his details. But don't get emotionally involved. He might be a nice enough man. But, equally, you don't know anything about him. The fact that he's separated from his wife is a red flag too, in my opinion. He's fragile, Hannah. I'm sorry, but the best gift you can give him you already have – forgiveness. I think you're underestimating the impact of you simply talking with him and being kind will have had. You have probably just given him the key to unlocking his healing. Leave him be, Hannah.'

'He said he's imagined me spitting at him or trying to tear his eyes out.'

'So, just consider what sharing your lunch with him might have meant then.'

'Hmm. I guess.'

'Please don't think I'm being horrible.'

'Never, Jo,' Hannah said.

'You being such a lovely person with a big heart makes you very vulnerable, Hannah. Clearly you were meant to meet him. But perhaps that's all it was meant to be.'

'And maybe it's more about him than me,' Hannah mused.

'I'm sure it is. Now, I want to show you something.'

Joanne led her outside to the community garden where there was a new wooden arbour with a timber bench beneath it.

'Eventually there'll be lovely pink climbing roses all over it.'

'Oh, it's beautiful,' Hannah said, looking around and taking it all in. As she read the brass plaque, her eyes filled and she had to keep blinking to clear her vision.

IN MEMORY OF DANIEL AND DAPHNE WHITE
TRUE FRIENDS TO ALL, TRAGICALLY TAKEN TOO SOON, 2015.

'Hey, I wanted to cheer you up, not upset you more,' Joanne said, draping her arm around Hannah and squeezing her tightly.

'It's okay. Oh, Jo, it's lovely. They would love it. Do you want me to donate for it? The village can't be …'

'The village didn't. The residents took up a collection and a couple of the men did the handiwork. They wanted it finished for the anniversary. Your parents were very much loved, as are you. Now, shall we go and see them?'

'Oh, I couldn't ask you to …'

'You're not, I'm offering.'

'You know, I've changed my mind. It's been such a big, emotionally draining day that I think I want to go home and cuddle the cats. Sorry, but I think I'll go another day. When I'm feeling differently.'

'Of course. You don't need to apologise, Hannah. If you ever want me to go with you, just ask. And if you decide you'd rather go alone or with someone else, that's entirely up to you.'

'You know, I'm not sure I ever want to go there, if I'm being completely honest,' Hannah said, her cheeks beginning to burn. 'I know I should, but ...'

'There's no *should* about it. If you want to, do, if not, don't. You hold them and your memories in your heart and that's wherever you are. That's what counts.'

'I'm glad I had them put somewhere – god, how awful does that sound? – but, you know, seeing your memorial makes me wonder if I did the right thing. I didn't exactly rush into it, but now I'm thinking I should have done something else.'

'There's nothing to say you can't do something else as well, and at any time. Hannah, there are no rules. Grief is hard enough without you putting more pressure on yourself. You have to do whatever feels right to you – and only you.'

'Speaking of which,' Hannah blurted, desperate to divert the conversation away from herself. 'Well, not really. I'm changing the subject completely. You should know, Sam's husband has left her. He's decided he's actually gay and has gone off to, I guess, find himself – or a man. If it wasn't my darling Sam involved, it might be a little bit funny.'

'Oh dear. How is she?'

'Sad. In denial. Bless her.'

'The poor darling. I think Sam's just gorgeous.'

'She is. I wanted to give you the heads-up – better in person than on the phone. I think I'll organise a lunch soon for all of us – remind her how many people love her. It's not a secret, so when the time comes or if you happen to bump into her there's no need to pretend you don't know.'

'Okay. I think a lunch is a lovely idea. The one you put on for your birthday was so special. When are you thinking of?'

'Oh, well, I've just only this minute had the idea. This weekend's a bit short notice. I'll ask around and see when everyone's free. How are you situated?'

'Free as a bird – at this stage I have no firm plans that I can't easily change at short notice.'

'Great. Pencil in Sunday week. I'll call you when I've decided. I'd better let you get back to work. Thank you so much for your friendship – it means a huge amount to me.'

'And to me. I'm so glad you dropped in.'

'Me too. I feel so much better,' Hannah said, hugging Joanne.

'Good. Drive safe and give the gorgeous Holly and her sweet little kittens lots of cuddles from me.'

Chapter Twelve

Hannah couldn't stop wondering what to make of Sam's text message.

Can you come over? Stay for tea. I need your help.

Hannah had replied:

Okay. See you at six?

Sam hadn't given Hannah cause to worry about her state of mind, but then she hadn't given her a reason not to either. Their contact had been confined to daily checking in via text messages and the odd brief phone call. It was clear to Hannah that Sam had withdrawn a little. She was just hoping it had more to do with Sam getting back into her art and not, as she suspected was the case, that she was upset over her marriage. Regardless, Hannah knew all she could do was sit back and wait for Sam to come to her if she needed to.

On the tram home from work Hannah tried not to think what might be behind the message. It clearly wasn't medical or urgent. It could be that Sam needed help carrying a particularly large or heavy artwork or something. Hannah couldn't quite shake the thought that Sam had chosen text message rather than phone call so she couldn't be interrogated. Perhaps she simply didn't feel like talking, or didn't want to disturb Hannah at work. Hannah almost laughed at herself – she'd never been one to let her head get this caught up in unknowns. She tended to accept that if she were meant to know something she eventually would. Sam was the one who couldn't stand a mystery and insisted on nutting everything out. Though, Hannah had to admit she had enjoyed the distraction of thinking about the text these last couple of hours.

She'd spent a quiet weekend at home reading and visiting with Beth and her cats. She'd hoped she might get bored enough to look forward to going to work, but her strategy was flawed considering the exciting book she was currently devouring. She continued to wonder how to change her feelings of disappointment around everything being a little too ordinary while carrying on and hoping the universe – yes, she had to admit she was now a firm believer – well, she was certainly starting to be – might show her a sign. Preferably the sign would be so obvious that she couldn't possibly miss it or the meaning behind it. She agreed with Joanne that what she was feeling most likely wasn't about her job. And she did feel she owed Craig her loyalty. So, while she wasn't entirely content, she was resigned to staying in her job. She'd largely managed to put Henry Peace out of her mind too, though she would call him about the trees at some point when she got her head a little straighter. If he asked for her help with something in particular she could consider it. But again Joanne was right – he had to sort himself out and couldn't be her concern.

Right now, she had to concern herself with Sam and the boys. After far too much thought, Hannah decided it really was unlikely that another major crisis was unfolding in Sam's life and that her best friend probably only needed her to hold the stepladder while she changed a light bulb, or something of that nature.

'Hann, thank God you're here!' Sam cried, throwing the door open before Hannah had even had the chance to ring the bell.

'Has something happened since you messaged me?' Hannah said, frowning.

'No.'

'It didn't sound like it was urgent. Sorry, I would have come straight away.'

'I know. I didn't want to worry you.'

'Well, you are now. What's up?'

'I'm a nervous wreck.'

Hannah's stomach flipped. *God, what now?*

'Perhaps I'd better come in,' she prompted with a gentle smile.

'Shit. Yes. Jesus. Sorry. Come in.'

'Where are the boys?'

'Sleepover with kids up the road.'

Ah, Hannah thought, *that doesn't help things.* Sam was good at putting on an act in front of the boys and hiding some of her true emotions. Sometimes Hannah thought Sam should be an actress rather than an artist, she was so good at it.

'How about you sit down and I get us a cup of tea?' Hannah suggested.

'Okay. That would be good. Thanks.'

'Yum. Something smells good,' Hannah said as they walked into the kitchen.

'Shepherd's pie. Not quite the weather for it, but still ...'

'Sounds perfect.' *Uh-oh*, Hannah thought, taking in the empty sink and spotless kitchen.

'Yes, it's the closest I'm getting to being creative at the moment,' Sam said, clearly reading Hannah's thoughts that procrastination was at play.

'Right. Now, slowly from the top, tell me what you need my help with,' Hannah said, placing two mugs of tea on the rustic table and sitting down.

Without a word, Sam picked up the landline handset sitting on the table, pressed a few buttons and put it back down again.

A bland female voice said: *'You have one saved message, received at two p.m. today.'*

And then a male voice came on, *'Hello, Samantha, this is Roger Huntley from Hill Street Art Gallery in Prahran. A friend of mine saw your work at the Southbank market recently and passed your details onto me. I'm having an exhibition starting early April and I've had an artist cancel due to illness. If you're interested in discussing your work and potentially exhibiting with me, please call me. The number is ...'*

'Wow, Sam, that's fantastic! See, I told you the markets were worth doing. So, what did he say? Which of your pieces is he interested in?'

'I haven't rung him. That's what I need your help with — do I call him?'

'What? Of course you bloody call him. Sam, what's got into you?'

'I'm a wreck.'

'Well, you need to pull yourself together. It's a great opportunity,' she said, her frustration bubbling over.

'What if he doesn't want me?'

'Then you wait for the next opportunity to come along or you go out looking for it yourself. But you won't know what this

Roger Huntley has to offer if you don't call him back. You can't let Rob leaving stop you from chasing your dreams, because one day you'd look back and see what you did and hate yourself for it. And him.'

'I can't do anything. I'm creatively paralysed.'

'Oh, don't be melodramatic, Sam! The juices will flow again, they always do. But if you believe they won't, well, then you've got no hope. Jesus, Sam, you're the strongest, most positive person I know. What's got into you?'

'I'm scared.'

'Of what?'

'Failure. Success. Oh, I don't know.'

'Sammy, darling, you need to pull yourself together. You've never been scared of anything. What's the worst that can happen? Seriously, what?'

'He likes my work and I can't do anything for him,' Sam suggested.

'Well, that's unlikely. The boys will be at school in a few weeks and you'll be bored and won't be able to help yourself. What else?'

'He doesn't like anything I've done.'

'So, we drown our sorrows in a bottle of gin and stick pins in a voodoo doll of him. You've always been so philosophical about how subjective art is, Sam.'

'That's all well and good until you actually care. And put yourself out there. I was never really serious about it like I am now.'

'I'm your friend, so this is said with all the love in the world. Samantha Barrow, you are being utterly ridiculous. Now, just pick up the god-damned phone and call the man and find out what he has to say. You can always stall him by simply setting up a time to meet. I'm sure that's really all he'll want right now, anyway.'

'Um, can you do it for me?'

'Sam!'

'No, seriously,' Sam said, brightening suddenly. She'd clearly just had an idea. 'Can you pretend you're my agent?'

'Oh. What?'

'Pleeeease. As you said, he probably only wants to set up a time to meet. But it's almost six o'clock – is it too late?'

'It's a mobile number. And if he doesn't want to answer, he'll send the call to voicemail,' Hannah said.

'So, you'll do it?'

'Hang on a second. We've got to think this through. I don't think it would be very professional to pretend you have an agent to call him and then turn up and meet him on your own. He'd reasonably ask where your agent is. Then you'd have to fess up to tricking him. Then you'd just look pathetic and that really wouldn't be a good start to a trusting business relationship, now would it? No, Sam, you'll have to phone him yourself.'

'Couldn't you meet with him too – as my agent? Like, *really* my agent? You know nearly as much about my work as I do.'

'Hardly.'

'Well, I can make sure you do. You'd be in a much better position than me to talk objectively about me and my work.'

'It's not exactly objective coming from your best friend, Sam.'

'Please, I need this, Hann. And I can't do it without you. You're always telling me I'm selling myself short. Pleeeeease.'

'Shhh. Just let me think a moment.'

Hannah's brain was spinning.

'Okay. All right. But …' Hannah said, feeling a surge of excitement. Ideas began to fire within her like fireworks.

'Oh, thank you. You're the best,' Sam said, tapping her feet on the floor.

'But, there are conditions.'

'Whatever you say.'

'Sam, I'm being serious.'

'Okay. What?'

'It's either all or nothing, no changing your mind later and taking over, going behind my back and agreeing to different prices or business details with him. If I'm going to be your manager, everything goes through me. Got it?'

'Uh-oh, I've created a monster.'

'Sorry, but this is not a game. This is your career, Sam. You have one chance to make a good impression with him. This could be your big break. Do you know anything about the gallery?'

'Yes, I've Googled him and printed out a heap of stuff. Some hugely successful artists got their start with him.'

'Excellent. My only big concern is the golden rule that you shouldn't do business with friends.'

'How about I agree to just do as I'm told?' Sam offered.

'Yeah, right. As if you could do that for longer than five minutes. I've known you for over a decade, remember? Hey, where are you going?' Hannah said as she watched Sam get up and go to a drawer in the kitchen bench.

'I'm getting paper so you can write us a contract. Oops, I've only got brown paper and crayons, I'm afraid,' she said with a smile. Hannah accepted the items with raised eyebrows.

'It doesn't matter how it's recorded. Go on,' Sam urged.

'Right. We'll start with the date,' Hannah said, unrolling the brown paper a little and selecting a blue crayon. 'Now, "I Hannah Ainsley agree to act as Samantha Barrow's agent in her dealings with Mr Roger Huntley on the proviso that Samantha listens to me, trusts me and does not interfere. I agree to discuss any major decisions with her prior to making them and to always act with her best interests in mind." How's that? Not exactly legalese. Anything else?'

'What am I going to pay you?'

'You don't have to pay me anything.'

'Yes I do if this is going to be a legitimate business relationship, which it is if we're having a contract.'

'Which, I might remind you, is handwritten on a roll of brown paper in thick children's crayons.'

'So? It's still binding, isn't it? I'm serious. How about fifteen percent of anything I make? That sounds fair, doesn't it?'

'Well, it would give me an incentive to work hard for you.' Hannah felt excitement course through her again.

'Exactly.'

'Are you sure?'

'Absolutely.'

Hannah added the payment clause to the contract. 'Okay, that's got the main things covered, hasn't it?'

'I think so.'

'I'll just add our names and then we sign.'

'Now we have to shake on it,' Sam said after they had both signed their names in crayons and Sam cut the paper on the edge of the table. She held out her hand and Hannah accepted. As she did, Hannah's stomach did a little flip. *Wow.*

'Oh, Hannah, thank you. This means so much,' Sam said.

'Well, I haven't done anything yet.' But nonetheless, she felt a bit giddy with the possibilities.

'Oh. My. God. I have an agent!' Sam said.

'Darling, not a real one. Let's not get ahead of ourselves.'

'Go on, ring him,' Sam urged.

'Listen to you, bossy boots.'

'You're working for me now.'

'Touché. I'll use my mobile in case he's put your number in – it might look weird for your agent to be phoning from your house. A real one wouldn't do that.'

'See, you think of everything. God. I'm going to have to get the business cards re-done with your details on. Lucky they were cheap.'

Hannah's fingers shook slightly as she put the number into her phone and then quickly and silently ran through what she was going to say.

'Hello, Mr Huntley, this is Hannah Ainsley returning your call to Samantha Barrow. I'm acting as her manager.'

'Oh. Okay. Great,' Roger said. 'Thank you for phoning back. I was excited to see the photos my friend took of Samantha's work at the market.'

'Yes, she's very talented.'

'I couldn't find a website to learn more.'

'No, the website is currently under construction – it should be available in the next few weeks,' Hannah said, looking away from Sam's astonished expression. 'Samantha has only recently decided to seriously pursue her art after many years honing her craft in private. She feels now the time is right and is looking for the right gallery to open the door for her.'

'I see. Good. Good. Well, I hope we might be the best fit.'

'You must understand, Mr Huntley, I am speaking to several other galleries.'

'May I ask which ones?'

'You may. But I am not at liberty to say, as I'm sure you would appreciate.'

'Yes. Of course. Now, would two p.m. on Saturday work for you – at my gallery at 645 Hill Street, Prahran?'

'Saturday two p.m. at your gallery at 645 Hill Street, Prahran, would be fine.'

'Could you please bring an up-to-date CV and portfolio?'

'Of course. Is there anything else you need?'

'No, that will suffice for now.'

'Excellent. I look forward seeing you then. And, thank you for this opportunity, Samantha really appreciates it, as do I.'

'It's my pleasure. Thank you for getting back to me. Bye for now.'

Hannah's heart was racing and her face was burning a little when she hung up.

'Oh my god, oh my god! What did he say?' Sam demanded.

'You heard most of it. Lucky I decided on Sunday instead for my lunch,' Hannah mused aloud.

'Did he say we have to take anything?'

'An up-to-date CV and a portfolio – that's all.'

'Shit.'

'You'll be fine. I'll help you put them together.'

'I can't believe you said you're meeting with other galleries.'

'Well, I couldn't have him thinking he has all the power, now could I?'

'God, Hann, you're good!'

Chapter Thirteen

A few times during the week Hannah had wondered if she'd get everything done in time. But as always, she thrived under pressure, especially when there were many tasks to take care of. Having done the final preparations for her high tea, she paused to consider if there was anything she'd missed. As had been the case several times since their meeting, her thoughts strayed to Roger Huntley and his gallery until the doorbell rang, jolting her from her reverie.

'Sorry I'm early,' Beth said, looking a little flushed as she hugged Hannah and then stepped into the hall. 'I had to leave while I was only half covered in cat fur. You'd think wearing dark would be fine, but oh no. Look at me.' She indicated her black pants and sighed with exasperation. 'But I do so love the precious monsters.'

'You look perfectly fine to me.'

'Where are your little darlings?'

'In the laundry. I felt terrible locking them up, but I don't want Holly suddenly deciding she'd like to be a street cat again and sneak out while everyone is arriving and the door's open. She's been well behaved, but I'm not taking any chances until she and the kittens are de-sexed and have had all their vaccinations. They probably couldn't get out of the back garden, but still ...'

'No, you can never be too sure. I caught Joseph sitting on top of the lounge-room curtain rod the other day. Cheeky devil.'

'Terrors,' Hannah agreed.

'We wouldn't be without them now, though, would we?' Beth said, beaming at Hannah.

'Yes, although I'm not sure what I'll be saying in a few months when the little ones start racing through the house at full speed. At the moment they're still small and slow enough on their feet for me to catch them.'

'Now, is there anything I can do?' Beth asked, looking around the kitchen.

'No, I think I'm all sorted. When everyone's inside, can I put you in charge of letting Holly and the kittens out?'

'You certainly can. Would you happen to have a lint roller? I'm starting to feel very self-conscious.'

'Here you are,' Hannah said, taking out a sticky roller from a kitchen drawer. She had several strategically placed around the house. 'But, seriously, what's a bit of cat hair between friends?'

'So says the one who was adamant there'd never be any pets inside, just a few short months ago,' Beth said, grinning.

'Yes, well, instant cat lady, just add water,' Hannah said with a laugh. 'My only hope is that there's no hair in any of the food.'

Half an hour later Joanne, Jasmine, Sam and Caitlin had arrived and Holly, Squeak and Lucky were out of the laundry and commanding all the attention. Eventually everyone was seated, the scones were cooked and added to the top tier of the cake stands, the food was placed on the table, the cork was popped out of the bottle of sparkling wine and the flutes filled.

'How gorgeous does this look?' Joanne said, and everyone agreed heartily.

'I'll just tell you what's here,' Hannah said. 'We have egg-mayonnaise and chicken ribbon sandwiches, mini quiches, chocolate cupcakes, lemon tarts, and caramel slice. And, of course, scones.'

'It all looks and smells amazing. And, look, Holly wants part of the action,' Caitlin said. Sure enough, Holly had hopped onto the spare chair at the end of the table. Hannah cringed. *Please, not on the table.* But she relaxed when the cat curled herself into a ball.

'Right, now, sorry if this sounds like a sermon, but I just wanted to say a few words before we start. Thank you for being here. I wanted to get us all together. It's so easy to get caught up in everyday things and then suddenly realise months have passed and we haven't seen this friend or that. As you know, I'm not into New Year resolutions, but I did make a vow to make sure we all catch up together regularly. Can you believe it's coming up to three months since we were last here? You'll never know how much it meant to have all of your support …' She felt Auntie Beth's hand close over hers.

'No, it's okay. I am not going to cry.' She swallowed hard. 'Anyway, you all mean a lot to me. I wanted to invite you here as another thank you from me. And also as a reminder to Sam that there's safety in numbers. Darling,' she said, gripping Sam's hand across the table, 'you're going through something really big right now, but we're all here for you. Aren't we, girls?'

'Absolutely,' Auntie Beth said, followed by Joanne, Jasmine and Caitlin.

'So, please don't shut yourself away or us out,' Hannah added, giving Sam's hand a squeeze before letting it go.

'Thanks, everyone. I really appreciate you all. But I'm fine. Really. I can't create, but other than that at this point I'm okay.'

'Well, when you don't feel okay, call me,' Jasmine said.

'Or me,' Caitlin said.

'You know where I am,' Auntie Beth said.

'And me,' Joanne said.

'And I have kittens to cuddle and a lovely mummy cat,' Hannah said, smiling warmly at her friend. 'So, please raise your glasses to friendship.'

'To friendship,' each person around the table repeated, clinked glasses, and then took a sip of their drink.

'And absent friends,' Beth added.

'Yes, and absent friends,' Hannah said solemnly, followed by Jasmine, Joanne and Caitlin. They were silent for a few beats before Hannah spoke again. 'Right, enough of the deep and meaningful, we're also here to celebrate. Our darling Sammy here has some very exciting news. It has been confirmed that she has been offered a spot in a joint exhibition in April.'

'It has? I have?' Sam said, her eyes wide.

'Hang on, how come you don't know?' Caitlin said.

'Because I just got the call from Roger at the gallery this morning,' Hannah said.

'Which brings us to the other exciting news,' Sam said, raising her glass again. 'To Hannah, my oldest and dearest friend who is now also my agent!'

'To friendship, new directions and great success,' Jasmine said.

'And gorgeous cats,' Caitlin said, nodding towards Holly who had sat up and was watching the proceedings.

'I think you should go into business as a caterer too,' Jasmine said. 'Your food is incredible.'

'Well, maybe I will,' Hannah said, with a laugh, touching the pearl pendant that had been her birthday gift last year from her parents-in-law, Raelene and Adrian. They'd told her it was to remind her that the world was her oyster. Only recently was she beginning to see the truth in that statement.

'I think you'll be an amazing agent,' Caitlin said, 'you're so professional and switched on.'

'Well, we shall see. It's early days.'

'It's just a pity I'm getting a spot in the exhibition because someone else was sick and had to pull out,' Sam said.

'So?' Joanne said. 'It's still a wonderful opportunity.'

'Exactly,' Jasmine said. 'If your work wasn't good enough, you wouldn't have been asked.'

'I know, I should feel more grateful.'

'Well, you've got other things clouding your feelings,' Beth said. 'Please remember to give yourself credit.'

'And Hannah. It's thanks to Hannah meeting him and selling me.'

'It's my job. And you're an easy sell. I'm excited to be able to do my bit.'

'Hannah, you've always done your bit – always supported and encouraged me.'

'Now I get to shout about your talent from the rooftops and you can't tell me off, Sammy, because it's officially my job. You're paying me to do it.'

'Only if we sell something. And I don't have anything to sell,' Sam said.

'It'll be fine. We'll work it out. But right now we have to eat the scones while they're still warm,' Hannah said, taking one from the plate stand in front of her. 'Please, tuck in everyone.'

'Oh my god, could they be any cuter?' Caitlin said as Lucky and Squeak wandered up to the table and let out little meows. 'Can I pick them up?'

'Of course. But remember, I'll be checking handbags before you leave – that goes for all of you,' Hannah warned, feigning seriousness.

A tittle of laughter made its way around the table.

★

When the plates had been cleared, Hannah took the portfolio she'd put together for Sam down from the sideboard.

'For show and tell this afternoon, I present Sam's portfolio,' Hannah said. She held the book up and opened the first page and commented on the contents, just as she had done with Roger at the gallery.

'No, Sam, no getting bashful,' she gently scolded. 'You need to start accepting praise because soon the whole of Melbourne is going to know your work.'

'It's a beautifully put together portfolio,' Jasmine said.

'Oh, that's all Hannah. I couldn't even colour inside the lines at this point. I've been a wreck,' Sam said.

'I'm sorry to hear that. I'm sure it will get easier soon,' Joanne said.

'I sure hope so. Because now it's not just about me – I don't want to let Hannah down. So what if I'm starting to look like the Steven Bradbury of the Melbourne art scene. Whatever it takes, right?' she added with a wry smile.

'Exactly,' Jasmine said.

'That's the spirit,' Joanne said.

'Well, it certainly looks like you have plenty of artistic talent too, Hannah, this is quite something,' Beth said.

'You're both inspiring me to get my act together and make a serious start on getting my business properly up and running,' Jasmine said. 'I need a portfolio, too.'

'It's only desktop publishing – easy-peasy. I could help you, Jas, if you like,' Hannah said.

'Oh, would you?'

'Of course. You do realise I spend my days at work doing a lot of this sort of stuff. It's just moving bits and pieces around to make it visually appealing on the page and tell a logical story.

'And while we're talking business, you each have to take one of my new business cards,' Hannah said. 'It's compulsory. I only needed one for the man at the gallery, but I had to get two hundred and fifty of the damned things printed! Oh, and speaking of business, take one of these too, in case you or someone you know needs their lawns or any other gardening done,' she said, handing them each a copy she'd made of Henry Peace's card.

'Who's this?' Caitlin asked.

'This is the driver of the truck involved in the accident that killed Tristan and Mum and Dad.'

'Oh. God, really?' Caitlin said. 'Why would you be handing out his business cards?'

'Have you seen him again?' Joanne said, looking a little concerned.

'No. I made some copies of the card he gave me. He's trying to get work so I thought it's the least I could do.'

'I'm still stuck on the fact you've met him,' Caitlin said. 'And that you seem okay with that.'

'Well, it was an accident. He shouldn't lose his life as well for something that wasn't his fault. I met him at the court. I forgot I haven't really seen you since to tell you.'

'I'm fine now, but I was off sick for a week, remember?' Caitlin said.

'That's right. I'm glad you're okay again,' Hannah said.

'Anyway, good on you for being so understanding about it. I'll pass his card on to Mum and Dad. They might need his services.'

'Thanks. I'm sure Henry would appreciate it. He seemed like a nice fellow – quiet and gentle – though I've only met him the once. I'm thinking of having him come and prune my fruit trees.'

Hannah noticed the silence around the table. 'Guys, it's okay. I'm not being scammed or taken for a ride, or whatever you're thinking. I appreciate that you're concerned that I could get hurt by caring too much, that I'm getting involved. And I love you for it. But it's just a business card that I hope will lead to more work for him. Perhaps if he had great friends like I do, then maybe he wouldn't have lost his way as he seems to. So, please don't look at me like I'm about to hand over all my money to a scam artist. I promise that the only help I'll give him will be practical – not financial,' Hannah said. 'Would that help put you all at ease?'

'Yes,' Sam said. 'You don't know anything about him.'

There was a collective mumble of agreement.

'You didn't tell me he was a gardener,' Joanne said.

'Didn't I? Oh well, he is.'

'Handy to know. I'm sorry, Hannah,' Joanne said, 'I was allowing my concern for you to get the better of me. You're a very kind and thoughtful person. Perhaps if there were more people like you in the world, it wouldn't be such a horrible, screwed-up place right now.'

'Yes. Hear, hear, Joanne,' Beth said.

'Thanks, Jo. I enjoy helping. I got such a kick out of doing Sam's portfolio and meeting with the gallery owner and negotiating on her behalf. I've been treading water, which I've needed to, but now I feel I have to do more. I'd really love to help you out with your portfolio, Jas.'

'Oh, thank you. You know, Craig told me the other night there was something different about you – that you were practically glowing. And you really are,' Jasmine said.

'Yes, you are,' Beth said. 'You've said how lucky you are to have us. I think the world is lucky to have you. Your parents and Tristan would be so proud.'

Chapter Fourteen

'Ready to go?' Craig asked, peering over Hannah's cubicle wall.

'Yep. Two secs.' Hannah grabbed her handbag. She'd been surprised when the day before, just as she was leaving, Craig had told her he was taking her out to lunch tomorrow. She couldn't remember the last time she'd had lunch out of the office alone with her boss. Had they ever?

'If that's okay with you,' he'd added.

'Yes. Of course. Great. I'd love to have lunch with you. Thanks. Do you want me to book somewhere?'

'No, no, it's all taken care of.'

Hannah almost gasped when they went into One on the corner of King Street – it was currently one of *the* most popular places to dine in Melbourne.

'I read about this in the paper the other week, I've been dying to check it out,' Craig said as they settled into the plush velvet booth. 'It's such a pity they're not open of an evening.'

They perused their menus while a friendly but brusque waiter moved around them delivering water and bread rolls.

'Thank you,' Hannah said, beaming, in an attempt to elicit some cheerfulness from the man. She wasn't a fan of stuffy service. She and her friends agreed it could ruin what might have otherwise been a lovely meal. They said they always preferred warm and friendly, and to leave feeling they'd been welcomed rather than they'd had the privilege of visiting the premises. Jasmine who was originally a Sydneysider and now a staunch Melbournian had a theory that the haughty places were owned by Sydney restaurateurs.

'So, how's things?' Craig asked when their orders had been taken: pumpkin ravioli entrée and the duck main for Hannah and scallops and then rib-eye steak for Craig, with green beans and fries. They'd look at the dessert menu later, though Hannah doubted she could do three courses. She'd said no to wine. When Craig had said they were in 'no rush' she figured he didn't mean they weren't going back to work at all that afternoon. Wine over lunch would make her sleepy and pretty much useless for the rest of the day.

'All good. I'll have those spreadsheets to you by close of business. Well, depending how long we're out for,' she said with a little laugh before taking a sip of water.

'I wasn't referring to work, Hannah, it was a general enquiry.'

'Oh. Right. Well, pretty good, thanks.' It was really odd to be sitting across the table from Craig, her boss, but also someone else's husband – particularly as she now considered Jasmine one of her most treasured friends. Hannah had never socialised with them as a couple and suddenly she felt all at sea. *This is weird.*

'Have you seen Henry Peace again?' Craig asked.

'No. I do need to call him to get him to prune my fruit trees. I'm not sure why, but I keep forgetting. Every time I think of it it's too early in the day or too late at night.'

'Jas gave me his card. I'm going to try him out. And how are the cats?'

'Good. The kittens are starting to wreak havoc now they're mobile. They'll need vaccinations and de-sexing soon.'

'Yes, one must be a responsible pet owner. Jas tells me you're now acting for Samantha. That's great. You'll be really good at that.'

'Thanks. It's early days and not exactly a viable career proposition. So, don't you worry, I'm not leaving you.'

'Oh, I wasn't worried about that. But, good to know.'

Hannah almost let out a huge sigh of relief when the waiter delivered their entrées. She gave him a beaming smile. 'Thank you, this looks wonderful.'

'Yes, it does look good,' Craig agreed, picking up his fork.

'Yum,' Hannah said, after her first mouthful.

'And where are your parents-in-law at the moment?' Craig asked when their plates had been collected.

'Kununurra right now. I think. Look, Craig, can we please stop with the awkward twenty questions. It's getting really weird,' Hannah said with a laugh. 'I'm guessing there's a reason we're out to lunch, considering I can't remember the last time we did this. What's going on? It's me, you can talk to me about anything, remember?'

'Yes. Please. Great. Thank you,' Craig said with obvious relief. 'Well, I have a proposition.'

'Okay.'

'I'm leaving to set up my own consultancy specialising in assisting organisations in the services sector with growth, expansion and diversification, implementing change and improving efficiency. I'm deliberately keeping my focus broad to start with. Anyway, I'd like you to consider coming with me – to set up my office, run it, and generally be my right hand.'

'Oh. Wow.'

'I've been chewing it over for years. But, as you understand only too well, you never know what's around the corner. So, no guts no glory, as they say.' He paused and took a sip of wine.

There's that damned ripple effect again, Hannah thought.

'So, what do you think? The thing is, it would only be part-time – probably two or three days a week. If we get lucky and become really successful, it might become full-time. But I can't guarantee it. I could try and get you a job-sharing role or I have some friends in recruitment ...'

'It's fine, Craig.'

'What's fine? You're not interested in leaving, or what?'

'Two or three days a week would be fine with me.' Hannah had never told anyone just how much she had received as the beneficiary of her husband and parents' estates – not even her best friend, Sam. The truth was she felt guilty about it. And a bit embarrassed to no longer be struggling like everyone else around her age. 'Yes, I'm interested. Very.'

'Oh, that's great.' Craig looked like he was ready to launch himself across the table and hug her. Instead he reached over and gripped both her hands. 'You've no idea how much this means. You're wasted at TLR. How do you feel about cold calling prospective clients, running a website and doing a lot of market-ing, along with all the stuff you do for me now?'

'I don't have any marketing qualifications.'

'That's not a problem. According to what I've seen and heard from Jasmine in regards to the market stall and what you're doing for Samantha, I'd say you've probably got more skills in market-ing than most graduates. You'll be fine. I'm sure you know more than you realise.'

'Well, as long as you're sure I'm the best candidate, because it's your business. I wouldn't be offended if you'd rather find someone more qualified. Honestly.'

'Hannah, there *is* no one more suitable than you. We're here because I want you. The question is, could you work just for me?'

'I already work just for you, Craig.'

'Yes, I know. But you currently have the buffer of an HR department and workmates to talk to. How do you feel about working from home – either yours or mine? That would be up to you. I know you're disciplined enough, but do you need the camaraderie? That, I guess, is the question.'

'I think I'd be fine. Either at your place or mine. I'm happy to play it by ear and see how we go. Maybe shift between the two, depending on what we're doing? We only live a few suburbs apart.'

Oh wow, Hannah thought again as she took a long drink of water.

'Sorry, I'm rushing you. Take your time to think it through, weigh up the pros and cons,' Craig said.

'No. You know what, Craig, count me in. I've been feeling a little restless and I think this might be just what I need. It'll be great to have more time for Sam, too. So, the answer is yes, I'd love to come and work for you,' Hannah said, beaming and holding her glass out to be clinked.

'Here's to the dynamic duo taking on the world – well, starting with Melbourne,' Craig said.

'Aim high, I say,' Hannah said with a laugh.

Craig beamed back.

'Oh, this looks amazing,' Hannah said when their mains were delivered.

'Yes, and at least now I can concentrate on enjoying it. Bon appétit!'

When they began discussing Craig's vision and the finer details, Hannah retrieved the notebook she always kept on her desk that she'd stuffed into her handbag as she'd left.

'Thank goodness I have you,' he said, grinning and lifting up his second glass of wine.

'Anything take your fancy?' Craig asked after the dessert menus had been delivered.

'Yes, everything!' she said with a laugh. 'But I'd better not.'

'Sure I can't tempt you?'

'I'm very tempted, believe me. But I might struggle to walk back to the office.'

'Do you fancy sharing something?' he asked.

'Oh, now you're twisting my arm.'

'No pressure.'

'I'll go halves in the salted caramel if you're keen.'

'Done,' he said, just as the waiter appeared again.

'That really was lovely, Craig, thank you,' Hannah said when they stepped from the restaurant into the warm afternoon.

'No, thank *you*. And lunch was my pleasure. Come on, we'd better get back before we get the sack. It's three o'clock,' Craig said.

'Yes. Golly. It would almost be worth it after that meal. I really enjoyed it.'

'I'm glad. Me too. I'll have to bring Jas here.'

'They're only open during weekdays, remember? And when I'm in charge, there'll be no slacking off,' Hannah said.

'Yes, ma'am. Better do it in the next two weeks, then. While I'm still a salaried employee and know I can afford it.'

'None of that, we're going to be hugely successful.'

As they walked back, Hannah thought how the last time she'd enjoyed a meal so much was when she'd stayed at The Windsor last year and taken the plunge and shared a table with Brad – the stranger who turned out to be a freelance journalist. She'd eaten out a lot with girlfriends, but that was somehow different – they chatted at a different level about different things. Oh, how she missed Tristan.

She was surprised to find her thoughts straying to the discussion she'd had all those months ago with Jasmine about setting up an online dating profile. Was she ready now to take that big step too? According to the rest of the world, it wasn't such a big move. But it was to Hannah Ainsley, who'd had her happy marriage suddenly snatched away from her.

Chapter Fifteen

'Hello, you two,' Hannah said, opening her front door to the twins standing in front of their mother.

'Hello, Auntie Hann.'

'How's school? Are you still enjoying it?'

'Yes, it's good, thanks,' said Oliver.

'I like colouring-in best,' Ethan said.

'That's great.' Hannah was at a loss. What else was there to say?

'Something smells yummy,' Ethan said.

'That's good.'

'Thanks for having us over for dinner,' Oliver said.

'You're very welcome. It's lovely to see you.'

'Do you have something yummy for us?' Ethan said.

'Ethan,' Sam warned.

'I hope so. How does lasagne sound?'

'Oh, yes. I love lasagne.'

'Me too,' Oliver said.

'Well, you'd better come in, then.' Hannah stepped aside and the boys ran past her. 'Are you okay?' she said, peering at Sam after giving her a hug.

'Well, other than being a bad mother, fine, I guess.'

'Why are you a bad mother?'

'Because they hate my food. Not that fish fingers and baked beans on toast can really be counted as mine.'

'I hope you not cooking is because you're too busy creating,' Hannah said, as she closed the front door.

'Hmm. Unfortunately not,' Sam muttered, as she followed Hannah into the hall where the boys were standing, looking around.

'What's up, boys?' Hannah asked.

'Where are the cats?' Oliver asked.

'Yes, can we please have a cuddle? Mum says maybe if we're really gentle,' Ethan said.

'Try the lounge room, they were in there earlier. And, yes, you can have a cuddle if you're careful and they want a cuddle.'

'How will we know?'

'Oh, you'll know,' Hannah said.

'But how?'

'You just will,' Sam said wearily. 'Go and sit in the lounge quietly and see if they come to you. Remember, quiet and gentle. They're only little. Okay?'

'Yes, Mum. We'll be very good,' said Oliver.

'Yes, very good,' Ethan said.

'Are you okay to wait a little while for dinner or do you need a snack to keep you going?' Hannah asked.

'I'm okay, thanks, Auntie Hann,' Oliver said. 'I had chips in the car after school.'

'And I had snakes,' declared Ethan.

'Good. Off you go, then,' Hannah said.

'See, bad mother, right here,' Sam said.

Hannah put the lasagne and garlic bread into the oven and then poured Sam a glass of wine.

'Oh, god, that's good,' Sam said after taking a large gulp.

'Yes, lovely. So, what's up?'

'I'm useless. I'm a bad mother, as you've seen. I can't create anything. The only reason I haven't taken to drink is because I have to remember to pick the boys up from school. Even then I have to set an alarm so I don't forget them. Good idea, by the way. And, god, I miss Rob. I never thought he did much, but just knowing I could call on him meant a lot more than I realised,' Sam said, her eyes filling with tears. 'I'm even missing his awful tuna mornay,' she said with a tight laugh. 'Well, not the mornay, as such, more him taking care of dinner occasionally. And him being here, generally.'

'What can I do to help?'

'Nothing. Thanks. I'll be okay, I'm just having a whinge.'

'You're allowed. Do you hear from him much?'

'He Skypes with us most nights.'

'That's good. Isn't it?'

'Yes, but, Hann, it hurts. Nothing has changed, yet *everything* has. He still tells me he loves me and blows kisses – to me, not just the boys. But he's not here and as much as I tell myself he's going to snap out of this – whatever it is – and come home, it's not going to happen, is it? I'm trying so hard to hold it together for the boys that I'm exhausted all the time. Why couldn't he just be an unfaithful arsehole so I could hate him?'

'But you wouldn't and you still wouldn't bad-mouth him to the boys. It's not you.'

'No, but it would be easier.'

'Maybe.'

'Anyway, I couldn't be angry with him while he's still good enough to be paying all the bills and letting me stay at home playing at being an artist.'

'You're not exactly *playing* now, Sam – you're a professional.'

'Hmm.'

'How are the boys coping with it all, do you think?'

'Oh, they're fine. They're probably in denial, too, and all the new experiences of school are keeping them distracted enough. You know, kids are a lot more resilient than we give them credit for. Or maybe that's just me telling myself what I want to hear – trying not to think about what long-term damage is being done. Though, that's just par for the course of being a parent. I'm sure we all screw them up one way or another, despite our best efforts.'

'I think you're being way too hard on yourself. You're a great mum and the boys are fabulous – because of you.'

'Thanks. If only I could get stuck into a project. You know me, I'm much better at life when I'm making things. I'm trying not to freak out about the exhibition. I don't know what to do for it. Roger's going to want to know soon, isn't he?'

'Yes. And he'll need something to photograph so he can get the marketing ball rolling early, and get cracking on designing the invitations and sending them out.'

'Fuck,' Sam said, running a hand through her hair.

'Sam, it's only been a few weeks since you made all those pieces for the markets. You worked like a machine for that. You're just a bit burnt out. You'll be fine again in no time.'

'But I don't know what to do.'

'You never do until you actually start.'

'This is different. Roger needs to know.'

'He especially liked your ceramic ladies and the linocuts.'

'I can't do the same thing.'

'Why not? Don't most artists have a signature style? You could do a series of little old men with hats, cravats … Sorry, I'm not helping. I know it's not that easy – the urge and passion has to be there. I guess what I'm trying to say is can you capitalise on what you've already done rather than stressing over trying to come up with new ideas?'

'Hmm. Oh, I don't know. I just don't want to let you down – now you're my agent.'

'Oh, Sammy. You could never let me down. And I'm your agent for you, not me.' Hannah draped her arm around Sam. 'You're always saying your best ideas come when you're not looking for them. I think you need to try to stop worrying about deadlines. Get back to basics. Take a soak in the tub, a long walk in the park, sit and doodle. The ideas will come. They always do. Your brain is just too busy.'

'Hmm.'

They lapsed into silence as they enjoyed their wine. Hannah thought about how Sam had so often said creativity couldn't be forced, that it didn't work under pressure or to deadlines. So how the hell had she got her assessment pieces done during her university degree? She was starting to feel a little frustrated. She wanted to point all this out to Sam, but it wouldn't help, would it? Sam would have to figure it out in her own time – alone. Except, now Hannah was her agent and dealing with the gallery she was feeling a certain amount of pressure herself. She was relieved Sam could see that as well. *Yes, my reputation is at stake too*, she found herself thinking. But, really, what reputation? When it came to being an artist's agent, she had no reputation. She'd simply made a phone call, put together a portfolio – a pretty damned fine one, if she said so herself – had a meeting, secured an exhibition spot that was practically going begging, and had some swanky business cards done. Business cards that didn't even have a title on them. For the umpteenth time recently, Hannah found herself thinking, *No, this is not about you. God, if you think it's frustrating for you, think how it must be for Sam!* But the truth was Hannah didn't like anything half-done. If it was worth doing, it was worth doing well. That was why Craig had so much faith in her.

Oh well, it's out of my hands. If Sam lets me down, then so be it. She just hoped Sam didn't let herself down. The state her friend was in, it might be her undoing. *Is it time for some tough love? Oh, god, I don't know*, Hannah thought.

'Right. Enough about me. What's going on with you? Distract me from my misery. With anything.'

'Well, I do have some news, actually. I've quit my job.'

'You've done what? Good for you. Why? Um, it *is* good news, isn't it?'

'Yes. Craig is going out on his own to become a consultant. He's asked me to work for him – run his office, do the marketing ...'

'Oh, you'll be fantastic. Well done. When do you start?'

'Two weeks. I handed in my notice today. I'm going to miss everyone at work, though.'

'Well you already see plenty of Caitlin, and Chloe occasionally.'

'I think it'll be the masses – the noisy kitchen at lunch time and morning and afternoon tea; the chitchat – that I'll miss.'

'You sound like you're regretting your decision already.'

'No, not really, just being realistic – preparing myself, I guess. It's only going to be a few days a week, too, so I can be around more for you, if you want. You know, moral support from your doting agent.'

'Will you be okay with just a few days work – I mean, financially?'

'I'll be fine. And if I do well and Craig gets busy enough it might become full-time. But I am looking forward to being here with the kitties.'

'Speaking of which, it's awfully silent in the lounge room – never a good thing with those two. I'd better check.'

'Aww,' Hannah whispered as she and Sam stood in the doorway and saw the boys lying together on the floor with a kitten curled up against each of them and Holly stretched out close by.

'Oh, bless,' Sam said. 'School really does tire them out. Shh. Don't move. I need a photo for Rob,' she said, tiptoeing back into the hall where she retrieved her phone from her handbag.

Just as the boys looked up and noticed them the oven timer dinged.

'Is dinner ready, Auntie Hann?' Oliver asked.

'It sure is. Have you worked up an appetite?'

'Yes.'

'Me too,' Ethan said.

'Did you enjoy playing with Holly and the kittens?'

'Yes. Thank you.'

'You'd better thank them.'

'Thank you, Holly,' Oliver said, bending down and kissing the cat. 'Thank you, kitten,' he said, picking Lucky up, kissing him and then putting him down gently and doing the same with Squeak. Ethan copied his brother.

'Lucky is the darker one and Squeak has the white paws,' Hannah said.

'Bye bye, Holly, Lucky and Squeak,' Oliver said as they got up.

'I like that you have cats,' Ethan said.

'Me too,' Hannah said. 'How are Inky and Oofy?'

'They're good. A bit naughty,' Oliver said.

'Yes, we need to distant them more, Mum says.'

'*Discipline* them more,' Sam corrected.

'I bet they miss you while you're at school.'

'Probably, but it's really just like when we were at kindy, only more days, Auntie Hann,' said the ever-knowledgeable Oliver.

'They do miss us,' Ethan said. 'They jump all over us when we get home.'

'And run around the house like mad things,' Oliver added.

'Hence the need for more discipline,' Sam said.

'Come on, dinner time,' Hannah said.

'Thank you so much for this,' Sam said as the tucked into their meals. 'I so badly needed a break.'

'Good. I'm glad.'

Chapter Sixteen

Hannah told the vet's receptionist her name and that she was there to collect Holly and Lucky and Squeak. Without the three cats in the house she'd spent all day feeling a little out of sorts, as if something major was missing from her life. And it had been. Again she'd wondered how she could have thought her life truly complete without a pet.

She'd planned to collect the cats after their 'snips' and vaccinations hours ago, but the receptionist had called, asking her to come later, just before closing time, because several emergency cases had taken priority over routine procedures.

'Hannah, hi.'

Hannah looked up at hearing the familiar voice and smiled back at the vet standing in front of her. Not so much cute as tall, dark and handsome, she thought, at the same time as her stomach flipped. She wondered if she now regretted turning down his invitation for a date. It was a little under two months ago. She certainly hadn't felt ready. So much had changed since then. Had that feeling changed too?

'Hi, Pete. Where's Charlie?' Hannah could have kicked herself. *Of all the things to say, you asked after his dog!*

'Do you mind if I sit down? It's been a long, difficult day. I just needed to escape the chaos for a sec.'

'No, not at all. Please,' she said, indicating the plastic chair beside her. 'Is everything okay?'

'I hope so. Charlie's out the back, keeping an eye on a couple of critical cases. Touch and go. At least if we lose them they had canine company,' Pete said sadly.

Hannah was struck by how despondent he seemed. While she didn't like seeing him distressed, or anyone for that matter, she did like seeing how much he cared. No doubt he'd been in this position many times, but still he showed so much emotion.

'He's a lovely dog.'

'Yes, he is. I'm sorry, Hannah, I'm a bit ragged. Not very good company. No matter how many times you go through it, it never gets any easier. Your Holly and kittens are just coming around and will be ready to go home soon. Everything went fine. They're really lovely cats.'

'They are. I've been a pathetic basket case without them today,' she said with a warm smile, trying to cheer Pete up a little.

'Well, I'd better get back out there,' he said.

As he stood up, Hannah found herself also rising. She got a flash of memory – the hug she'd shared with Brad just outside the lift on the fourth floor of The Windsor Hotel all those months ago.

'Um, Pete?' she said.

'Yes?'

'Would a hug help?' she said, opening her arms out wide.

Without a word, Pete wrapped his large arms around Hannah and held on tight. She could feel his breath in her hair at her neck.

He held her so tightly she could also feel his heart beating against her – fast, but as the moments passed it slowed.

'Thank you,' he said, slowly releasing with a sigh. 'I needed that.'

I thought you might. 'You're welcome,' she said, reaching up and putting a hand gently to his face. As she did she thought how good it felt to give to someone else what Brad had done for her that night. By the look on Pete's face it really had helped.

Hannah watched, almost mesmerised as he took hold of her left hand, raised it to his lips and planted the lightest of kisses on it before letting it go.

'I'll see you 'round,' he said, and turned away.

'Pete?' Hannah found herself calling.

He turned. 'Yes?'

'Would you like me to cook you dinner? Um, tonight? Now?'

He looked at her. 'I would. Very much. Um …'

'Of course, if you've met someone else or … I'm being too forward. Sorry.'

'I haven't. And you're not.'

'It's just you look like you could do with someone taking care of you tonight. And I could do with a vet on hand since I'm a complete novice at being a cat mum and all,' she said, grinning and trying to defuse what had the potential to become an awkward situation.

'You seem to be doing a pretty good job from what I've seen,' he said as he glanced down at what he was wearing.

'Please, just come as you are.' He looked presentable enough to Hannah. 'Do you like spaghetti bolognaise?'

'It's actually one of my favourite comfort foods.'

'Brilliant.'

'Are you sure?'

'I am. Just a quiet evening in. Charlie is welcome too, if he likes.'

'No, Charlie will insist on staying here tonight with his patients. But I will take you up on your very generous offer.' Hannah tried to hide her relief – as soon as she'd offered Charlie's invitation she'd regretted it. It wouldn't be fair on Holly and Lucky and Squeak to have a German shepherd in their house during their recovery, no matter how well behaved he was.

They looked over when a nurse carried the cat box out. 'All ready to go,' the young woman said.

'I can leave now, so I'll follow you,' Pete said. 'I'll just get my keys and do a quick final check on the patients and say goodbye to Charlie.'

'Okay,' Hannah said, taking her wallet out as she moved towards the desk. 'Take your time.' She watched after him, her heart flipping between a yearning to take care of him and huge, swelling respect for his kind, generous soul.

She handed over her credit card before squatting down and looking into the cat box. Three pairs of eyes opened briefly, and then closed again. 'Hello, darlings,' Hannah said. 'Are you okay?'

'They're still a bit sleepy,' the nurse said. 'And they'll be unsteady on their feet for a few hours, so put them somewhere where it's quiet and comfortable.'

'Okay. Thanks.'

As she drove home, Hannah was surprised she didn't feel at all nervous about her first date with Pete. It was as if they were old friends, which they weren't. They didn't know each other very well. Granted, it wasn't exactly a conventional first date – no days of anticipation, wondering what to wear, et cetera, et cetera …

'Thank you for this, Hannah, I feel much better already,' Pete said when he was ensconced at Hannah's kitchen bench with a glass of wine in hand.

'I'm glad. Cheers,' she said, raising her glass.

'Cheers,' he said. 'Um, is this our first date?' he asked hesitatingly.

'I think it might be,' Hannah said shyly.

'Well, to our first date,' Pete said, 'may it be the first of many.' They clinked glasses and then Pete leaned over and pecked Hannah lightly on the lips.

As she put the spaghetti into the boiling water, Hannah thought how lovely this was. Nice and easy and relaxed.

'Please tell me if there's anything I can do,' Pete said.

'Thanks, but it's all organised. I just need to cook the pasta and make a quick salad. I made the sauce this afternoon.'

'I have to say, Hannah, I'm very impressed at how at ease you are with me watching you cook. I often feel nervous if someone watches me – though I'm probably not as competent a cook as you seem to be.'

'Oh, I could practically do this with my eyes closed – well, not exactly with the knives, but you know what I mean. I made my first spaghetti bolognaise when I was twelve. I love to cook – it relaxes me.'

'I love to eat, so we're a match made in heaven!'

'It's great to have someone to cook for. I miss that.'

'Yes, I know what you mean. The company, companionship. It's been eighteen months since Rachel died, but the cancer took her vibrancy – and her appetite – a year or so before that. You know, I used to suffer terrible guilt enjoying a meal in front of her, too, when most of the time, especially near the end, she could barely force down half a cracker. It took me ages to allow myself to properly relish food again. Though, of course, the grief doesn't help with that, does it?'

'No.'

'Sorry, I didn't mean to get morose.'

'It's okay. I completely understand if you need to talk about it. About Rachel.'

'Thanks, but I'm fine. It must be just the tiredness getting to me.'

'Here we go,' Hannah said, putting steaming bowls on the bench. 'We can sit here or in the dining room. Your choice.'

'Right here's perfect.'

'Okay. Tuck in then.'

'Oh, this is good, Hannah. And just what I need. You're an absolute saviour. You've no idea.'

Hannah beamed back.

'So, how have you been?' he asked when they'd settled into their meals.

'Good. Better,' she said thoughtfully. 'Finally now I have more good days than bad.'

'So, do you cook for a living, if it makes you so happy?'

'Oh no, I'm an executive personal assistant. Well, I guess I still am.'

'Oh?'

'I'm in the process of changing jobs. My boss has just left the firm to go out on his own so I'm going too – to run his office and him, essentially.'

'I can see how you'd be very good at that. You're strong, but you're also a nurturer. You take care of people – that's where I think your true passion lies.'

'You've got me sussed,' she said with a laugh. It was quite special and a little unnerving to have a relative stranger *get* her so completely, so quickly. Especially when she'd only recently discovered this about herself. 'You know, I've also become an agent to an artist – my best friend, Sam.'

'Oh wow, how exciting.'

'Well, not really. She's just starting out.'

'I love art. What does she do?'

'All sorts. She's very talented in a number of media, but still finding her *thing*. She's actually having her first exhibition – a joint one – in a little under two months. That's the portfolio I've done up for her on the end of the bench there,' Hannah said, pointing. 'Feel free to have a look through.'

'I will,' he said, pulling it towards him. 'Oh, I see what you mean. She does seem very talented. And in so many media, like you say. That's amazing.'

'Well, at this point, it's proving a bit of curse because she's freaking out about what to focus on. She's also got a lot else going on. Her husband has just announced he's gay and disappeared to run his company's office in Singapore, leaving her to look after their twin six-year-old boys.'

'That's a lot for her to deal with.'

'Do you think everything's connected?'

'Um. Everything in what sense? Do you mean spiritually? You should know I'm anti organised religion. But please don't ask me to explain my views now – I'm a bit too tired for such a deep, important subject.'

'I'm against organised religion too, but I am starting to see there's a powerful force out there pulling strings,' Hannah said. 'I've never really got it. Until recently. It's strange how everything does seem connected.'

'Tell me.'

'Well, like the accident that claimed my family. You think it's really only those who are directly impacted that suffer. Sure, friends and extended family are sad and empathetic, but until recently I never realised to what extent they could be affected too. Sorry, I'm not making sense. It's hard to explain.'

'I'm listening.'

'It's the ripple effect. Well, that's what I'm calling it. So, Rob, that's Sam's husband, realises he's sick of living a lie – as a result of seeing just how quickly things can change because of what I went through. My Tristan and he were dear friends. And then my boss, Craig, he's decided life's too short so now he's starting his own business after procrastinating for several years. And, Sam, well, she's suddenly decided she's determined to have a career as an artist after all these years of dabbling. I know she's been busy raising the boys, but there's suddenly a fire in her belly that wasn't there before. Well, there is behind the doubt and indecision. That's hard to explain too.'

'I think it's good that people, especially those you care about, are using what's happened as a catalyst for change in a good way,' Pete said. 'I think it's especially sad when really bad things happen in vain.'

'I met the driver – you know, the guy who drove his truck into … No, that sounds terrible. It was an accident and he was cleared of all wrongdoing. Anyway, I met him.'

'Really. How was it?'

'Strangely good. I think. He seems nice, but badly affected by it all.'

Hannah proceeded to tell Pete the story of her meeting Henry Peace and how she felt annoyed with him and frustrated that she couldn't help.

'You are an exceptional human being, Hannah Ainsley,' Pete said, shaking his head slowly.

'Oh, I don't know about that,' she said, blushing. 'I just can't not care. And I can't stand seeing someone sad and not at least try to help. It's just who I am, I guess,' she added with a shrug before taking a sip of wine.

'Well, I'm really sorry such a kind person as you had to go through something so horrible and lose so much,' Pete said.

'Thanks. Ditto. I'm learning to be okay with it all.'

'Me too.'

'What choice do we have?'

'Exactly.'

They looked around at hearing a squeaky little meow. There were Holly and the two kittens making their way unsteadily across the kitchen tiles. Hannah got off her stool and gently scooped Holly up, taking care near her shaved belly and stitches.

'You darling little thing,' she said.

Pete picked the two kittens up. 'You're a pair of little cuties,' he said, nuzzling them.

'Do you ever get tired of animals after seeing them all day?' Hannah asked.

'Nope. They're each a little different. If work called me right now I'd go back in. I hope they don't, but I'd go. Like you, I just want to help. It's my calling. I'm afraid I am a bit of a workaholic. Though that may have been a coping mechanism. I still can't believe you're such a new pet owner, you're a natural,' he said.

'It's not hard. These guys are just so lovely. They say cats are arrogant and aloof. Not Holly, she's an absolute sweetie. And the kittens – I'm sure they'll be naughty, but at the moment they're just plain cute.'

'She knows how lucky she was to find you. I think they understand a lot more than we give them credit for.'

'Are you guys hungry?' Hannah said, putting Holly down. 'Is it dinner time for you? Just a little bit while you're still feeling fragile. More later. Okay?' she said, dishing out a third of their usual allowance into the bowls. 'No wolfing it down, Lucky and Squeak,' she warned. 'You'll make yourselves sick. I hope I'm doing the right thing by them – I'm a bit clueless,' she said, watching the cats eating.

'I think you're doing great. And you can always ask me or phone the clinic if you ever have any questions.'

'So, that doesn't bug you, either – ignorant people picking your brains all the time and you never getting a break?'

'Not at all. I'd much rather someone ask than run the risk of harming their pet. If only more people thought to ask questions.'

'Hmm. Fair enough. Right,' Hannah said, coming back to the bench after washing her hands. 'Can I tempt you with a warm chocolate brownie with cream or ice-cream – or both?'

'Is there no end to your cooking skills? Your spaghetti bolognaise was incredible, by the way.'

'Thank you. I'm afraid the ice-cream isn't my doing. If I wasn't pretty much addicted to the stuff, I would have bought myself one of those fancy churner machines. As it is, I have to exert all my willpower to not polish off a whole tub in one sitting.'

'So I'd be doing you a favour, then?' Pete asked, smiling cheekily.

'Yes, you would.'

'Well then, how can I resist? Both cream and ice-cream, thank you,' he said, beaming.

'Come on, let's go into the lounge room,' Hannah said, carrying their desserts from the kitchen. 'Feel free to kick off your shoes and make yourself comfortable.'

'God, I feel so much better now after that crazy day,' Pete said, stretching as he put his bowl down on the coffee table. He yawned. 'Sorry. I'd better get going before I embarrass myself by falling asleep. I blame your wonderful food.'

'You're welcome to stay if you'd like. The spare bed is all made up. I don't want you driving if you're exhausted.'

'Would you mind? Would it be too weird?'

'No, I offered. And, no, not at all, but I, um, I ...'

'It's okay,' he said, holding his hands up. 'I completely understand. Slow. I know.'

'Come on, I'll get you a towel and show you where everything is.'

*

Hannah woke up feeling surprisingly refreshed. She'd gone to bed and laid there wondering how she'd get to sleep as she'd switched between feeling bewildered, disappointed and a little relieved at Pete's apparent lack of romantic inclination towards her. But if she were being honest with herself, she wasn't entirely sure she was ready for full-blown intimacy just yet. She thought he was handsome – a handsome man who clearly had a kind, wonderful heart and soul. She felt a strange sense of gratitude for having met him, similar to what she regularly felt for Holly when she watched the cat who had brought so much good into her life.

She looked over the side of the bed to where she'd placed a soft cat bed in a basket on the floor in the hope Holly wouldn't put her stitches at risk by jumping up onto the bed. She'd also placed a chair with a small box next to it, to create a set of makeshift steps.

'Hello there, kitties.' She noticed they'd made use of the basket. 'Is it breakfast time?' She pulled her bathrobe on and quietly made her way down to the kitchen.

Hannah was surprised to find Pete at the bench fiddling with his mobile phone.

'Good morning,' she said, 'how are you?'

'Good morning. I'm good, thanks. That bed is amazing. I slept really well.'

'That's great. You're up early for someone who slept well,' Hannah said with a laugh. It suddenly felt very awkward having a man she barely knew in her kitchen looking like he belonged there and her dressed in a robe.

'No matter how well or how poorly I sleep, I always wake up at five-thirty.'

'Me too, but it's usually closer to six for me. You could have helped yourself to coffee.'

'I didn't want to overstep the hospitality or risk waking you. It is Sunday morning after all. I've just been texting with the surgery. My patients made it through the night. I'm so relieved.'

'Oh, that's great news. I'm so pleased for you. And them.'

'They've still got a long way to go, but this is an important milestone. Speaking of patients, how are you and your little ones this morning?' he said, speaking to Holly and the kittens who were sitting patiently by their bowls.

'They seem fine. And hungry.'

'That's the best sign of all.'

'Do you think they can have their full allocation now?'

'Yes. They should be okay. And then could I interest you in breakfast out?'

'Oh, yes. I love breakfast out.' It had been one of Hannah and Tristan's favourite things to do on a Sunday morning.

'I'm not too unpresentable, am I? I could go home, but I do want to stop into the surgery and check on things for myself, and collect Charlie.'

'I think you look fine, but I need a quick shower.'

'How about we take separate cars and you meet me at the surgery in, say, forty-five minutes? I can shower there. How would that be?'

'Okay.'

'Well, I'll get going.' He held her by the shoulders and pecked her on the lips. 'Thanks again for taking such good care of me last night. It was just what I needed.'

'You're very welcome,' she said as she walked him to the door. 'I'll see you soon, then.' She closed the door behind him and rushed to get organised. She'd had plenty of meals out recently, but hadn't had breakfast out for ages. She couldn't remember when the last time had been. None of her friends were true morning people. Sam would have been keen before the twins had come along. Now she preferred to dine out without them, even if she could get them dressed and in the car before noon. Without ever acknowledging it out loud she, Rob, Hannah and Tristan had made a pact to not bother trying for breakfast together anymore.

As Hannah drove towards the vet practice, she began yearning for eggs on heavily buttered sourdough toast and cooked tomato and crispy bacon. She often cooked herself a big breakfast on a Sunday, but there was something exquisite about it appearing without any effort. She hadn't realised how much she'd missed it, she thought as she parked beside Pete's car.

'Hello, Charlie,' she said to the dog as she walked in. She gave his ears a good ruffle.

'Come on through,' she heard Pete call. Hannah walked into the surgery. She felt sad when she saw the rows of cages with listless animals inside. 'I won't be a minute, I just want to change this dressing,' Pete said. He stood at a stainless-steel bench with a small dog stretched out in front of him. Hannah's heart lurched and her stomach turned at hearing the whining and seeing the huge jagged wound that had just been exposed. She nodded and smiled weakly in greeting at the nurse who stood on the other side of the bench, holding down the squirming dog. Hannah swallowed and tried to ignore the light-headedness she was feeling. She felt the blood drain to her feet and she became clammy all over. Suddenly the clean smell of the room became intense and overpowering.

'I'm just going to wait in the other room,' she said and hurried away back the way she'd come.

As she sat on one of the chairs in the waiting room she was thankful she'd managed to not throw up. She'd probably come very close. Thank goodness she hadn't eaten anything this morning. She tried to ignore her thumping head as she ran a hand through Charlie's fur – the faithful dog sitting beside her.

'Sorry about that,' Pete said as he came out drying his hands on paper towel. 'Are you okay? You look a little pale.'

'I'm fine. I think my stomach's weaker than I realised.'

'Right, come on, breakfast time. Hopefully you'll feel better with some food in you. Do you want to come, Charlie, or stay here and look after your patients?'

Hannah was stunned when the dog tilted his head as if to ponder the question and then got up and trotted towards the reception desk and disappeared behind it.

'Well, I guess it's just us, then.' Pete put a protective arm around Hannah as he held the door open and ushered her out.

At a café just down the road Hannah ordered what she'd initially craved, but wasn't entirely sure she could face it now. She was unable to shake from her mind the icky image of what she'd seen. And the smell. Also, when she'd sat down, she'd suddenly remembered with a jolt that the last time she'd been out to breakfast with anyone it had been Tristan. She suddenly felt desperately sad.

Hannah moved her food around a little while Pete attacked his with gusto, oblivious. Even though she scolded herself for wasting food, she couldn't eat more than half of her meal.

'What you saw back there has put you off your breakfast, hasn't it?' Pete said as he put his knife and fork down on his almost empty plate. 'I'm so used to it, I didn't think. I'm really sorry.'

'It's okay. It's not your fault. Maybe I'm just not as hungry as I thought I was.' *It's only a meal, only food*, she thought. But it didn't help. She suddenly so desperately wanted to have Tristan across from her, reading out items from the paper in one of the various voices he was so good at putting on – butch sports reporter, posh food reviewer. *Oh, Tris.* She knew Pete would understand, but if she tried, she might just cry. And doing that in public was the worst.

'Okay, then, if you're done, I'll get this. And then I'd better get back,' Pete suddenly announced when he'd pushed his plate aside and drained his coffee cup.

'Yes, sorry, it was very nice, but I can't manage any more.'

'That's okay. You might be coming down with something. There were a few sniffly people in last week, so there are definitely bugs around.'

'Hmm. Yes, I probably am.'

'Well, come on then, let's get you home.' Hannah longed to have him take her back to her house, tuck her into bed and leave water and paracetamol by her bed, and generally take care of her. But instead she was deposited back at her car and then given a quick kiss on her forehead and a hug.

'Feel better soon,' he said as he closed her car door for her. And that was it.

Back at home Hannah stood with her house keys in hand and toyed with going inside or popping across the road to see if Beth was home. She felt fine now, still a little sad, but not actually unwell.

She heard a distinctive 'Yoo-hoo' and looked up. She smiled at seeing Beth waving with one hand and holding up a teacup in her other. Hannah hurried across the street.

'I saw a different car parked in your driveway overnight,' Beth said as she put cups of steaming tea and a plate of buttered date loaf on the table and sat down in her usual spot at the end.

'You don't miss anything, do you?' Hannah said with a faint chuckle.

'Not if I can help it,' Beth said cheerfully. 'So, tell me.'

'There's nothing really to tell. It was Pete, the vet who owns Charlie the dog. I invited him back for dinner because he'd had a really bad day.'

'And then he stayed the night,' Beth prompted.

'Yes, in the spare room.'

'It makes no difference to me,' Beth said, raising her hands palms out.

'He took me out to breakfast this morning and now here I am.'

'Right. So why do you look more like you've been to the dentist than been on a date with a nice man? I take it he *is* a nice man.'

'Oh, yes, he's lovely.'

'Also, why have you eaten two slices of cake if you've just been out for a meal? Were you too excited to eat?'

'No. Oh, Auntie Beth,' Hannah said, and dissolved into tears.

'Darling, there, there, let it all out,' Beth said, rubbing Hannah's shoulder. 'What's up? Did he say something to upset you?'

'No. He was lovely. He *is* lovely. I think.'

'So, what's wrong?'

'He's not Tristan.'

'Oh. Oh, darling.'

'He's nothing like Tristan.'

'Maybe that's a good thing. I know you can't help it, but do you think it's wise to make comparisons?'

'And I've got a weak stomach.'

'Sorry, whatever do you mean?'

'He took me into the back of the surgery and there was a dog with all these stitches and …'

'Well, that's some date he took you on. What a charmer.'

'He just didn't think. He needed to check on something and …'

'Sounds like you need a do-over, as they say – rewind and start again. Have another go.'

'Yes, all of the above. Maybe I'm just expecting too much.'

'Like what?'

'Is it too much to want to be wooed?'

'It is if you're not ready. Don't forget you turned him down that time. His pride is hurt, so he's not going to be in a hurry to do candlelit dinners and send flowers. And he mentioned being friends. Have you told him you want something different now?'

'I don't know what I want. Just not that – this morning.'

'Dear, men are simple creatures. And a lot less brave than we tend to give them credit for. So, what changed, anyway? You weren't interested in him a few months ago.'

'I didn't think I was ready then.'

'Do you feel ready now?'

'Honestly? I don't know. Maybe. I thought I was.'

'How did last night come about, anyway? It might help if you start from the beginning.'

'I offered to cook him dinner because he looked so shattered – I was at the surgery to pick up Holly and the kittens. They had their operations yesterday.'

'Oh, the little darlings. How are they?'

'Bit under the weather last night, but fine this morning.'

'Sorry, back to the problem at hand.'

'It's okay, Auntie Beth, you don't need to solve it. I guess perhaps I wasn't ready after all.'

'Or he's the wrong one. I don't think it helped that you took him in and mothered him. It's nice of you, but hardly romantic.'

'Oh. Oh! We've put each other into the friend zone, haven't we?' Hannah's eyes were wide.

'I don't know what that means, but I think it would have helped if the first date was left to him to take the lead. Though, I don't know the man from Adam, obviously.'

'I've blown it, haven't I?'

'If it – whatever *it* is – has been blown, I blame him,' Beth said defiantly. 'You deserve to be treated like a lady – and wined and dined. Pampered.'

'Thanks, Auntie Beth.'

'Maybe he'll realise the error of his ways and make it up to you. Maybe he's out of practice like you and he needs to be told what's expected – not hinted at. Men don't get hints. They need to practically get smacked over the head to learn anything.'

'Oh, Auntie Beth, you're just what I needed.'

'I'm glad. Hannah, just take it as it comes. I know you've come a long way. But you're still fragile. And you're not the same person you were when you met darling Tristan, or when you lost him.'

'Hmm. Thanks, Auntie Beth, you're so wise,' she said, getting up, moving around the table and hugging her dear friend from behind.

'Well, I'm not sure about that. But I am sure we need more to eat and drink,' she said, patting Hannah's arm at her chest before beginning to gently push her chair back.

Chapter Seventeen

It was a little odd to Hannah – and probably everyone else – that her final day at TLR was on a Tuesday. But Craig had been keen for them to leave the company together and Tuesday suited him best. As she'd sat on the tram that morning, Hannah was relieved to have this unusual day ahead of her, to take her mind off Pete. Not that she was worrying about the situation, but she'd spent the last few days feeling more disappointed every time he crossed her mind.

Her to-do list was almost completed by the time she came back from an informal farewell lunch with the junior staff, and she was starting to wonder how she'd fill the afternoon. She needed to keep busy or she might start regretting her decision to leave. A few times she'd stopped whatever she was doing and thought about her time at the firm. She always came back to the fact TLR had been her life preserver after the accident. If she hadn't had her work, the buzz of people around her – normality – a support network of people here keeping a careful eye on her, she might have completely crumbled. Was it really time to move on or had she made a mistake?

She stood up and looked over the top of her cubicle to the back of Craig's head on the other side of the glass wall of his office. There was the answer. It wouldn't be the same place without him here. Really, *he* was the lifebuoy she'd needed. She strongly felt that. She just had to remind herself when she got jittery. Like now. Any change was hard for someone like Hannah who had sailed through life unscathed and barely even bruised until that dreadful Christmas morning. Her lovely parents, bless them, hadn't adequately prepared her for such upheaval. But she had found a way through. She'd survived.

This is the right time to go, Hannah reminded herself. *It's only the change factor making you question it.* She wondered if her position would become redundant anyway. She'd heard that with the belt-tightening going on Craig's role would be absorbed by several partners.

'Are you coming?' Craig called, startling her from her reverie. She looked up. He was standing in the open door, his hand on the brushed aluminium frame. She hadn't even noticed him getting up from his desk, even though she'd been looking that way.

'Sorry?'

'Farewell drinks in the boardroom.'

'Maybe for you,' she said.

'And you. Come on. You don't want to make me late, do you? Bring your things, we're not coming back. And then there's dinner with Jas, so no getting rolling drunk.'

'Yes, sir.'

'Sorry, I didn't mean to sound bossy. That last bit was more a note to self,' he said.

Hannah detected a little nervousness in his voice. While leaving was a big step for her, it was huge for Craig – he had everything riding on his future success.

She took a last inventory of her desk, straightened the cube of brightly coloured sticky notes, grabbed her handbag and waited in the hallway while Craig turned out the light in his office and closed the glass door.

'Feeling okay?' he asked.

'No, I'm not sure I should be going to partners' drinks.'

'I meant about leaving. You most certainly *are* meant to be at drinks.'

'A little sad about leaving, but excited to see what's in store.'

'It's not too late to change your mind.'

'I think it is considering we're about to go into farewell drinks.'

'Yes, probably. Well, you can always change your mind later.'

'And leave you to your own devices? I don't think that would be wise,' she said, grinning, the butterflies subsiding. She was actually looking forward to a more challenging role now it had been offered – a more meaningful partnership. She hadn't realised it was something she might want until Craig had asked her. Now she couldn't wait to get her teeth into marketing and helping build his new business.

And it is pretty cool to be invited into the boardroom for drinks, she thought. Hannah was surprised to see most of the staff there – no one had mentioned it during lunch. She was only halfway through her glass of sparkling wine when the head partner, Bill English, called for their attention. Bill had been on the interview panel when Hannah had been offered her full-time position. She'd always liked him – he was a quiet, kindly man who seemed a little grandfatherly despite only probably being in his mid-fifties.

'Don't worry, folks, just a few words. There'll be plenty of time to enjoy the spoils. We're here to farewell ... Hannah, where are you? Come on up here, please. And you, Craig.' Craig who was already near the front shuffled over to stand beside Bill. Hannah, pink faced, made her way through the crowd to stand with them.

'Hannah, you've been a wonderful asset to this firm for ten years. You're a talented young woman and a hard worker and you have a truly lovely soul. The fact you were able to pick yourself up so well and continue to be such an important part of this place is a tribute to your wonderful, giving character. We're going to miss you greatly. But I think Craig is going to need you more. And if he proves too much, remember there will always be a place for you here.' He grasped both her hands and looked into her eyes.

'Thanks, Bill,' Hannah mumbled, trying not to cry.

'Craig. This place won't be the same without you, but we really do wish you all the best and look forward to working together in some capacity in the future. Good luck, mate,' Bill said, grasping Craig's hand and shaking it furiously.

'Thanks, mate,' Craig responded. 'I really appreciate the support and friendship of everyone here, as I know does Hannah,' he said, putting an arm around her and pulling her close. Hannah nodded. 'This is a great firm with a wonderful culture, thanks in large part to Bill's leadership. But there comes a time when it feels right to fly the nest. So, thanks, everyone. I look forward to staying in touch. And if you or any of your friends or network need any business advice, call. I've left a pile of my cards on the table back there by the door.'

'Of course he has,' someone called out.

'Ever the opportunist,' Tom, another partner, called out, and chuckled. A few wolf whistles sounded.

'Tom, opportunities are everywhere if you only look,' Craig said good-naturedly. 'Just you remember that. But, seriously, please keep in touch. I've enjoyed working with you all and I'm going to miss you. Even you, Tom. *We're* going to miss you all, aren't we, Hannah?'

Again Hannah nodded. And then she was surprised to find herself speaking, and with strength and clarity. 'Yes. Thank you all for a wonderful ten years, and for helping me through a really difficult time.' *Don't cry*, she told herself and bit the inside of her cheek hard enough to make her wince. She nodded and took a half step back to signal she'd finished.

'Okay, Craig and Hannah, we wish you goodbye and good luck,' Bill said, raising his glass. There were mumbles of assent and then the room erupted into cheers and applause.

'You okay, kiddo?' Craig whispered when everyone had turned their attention back to their drinks and chatter.

'All good, thanks.' Hannah loved it when he was so protective of her. 'And you?'

'Fine, fine. Jas is picking us up downstairs at six, so don't let me forget,' he added.

'Yes, boss,' Hannah said, putting a hand to her head as a salute.

'Note to self, just one more.'

'Make sure you eat something to soak up the alcohol. Those pinwheels are good.'

'Yes, ma'am,' he said.

They left with calls of 'Goodbye' and 'Good luck' following them. Right on schedule Jasmine pulled up at the kerb.

'In you get,' Craig said, opening the front passenger door for Hannah.

'Are you sure?'

'Yes. I know my place. In the back is where I belong,' he said cheerfully.

'Oh ha-ha,' Hannah said, getting in. 'This is very good of you,' she said, leaning over and hugging Jasmine.

'My pleasure. How was it?'

'Good. I even got invited to the partners' drinks.'

'Yes, it was a lovely send-off,' Craig said.

'Are you still feeling okay about it all, Hannah?'

'Yes. Absolutely.'

'Good, because I can't do it without you,' Craig said.

'Yeah, right,' Hannah said.

'Well, I wouldn't want to,' he said. Hannah smiled to herself.

'You big old softy,' Jasmine said, putting a hand back between the seats.

'Oh, well, there could be worse things to be.'

'That's right, darling. And we love you just the way you are,' Jasmine said.

Hannah's phone pinged with a message. It was from Sam, and made her smile:

I hope they gave you the send-off you deserve and you're feeling awesome about leaving. If not, just think of all the extra kitty cuddles you get now. But, seriously, you've made the right decision. So proud of you! Xxx

Hannah hugged the phone to her, savouring the warm and fuzzy feeling surging through her. She did feel happy about her decision to go and work for Craig and was excited to be going to dinner with such good friends. What a great day!

'Oh, this is lovely. I haven't had a chance to come here yet,' Hannah said, looking around the foyer of the restaurant. It was quite new and she'd watched it take shape from the tram on her way to and from the city. For the past few weeks, since it had opened, she'd been wondering about its décor and menu, other than modern and moody.

'Ah, white tablecloths,' Jasmine said. 'I do love crisp white tablecloths.'

'This we know, dear,' Craig said.

They smiled and thanked the friendly but efficient waiter when he delivered their menus.

'Now, before I forget,' Craig said, 'a few housekeeping things ...'

'Darling ...' Jasmine said.

'I won't be long.' He fossicked in his briefcase he'd put beside his chair, which Hannah only now realised he'd brought in with him. 'This is for you,' he said, bringing out an envelope. 'It's your access to the business account – and credit card attached.' He handed it to Hannah. 'So you can take care of things without too much mucking about. Here,' he said, taking a pen from the inside pocket of his jacket and handing it over, 'to sign the back.'

'Um. Okay. Thanks.'

'Don't be weird about it, Hannah. It won't bite. And you might not ever need it, with most things happening online. Though I do want you to make a trip to buy stationery – for your office and mine. Anyway, there it is. The other thing is, are you still good to start next Monday?'

'Yes. If that's okay with you.' Hannah had decided a couple of days break would be a good idea. She could get a few things done at home and then fully immerse herself in her new job. Though it was going to be a bit of a play-it-by-ear process, as they'd discussed. The trickiest thing was geography. She hadn't been able to decide if she should work from her place or at Craig and Jasmine's house. Though that might get a little crowded with Jasmine trying to run her business from there too – and coming and going. Of course most information would be kept online on the cloud and most business done via email, but hard copies of certain things had to be kept. And Hannah did pride herself on keeping a well-organised filing system. So the other problem was where to keep any physical files or printed information.

'Perfect. It will be a big day for both of us,' Craig said.

'I'll probably make a shopping trip to the stationers beforehand so I'm all ready to go first thing.'

'No worries – just record your hours. Keep the receipts. And make sure you keep track of any other expenses – like phone calls, et cetera. When your mobile plan comes due we'll look at that then. Okay?'

'Okay.'

'There's a lot to organise and think about,' Jasmine said.

'Yes, and you'd better take note since this will be you too soon, my sweet,' Craig said. 'Watch the master Hannah at work.'

'Is there anything particular you need me to buy in the way of stationery – or anything else for that matter?' Hannah asked.

'No, I'll leave it in your capable hands. We're starting from scratch, so anything you think we'll need. Plenty of sticky notes – we know how you love those things.'

'Yes, I do!' Hannah grinned and had to consciously stop herself from clapping her hands with glee. Oh how she loved stationery, full stop! One of her favourite things to do at the office had been to stand in front of the massive cupboards full of pens, mechanical pencils, blocks of coloured sticky notes, pads of paper and breathe in the scent while marvelling at the order and neatness – her doing – for a few moments before making her selection.

'So, whatever you need – desktop printer or colour laser. Whatever you think. Just use the card.'

'I think I'll wait and settle in and see what we really need before I go crazy with major hardware purchases.'

'Right. Entirely up to you. And the other thing is. Here. For you.' He handed her a set of house keys.

'Are you sure?' she asked, looking from Craig to Jasmine.

'Of course,' Craig said.

'Absolutely,' Jasmine said.

'Okay. Thanks,' she said, and put them in her bag with the new credit card.

'I think that's all, isn't it, Jas?' he asked, scratching his head. 'Oh, make sure you start recording your work-related car mileage to claim from me or off your tax – we'll decide which way to go later. I think that's it for now,' he said, picking up his menu and opening it.

'This looks good,' Craig said. 'Even the desserts.' While he indulged in the odd dessert, Craig was more a meat and veg man.

'Oh, yes,' Jasmine said.

'Incredible,' Hannah agreed. She chose the duck main and the orange parfait for dessert and closed her menu – one of her quickest choices in history.

'Did you tell Hannah about Henry?' Jasmine said after they had given their orders.

'Oh, yes. I mean, no. Hannah, I had your Henry around.'

'My Henry?'

'Yes. Henry Peace. I had him do the lawns and trim some shrubs the other day.'

'Oh. Right. Great.' *I hope.*

'Yes, Craig was being all fatherly ...' Jasmine said, stroking her husband's arm.

Hannah wasn't sure what Jasmine meant, so stayed silent.

'Come on, dear, you're making me sound old.'

'Well, protective then,' Jasmine said.

'Yes, I wanted to check him out.'

'Oh. Okay. And ...?'

'He seems okay, did a good job with the lawns and pruning, but I'm not so sure he's a very switched-on businessman. I didn't let on why I'd called him, specifically. He didn't ask. Number one rule in business, know where your clients are coming from and reward your referees. Well, okay, two rules,' he added, just as the waiter appeared and began pouring the sparkling wine Craig had chosen.

'Now, we're here to celebrate. To us and taking on the world,' Craig said, raising his glass. 'And to Jasmine, love of my life, who has secured her very first client.'

'Really?' Hannah said.

'Yep,' Jasmine said.

'Oh, that's fantastic. Well done. I'm so excited for you.'

'Well, it's a little daunting, but it's a start.'

'If you need any help from the admin side of things, let me know.'

'Careful what you offer. I'm not sure running a business is my forte,' Jasmine said.

'Ah, I'm sure you'll be just fine.'

'Thank you, Hannah, that's what I keep telling her,' Craig said, reaching over and taking his wife's hand.

They enjoyed their meals, but didn't linger, laughing as they walked to the car about how exhausting socialising was.

Chapter Eighteen

As Hannah drove to Sam's she wondered what she'd find. Today was 'D' day. Would she be pleased with what she saw or would she be itching to get out of there and phone Roger at the gallery so he had as much time as possible to find another artist? Hannah had no idea how things stood with Sam. They'd shared daily texts and the odd phone call, but Hannah had avoided what was now necessary to address. Once her enquiries could only be seen as genuine interest from a supportive, caring friend. Now she could see how her questions might come across as nagging or even self-serving, since she and Sam were in this together to some extent.

Hannah took a deep breath as she raised her hand to the doorbell and steeled herself to be cool with whatever she found.

'Hann, hi,' Sam said, opening the door wide and pulling her into a hug. 'How's things? How are you feeling about having left TLR – still okay?'

'Yes. Good. Thanks so much for your gorgeous text. You always know the right thing to say at the right time. So how are you? And are the boys still enjoying school?'

'Yes. Bless the little darlings. That certainly makes life easier. Come through.'

As Hannah followed Sam, she took in her friend's appearance. Uh-oh. Though unkempt could go either way with the artistic Sam – in a funk or too busy creating to shower and change into clean clothes. Hannah tried to look for signs of paint or modelling clay on Sam's clothes – nothing. Her heart sank further. Not for herself, but for Sam. Sam needed to create to keep her going at the best of times. With the boys at school and Rob having left, she might be at risk of completely falling apart if she remained blocked for too much longer. *And here I am about to play bad cop.* Hannah stayed silent while Sam made coffee. She took a seat at the table and looked around. The kitchen was neither clean nor messy, which was another disconcerting sign. Sam didn't really do in-between – with her it was all or nothing.

'Oh, that's good,' Sam said after taking a long slug from her mug.

'Yes, it is.'

'It's deadline day, isn't it?'

'It is. So, what have you decided?' Hannah said.

'Hold that thought. I need to show you something. Close your eyes. Back in a sec.'

'Okay.'

Sam left the room then came back and sat down at the table.

'All right. Open. What do you think?'

Hannah looked at the object sitting in front of her and blinked. She bit her lip as she looked up at Sam across from her. Her friend had an expectant, fearful expression etched in her face.

'It's ...' Sam started.

'Yes. I can see.' *It's Tristan and me and the cats.* 'Oh, Sammy, it's amazing.' She blinked back the welling tears so she could see clearly. There in front of her was a sculpture of two people sitting at a desk or table, only the two people were sort of one – moulded together and only separated by the pale blue wash over the one that was placed slightly to the side and behind. Tristan's favourite colour – Bermuda blue. How did Sam know that? It wasn't something they'd ever discussed. And the balloon behind Tristan's head – she'd never told Sam about the discussion she'd had with her mother-in-law at the funeral parlour that day either. On the flat surface in front of the figures was a representation of a cat curled up with two kittens.

'It can be a sculpture or a paperweight – though it might be a bit big for your desk.'

'Oh, Sammy, it's perfect.'

'So, you like it? It's okay?'

'Samantha, are you kidding me?' Tears spilled down Hannah's cheeks and dropped onto the piece. 'Oh, shit,' she said, dragging out a tissue from her sleeve.

'It's okay, it's glazed ceramic. It can be washed,' Sam said gently. 'I didn't want to upset you, Hann.'

Hannah wiped the tears away and then picked up the object and turned it around to study it closer. *God, Sam's amazing. This must have taken her weeks.*

'Do you think it's good enough for the exhibition?' Sam asked tentatively.

'Of course it's good enough! But it's not for sale. I'm buying it.'

'No you're not – I'm giving it to you.'

'Why balloons, Sam, when you hate them?' Hannah said, pointing to the perfectly round balloon a little above Tristan's head.

'I know. It just felt right. I don't even believe in god or heaven and all that rubbish, as you know, but it felt right for him to be holding a balloon. You can't argue with the creative juices. I'm just a conduit,' she added, with a shrug.

Hannah was stalling. How did she tell Sam one piece wouldn't cut it, no matter how brilliant – especially if that one piece wasn't even for sale?

'So, do you think you've found your *thing*?' Hannah ventured.

'Maybe. For now.'

'This must have taken you ages. Are you working on something else?' Hannah's head was whirling. They could use this piece for the brochure and invitations, and that would buy Sam some time – perhaps as much as four weeks. How many more pieces could she do in that time? And did she want to? Maybe this was a one-off. But would using this piece for marketing purposes while it would not be for sale be considered false advertising, dishonest even?

'You mean, have I got my shit together enough to go ahead with the exhibition, don't you?' Sam asked.

'Well, it is deadline day. I need to give Roger his answer. So …?'

'Come with me. I need to know what you think.'

As she followed Sam, Hannah started to worry about the prospect of having to be more objective about her friend's art. She was used to just being kind and supportive, not that she'd ever been dishonest. She hadn't needed to be. But now she would have to be more calculating. What if Sam had done something she didn't like, or didn't see as saleable? Oh, who was she kidding – what would she know about what was saleable or not? That was Roger Huntley's job.

'Now, I want you to be totally honest – I need you to be,' Sam said as she opened the door to her garage studio. 'Because, this is serious. No more mucking around dabbling.'

Hannah stood at the large bench draped in a white sheet, which was raised here and there by objects hidden underneath. Sam carefully gathered the fabric and lifted it off, rolling it into a ball as she went, which she clutched tightly to her while she awaited Hannah's response.

Hannah's mouth dropped open. She made her way slowly right along the bench. 'Oh my god, Sammy. You're a bloody genius!'

'Do you think these pieces will work as an exhibition?'

'Of course they'll work. What's here – eight pieces?' she counted.

'Nine including yours. And I've got ideas for about four more, if you think it's a goer.'

'We're not selling mine.'

'We can still exhibit it, though, can't we? Galleries do that all the time – have a not-for for-sale sticker on it, or Roger can just put a red dot on it straight up.'

'Oh. Yes, I suppose so.' Though Hannah didn't want to let it out of her sight for a moment.

She stood staring at the pieces trying to work out what they each meant.

'It's the ripple effect,' Sam said. 'That's what I think the theme should be. See, that's Rob in Singapore. Your parents on their bench at the retirement village. Henry and his lawn-mowing. I don't even know what he looks like. It's not too morbid, is it?'

'No, they're lovely sculptures in their own right. Are you going to do a little story for each one?'

'I haven't decided.'

'You do realise you're as good as ensuring they all sell. How can I not buy every one of them – they all mean so much to me.'

'Well, I won't let you. And, you said yourself they could pass as just interesting sculptures. See, you know that as Charlie the dog and you on the park bench, but it could be anyone.'

'Hmm.'

'You don't mind that I've used you and your experience as inspiration, do you?' Sam asked, misinterpreting Hannah's silence. She was being drawn back to her trip to New York as she stared at one piece.

'This one is a little more random,' Sam said, pointing to the sculpture Hannah was looking at – an unusually large ladybug sitting on a leaf. 'Though, there are nine spots,' she added as Hannah counted.

'Well done, you,' Hannah said, draping her arm around Sam and pulling her close. *Thank you for coming through*, Hannah thought while she tried not to let out a loud sigh of relief.

'Thank you for inspiring me and for giving me the push I needed.'

'It was a pretty bloody big shove from what I'm seeing here,' Hannah said.

'Which I clearly needed. It feels so good to be going hard at it again – and have a real purpose. Though, I feel for those poor, neglected little boys. You know, I'm not sure I should have had kids.'

'That's just your exhaustion talking. You love them to bits and wouldn't part with them for the world.'

'I know, but I can't help wondering if perhaps you can't really have both – be a good mother *and* a successful artist.'

'Come on, you've just shown me this amazing work. And the twins adore you.'

'Yes, but is that right? Is that enough? I'm a bloody train wreck, Hann.'

'You know damn well you'd do anything for them. *Anything.*'

'Of course. Without a second thought.'

'That's what being a great mum is. You can absolutely be a great artist at the same time. You already are.'

'But I saw online that ...'

'Since when have you ever taken any notice of something you read online?'

'Erm, since I've started to think seriously about my art as a career.'

'Well, don't. You need to leave the business side of things to me and focus on the creation side. And getting the kids fed, dressed and off to school and back again.'

'I forgot to bath them last night.'

'So? I read somewhere we all wash too much – it's bad for us. Anyway, they won't start to stink until they hit puberty. You've got a few years up your sleeve yet.'

'Oh, Hannah, you're too funny.'

'Darling, just be your wonderful self and you and the boys will be fine. Now, back to serious matters. What do you say about tidying yourself up and coming with me to meet Roger and show him your work?'

'Oh, Hannah ...'

'You have to meet him sometime. And, no, not for the first time on opening night. Go on, you've got time for a shower.'

'You're saying the dishevelled, crazy artist look isn't the right way to go?'

'Not when you smell like you haven't showered in a week.'

'See, that's what I love about you – your honesty.'

'Off you go,' Hannah said, turning Sam by the shoulders and giving her a gentle shove.

Hannah stayed where she was, staring at the sculptures while shaking her head slowly with admiration.

Chapter Nineteen

'Stay,' she told Holly, Squeak and Lucky when she heard the doorbell ring. She'd just come back from shopping and the cats were tripping her up in the hallway, sniffing at the bags of groceries.

'Hello, Auntie Beth. Come in out of the heat. Oh, they're gorgeous,' she said, looking at the bouquet of flowers her friend handed her.

'They're for you. They were left earlier and I rescued them before the sun hit the porch.'

'Oh. How lovely. Thank you. They would have withered in minutes today. Hmm, there doesn't seem to be a card,' Hannah said, peering amongst the blooms.

'No, I couldn't see one, either. Not that I was snooping.'

'They're probably a farewell gift from the office, though they did give Craig and me a lovely drinks send-off,' Hannah said as she carried the box of flowers through to the kitchen and put it carefully on the bench. 'How are your cats settling in?' Hannah asked as she got them each a glass of iced water while Beth pulled out a stool at the bench.

'Oh, they're precious. I can't tell you what a new lease on life they've given me.'

'That's wonderful to hear.'

'Speaking of which – you seem extra chipper today.'

'Oh, Auntie Beth, I've had just the best day. I went to see Sam and you should see what she's done for the exhibition. She blew even me away.'

'So, it's going ahead, then?'

'Yes. I took her with me to meet with Roger Huntley, the gallery owner, and he was thrilled with her work too. So, it's full steam ahead. The opening is April eight.'

'Goodie. I can't wait.'

'We want as many people at the opening as possible so I'll need the names and addresses for all your friends who might be interested.'

'Oh, they'll be thrilled to be invited to the opening of an art exhibition.'

'I'm determined it's going to be a huge success, and I want a crowd there. Thank goodness I'm only working part-time now.'

'Tell me, have you heard from your dashing vet?'

'No, but hang on, the flowers could be from him. I wish there was a card. You can't exactly ring someone and ask if he happened to have sent you flowers, can you? Come on, there must be a card here somewhere,' she said as she lifted the container of flowers out of its decorative box and peered inside. 'Ah-huh,' she said, holding up a long envelope.

'I'll go so you can read that in peace,' Beth said, easing herself off her stool.

'No, don't. As long as you don't mind me being rude and reading it while you're sitting here.'

'Hannah, dear, as if I would mind. Go ahead.'

'Okay. Here goes.' Hannah opened the envelope and took out a folded sheet of paper and raised her eyebrows at Beth. She was suddenly nervous. But what could he possibly say that was worth being nervous about? She quickly scanned the first few lines before starting from the beginning and reading aloud:

Dearest Hannah,

I have it on good authority – my sister – that I am an idiot and have behaved abysmally. Please accept these flowers as a token of my apology and for being a clueless fool with regards my treatment of you on our first and second dates – if you can call them that. I am so sorry for taking you for granted, for being so unromantic and for being so distracted by my work. Please don't take it as an indication of my lack of interest in you romantically, because that is certainly not the case. Instead, and while I don't wish to make excuses, please accept, as I have, that I am very out of practice in the dating department. Please will you have dinner with me on Friday night – dinner at a nice restaurant with white tablecloths, not the sort of casual dining I subjected you to on Sunday for breakfast. Feel free to dress up – or not, if you wish; no pressure – as I will be making an appropriate effort. I am not a man for wearing ties, but I do own a suit. Apologies for the over-sharing, but I don't want there to be any misunderstandings. Please have dinner with me Friday night. I am not begging. Well, I sort of am. If you are willing to forgive me and give me a second chance – give US a second chance – please text me. A simple yes will suffice. I await your reply with bated breath.

Yours truly, Pete.

Hannah stared at Beth, a grin pulling at the corners of her mouth.

'Well,' said Beth. 'So, what do we think about that?'

'I was just about to ask you that question. He's pretty full-on, isn't he?'

'I think it's rather delightful. He's clearly smitten with you. And apologetic.'

'He doesn't use paragraphs. It's like he hasn't taken a breath.'

'I like that. It means it's come from the heart. I think it's terribly romantic. It's probably not very often you get handwritten notes these days.'

'You're right, it is pretty sweet,' Hannah agreed.

'So, what are you going to do?'

'Well, I can't really say no after reading this.'

'Of course you can. You are your own woman. You're allowed to spend your time however and with whomever you wish.'

'I liked him – even …'

'I know you did – it was written all over your face.'

'Do you think he sounds a little bit dorky?'

'Maybe. He's a vet, so he's clearly kind and well educated – even if he didn't use paragraphs. Sometimes really intelligent people struggle with social norms. But he's being honest and in my book that's important. He didn't have to write all that. He could have simply tried to woo you with flowers, chocolates, champagne. In this case, dear, I think the words are speaking louder than the actions.'

'I'd like to meet his sister. She sounds like my cup of tea. I love that they're clearly so close, too. I'm going to go – give him another chance.'

'Good for you. If nothing else, I'm sure you'll have a lovely meal. And it will be good practice for you,' Beth said.

'The poor guy. It was probably his first date in years and he thought it went well only to be told he'd failed.'

'Well, thank goodness someone told him. Men really don't have that much of a clue. Oh, the stories my friend Myrtle tells me about her Gerald. It makes me glad to be living alone.'

'And here you are encouraging me to go on a date, Auntie Beth!'

'Oh, you're far too young to be shutting that door just yet, dear, as you well know. Go on, text the poor fellow and put him out of his misery – these arrived hours ago.'

They were silent for a few minutes while Hannah tried to find the perfect phrase.

'Okay. What do you think of this? *Thank you for the gorgeous flowers and heartfelt letter. I would love to accept your kind invitation to dinner on Friday night. Hannah.* How's that?'

'Good. Send it before you start second-guessing yourself.'

'Okay. It's gone.'

Seconds later she received a reply.

Yay! Thank you. I won't disappoint you again. I'll pick you up at 7 p.m. unless I hear otherwise. Pete

'Thank goodness he didn't add kisses or hugs or smiley or winky faces or any other sort of emoji or anything.'

'You're going to have to explain what you just said, because it sounded like gibberish to me!' Beth said.

Chapter Twenty

Well, he's punctual, Hannah thought when her doorbell rang at two p.m.

'Hi, Henry. Thanks very much for coming,' she said, after opening the door. In his stressed, slightly haggard state at the court, Hannah had pegged Henry Peace's age at late forties. Now she surprised to realise he was probably only ten years older than her – definitely nearer forty than fifty.

'No problem. Thanks very much for thinking of me. I really appreciate it.'

'I'm sorry it's taken me so long, I …'

'Ah, no worries.' He gave a slightly nervous laugh. 'Better late than never, as they say.'

She shook his hand and noticed the roughness of his skin. She thought she was perhaps being a little too formal in offering her hand, but in the next breath she asked herself how else she should be. She'd met the man once – weeks before – in what had become an intimate moment that had felt right. But that was then. Craig had sized him up and given his approval, but Hannah didn't know

Henry well at all. And here she was inviting him into her home. She closed the door behind him.

'So where's this garden of yours that needs taming,' he said, his voice a little higher pitched.

She wanted to say, 'It's okay, there's no need to be nervous.' Instead she said, 'This way, out the back.'

'You have a very nice home,' he said, as they made their way through.

'Thanks. I've lived here my whole life. Tristan and I took it over when Mum and Dad went to live in a retirement village,' Hannah was surprised to find herself saying. But while they were mere acquaintances, they were also so much more than that. Bound by the tragedy. 'I've given your details to a few of my friends, so I hope you'll be getting some more work.'

'Thanks very much. That's very good of you. Things have picked up a little, come to think of it.'

'Here we are,' she said, opening the back door and stepping onto the deck. 'It's mainly those fruit trees,' she said, pointing. 'They weren't done last year either. I don't think.' Suddenly she couldn't remember. The thoughtful men in her street had done her lawns and weeding for many months. Had they also done her pruning?

'You know, I can't remember now if they were done or not.'

'It's okay,' Henry said, placing a hand on her arm. 'It doesn't matter,' he added as she stared at his hand. 'It really is a beautiful garden.'

'Thanks, though I can't take any credit. It was all Dad. I've thought about putting in a pool, actually.'

'Oh. Well, that might be nice, too. Okay, so prune the fruit trees. Would you like me to tidy up those shrubs along the fence as well?'

'That would be good, thanks. Whatever you think should be done. I don't really have a clue of what needs what.'

'Your dad did a great job of designing a relatively low maintenance garden, so there's not a whole lot to do other than the pruning and just a bit of a tidy. You're only talking about three hours work. I'd be happy to do it now. And I'd be happy to do it as a favour – on the house.'

'No, we discussed that. You're not doing it for free. You're running a business, Henry. Please, do a proper quote.'

'How would one hundred and twenty dollars be?' he said with a resigned sigh.

'Fine with me, as long as you're not short-changing yourself.'

'I'm happy if you're happy.'

'Okay, then. The only thing is I'm not sure I have that amount in cash on me.' Hannah only liked to keep a maximum of one hundred dollars in her wallet. How much did she currently have? 'I'll have to check.'

'Ah, not a worry. We can always sort it out later.'

'Okay. Is there anything you need? There are some tools in the shed.'

'No, thanks, I have everything in my trailer. Do you have a side gate I can use? I don't want to bring ladders and things through the house and make a mess.'

'Yes, just around that side,' Hannah said, pointing.

'Great. I'll get cracking, then.'

'Yell out if you need me.'

Hannah found herself standing at the back door and watching Henry getting set up and then working. Had he always been so hunched over, looking weighted down and resigned to what his life had become, or was that a result of the accident too? It made her sad to watch him move as if he were an old man instead of someone supposed to be in his prime. When he looked up and caught her eye and waved, she moved away. The man deserved to get on with his work and not feel spied on, distrusted. She went to check her wallet for cash to pay him.

*

'Hannah?' Henry called from the back door and knocked. Hannah hurried out.

'Yes, I'm here.'

'Can you just check you're happy with what I've done and there isn't anything I've missed?'

'You were quick.'

'Three hours, like I said.'

Hannah had the strange feeling time had skipped. After he'd started work, she'd retrieved what cash she had and then sat in her office, first reorganising papers that didn't need reorganising and then scrolling through Facebook on the computer. She hadn't really been able to settle and could now see what her mum had meant about not being comfortable having a cleaner – or any other help – come in.

'That's great. Thank you so much,' she said after looking around the garden.

'It was my pleasure.'

'Would you like a cup of tea or coffee or a cold drink before you head off?'

'That would be lovely. I'll just pack everything away if you're sure there's nothing else you want me to do.'

'No. I think that's all. You've done a great job.'

'Thanks. It's amazing how a bit of pruning goes a long way towards giving the whole garden a neater, fresher look.'

A few minutes later, Hannah heard a gentle tap on the glass of the back door.

'Come through,' she said. 'The bathroom is just there if you need to wash up.'

'Thanks, but I'm all good. It's unusual to have anyone home so I'm completely self-sufficient.'

'Before I forget,' she said, 'here's seventy dollars. It's all I've got on me. So if you could just give me your direct deposit details, I can do a transfer for the rest right now on my phone.'

'Oh. I'm afraid I don't have them. Louise always took care of that side of things. Could you write out a cheque?'

'Um, no, I'm afraid not. I don't have a cheque book.' Hannah couldn't remember the last time she'd seen one, let alone written out a cheque. 'Can you log into your online banking on your phone and get the BSB and account number that way?'

'Oh, well, I'm not sure.' Henry pulled out his phone and stared at it as if he'd never seen the device before.

Hannah suddenly felt very young. And a little annoyed and frustrated. She hated things left unresolved.

'How about I text you so you have my number and then when you get home and find the details you text them to me?' Hannah suggested.

'Why don't we just not worry about it – it can be my treat,' he said.

'No, Henry, that's no way to run a business,' she said, trying to hide her frustration. He'd been split up from his wife for months, if he couldn't take care of the most basic things, it was no wonder he was struggling with his business. 'So, what can I get you – tea or coffee, or would you prefer a glass of cold water?'

'Tea would be good, thanks. White with two.'

'Okay. Coming up.' As Hannah put some slices of cake on a plate, she told herself to calm down. Not everyone was well organised. *It takes all kinds* had been a favourite saying of both her parents. She'd get the money to him somehow.

'Here we are,' she said, putting the cake and mugs down on the table and taking a seat.

'This is good. You really know the way to a man's stomach.'

'Thanks. I'm glad you like it.'

'So, how come you're home on a Friday?' Henry asked with his mouth still half full.

'Oh. I've gone part-time. And I'll be working from home. My boss has started his own business so I'm going to be working for him – doing his marketing and running his office.'

'That's great. I need someone like you to keep me on track,' Henry said with a tight laugh.

What about your wife? Hannah wanted to say it, but couldn't make the words come out. He was clearly depressed, maybe a bit on edge as well as being down. She didn't want to upset him and risk making him angry.

'You'll figure it out,' she said instead, and took a sip from her mug. As much as she wanted to help and didn't like anyone feeling out of their depth when she could see a way through, she also knew that it wasn't for her to sort out. Of course she could offer to take over his books, sort out his business affairs, but she realised that wouldn't help Henry in the long run. She could give him some tips right now, but he seemed a little fragile. He wasn't ready to hear constructive feedback. He needed to climb out of his pit of self-pity first. She could be completely wrong, and she was no psychologist, but Hannah thought that maybe Henry had to stop feeling sorry for himself and get his act together. Jesus, he'd lost his job, but losing his family was about him walking away from them, not actually losing them. Hannah took a large bite of cake to stop herself from inadvertently expressing her views.

'Can I get you anything else?' she asked.

'Actually, a glass of water would be nice. Just out of the tap is fine.'

Hannah leapt up, got it, and returned. She stayed on the edge of her stool in the hope she looked restless and he'd head off. Too much longer and she might just begin to share her thoughts. She made a point of looking at her watch, and said 'Oh' quietly. Unfortunately Henry chose that moment to pick up his glass and look around the kitchen, and completely missed her hint.

'You really do have a lovely home.'

'Thanks. I like it.'

'Louise and I bought a little fixer-upper-er when we got married. A weatherboard. In Yarraville. It's been a labour of love. I guess it will have to be sold.'

'I'm sorry to hear that,' Hannah said.

'Thanks.'

'I'm really sorry to cut this short, Henry, but I'm going out to dinner and I need to get ready.'

'Oh, I'm sorry. Here I am going on.'

Tristan had always said she was a terrible liar. The few occasions she'd tried to organise a surprise, keep a secret, or tell a white lie about something she'd failed. She got away with it at work when screening Craig's calls or deflecting annoying sales people because they couldn't see how red her ears became when she lied. Like now, damn it!

As much as she cared about Henry's welfare, she could already feel her spirits being dragged down. She'd been so looking forward to seeing Pete again – going on a proper date, getting to know him on a different level.

'A date, I hope?'

'No, just dinner with a friend,' she said, and cursed how hot her ears had suddenly become. Why did she feel the need to lie?

More to the point, why did Henry feel the need to pry? She was more annoyed than embarrassed now.

'Sorry, I seem to be putting my foot in it everywhere at the moment,' he said, smiling sadly. And Hannah softened.

'Don't be so hard on yourself.'

'I know I said it that day at the court, but I'm so glad you're okay, that you've kept it together.'

'Well, it hasn't been easy, as I told you then.'

'Yeah,' he said, rubbing the side of his glass. 'God, I miss Louise.'

Well, have you called her, talked to her, made any effort at all? You're the one who left, you stupid, stupid man! Hannah closed her eyes briefly to will away the fury she felt. What sort of an example was he showing his child?

'You know, while there's life there's hope,' Hannah said, trying to keep the annoyance from her voice. 'I'm sure it's not too late for you to try and sort things out. If you want to.'

'Hmm,' Henry said as he got up.

Hannah hoped that was a 'Hmm, you might be right' and not a 'Hmm, what would you know?'

'Well, thanks again for coming around,' she said, getting up and following him out.

'Thank you for the work. And for the wonderful hospitality,' he said, holding out his hand when they were at the front door. Hannah accepted it, but suddenly found herself being pulled into a tight quick hug.

'I'm so glad you're okay,' he said again, stepping out.

'You can be too, Henry. You can get through this. Small steps. But you have to try. And you have to be strong,' she said, and then began closing the door in case he stopped to talk again.

Chapter Twenty-one

Well, I guess I'd better get ready, Hannah thought, suddenly feeling a rush of sadness grip her so tightly she almost gasped. She leaned against the hallway wall as an ache filled her entire being and she struggled to breathe. She noticed Holly and the kittens look up from their cushion on the lounge. She went in and sat beside them.

'Oh, Holly girl, I'm so sad,' she said, stroking the cat who looked up at her. *Oh god*, Hannah thought as her eyes filled and spilled over. A moment later Holly crawled into her lap and the kittens climbed onto her legs behind their mother. The ball of sadness inside her started to break apart.

'I'm not ready, am I? Will I ever be?' Holly licked her hand. 'Pete's a good man. You liked him, didn't you, guys? You would have *loved* Tristan. He was lovely. Really beautiful,' she said, her throat sticking. 'Oh, Tris. I don't want anyone else.' Hannah began to sob. Through her tears she saw Holly sitting up in her lap, staring up at her. Hannah didn't think cats could change their expressions, but Holly definitely looked concerned. Lucky and Squeak joined their mother in sitting to attention and looking up at her.

'It's okay, I'm okay,' Hannah said, wiping her eyes. 'Mummy's just a bit sad.' *And scared. Am I scared?* Hannah suddenly wondered. Terrified. Terrified of letting go of Tristan, her memories of him fading, as much as being afraid of what lay ahead or possible heartbreak with Pete. Her heart could never be hurt again as much as it was by losing her darling Tristan. But she was a little afraid of it not being as easy.

Right from day one she and Tristan had been in sync – their values, their shared sense of humour and vision for the future. They'd had wonderful intellectual debates, but never fought. Would they have down the track if she hadn't lost him? Hannah knew she most likely had an idealised set of memories around him and their life together. But she'd been happy. Really happy. She knew that. She could hold onto those memories and spend her life alone if she chose. It would be a perfectly reasonable reaction, excuse even. *Maybe if you were Auntie Beth's age.*

Being scared was no reason to not do something that held her in no mortal danger. What was the worst that could happen? *Small steps*, she reminded herself. *I have to try, I've just finished telling Henry that.* Hannah thought about what she'd faced up to and survived in the past year.

'Oh, you guys,' she said, and smiled as Lucky and Squeak stood up and began climbing up her chest. She probably should stop them before they ruined her knitted top with their needle-like claws, but they were too cute.

Hannah began to giggle. They were now perched on each side of her shoulders. She wondered how long it would be before they were too big or heavy to do this. She turned to her left and kissed

Lucky on the head and then turned right to do the same with Squeak.

Darling little things, she thought, her heart swelling. *You're just beautiful.*

When they both began licking her ears she started to squirm and laugh before plucking them off their perches. She leaned back, put them on her chest and stroked them, igniting their little motors. She loved the feeling of their vibrating chests against hers. Too precious for words.

'Okay, everyone, I'd better get ready if I'm going to do this,' she said, putting the kittens down on the floor and gently removing Holly from her lap. The sadness was still there as she made her way down the hall, but it was manageable.

In her bedroom, Hannah opened the wardrobe to choose an outfit. There were plenty to pick from, but two dresses caught her eye – a simple black dress and an emerald one that had been Tristan's favourite. He'd always said it made her eyes shine a lovely shade of green. When had she last worn it?

Oh. Her heart sank as she remembered: Sam and Rob's Christmas party just days before The Accident. She touched the fabric, stroked it as she remembered what a lovely night they'd had and how she and Tristan had sat up talking into the early hours of the morning. Had she worn it since? Surely she had. Or had she avoided it? She actually couldn't remember even opening this side of her wardrobe since it had happened. No, she hadn't. She'd avoided most functions – she'd barely been *functioning* herself for that whole year.

Yes, it's time. But she still couldn't decide between the two dresses of completely different styles. You could never go wrong with a little black dress with a light, colourful wrap. The question was, did she want to wear the more fitted design to show her curves or the floatier one that highlighted her eyes? As she stood there she briefly wished she'd thought to ask Sam or Jasmine or Auntie Beth. She could phone Beth to come over or send photos to Sam or Jas and ask their opinions. *Seriously, Hannah, you're a woman of over thirty! You can do this. Get a grip. Okay, I'll decide after my shower*, she thought, and laid the dresses on the bed.

Hannah returned from the bathroom to find Holly and both kittens sprawled across the black dress. 'Oh. So do you choose this one – it's the nicest so you're sitting on it, is that right? Good choice. Mine too. But you all have to get off now.

'Thank goodness for sticky lint rollers, is all I can say,' she said after hanging the green dress back in the wardrobe. She surveyed the damage. The whole front was covered in a fine layer of grey, white and other shades of cat fur she couldn't name. *Oh, well, at least Pete will understand.* And she smiled. Pete *would* understand, and not just about the cat hairs. He would understand her fear, trepidation, the need to take things slowly. If there was a perfect man to take her on her first proper date since Tristan, then he was the one. She felt a slight flutter in her chest and a warm feeling filling her. Pete was a lovely man. Suddenly Hannah started to feel excited about the evening.

'It's okay, kitties, I'm going to be okay,' she declared, more to herself than the slumbering cats. They looked up at her, yawned, stretched and curled up again.

Hannah was just finishing getting ready when her phone pinged with a series of text messages.

Sam: *Have an awesome night. No chickening out! Xx*

Jas: *Happy first date! Can't wait to hear all about it.* ♥ *xx*

Beth: *Enjoy your evening. Thinking of you. Lots of love, A. Beth xx*

She replied to each of them, but with the same message:

Thanks. Excited but terrified! Nearly chickened out, but am okay now. Speak soon. Xxx

'So, how do I look – passable?' she asked the cats, and did a twirl. They each went through the same ritual of opening their eyes, stretching, yawning and curling back up. 'Geez, thanks, you guys. Hey, ease up with the compliments, they might go to my head,' she said with a laugh, grabbed her handbag, and left the room.

She practically skipped down the hall and was still smiling when the doorbell rang moments later. The wings of a swarm of butterflies beat against her insides as she opened the door.

'Hi, Pete, you're looking dapper,' she said to the decidedly nervous looking man on her doorstep.

'Hannah, hi. Thanks. You look absolutely stunning,' he said, leaning in and kissing her cheek.

'Thank you. The cats chose this evening's outfit for me,' she said.

'Oh. Right. Okay then,' he said, clearly puzzled.

She closed the door and grasped his arm. 'I had two dresses I was struggling to choose between,' she explained as they made their way down the path. 'I made the mistake of leaving them on the bed while I had a shower – still getting used to being a pet person. Anyway, I came out of the bathroom to find them all sitting on this one. Hopefully I've got rid of all the fur,' she said, looking down her front.

'You look perfectly fine to me.'

'Thanks. So, they decided for me,' she added.

'You know,' he said, grinning as he held the car door open for her, 'maybe that's the dress they *didn't* choose. Maybe they avoided the other one to keep it pristine for you to wear. Or they were sitting on this one so you wouldn't pick it up.'

'Oh. I hadn't thought of that. Good point. If only they spoke – English,' she said, grinning.

'So, I thought if we had time we might go and see a movie after dinner, if you like,' Pete said as he pulled away from the kerb.

'You mean, if we run out of conversation?'

'I did, actually,' he said a little sheepishly.

'I haven't been to a movie for ages,' she lied. *Well, not with a man.* 'That would be lovely.'

'No need to decide yet. There's a session of *Bridget Jones* at nine-thirty, but I haven't bought tickets or anything, so we can play it by ear.'

'Sounds perfect,' Hannah said, and settled back into her seat. She was pleased to see Pete starting to relax too. 'So, how was your week?' she asked.

'Good. It was a good week.'

'How did your critical patients end up?'

'They've all gone home. A great outcome,' he said, beaming. 'Have you started your new job?'

'Not officially. I've done a few bits and pieces to get the office ready, but I'm starting on Monday. It's only going to be a couple of days a week to start with.'

'And you're starting on a Monday? Clearly you don't suffer from Monday-itis.'

'Nope, never really have.'

'Me neither. Well, not really. Every morning can be a bit daunting when you don't know what cases will come up that day.'

'Yes, I can imagine. I'm not sure how you deal with the heartbreak that must be such a big part of what you do.'

'It's the joy in sending a family home with a pet they thought they might lose and educating new pet owners that keeps me going. You've no idea how much I get out of simply watching the interaction between owners and their pets. The genuine love they have for each other.'

'Oh, you old softy,' she said, patting his leg.

'Yep. That's me. But, seriously, it's more than just a job or a means of making money. Here we are,' he said, turning into a carpark. 'I've been watching this place come to life and been dying to try it.'

'Me too,' Hannah said, trying not to smile too broadly at the restaurant Craig and Jasmine had taken her to on Monday night.

'Oh, hello there,' the maître d' said as they entered. 'Back again so soon. This is good.'

'Yes. It was such a lovely night,' Hannah said.

'Have you already been?' Pete said, looking crestfallen. 'We can go somewhere else.'

'Not at all. It's absolutely worth a second visit. My boss and his wife brought me here to celebrate our new beginning,' she explained. 'Please don't feel weird about it. You weren't to know,' she said, putting a hand on Pete's arm.

'Booking for two under the name Pete Shaw.'

'This way, please,' the maître d' said, and led the way through the almost full restaurant.

'I actually wanted to come back because I had my eye on another dish on the menu. I can recommend the duck main and the orange parfait for dessert. I don't even really need to look at the menu, I'm having the pork main and the caramel dessert,' she said, giving the items a cursory scan.

'It's a good looking menu,' Pete said. 'I avoided checking it out online. Modern Australian and European tells me all I need to know. And it got a great write-up in one of the papers recently.'

'Hah, we're different there. I love looking up the menus online. I have been known to spend far too long deciding on what to have,' Hannah said. 'At least by knowing beforehand I only have to think about any specials on offer.'

'Or if the menu isn't up to date,' Pete said.

'Yes, and that.'

'I used to look at the menu online, but a few times I got disappointed when what I'd chosen wasn't available. What wine would you like? I'll only have the one glass and I'm not fussed about matching it to food. I love a rosé, especially during summer. It's probably not considered very manly, but hey,' he added with a shrug.

'I like a man in touch with his feminine side,' Hannah said, a little surprised to hear the slightly flirty twang to her voice.

'Do you now?' Pete said with a wink. 'Well, I like a woman who can embrace a bit of pet fur.'

'Ha-ha. Cheers to that!'

Chapter Twenty-two

Hannah didn't like loose ends. She'd sent Henry a text asking for his banking details, but he'd replied with:

Don't worry about it – we'll sort it out next time.

Hannah was too frustrated to reply. She went for a long walk and took some rolled oats to the ducks by the river in the hope of letting the feeling go. It was an enjoyable morning, but thoughts of Henry kept creeping in, even overshadowing her memories of her delightful evening with Pete. They hadn't ended up going to a movie, had decided to instead call it a night. He assured her he was just tired and that it wasn't because he wasn't enjoying her company. Hannah had lied and said she was feeling a little tired too. She'd waved him off after he'd given her a goodbye peck on the cheek, and she'd gone inside feeling the tiniest bit disappointed again. She really did enjoy being with him and she wasn't going to waste energy thrashing it about in her head. He had a busy, demanding and very meaningful job – of course he'd be tired at the end of the week.

Back at home, Hannah sat with a mug of tea overlooking her neat garden. Henry had done a good job, not that she knew anything about the correct pruning angles or anything technical like that. She'd only know if the trees continued to bear fruit and didn't die, but they certainly looked neat and other than that you wouldn't know he'd been. He'd taken away all the pruned branches.

But the longer she sat there and thought of him the more annoyed she became. She so badly felt the need to help him get his life back on track. But how? What could she do that wouldn't be considered stepping over the line? Also, she couldn't risk him getting the wrong idea and setting his romantic sights in her direction. Not that she thought he might – it's just that he was vulnerable and clearly not very strong. Most likely he'd love a woman to take charge. So, what was the story with his wife, Louise? Was she weak and mouse-like?

Suddenly Hannah knew she had to know. She went back inside, put her mug in the sink and went through to the office. She dug out Henry's business card she'd filed and put it on her desk. The landline number was crossed out, but it was still decipherable. She turned on her laptop and brought up the White Pages website. He'd said he lived in Yarraville. She put in the details, pressed the search button and held her breath while she waited. *Bingo!* she thought as the results revealed just one result. Thank goodness they hadn't had their number delisted. She quickly wrote down the details. Next she brought up Google Maps and put in the street address and her own and then printed out the map and directions. With her printed pages in hand she stepped around the cats who'd just entered the office. 'I'll be back soon,' she told them and strode down the hallway where she collected her mobile, handbag and keys from the small table.

As she was closing the front door she paused to look at her attire. She probably should change. But if she went back inside she might talk herself out of this. And, anyway, most of Melbourne's cafés would be filled with women in their 'active wear'. At least she'd actually been active that morning!

Hannah parked across the street and took in the neat, well-maintained picket fence, front garden and house. Someone must have researched heritage colour schemes. Or perhaps this was a designated heritage area and Henry and Louise hadn't had a choice. Though Henry had spoken with clear affection of the house and from his comments Hannah gathered that he'd lovingly restored it. She wondered if he was still coming around to take care of the lawn and garden despite being estranged from his wife.

With her heart beating hard against her ribs, Hannah suddenly asked herself what she was doing here. There was a loud whooshing sound in her ears distracting her. As she looked at the house she wondered, did she really want to meet Louise Peace? Would Louise want to meet her? What would she say to this woman? She really hadn't thought this through. Uh-oh. *This is a bad idea. I should just go.*

As she was about to put the car back in gear to leave, Hannah remembered the money she'd taken out from the ATM. That's right, the whole reason for her being there was to get the remaining fifty dollars to Henry. How could she have forgotten? Perhaps Louise asking him to come and get the money might help them in some small way. Or perhaps keeping it might help Louise in some small way. Hannah knew most people would think she was obsessed about it – it was, after all, only fifty dollars, and it wasn't like she hadn't already tried to pay Henry. But she felt very strongly about not owing Henry, in particular. She wasn't sure why. But he wasn't a friend and she wanted things to be kept professional between them. *God, human beings can be complicated*, she thought. She reluctantly left the warm car and made her way across the street.

Hannah's hand was shaking slightly as she lifted it to turn the knob of the old-fashioned doorbell. Her heart began to race when she heard muffled footsteps and voices. *Uh-oh, what if Henry's here? Then you give him the money, silly. You're not hiding or doing anything wrong.* She almost laughed at her idiocy. But then her mind clouded as she wondered what to say.

The door opened and a pleasant looking woman in jeans and a crisp, freshly ironed floral shirt peered out at her. She looked even younger than Henry – probably not yet forty.

'Hello?' she said.

'Mrs Peace? Mrs Louise Peace?'

'Yes.'

Hannah could see Louise taking in her appearance and felt a little embarrassed.

'You're not media, are you?' Louise asked.

'No. I'm Hannah. Hannah Ainsley. Um. Your husband, Henry, did some gardening for me but I didn't have enough cash. Here,' she said, thrusting the fifty dollar note out towards Louise.

'Oh. Okay. Thank you. Would you like a receipt?' Louise was frowning slightly.

'No, that's okay.' Hannah turned to walk away.

'Hang on.'

Hannah turned back.

'Hannah Ainsley? *The* Hannah Ainsley? The one who lost her entire family …?'

Hannah nodded as she watched the blood drain from Louise Peace's face. 'Um, yes. I'm so sorry to intrude. I wanted to bring the money. But I also wanted to meet you and tell you that I don't hate your Henry. It was an accident. I know that. I don't want Henry throwing his life away – and yours too.' Hannah shut her mouth on the torrent that threatened to continue. She was already coming close to sounding like a crazy person.

Suddenly she found herself in Louise's arms being held very tightly. She gasped.

'Thank you,' Louise said when she had released Hannah. 'It means so much to have you say that. Henry was right about what an incredible woman you are.'

Hannah, feeling a little embarrassed and not sure what to say, looked at her feet.

'Would you like to come in?' Louise asked.

'Oh, well I don't want to …'

'Please. But only if you can spare the time.'

Hannah smiled. 'Um, okay. I'm not in any rush.'

'Mummy, who's this?' said a little boy about the twins' age, who was half hiding behind his mother and holding onto her legs.

'Felix, this is Hannah, a friend of Mummy and Daddy's.'

'Hello, Felix,' Hannah said, squatting down and holding out her hand, which Felix tentatively took hold of and shook gently. 'It's really nice to meet you.'

'It's nice to meet you too,' he said, and let go of her hand.

'Now, Felix, darling, how about you go and play outside with Bertie for a bit.'

'Okay,' Felix said and ran off down the hall.

'Bertie's our dog,' Louise explained to Hannah, who nodded and smiled in reply.

'Come through.'

'You have a beautiful home, Louise,' Hannah said when she was seated in the kitchen.

'Thanks. It's rustic, but I love it.'

'I love old furniture too,' Hannah said, taking in the leadlight cabinet and oak table and chairs.

'Thanks. I have a fondness for the nineteen thirties. It's been a great era to collect because no one really appreciated it until quite recently. Thankfully before people twigged I had all I needed,' she said with a smile.

'Solid timber has so much character and warmth, doesn't it?'

'Yes, and it is nice and sturdy too. They certainly don't make things like they used to, do they?'

'No, they don't,' Hannah said smiling in return.

'I was about to put the espresso pot on if you're interested.'

'Espresso sounds lovely. Thank you.'

'It was always instant in this house, but when Henry left I decided I'd damned well have decent coffee if I want it, especially now I'm working again. It's my little luxury,' she said, putting the pot on the hotplate and turning it on.

'I'm sorry he left,' Hannah said.

'Me too. But I can't be sitting around crying about it. Someone has to step up, especially when there's a child to be taken care of. It's all very well for Henry to drop his bundle. Silly man. Don't get me wrong. I love him to bits, I'm just disappointed.'

Hannah nodded.

'God, listen to me going on.' Louise suddenly sat down at the table and gripped both of Hannah's hands in hers. 'I am so, so sorry for your loss, Hannah. I can't begin to imagine what you've been through. If there's anything I can do, please just ask.'

'Honestly, I appreciate the gesture, Louise, but I'm fine. I can't say it hasn't been hard – my world has been turned upside down, but, like you, I'm getting on with things.'

'Like me? Hannah, my situation is nothing like yours. You poor thing.'

'I try not to think of myself as a victim,' Hannah said, not wanting to sound defensive. She was beginning to wish she hadn't accepted Louise's invitation. It was getting a little awkward. She looked down at her hands, desperate to pull them away. But she didn't want to cause offence.

'Of course you are. I'm sorry. I didn't mean to ...' Louise said, letting go of Hannah's hands as if they were suddenly too hot to hold.

'It's okay.' Hannah was thankful for the distraction of the spluttering and gurgling pot on the stove, which Louise jumped up to attend to.

'Now, I like plenty of milk and one and a half sugars. How about you?'

'Sounds perfect,' Hannah said, relaxing. She was here and couldn't leave without it looking rude.

Louise took the lid off a plastic container and put it on the table.

'They're gorgeous,' Hannah said as she selected a cupcake covered in pink icing and small silver balls. 'Yum,' she said peeling off the paper case and taking her first bite. 'So you said you're working. Are you enjoying it?'

'Yes, surprisingly. It's just a few days in an office, but I'd forgotten how good it feels to be useful as more than a mum and wife. I like the renewed feeling of independence, too. Not that Henry isn't a good provider. Well, he was. He does his best, but he's a bit lost. Ah, who am I kidding? He's being a bloody fool. Speaking of being a victim. Seriously, sometimes I just want to shake the shit out of him. Oops, sorry.'

'No problem at all,' Hannah said, trying not to smile too broadly at Louise's frankness.

'Seriously, he's a pretty smart man, but he's not behaving like one at the moment. It's one thing for me to see it, but what I worry about is what message it's sending Felix. Sadly Henry is too caught up in his poor-me syndrome.'

'Is there anything I can do to help?'

'Sadly, no. But, thanks for asking. I think he has to either hit rock bottom – which I'd rather not see – or somehow wake up to himself. I haven't told him I'm working and I'm keeping the money in a separate account in the hope he'll think we *have* hit rock bottom. I guess I'm also trying not to emasculate him even more. I want him back. I want my family back together. He may be a big boofhead, but he's my big boofhead,' she said sadly and sipped on her coffee. 'But I can't exactly drag him back kicking and screaming. I guess I've just been hoping he'll suddenly step up. Maybe I'm kidding myself.'

'I think he'd be very upset to see the house sold,' Hannah said quietly.

'So, what's he bloody doing about it, then?'

'I think he's getting more gardening work. I've given his details to a few friends of mine.'

'That's lovely, but as good as he is at lopping limbs and cutting lawns, he's really not quite the businessman. He needs a boss.'

'He mentioned you did the books. I wanted to pay online, but ...' She shrugged in a helpless gesture.

'I keep offering to help him. I've told him I'm happy for it to continue to be a partnership. But the silly man has got it into his head that he's failed and can barely look me in the eye.'

'So, what are you going to do?'

'Wait it out, I guess. And just hope he doesn't do anything silly. That's my greatest fear – that he'll, you know,' she said, tears filling her eyes. 'He knows Felix and I love him and will welcome him back in a heartbeat. It's up to him. Meanwhile, I'm a single mother doing my best.'

'I think you're doing really well.'

'I'm sorry to lump all this on you. I'm suddenly feeling very embarrassed about my verbal diarrhoea.'

'Don't. It's quite all right. A bit of venting is good for the soul,' Hannah said, smiling warmly. Louise's down-to-earth, forthright nature reminded her a little of Sam.

Suddenly she noticed Felix hovering in the doorway.

'It's okay, darling, you can come in,' Louise said and the little boy rushed over to the table.

'Mum,' he said, and looked pleadingly at Louise.

'I know. It's okay. I'm really sorry to cut this short,' Louise said to Hannah, anguish clear on her face, 'but Felix has a birthday party to go to.'

'No problem. I'm sorry to hold you up.' Hannah rose from her chair. 'You should have said.'

'It's okay. We're not late yet. Felix, you go and get the present. I'll meet you at the car. Say goodbye to Hannah.'

'Bye, Hannah.'

'Bye, Felix, enjoy your party.'

'I will. Thank you.'

'I'll walk you out,' Louise said. 'Sorry again for getting so deep and heavy. I think I was a little overwhelmed to have you here, which if I haven't already said, I really appreciate. Thank you. It's been really lovely to meet you. I couldn't imagine having the courage to do what you did – coming here today, meeting Henry, and of course ...'

'I'm glad I came,' Hannah said, smiling warmly. She was a little surprised to find herself drawing Louise into a firm embrace. She felt a sudden strong warmth towards this outspoken but seemingly kind-hearted woman, knowing that they were loosely joined by a tragedy. 'I hope you and Henry can get back on track.'

'Me too, but I think the ball's in his court now.'

'Okay. Well, bye, then,' Hannah said, stepping down off the porch. As she did, a thought struck her. She stopped and turned back. 'Actually, completely off-topic, but my friend Sam is an artist and she's having her first exhibition in early April. Would you be at all interested in coming to the opening or at least receiving an invitation?'

'Oh. I'd love to go to an art exhibition opening – I've never been to one before.'

'Muuum!' Felix called.

'Sorry, I'd better go.'

'I'll send you an invitation. Feel free to bring a friend if Henry's not interested. The more the merrier. Here, I'll give you my number in case …' *In case of what?* Hannah wondered as she dug in her handbag for one of her business cards to give her.

'Great. Thanks. I'd better go before I get the royal hurry-up,' Louise said.

Hannah waved as she drove away from the kerb. *Wow,* she thought. *What a morning.*

Chapter Twenty-three

From the gallery Hannah drove straight to Sam's house. A few times she thought she should pull over and phone or text her friend and make sure she wasn't making a wasted trip, but she didn't want to ruin the surprise. She just hoped Sam hadn't suddenly started going out for coffee with other mums after school drop-off.

'Hey, Hann, what are you doing here?' Sam cried and threw her arms around Hannah.

'I come bearing gifts, well, maybe not a gift as such. Exciting news, anyway. I've brought the invitations to show you.'

'Ooh, goodie. Well, you'd better come in, then,' Sam said, ushering Hannah in.

'Let me see,' Sam said, clapping her hands, when they were seated at the kitchen table. Hannah took out the sample from her handbag and handed it over. She sat in silence while Sam stared at it, turned it over, read both sides twice and stared at it again. The drawn-out silence started to worry Hannah.

'Is there something wrong?' Hannah asked. She'd gone over the proof online a week ago and printed it out, double-checked it and then checked the finished product at the printer before leaving.

Sam shook her head.

'What is it?'

'It's beautiful,' Sam said, and burst into tears.

Hannah laughed. 'Sammy, you're meant to be excited, happy, not drowning in tears,' she said, putting her arm around her friend. 'Of course it's beautiful, it's got a picture of your work on it.'

'I am happy. It's just … I never thought I'd see the day. Look, it's *my* name, *my* art.'

'Yes, darling, I know. Isn't it wonderful?'

'I can't believe how good it looks. My sculpture looks, looks … I don't know, *real*.'

'It is real, silly.'

'No, I know, but you know, like a professional has done it.'

'You *are* a professional, Sammy.'

'Not until I've sold something I'm not.'

'You sold all those pieces at the market, remember?'

'But that was just a market. Okay, so a very good design market, but still … This is a proper gallery. Oh, Hann, thank you. This is all because of you.'

'No, it's not. You're the artist. This is all you.'

'But without you being my agent, I could never have made this happen.'

'Don't be bloody ridiculous. You've really got to start believing in yourself,' she said, putting the invitation down.

'The piece looks so incredible,' Sam said, picking the card up again.

'You took the photo,' Hannah said.

'I know, I'm just so blown away.'

'Well, believe it, Sammy, because it's real. It's happening.'

'Pity I have to share the exhibition with another artist,' Sam said. 'Though I quite like Zoe's style. I'm looking forward to seeing what else she's done.'

'I think it's great – and lucky – that you are so different.'

'Yes, it's a good contrast. Hopefully something for everyone,' Sam said.

'You'd better do some more pieces, because there are over two hundred of these babies going out.'

'All up, including Zoe's?'

'No, that's just yours.'

'No way! Do I even know that many people?'

'Probably not. Jasmine and Beth and even Pete have added some names to broaden the reach. Zoe doesn't have many on her list because she's from overseas or been living overseas for ages, or something,' Hannah said.

'Wow. Thank you.'

'Now, don't get too excited. I think if we get sixty turning up from our side we'll be doing well. Some of the invites are a bit random.'

'I need a Bex and a lie down. It's quite overwhelming.'

'I'm sure it is. Actually, I'm a bit hungry, do you have anything to eat?'

'God, you sound like the boys. There's chocolate cake in the tin on the bench.'

'Oh. Okay.'

'Don't worry, it's from Joan across the way and has received the boys' seal of approval.'

'Brilliant! Yum.' Hannah said, instantly regretting her sudden enthusiasm. Oh well, Sam was fully aware of her failings in the kitchen.

'So, who's enveloping them and putting the stamps on and everything?'

'Don't worry, Roger has it all sorted. We don't have to do a thing,' Hannah said, putting down the plate with two slices of cake and two forks.

'That's good of him.'

'Well, he is taking a decent commission from sales, don't forget.'

'Right, of course,' Sam said. 'So, how's the new job?'

'I love it, Sam, I really do. I know it's only been a couple of days, but so far so good. It's challenging and it's interesting. And best of all, I get to be home with the cats. Although, they do limit productivity somewhat. They love sitting right under the heat of the desk lamp or in my lap or on the keyboard, or anywhere else my attention is when it's not on them. They're seriously cute, but there's a limit. Well, there should be. I've lost half my desk space to a bed for them in the hope they'll settle and be less disruptive.'

'Hannah, you can put them on the floor and say no, you know.'

'Oh, but you haven't seen their little faces.'

'You'll sort it out. So, what is it you're actually doing for Craig?'

'Everything. This week I'm mainly concentrating on writing the copy for the website and getting quotes for web designers and hosts. I even managed to get Craig in for a coffee meeting with the CEO of one of the biggest electricity companies.'

'Wow. Go, you.'

'It doesn't sound very exciting or glamorous, but it feels good to have so much at stake and be such an important cog in his business machine. I know he's always valued me, but this is different.'

'Whatever floats your boat. God, I'd love a personal assistant right about now. I came so close to forgetting the boys yesterday. Made it by the skin of my teeth. I was so engrossed I didn't hear the alarm I'd set. Thankfully I got that pesky feeling I was forgetting something and it wouldn't let up until I realised. I can't wait until they're old enough to catch public transport on their own so I can get a whole day to myself,' Sam said.

'Well, if you're feeling like a taxi service now, imagine what it will be like when one decides he wants to play soccer and the other wants to pursue piano, or whatever.'

'God, don't remind me. That's the other reason I need Rob here,' Sam said sadly.

'I'm sorry. I didn't mean to upset you by bringing things up.'

'It's okay. It's not your fault my life is a mess.'

'It's not a mess, Sammy.'

'Well, it is what it is,' Sam said soberly with a shrug. 'At least I have my first exhibition to distract me.'

'That's the spirit.'

Hannah wondered about the level of Sam's despondency. She was such a strong, independent woman, it was hard to believe she might be falling apart. But then she had the twins, who were most likely wearing her down with constant questions of where was their dad and when was he coming home. She really hoped the exhibition was a roaring success and Sam would start to feel better all round.

'So, how's it going with Pete?' Sam asked.

'Oh. Well …' Hannah hesitated. The last thing she wanted was to make Sam feel worse.

'And no censoring. Come on, I need you to remind me that maybe just maybe I won't end up a lonely dried up old prune.'

'As if, Sam! Anyway, you'll always have me.'

'Not if you're off with Pete. So …?'

'We're taking things slowly, but proper date number two was the other night. We were going to see a movie and have pizza but decided we'd save that for when the weather isn't so nice.'

'Looking into the future – that's a good sign. What did you end up doing instead?'

'We went down to Port Melbourne and walked along the beach and had fish and chips and then ice-cream.'

'Now *that's* romantic.'

'Yes, it was really lovely.'

'You know, I don't think you can go wrong with someone who cares for both people and animals like a vet does,' Sam mused. 'And he is quite scrummy, in a gentle yet rugged way – if that's possible.'

'Hmm. What? Hang on, how do you know?'

'I have a confession to make.'

'God, don't tell me you've gone and stalked him.'

'I didn't stalk him, Hannah, you didn't let me finish,' Sam said with a laugh. 'It was accidental. I took the dogs in for their annual jab and check-up and my usual vet wasn't there. I didn't even realise until after, actually. His name tag said Dr Shaw and I don't remember him introducing himself. He seemed in a bit of a rush. Or maybe I was too busy looking into those hazel eyes or checking out his …'

'Sam, don't be ridiculous. He's not even *that* good looking. Handsome, yes, but not drop dead gorgeous or swoon-worthy.'

'Oh I don't know. I thought he was quite divine. Nice gentle hands too. And the dogs seemed to like him, though giving them treats helped. Greedy things.'

'So how did you figure out that he was Pete?'

'When I was paying. He was hovering nearby and someone called his name from the back of the office and off he went. Then it clicked. Anyway, he has my seal of approval. You lovebirds have my blessing.'

'Why, thank you very much. But, really, it's early days. And I'm still not entirely sure I haven't been put into the friend zone.'

'Why, what do you mean? What about the romantic walk along the beach?'

'Well, he hasn't even tried to kiss me, except for a couple of times that were more of a quick peck. He did hold my hand and put his arm around me. God, I've missed that safe, secure feeling of being held by strong arms. But that was as far as it went, intimately,' Hannah said.

'You did say you were taking it slow.'

'Maybe that's just the excuse I'm using so I don't feel hurt.'

'He knows your situation. And he's bound to be cautious too. If you want it to be different, you'd better tell him that.'

'I think it's a little soon to be saying, "Pete, we need to talk". Also, I don't know what it is I want. Sometimes I think I'd like some nice sex or maybe even just to curl up with some strong arms wrapped around me.'

'I hear ya,' Sam said wistfully.

'But then the thought of casual sex freaks me out. You don't get anything nice without getting emotionally involved. Well, I can't see how I could, anyway. And then just the thought of being that intimate with someone makes me feel guilty and miss Tristan. I know deep down he wasn't perfect and *we* weren't perfect, but I keep having the feeling that no one is ever going to measure up.'

'Poor Pete. That's a lot of pressure,' Sam said.

'Exactly.'

'Maybe you're just not ready.'

'Perhaps you're right. He's going away for a few weeks to do some locum work for a uni friend. He's hoping to make it back in time for your launch, but there are no guarantees. The time apart might be useful.'

'Well, they do say absence makes the heart grow fonder. Long chats on the phone might be good for getting to know each other better.'

'I get the impression he's not really into spending hours on the phone.'

'Maybe some quick phone sex to spice things up, then,' Sam added with a cheeky grin.

'Eeew! No way!'

'Only kidding. Maybe he'll write romantic letters or emails instead. He has form in that department,' Sam said a little more seriously.

'Hmm.'

'Don't overthink it. You've come a long way, but this is a whole different ball game. Be grateful he isn't pressuring you into bed and he clearly wants a deeper, more meaningful relationship.'

'You're right. Oh, Sammy, I don't want to feel so damaged, so broken,' Hannah said with a sigh.

'Hmm. Imagine what a basket case I'm going to be if I ever decide to start dating again,' Sam said. 'What a fine pair we are.'

Hannah leaned over and hugged her friend. Oh how she loved her dry wit. 'Yes, but as you say, at least we have each other.'

'I know. But, god I miss him, Hann. And he's still being such a good dad, even from a distance. I didn't tell you this, but he's bought a stack of books the same as what the boys have here and reads to them every night while they follow along here.'

'Aww, bless him.'

'Why can't he have turned out to be an arsehole instead of gay? Damn it,' Sam said.

'It would make it easier for me too, you know. In these situations friends are meant to take sides, but I can't. I blame you.'

'Why, because he's even more loveable to you now he's gay, right?' Sam said.

'Yup, afraid so,' Hannah said, laughing.

'Have you spoken to him?'

'Just the once. I hope you don't mind. He called soon after he arrived in Singapore. I didn't want to get put in the middle, but I didn't feel I could … Especially when you said things were okay between you.'

'No. It's fine. Honestly.'

'I still felt like I'd betrayed you a little. That's why I didn't say anything.'

'Don't worry, it's a weird situation all round. Hann, you have my permission to be in touch with him however much you want. As I've said, I want to hate him, but I just can't. Actually, I don't think I've ever loved him more than I do right now. I hate *that*! He's just such a bloody decent bloke.'

'Yes, that he is.'

Rob! Oh! Should I invite him to the opening? Would that help or make things worse? Would Sam see it as rubbing it in because he's left her or would she appreciate such a show of support? He should definitely be here, Hannah concluded. *But Sam doesn't like surprises. It would have to be a surprise, wouldn't it, if I'm going to keep her at least a bit calm and focussed? She's already on a knife-edge.*

The more Hannah thought about it, the more convinced she was that Rob should be there. About the surprise factor and getting in trouble with Sam, Hannah decided she'd cross that bridge if and when she came to it. Hopefully the risk would be worth it.

'Bastard!' Sam said with a sob.

'Come on, no tears,' Hannah said kindly.

'Everything will work out, won't it? Eventually?' Sam said.

'So you've always said.'

'I know I've said it before, probably a million times, but I don't know what I believe anymore.'

'I know. Me neither. Let's just believe that the best will happen – I don't want to become a bitter old woman. And you need to set a good example for those precious boys.'

'Oh, to be so young and carefree,' Sam said wistfully.

'Darling, we're not ninety.'

'Sometimes I feel like I might be.'

Chapter Twenty-four

Sam: *Eek, the opening is tonight! Freaking out a wee bit here.*

Hannah: *You'll be fine. The hard work is done. Tonight is to be enjoyed. Just enjoy a quiet day chilling with the boys. Go for a long, relaxing walk. That's what I'm off to do now. Xx*

Sam: *So you don't need me for anything?*

Hannah: *Nope. All under control. Enjoy your day. See you later, superstar. Xx*

Sam: *Okay. Thanks for everything. Love you. Xx*

Hannah: *You're welcome. Love you too. Xx*

Hannah put her phone down and was tying the laces on her second running shoe when her doorbell rang.

She opened it to find Rob standing on her doorstep.

'Oh my god! Rob! Hello. You came! It's so good to see you!' She pulled him into a tight hug. 'And, you do give the best hugs. I've missed you so much.'

'I'm not calling too early, am I?'

'Not at all. You know any time after six-thirty is fine with me. Come in,' she said, and led the way through to the kitchen. 'I'm so glad you're here. How are you?'

'You know, right now I'd give my left arm for a decent coffee,' he said, sitting on a stool at the bench.

'Coming right up.'

'Are you on your way back in or were you on your way out?' Rob asked as Hannah took her shoes off once the coffee machine had been set in motion.

'On my way out. But just for a distracting walk. No biggie. I'd much rather be distracted by you. So how's Singapore?'

'Same as last time you asked me. Big city, lots of people,' he said.

'Fair enough. Have you met any nice people? Have you met anyone special?'

'Have I made new friends? Hann, darling, we're not in school and you're not my mother.'

'Just being interested, making conversation,' she said, putting his coffee down in front of him.

'God, that's good,' he said after a long sip.

'You must have got in very early,' Hannah said.

'Yeah, most of the flights are overnight. Anyway, it's better than losing a whole day. Well, except for losing most of a night's sleep. And I have met someone, actually,' he added quietly.

'How long are you here for? Hang on, met someone – as in a man, a *special* man?'

'I think so. I'm hoping so.'

'That's great. Well, come on, tell me.'

Rob pulled out his mobile phone, scrolled through some photos and handed it over. Hannah felt a little jolt of shock at seeing Rob with his arm around a blond guy.

'Nick,' Rob said. 'He's really nice.'

'I should hope so.'

'Are you really shocked?'

'No. Well, maybe a little. It's just a bit different.' Hannah wanted to say, 'It's too soon, isn't it?' But then she reminded herself he'd been gone for four months. Anyway, he'd most likely been waiting for this for his entire adult life. 'I'm happy for you, Rob, I really am. I'm just a bit sad for Sam, that's all. She really loves you. We *all* really love you.'

'You have no idea how much that means. I love you all too. Oh, so much. God, she's amazing.'

'Yes, she is. But she's freaking out a little about tonight, so I'm glad you're here.'

'Thanks so much for giving me the push I needed to come over. I'm really pleased I'm here. I just hope I'll be a calming influence and not the thing that sends Sam over the edge.'

'Well, we won't know until we know,' Hannah said, smiling. 'So, how come you didn't tell me you were coming? And where are you staying? There's plenty of room here. You're welcome to stay.'

'Thanks. Okay, to answer one question at a time. I didn't tell you in case it all goes pear-shaped. I didn't want to put your friendship in jeopardy by risking you having to lie – even by omission. This way if Sam gets angry and tries to turn on you, you can legitimately say you didn't know, even though you and I know that you sent me the invitation.'

'Thanks, I appreciate that.'

'You're best friends. I couldn't, and wouldn't, do anything to risk that. Ever. I'm so thrilled you're her agent now too – she couldn't be in better hands.'

Hannah felt a new rush of warm love for Rob. And realised for the first time just how much she missed him.

'I'm booked to stay at a hotel in the city. I've got some meetings while I'm here so work's paying. I'm sort of playing it by ear. I'm staying for the week and hoping to spend some time with Sam and the boys for school holidays and Easter.'

'Oh, that's great.' Hannah felt herself relaxing. She liked that Rob wasn't flying straight out again on Monday. 'So, tell me more about Nick. What does he do? Where's he from? He didn't come with you, did he?'

'No, we decided it's too soon. And this is Sam's gig. My turning up unannounced will be a big enough distraction as it is. He's tall, blond and handsome, as you can see. He's an architect from Sydney. We work in the same high-rise and met in the lift one day.'

At that moment the doorbell rang again. 'I wonder who that is. I'm not expecting anyone,' Hannah said as if to herself, and got up.

'It won't be Sam, will it?' Rob asked. 'I don't want her to see me until tonight. Just to be sure, I'll go and hide in your bedroom. Okay?'

'Okay.'

Hannah waited until Rob was out of sight before opening the door. She blinked at seeing her parents-in-law, standing there on the step with Beth hanging a little behind them.

'Surprise!' Raelene and Adrian said together.

'Wow, it certainly is! And a wonderful one,' Hannah said, throwing her arms around Raelene first and then Adrian. 'What are you doing here?'

'We heard there was an art exhibition opening by the soon-to-be-famous Samantha Barrow and thought we'd better be here to see history made,' Adrian said.

'And it's too long since we saw you in person,' Raelene added.

'Yes, and that. When Beth phoned and offered to have us stay, we couldn't resist turning it into a surprise,' Adrian said. 'We hope you don't mind.'

'Not at all. I'm so glad you did. Oh, you've no idea how good it is to see you,' Hannah said, ushering them inside.

Beth hung back. 'Hannah, dear, I hope I haven't overstepped the mark, I just thought you'd be busy and have enough on your plate.'

'Auntie Beth, I think it's a wonderful surprise. And I might have got in a flap if I had house guests to prepare for as well. So, thank you.'

'Okay. Well, I'll leave you to your catching up,' Beth said.

'Oh, you don't need …' Hannah started.

'No arguments. I'll see you tonight,' Beth said, and left with a wave of her hand.

'Before we get settled, I need to show you something. Rob, it's okay, you can come out now. Meet us in the study,' she called up the hall. 'It's a day full of wonderful surprises,' Hannah explained as they made their way through the house. 'Rob's just arrived from Singapore. I didn't know about that, either. You're all dark horses. I sent you an invitation to keep you in the loop. I didn't think for a second that you'd come all this way. But I'm overwhelmed and so happy that you are here. Wow, what a day.'

They all greeted Rob with warm hugs in the hallway before following Hannah into what was now her office.

'Look,' she said, pointing to the sculpture Sam had given her. Hannah had brought it home the other week when they'd agreed Sam had enough pieces to show. Hannah had been a little torn. On the one hand, she felt it was Sam's best piece and wanted the whole world to see it. On the other, she didn't want to share it with anyone because it was so personal to her. They'd agreed that since it wasn't for sale anyway, there was no point in including it in the exhibition.

'This, Rob, is the work of your extremely clever wife, I mean your, um …' Hannah gave up. She didn't want to risk ruining the moment. 'Raelene and Adrian, this is the quality of art you've flown so far to see tonight.'

'Bloody hell, that's good. Amazing,' Rob said.

'Oh, my,' Raelene said, bringing a hand to her heart. Hannah noticed her eyes had filled with tears. 'It's beautiful, but oh so, so sad.'

'Yes, it's very moving,' Adrian said quietly.

'I know. I'm still trying to decide if I can have it beside me all day every day,' Hannah said. 'One moment I look at it and feel inspired, the next it makes me sad.'

'Well, at least it makes you *feel*. That's a sign of great art, in my opinion,' Adrian said, putting one arm around his wife and the other around Hannah.

'Yes, I suppose so,' Hannah said.

'She's very good,' Raelene said.

'Yes. She seems to have really stepped it up to a whole new level,' Rob said.

'We are in for a wonderful treat this evening,' Adrian said, breaking the heavy silence.

'I really should go. I don't want to intrude,' Rob said as they left the room.

'Intrude? Don't be silly. You're practically family,' Hannah said.

'Yes, don't go on our account,' Raelene said.

'You won't be able to check into your hotel for hours,' Hannah said. 'Come and have another cuppa and then a lie down if you need to recharge.'

'Well, if you're sure …?'

'Absolutely,' Hannah said.

'And please don't feel at all uneasy about anything,' Adrian said almost out of Hannah's hearing. 'Hannah filled us in during one of our Sunday phone calls. You're amongst friends, Rob. It's your life to live as you wish.'

'Exactly. There's no judgement from us,' Raelene said, rubbing him on the shoulder.

'Thanks. That means a lot. It really does. Not everyone is so understanding.'

'Well, not everyone can be or should be counted as a friend,' Raelene said sagely.

★

'Thank god you're here,' Sam said, ushering Hannah inside.

'What's wrong? I'm not late. I said I'd be here at five.' Despite knowing exactly what time it was, having kept an almost constant eye on the time all afternoon, Hannah checked her watch with a frown. 'I'm actually five minutes early. How come you're not dressed?'

'I can't decide what to wear,' Sam said, leading the way through to her bedroom.

'But we went through all this the other day and decided on the black pants with the green top.'

'Now I'm thinking of going all black.'

'Fine, if it's going to make you feel more comfortable and less stressed. You'll look fabulous in whatever you wear.'

'Oh, I don't know which one now,' Sam said, running a hand through her hair. 'You look good. I love that top.'

'Thanks.'

'I'm so nervous, Hann, I think I'm going to have a heart attack or throw up.'

'No, you're not.' Hannah took her friend's hands gently in hers and looked into her stricken face. 'You are fine. There is nothing to be worried about. Slow, deep breaths. Come on, just like me.' Hannah demonstrated. 'That's better. Now, Sammy, you're going to be amongst friends and people who only want the very best for you. There's nothing to be freaking out about.'

'I keep telling myself that, but it doesn't help. Do I really have to speak?'

'Yes, you at least need to thank everyone for being there to support you and ...'

'Can't you do it for me? Or Roger?'

'No. You have to say *something*. It's your night, Sammy. Seriously, it's only about ten seconds of your life. And, again, it's in front of people who love and respect you – not strangers. Well, hardly any. Honestly, you'll regret it later if you don't thank them. You might not be able to see it now, but tonight is the door opening onto what will quite likely be a hugely successful career for you. Sometime you'll look back at this evening's event and realise what a pivotal moment it was. Your memories need to be fond, not, "Damn it, I wish I'd had the guts to say something, acknowledge it. How rude of me not to at least thank everyone for coming." Remember how well you did with those assessment tutes you had to run at uni – your lecturers and tutors all said you were a natural, remember?'

'But that was ages ago.'

'Not so long ago that you don't remember how to do it. Remember how nervous you were doing them? You always swore you were going to be sick right up until you stood up and spoke. Then you nailed it. Every time.'

'I suppose.'

'You've done plenty of other scary things since then, too, without even batting an eyelid.'

'Like what?'

'Erm, like giving birth to twins?'

'Darling, I can tell you I batted a lot more than an eyelid doing that! I was screaming as I went into the delivery room, saying that I'd changed my mind.'

'Ha-ha, oops, yes, I remember you told me that. Okay, sorry, bad example. Please, Sammy, just calm down. I have full faith in you. A lot of people do. You can do this. But we'd better get cracking – we can't be late. Unless you want to make a dramatic entrance?'

'Hell, no. Right, the green it is,' Sam said, pulling the top from its hanger.

*

'Okay, deep breaths,' Sam said when they were backing out of the driveway in Hannah's car. 'So, distract me. What did you get up to today? I took a long, relaxing bath, which helped, but clearly not enough, or the effects have worn off. Did you?'

'No, I didn't get a chance to do that in the end. You'll never guess who turned up. I had no idea they were coming.'

'Who?'

'Raelene and Adrian.' Hannah was pleased to have her in-laws to talk about as a diversion without the possibility of accidentally mentioning Rob.

'Oh my god. Now I'm really nervous.'

'Why?'

'Because they've flown in specially, haven't they? Nothing like a bit of added pressure.'

'Sam, as I've said, all you need to do is be yourself, revel in your big moment, and be proud of your achievement in getting this far. This is your big break. Enjoy it and don't let nerves ruin it for you.'

'I'll try.' Sam took a deep breath and let it out loudly. 'How come you're not nervous, anyway? I might completely embarrass you.'

'You couldn't, Sam. I'm far too proud of you. I know you're going to do your best, you always do, so I have nothing to be worried about.'

But the truth is, I'm very uneasy, but more because I'm not sure how you're going to react to Rob's presence.

'I love you so much, Hann.'

'I love you too.'

Chapter Twenty-five

'Oh no, they've even blocked off parking for us right out front!' Sam said in awe as Hannah pulled up.

'Yep, VIP treatment, baby!' Hannah said, grinning.

'I feel a little bit special,' Sam said in barely more than a whisper.

'You're a lot special, Sammy. Enjoy.' Hannah was relieved Roger hadn't run a red carpet out from the doorway to the kerb – that might have completely overwhelmed Sam. The large red mat was a lovely, understated touch.

'Welcome, welcome,' Roger said, as he opened Sam's car door while Hannah made her own way, locking the vehicle behind her. 'Perfect timing,' he said, gently embracing first Sam and then Hannah and air kissing them on each cheek.

'You're both looking absolutely stunning,' he said. 'Not too nervous, I hope?' he asked Sam.

'Terrified,' Sam said with a laugh.

'Oh dear. Perfectly understandable. But you're not to worry about a thing. Everything has gone like clockwork. It's going to be a fun night. Come on, lovely ladies, let's get you a drink to take the edge off,' he said, crooking both arms for Sam and Hannah to take hold.

'Have a look around while I find us some drinks. Back in a moment,' Roger said, releasing them once they were inside.

'Wow. It looks amazing,' Sam said, gazing about.

'It certainly does,' Hannah said. She thought the space had been put together really well – nicely balanced – not too cluttered, not too sparse, and with plenty of room for the hordes of expected guests. Still, she couldn't quite see how everyone would fit in. A few people were already making their way around the exhibition. She leaned closer to one of Sam's pieces and was a little stunned to see the price. She moved to another and found it was the same. Wow. Would someone pay twelve hundred dollars for one piece? Sure, they were good. Sam had put a lot of thought and work into them, but she was an unknown artist.

'Golly! Who's going to buy anything at these prices?' Sam said.

'Take it as a compliment. Roger obviously sees your worth,' Hannah said.

'And Zoe's. I like her work much better in the flesh,' Sam whispered. 'It's really rather good.'

'That's the spirit. I wonder where she is,' Hannah said, looking around despite not knowing what Zoe Raven looked like.

'It's quite crowded. It makes me a little relieved I decided not to bring the boys. I've been feeling a bit guilty about it this afternoon, to be honest.'

'Oh no. You should have said. I could have kept an eye on them or I'm sure Jasmine wouldn't have minded doing it.'

'Thanks. I know. But I'd still be worrying about them knocking something over or being general tearaways. You know how they can get sometimes. God, could you imagine if there was a loud crash in the middle of speeches or something? I'm stressed enough as it is.'

'Did they ask if they could come?'

'No. I explained where I was going and what I was doing, but they were too excited about their sleepover to show any interest.'

'Well there you go, then,' Hannah said. 'I'm sure you've done the right thing. And I'm certain there will be other openings they can attend when they're a bit bigger and understand the significance of the occasion and the need to behave.'

'Here we are, champagne for two,' Roger said, appearing beside them.

'Thank you,' they said in unison as they each accepted a tall glass.

'Would you excuse me, I need to keep a watch out for Zoe.'

'Of course,' Hannah said.

'No problem at all,' Sam said.

'This champagne is rather good,' Hannah said, after taking a sip.

'Yes. Oh. My. God,' Sam suddenly said. Hannah turned to follow her gaze. Rob and Adrian had just come in. Hannah could practically see the blood draining from Sam's face as she stared at Rob, who was walking towards them. *Uh-oh*, she thought.

'Oh, Rob, thank you for coming. It means so much to me,' Sam said as she threw her arms around him.

Hannah breathed a sigh of relief.

'I can't believe you didn't tell me,' Sam said, looking from Rob to Hannah and back again.

'I only found out this morning when he turned up,' Hannah said, feeling enormous gratitude to Rob for his foresight in preventing her from having to lie.

'Yes, don't be annoyed with Hann. It was all me. I decided it was a risk worth taking,' Rob said.

'If I'd known, you could have helped me choose what to wear. I was freaking out.'

'Oh. Well you clearly did okay. You look amazing.'

'Thanks. It really is good to see you, Rob,' Sam said.

'I'm glad. It's great to see you too.'

'The boys will be so disappointed to have missed you, though,' she said, her face clouding.

'I'll see them. I'm here for a week.'

Sam beamed. 'Really?'

Rob nodded. 'Yup.'

'Oh, you've made my night! I don't care now if no one else turns up and nothing sells,' she declared.

'Yeah, right,' Rob and Hannah said together.

'Well, okay, maybe just a bit.'

'You've done an incredible job, Sammy. I'm so proud of you,' Rob said, glancing around him.

Suddenly Roger appeared beside them with a decidedly nervous young woman in tow.

'Sam, Hannah, I'd like to introduce you to Zoe.'

'Lovely to meet you,' Hannah said, holding out her hand.

Sam followed suit and said, 'Yes, lovely to meet you. I think your paintings are really wonderful.'

'Thanks. And I think your sculptures are incredible,' Zoe said, looking instantly more at ease.

A man appeared with a tray holding a selection of drinks. Rob and Zoe each took a glass of sparkling wine.

'Here's cheers to a great night,' Rob said, to which they all agreed and clinked glasses. Another young man came over with a tray of food.

'Mini vegetarian pizza, beef with horseradish mayonnaise on cucumber rounds and mushrooms stuffed with creamy egg,' he explained.

'Oh, yum,' Sam said, and took a mini pizza. Hannah was pleased Sam's nerves had eased enough for her to be interested in food.

At that moment Jasmine arrived and pulled Hannah, Sam and then Rob into hugs. And then it was Craig's turn.

Gradually the room filled up with people and the sound of exuberant chatter.

Over Craig's shoulder Hannah could see the front door. She didn't stop her mouth from dropping open in time. *Is that …? Oh, my god, it is. Brad!*

Hannah almost gasped at seeing the man she'd had dinner with at The Windsor Hotel all those months ago – a time when she'd been struggling to put herself and her life back together. It seemed so strange to see him here. She felt her heart leap and swell and found herself moving forward towards him.

'Hannah. Wow. Hello.' *He remembered my name? Well, you remembered his, silly. Good point.*

'Brad. What are you doing here?' she said, a little breathlessly.

'I could ask you the same question,' he said with a laugh. 'I'll have you know, I'm quite the art connoisseur. Seriously, though, I did a story on Roger's gallery when it first opened and we hit it off. So, now I come along to most of his exhibition openings. Just call me rent-a-crowd!' he said, grinning.

Oh, that smile, Hannah thought, feeling herself melt a little.

'It's so good to see you,' Brad continued. 'I've often thought of you, wondering how you're doing. Come here, let me give you a hug.'

Oh, yes, please. 'Me too,' she said, holding on and feeling that she never wanted to let go as she breathed in his comforting scent.

Oh how good he felt. He still gave the best hug in the world. Even now when she was in such a different, better place.

'Okay. So, you now,' he said when they had separated.

'Sorry?'

'How do you come to be here?'

'Oh. Well, Sam's my best friend – one of the artists.'

'She's actually my agent,' Sam said, appearing beside Hannah. 'Sam Barrow,' she said, holding out her hand.

'Brad Thomas. Wonderful to meet you.'

'Brad Thomas? Why is your name familiar? Have we met?'

'No, I don't think so.'

'Brad and I met at The Windsor last year,' Hannah said.

'Oh! You're *that* Brad!'

'I suppose I am,' Brad said, looking amused.

'I've heard all about you. It's great to put a face to the story,' Sam said.

Hannah blushed and looked to the floor for any potential opening up and swallowing properties.

'Agent, eh? That's great. How exciting,' Brad said, beaming.

'Yes. Actually, let me know if you want to interview Sam sometime,' Hannah said, leaping into business mode and taking a card out of her bag.

'Okay. Maybe I will,' he said, handing her one of his own cards. 'And maybe you'd like to catch up for coffee sometime?'

'Oh. Are you in Melbourne for a while, then?' Hannah asked.

'I'm a permanent fixture now.'

'Right. Okay, great.' At that moment Hannah looked up and noticed Pete standing just inside the front door and glancing around as if he were lost. 'Excuse me,' she said to Brad, and rushed to Pete's side.

'You made it!' she said, kissing him on the lips, which she noted seemed to startle him a little. 'I'm so glad you're here. How was your trip back?'

'Long, but thankfully uneventful. But I could use a drink. And, oh, I smell food. I'm famished,' he said, touching her arm and moving past her. Hannah looked after him feeling a little perplexed. *What just happened? Did he just give me the brush-off?*

She pushed it aside. There were people coming in – maybe he didn't want to block the doorway. Or maybe he wasn't comfortable in such a large crowd.

By seven o'clock the gallery was so tightly packed the wait staff were having trouble getting through and Hannah began to worry about the safety of Sam's fragile sculptures. Suddenly a different noise crept over the babble of voices, gradually becoming louder as the crowd quietened.

Roger was tapping his glass with a spoon. 'Bit of shush, thanks, everyone,' he said. 'Thank you all for coming along to the opening of our exhibition, titled *Life*. Standing beside me on my left is our ceramicist, Samantha Barrow. And on my right is our abstract painter, Zoe Raven. I'm sure you'll agree that their work certainly doesn't show them to be debut artists having their first exhibition.' He paused as cheering, whooping and whistling erupted and waited it out for a few moments.

'I look forward to proudly telling the world that they got their start at this gallery. Because I believe both of these artists are going to set the international art scene on fire – you mark my words. So, please enjoy their work – make a purchase or two – partake in a few drinks and some of the wonderful food. But before we go back to our mingling, I believe our artists would like to say something. Sam?'

'I'd just like to thank Roger for this wonderful opportunity,' Sam began, her voice a little shaky. She paused and took a breath before continuing. 'It means so much to be given a chance and be believed in by someone other than well-meaning family and friends.' Zoe nodded her agreement while a titter of laughter made its way around the room. 'I'd also really like to thank my best friend and agent, Hannah, and Rob who have always been a huge support. Thank you all for coming along. Some really special friends have travelled a very long way to be here,' she said, looking at Rob and then Adrian and Raelene, 'and for that I'm truly humbled and grateful. Thank you, again, so much,' she said, choking up. Roger stepped back so Sam could pass Zoe the microphone.

'Yes, thank you,' Zoe said. 'I can't say it better than Samantha has. Unfortunately, being from London and relatively new to Melbourne has meant a lot of my friends and family couldn't be here. So, huge thanks again to Roger, Sam and Hannah and their family and friends for welcoming me with open arms and making this such an amazing night.' She turned and blew Sam a kiss as the applause erupted around them.

'That was perfect, all you needed,' Hannah said, hugging Sam. 'Well done.'

'Thanks. I'm so glad it's over,' Sam said, letting out a loud breath.

'Well, you can forget all about it now and go and enjoy yourself.'

'You know, I can even see a few red dots on my things. Phew for that.'

'Sam, please, of course they're going to sell – they're incredible. Oh, hang on, there's Henry and Louise Peace.' Hannah returned Henry's wave. 'I just want to go and make sure they feel welcome, and see if I can introduce them to Brad Thomas. Where's he gone?' she said, looking around.

'What a coincidence that he's here – you haven't been in touch since, have you?' Sam asked.

'No. I had no idea he'd be here.'

'He's a bit dishy.'

'Sammy, you sound like Auntie Beth. Anyway, he's married, remember?'

'Is he still? As you well know, a lot can happen in a week, let alone several months.'

'Doesn't matter, I'm seeing Pete. The vet, remember?'

'Is he here?' Sam asked, looking around again. 'I haven't seen him.'

'Yes, he's here. I saw him briefly earlier.'

'Oh, there he is,' Sam said. 'He's looking our way.'

'I'd better go and see him. But, oh, damn, Henry and Louise look like they're leaving. I think now Henry was actually waving goodbye before,' Hannah said.

'Go,' Sam said, seeing the indecision and slight anguish on Hannah's face. 'I met Henry and Louise earlier. I'll go and see Pete. He might like getting a personal tour by one of the soon-to-be-famous artists,' Sam said with a cheeky grin and a wink.

'Thanks. Tell him I'll be there soon,' Hannah said, and rushed over to the far side of the room.

'Henry, Louise, it's wonderful to see you. Thank you for making the effort,' Hannah said. Instead of having her proffered hand accepted, she was a little surprised to be hugged, first by Louise and then Henry.

'Thank you so much for the invitation. We've had a lovely time, we really have,' Louise said, now holding both of Hannah's hands and looking at her intently.

'But you're not going so soon, are you? We haven't had the chance to catch up properly.'

'We're going to get a meal – not that the food here isn't wonderful. It really is, but …'

'It's okay. You don't need to explain. Go and enjoy yourselves,' Hannah said.

'It has been a truly enjoyable evening,' Henry said.

'Thanks again,' Louise said, giving Hannah another hug. 'You've no idea how much you've helped,' she whispered. 'I'll call you and tell you all about it.'

'Oh, good. Okay. Yes, please do.'

Hannah beamed after them as they left with their arms around each other. She had the overwhelming urge to rub her hands together and say, 'Well, my work here is done.'

Damn, though, I didn't get to introduce them to Brad. God. Poor Pete – she'd barely spoken two words to him all evening, either. Oh well, he was a big boy. She was suddenly exhausted and desperate to take the weight off her feet. It didn't help to see out of the corner of her eye Raelene, Adrian, Beth and Rob occupying the ottomans. Next to them was Brad. Hannah got out her phone and snapped several sneaky photos through the crowd. And as she did a thought struck her: *Has anyone else been taking photos?* She didn't remember seeing a dedicated photographer walking around or notice any flashes going off. She quickly snapped a few more shots.

'Don't worry, Craig and I have taken heaps of photos,' Jasmine said, appearing beside Hannah. 'We figured you might have been too busy to take any.'

'Thanks so much. People are starting to leave and I've only just thought of it. I'm sure Roger has had someone roving about, but whoever it is has been very good at being inconspicuous, because I didn't see them. Or perhaps I've just been too distracted to notice.'

'It's been a great evening,' Craig said, 'you should be very proud.'

'It's been all Sam and Zoe and Roger's doing. I'm feeling very proud of Sam. Craig, see that guy over there, next to Rob?' she said, nodding towards the ottomans. 'That's Brad Thomas. He's a freelance journalist. I'm going to try and meet with him to see if he can give us – well, you, your business – some free publicity or at least give some hints on how to get some.'

'Listen to you, always thinking, keeping all the balls in the air all the time,' Craig said, looking bemused. 'But, seriously, Hann, that's a great idea. Let me know how you go and if you need me.'

'Who does he write for? The name's familiar,' Jasmine said, frowning.

'I have no idea. I know him from having dinner with him while I was staying at The Windsor.'

'Oh. Wow!' Jasmine turned and stared at Hannah, then looked back at Brad. 'The one that gives great hugs?'

'The very one,' Hannah said, looking over to him. When he turned, caught her eye and smiled broadly, she felt her stomach flip again.

'I'm clearly missing something here. Anyone care to fill me in?' Craig asked, looking genuinely perplexed.

'Later, darling,' Jasmine said, and patted him on the arm.

'Pete has bought my piece *Man's Best Friend*. How exciting is that?' Sam said, suddenly appearing with her arm tucked through Pete's.

'Wonderful. Craig, Jasmine, this is Pete Shaw. Pete, Craig is my boss.'

'Ah. Great to meet you,' Pete said, putting out his hand.

'Likewise,' Craig and Jasmine said in unison.

Gradually the crowd thinned and only Hannah, Sam, Rob, Raelene, Adrian, Beth and Brad remained. Hannah couldn't see Pete when she looked around. She felt a little bad about neglecting him.

'I'm absolutely shattered,' Beth said.

'I'm not far off not being able to stand up anymore myself,' Raelene said. There was a chorus of agreement.

'Well, I'd better get going,' Brad said. 'Is anyone in need of a ride? I'm heading south-west.'

'I think we're all good, thanks,' Hannah said.

'Okay then. Let me know about catching up,' he said, kissed her on the cheek and left.

'Hannah, are you okay to take Adrian, Raelene and Beth home? I'm going to drive Sam home,' Rob said.

'No problem at all,' Hannah said.

'Hopefully we'll get the chance to catch up again before I head back,' he said as he hugged Hannah.

'Don't stress. You focus on Sam and the boys. And enjoy. If we don't catch up, I'll understand. We can always Skype,' Hannah said.

*

'Well, that looked like a huge success all round to me,' Beth said in the car and on their way home.

'Yes, I think there were red dots on most pieces.'

'What a great night,' Adrian said. 'I'm so glad we came.'

'That Henry and Louise Peace were nice,' Raelene said. 'It's such a shame they've been so badly affected by the accident too. It's really sad. He was just in the wrong place at the wrong time, just like Tristan and Daphne and Daniel. So tragic.'

'I'm glad you got to meet them,' Hannah said. 'I meant to introduce you.'

'Your lovely Craig took care of it. Aren't they a nice couple – Craig and Jasmine?'

'They are,' Hannah agreed. 'I'm so glad you're here,' she said smiling into the rear-vision mirror to her parents-in-law. 'Thank you.'

'Thank *you* for such a wonderful evening, and for being you,' Adrian said, reaching forward and giving her shoulder a gentle squeeze.

'Goodness, I really am completely done in,' Raelene said, as they turned into Hannah and Beth's street.

'I'm not sure I'll be able to carry you, darling heart,' Adrian said. 'I can barely carry myself,' he added.

Chapter Twenty-six

The Sunday after the exhibition opening had been quiet for Hannah. She'd stayed in bed late cuddling with the cats and then whiled away the day with a book. When she'd phoned Beth to check on her and her guests, she'd been a little relieved to hear that they were also taking it easy. They'd shared a laugh about how no one could even be bothered making their way across the street.

On Monday Hannah found herself still functioning a little slowly. She emailed Brad to tee up a meeting, rang Beth and invited them all to come over for dinner and then retreated into the kitchen to take her time putting together a lasagne. She thought about inviting Sam, Rob and the boys, but decided to leave them be. Sam had sent her a text thanking her again for everything and for encouraging Rob to come back for the opening. Clearly Rob had now told her that part of it. Hannah wondered how it was going between them, and how the boys were feeling and reacting to having their dad home.

She was just finishing putting together garlic bread when the doorbell rang. She frowned slightly as she checked her watch on her way out of the kitchen. Beth, Raelene and Adrian were on-time people, sometimes a little early, but never half an hour early.

'Pete! Hi! Wonderful to see you. Come in,' she said.

'Thanks.' He kissed her on the cheek. 'These are for you,' he said, holding out a bunch of pale pink roses wrapped in layers of purple, green and white tissue paper and bound in clear cellophane with a purple bow.

'They're gorgeous. Thank you,' Hannah said, instinctively putting her nose to the blooms. She was disappointed. As usual. Why didn't commercially grown roses have a scent? And more importantly, why did she – and everyone else according to the movies – always test them, despite knowing the answer? 'Lovely,' she said. 'Come through.'

'Yum, something smells good,' Pete said.

'Lasagne. You're welcome to stay for dinner. Beth from across the road and my parents-in-law, Raelene and Adrian, are coming over.'

'Thanks, but I can't stay.'

'Glass of wine?'

'No, thanks. Better not.'

'Coffee, then, or tea?'

'No. I'm okay, thanks. I came to talk to you.'

'Well, at least sit down. As my dad used to say, you're making the place look untidy,' she said with a laugh, and pulled a stool out from the bench for him.

She sat down and as she looked across at Pete she realised she'd put the wide island bench between them. She hadn't meant to, but she couldn't exactly move now without it looking odd.

'I hope you enjoyed the event. Thanks so much for coming. I'm really sorry I was running around like a lunatic most of the night and barely got a chance to see you.'

'You *were* rather preoccupied. But I understand.'

'So, how's things? What's been going on?' Hannah felt a little stifled and then perplexed. Why was talking to Pete suddenly so hard? 'Oh. I'll just pop these in some water,' she said, leaping up. She unwrapped the flowers, quickly trimmed the stems and placed them in a large cut-crystal vase – her mother's favourite – and put it on the end of the bench. 'Lovely,' she said again and couldn't drag her eyes away from them. She felt like an awkward teenager unable to look at a boy she had a crush on.

'Hannah?'

'Yep?' She forced herself to turn back to Pete.

'I need to talk to you?'

'Okay.'

'This, *us*, isn't working,' he said with a long drawn-out sigh. 'I so badly wanted it to – maybe I wanted it too much, but …'

Hannah blinked. 'Oh. Right.' She wasn't sure what else to say. It was a long time since she'd been in this position. She found herself wondering if she'd ever been in this position. 'Because I didn't give you enough attention the other night, is that it?' She desperately tried to keep her voice even and the rising irritation at bay.

'No. God, Hannah, of course not. We're adults, we don't need coddling, well, we shouldn't.'

'So, what are you saying, exactly? That we're not going to be seeing each other anymore? We're not compatible, or something?'

'Yes. I'm sorry, Hannah. I can't really explain it. I liked you. I *like* you, Hannah. I still do.'

'I like you too. A lot.'

'I'm glad. As clichéd as it is, I guess all I can say is it's me not you,' he said apologetically.

'Which never actually means that, does it?'

'I don't know. Doesn't it?' he asked with a laugh. 'Oh, I don't know, I'm new at this dating thing and clearly not very good at it. Maybe it's just too soon for me.'

'And maybe you're just using that as an excuse to give up,' Hannah said. 'Maybe I'm not ready either, but at least I'm not throwing the towel in after two dates and a weekly text message for three weeks.'

'What are you saying?'

'I don't know, but it takes more than flowers and dinner to make a relationship work. Your letter was very promising. Look, hey, don't get me wrong, I'm not angry. Sorry, I didn't mean to have a go at you. I'm just disappointed. And I really do appreciate you coming around in person rather than you phoning or standing me up somewhere.'

'I would never do that.'

'Well, I wouldn't really know, Pete, I don't feel I got to know you very well at all.'

'I know. I'm sorry. It probably didn't help that I was away for so long.'

'No, but it was what it was. If it was meant to be, I guess it would have,' Hannah said.

'Here's another cliché. Do you think we could be friends? Please,' Pete said.

Hannah couldn't help laughing at the boyish, pleading look he gave her.

'I don't see why not. I don't want to have to change vet practices.'

'I don't want you to, either. Okay. So, we're good then? Or at least okay?'

'We're fine, Pete. I am disappointed, but I'm not going to go all psycho on you.'

'Oh, well, that's a relief.'

'No, no restraining orders needed here,' Hannah said, smiling weakly.

'Well, I'd better get going. Again, Hannah, I'm really sorry it didn't work out.'

'Me too.' She walked him out and gave him a farewell hug. It seemed the right thing to do. No hard feelings.

'Thanks for being so good about it. And, please, if you ever need me as a friend, you know where I am, Hannah. I mean it.'

'Thanks. Ditto.'

'All the best, Hannah. Oh, and give that Brad guy a call. The way he was looking at you, he's definitely interested.'

'Sorry? Oh. No, he's married.'

'Really? Well, could have fooled me. Oh well, must be a player, then,' he said, and shrugged. 'In that case, watch out for him,' he added, laughing, and left with a wave.

Hannah stood watching Pete go down the driveway, feeling a strange mixture of emotions. But she didn't have long to consider how she felt because she saw Beth, Raelene and Adrian making their way over.

Hannah closed the front screen door behind her in case the cats decided to run out and waited in the cool, still evening for her guests to arrive.

'I was hoping your young man would be joining us,' Beth said as she hugged Hannah hello.

'Yes, we saw him at the opening, but didn't get a chance to meet him properly,' Adrian said.

'He's not my young man anymore,' Hannah said.

'Oh?' Raelene said.

'Apparently I've just been dumped.'

'Oh, no. I'm sorry to hear that. I liked him,' Beth said.

'So did I. Come in,' Hannah said, holding the door open for them. 'Who else is in need of a glass of wine?' she said when they were in the kitchen.

'I'll do the honours,' Adrian said, holding up the bottle he'd brought.

'Okay, great. I just have to make a salad and heat the lasagne and garlic bread and we're done. You guys are welcome to sit in the dining room or lounge if it's more comfortable. I won't be long.'

'I'll keep you company in here,' Beth said.

'Me too,' Raelene said, joining Beth at the bench.

'Well, I'm not going to sit in there on my own,' Adrian said.

'Lovely flowers,' Raelene said.

'Pete brought them.'

'Oh. Why would he bring flowers if he's going to dump you?' Raelene said.

'Beats me,' Hannah said.

'Sounds like a guilt-offering to me,' Adrian said, though. 'Maybe he's met someone else.'

'So, what did he say? Or don't you want to talk about it?' Beth said.

'I'm not sure, really. It's not you, it's me, was about the gist of it,' Hannah said with a shrug.

'He didn't! What a cop out,' Raelene said.

'Sorry, I'm sure this is uncomfortable for you to hear, given you're my parents-in-law. I'll stop.'

'Only if you want to. We don't mind a bit, Hannah, do we, Adrian?'

'Not at all. We wouldn't for a second expect you to spend the rest of your life alone and celibate. Life is to be lived.'

'Thanks. I guess the timing just wasn't right.'

'Or maybe he's just not right for you,' Beth suggested. 'You did say he was a bit aloof these last few weeks while he was away. Only the odd text message?'

'That's no way to treat a young lady you really like and if you don't want her to look elsewhere,' Adrian said.

'You've probably dodged a bullet, isn't that what you young ones say?' Beth said. 'At least he didn't get the chance to break your heart.'

'Yes, but she can't not get involved out of fear of having her heart broken,' Raelene said.

'She didn't dump him, he dumped her, remember?' Beth said.

'Hey, guys, I'm right here,' Hannah said with a laugh. 'If I'm being really honest with you and myself, I'm not sure I felt enough for him. I liked the company and of course the bit of attention, but I'm not sure I felt or ever would have felt swept off my feet. I don't think he had the capacity to be very romantic without coaching.'

'Yes, remember that letter he sent? It was his sister who had pointed out the error of his ways,' Beth said.

'I don't think I'm very high maintenance, but I would have liked a bit more. I guess I'd like to feel all fluttery, weak at the knees maybe. Like I did with Tristan.'

'And you deserve to,' Beth said.

'Don't settle for less than you want or deserve,' Raelene said.

'What about that Brad fellow?' Beth said. 'I couldn't help noticing the way you looked at each other.'

'I don't think so.' *Not you too.* 'Anyway, thanks for listening. I think we can conclude that Pete just wasn't right for me.'

'Plenty more fish in the sea, as my dear old mum used to say,' Adrian said.

'I'll drink to that,' Hannah said, raising her glass. 'Not that I'm really looking.'

'That's good. That's when they turn up,' Raelene said.

'Here's to kissing some more frogs,' Beth said.

'No, thanks,' Hannah said.

Chapter Twenty-seven

From the tram, Hannah watched the glow of the setting sun behind the tall city buildings. She enjoyed being at home and not travelling into the city each day, but she did sometimes miss being a part of the hustle and bustle.

She got off and made her way along Spring Street, pausing at each crossing to take a fortifying breath. She wasn't sure why she was a little nervous. *It's only business*, she reminded herself. Though that didn't really help – she was new at this doing business caper and she felt a certain amount of pressure to succeed for Craig. She'd been pleased to have this to look forward to and to keep her distracted. Raelene and Adrian had left, Beth had gone to stay with a cousin to help out while she was unwell, and Rob was leaving this evening to go back to Singapore. She was disappointed she hadn't had the chance to catch up with him properly again because they'd gone to Daylesford at the last minute for Easter. Oh well. The most important thing was that Sam and the boys had spent a decent amount of quality time with him. And that his surprise arrival had been welcomed.

Hannah paused to look around her after stepping into the foyer of The Windsor Hotel. Oh how she loved this place with its plush, traditional décor. She made her way past the concierge desk and sweeping staircase to the restaurant entrance and waited for the maître d'.

'Hello. Booking for two under the name of Brad Thomas, I believe,' Hannah said to the young woman.

'This way please.'

Hannah was led to the same table as last time. She momentarily thought about sitting where Brad had sat to mix things up, but didn't want to cause a commotion when the maître d' pulled out the other chair for her. Seated, she checked her watch. She was five minutes early. That wasn't the same, she thought. Last time Brad had already been settled when she'd braved eating alone in the hotel's restaurant – a first for her, and one of many firsts that year. That week, fleeing the media camped outside her house to the security of The Windsor and then meeting Brad had turned out to be quite a turning point for her. She couldn't really put her finger on how, exactly, but she'd felt different after staying here – better – and he'd been a big part of that. She looked around. The restaurant was filling up. There was a buzz of cheerful, earnest chatter. Hannah waved when she saw him enter.

'Hannah, wonderful to see you,' Brad said. She leapt up to hug him.

'Thanks for suggesting this,' she said. 'It's nice to be back.'

'Thanks for agreeing. I have to confess to being a bit of a sentimental old bloke,' he said, sitting down.

'You're hardly old and, anyway, I think it's rather lovely.'

'I'm thinking of being really sentimental and ordering what I had last time – if it's still on the menu, even down to the Shiraz. Oh, and sharing dessert with you again if you're game – hopefully they still have that decadent chocolate pudding and delicious cheese platter.'

'You've got a good memory.' Though Hannah, too, had remembered.

'For some things. And if I remember correctly, you were very sensible and didn't drink.'

'I was in a very different place then. I'll join you in a glass tonight.'

'Don't feel pressured.'

'I don't.'

'Great. How about the Pepperjack?' he said, studying the menu.

'Sounds good to me,' Hannah said.

'I'm sure there are reviewers who would be scathing of their unchanged menu, but I like it,' Brad said.

'At least you know what you're in for. I don't think you can go wrong with sticking to the classics.'

'It really is wonderful to see you, Hannah,' Brad said after the waiter had taken their orders and left. Suddenly he was reaching his hands across the table and gently unwrapping Hannah's from the water glass that she was clutching as a bit of a security blanket. She was a little stunned. It felt very intimate, not at all like the business meeting she'd envisaged. And she found she didn't mind one little bit. *Was that wrong?* she wondered as she stared at their entwined hands. Oh how good it felt to be touched – skin on skin. She had to consciously stop herself closing her eyes in ecstasy.

Hang on, what are you doing? You're married! She wanted to pull her hands away but at the same time she didn't want him ever to let go.

As he dropped her hands and leaned back Hannah tried not to look at him, instead studying the table and the shiny cutlery. Anything to distract her from this awkward tension growing between them.

'You said at the opening that you're a permanent fixture in Melbourne now. How did that come about?' Hannah asked, almost barking the question.

'Oh. I got sick of all the travelling back and forth and living out of a suitcase.' Something in his slightly evasive tone made her look up and study him closer. He was looking decidedly uncomfortable. And then something dawned on her.

'Oh no, have you been through a separation or a divorce since I saw you? How awful.'

'Sorry?'

'You're not wearing a wedding ring, but you were last time,' Hannah said, nodding at his bare finger.

'Wedding ring? Oh. About that.' He stared with a slight frown at his hands as if seeing them for the first time.

'I'm not married. I've never actually been married.'

'But you were wearing a wedding ring the night I met you.'

'Yes. I was. I always do when I'm travelling and don't want to *pick up* or *be picked up.*'

'Oh.' Hannah felt quite disconcerted. She was honest to the core and didn't like the idea of this deception.

'Please don't be weird about it, Hannah.'

'I am a bit, to tell the truth.'

'I enjoy the company of women and it's just a way to put them at ease. You probably wouldn't have considered sharing my table that night if I hadn't been wearing a wedding ring and assured you I was happily married, would you?'

'No, probably not.' Hannah relaxed slightly. She'd brought a book with her to pretend to read so as not to be disturbed. Had his prop really been very different from her book? A voice in her head told her there was no comparison, but she chose to ignore it. At that moment two glasses of red wine were delivered.

'To us, friendship, and getting to know each other,' Brad said, raising his glass.

'To us,' Hannah said, lifting her own glass and tilting it towards him. They held each other's gaze as they clinked glasses and then took their first sips.

'So, you've changed jobs, you were saying at the exhibition launch,' Brad said.

'Yes. Thanks so much again for your amazing review. Sam was really chuffed with it.'

'You've already thanked me, and you don't need to. It was an honest, unbiased review, I can assure you. So, your new job? Tell me about it.'

'Well, it's why I wanted to meet, actually. I'm in charge of marketing and business development for a new consultancy firm specialising in the services sector. We're looking for small to medium sized organisations that might be interested in advice on their growth strategy and improving their business. As it's a new company we're deliberately keeping the approach broad. Craig's all about forming strong, long-term working relationships. I wondered if you might have some contacts or could at least point me in the right direction for some leads. I've never done this sort of thing ...'

'Oh. Okay. I'd need to give it some thought.'

'Any help at all, no matter how insignificant you think it might be,' Hannah prompted. 'I guess it's about getting Craig in front of the right people – networking in the right spaces.'

'I'm going to an event next week that would be good for him to get along to. I can forward the details now I've got your email address.'

'Thanks so much. Here's one of his cards,' Hannah said, fishing one of Craig's out of her wallet. 'He's got some great contacts of his own, but ...'

'You're trying to prove your worth?'

'Yes. I don't have marketing or business qualifications, so ...'

'Hannah, Craig wouldn't have given you the job if he didn't believe in you. But I will absolutely do all I can to help. I'll put my thinking cap on and get back to you,' he said, tapping Craig's card before sliding it into his wallet.

'Thanks so much.' Hannah relaxed a little thanks to the wine and having got the business talk out of the way.

Their meals arrived and they thanked the waiter.

'Yum, just as lovely as I remember,' Brad said after his first bite.

'Yes, perfect.'

'You know, I'm sure I met Craig at the event,' Brad said, between mouthfuls.

'Yes, you probably did.'

'I tell you who else I met at the launch. Henry and Louise Peace.'

'They're lovely, aren't they? Well, a bit troubled, but I'm sure they'll get back on track eventually. I really hope so.'

'If they do, it'll be thanks to you.'

'I'm not sure about that. I don't know them very well.'

'I'd like to do a story about your forgiveness of Henry. Would you do an interview with me?'

'There is no story, Brad. There was nothing to forgive – it was an accident and no fault of Henry's.'

'But socialising with them, Hannah? That goes way beyond what you would have ever been expected to do.'

'Henry's having a tough time. He's lost his job. If there's a story to tell, maybe it's about how his employer abandoned him.'

'And the kindness shown by strangers who have no reason to when others who should show their kindness don't.'

'There's never a reason not to be kind or show someone empathy. It's just being a decent human being.'

'Hannah, what you've done is remarkable. I felt you were special the moment I met you. But this …'

'I disagree. There's nothing remarkable about not bearing someone ill will when they've done nothing wrong, or at least whatever they've done is or was beyond their control.'

'You have every right not to want to have anything to do with the man. Instead you go out of your way to hand out his business cards, help him to get more work – yes, he told me – invite him to social functions with all your friends …'

'Brad, I don't have a story. *I'm* not a story. My life is okay. Different, but okay. I'm getting on with it. End of story. Help Henry by telling his story if you want. Or do something on Craig – like a profile of a new business.'

Silently Brad reached down and picked up the leather compendium he'd put next to his chair when he'd sat down. He unzipped it, pulled out a photo and pushed it across the table towards her. Hannah's eyes opened wide and her mouth dropped open slightly. There was a clear image of her face, with her eyes closed, and Henry's back as they hugged on the bench at the court.

'You were stalking me? Jesus, Brad, that's creepy,' she said, trying to keep her voice down.

'No, I have a friend who is a court photographer.'

'Stalking by proxy. Are you bloody serious?'

'Hannah, I only …'

'Well, this doesn't seem right to me,' she said, poking at the photos with her finger. 'It's creepy. Have you shown it to Henry?'

'No, I haven't met with Henry other than at the gallery the other night. I wanted to speak to you first.'

'This was months ago. Why now? Anyway, who's to say that's Henry – that could be the back of anyone,' she said a little defiantly and sat back in her chair.

'Maybe, but this couldn't.' Brad slid two more photos across the table. One was a clear shot of Henry in his distinctive suit – there was no mistaking that person as the man being hugged on the bench in the other photo. The second shot was of Hannah, Henry and Louise standing together at the art gallery event. It was a lovely photo.

Hannah looked up when the waiter appeared to take their plates. She nodded and smiled her thanks.

'No, Brad, I'm not interested,' Hannah continued when they were alone again. 'There's nothing stopping you interviewing Henry and Louise.'

'But they're only half the story. I'm going to write it, Hannah, with or without your blessing. It's too important.'

'Of course you are. So why are you even asking me?' Hannah stood up and pushed her chair back.

'Hannah, I didn't mean to upset you. Don't go. Please. Stay and have dessert.' He stood up and reached for her hand, but she snatched it back and left, while attempting not to draw attention to her hurried exit.

Outside in the cool breeze, Hannah's eyes began to water. She strode briskly back down Spring Street towards her tram, her fury gradually turning to disappointment and then sadness as she went. She'd really liked him. Why did he have to turn out to be a selfish, creepy arsehole?

Stay angry, she told herself, on the verge of tears. She bit the inside of her cheek so hard she made herself wince. Her phone beeped with a text message. Instinctively she checked it. Through the distortion of her tears she deciphered:

Hannah. Stop. Please. I'm sorry. Come back. Brad.

She pictured him standing at the doorway to The Windsor and watching her making her way down the street. *God, don't you dare come after me,* she thought. Thankfully she'd probably cross the first set of lights by the time he'd paid the bill and managed to get outside. Or perhaps he wasn't there at all, but was sitting with the chocolate pudding with two spoons and the cheese platter in front of him.

Back at home, Hannah sat in the lounge and sobbed with Holly in her lap and Lucky and Squeak fighting for attention on either side of her.

Eventually the tears stopped and she wondered at her extreme reaction. What had she been expecting, anyway? They'd been on a business meeting – dinner only because of their history. Out of sentimentality. But, no, he'd alluded to more, hadn't he, when he'd grasped her hands like that? God, the wedding ring. She'd momentarily forgotten about that.

'Icky all round,' she told Holly and the kittens peering up at her. 'Yes, I'll feed you, but just a bit and only because I'm a sucker,' she told them as she moved them carefully and stood up.

As she spooned out small portions of tuna from the tin, she couldn't shift the hard ball of sadness in the pit of her stomach. She'd felt a strong connection with Brad right from the start, perhaps the same as what he said he'd felt with her. They hadn't so much as kissed. She'd had much more with Pete, but didn't feel devastated when he'd broken it off with her the way she did now thinking about Brad. It hurt. *She* hurt. *A lot.*

She went to bed, turned her phone onto silent, curled herself around a pillow and began to cry.

Chapter Twenty-eight

Hannah wanted to stay in bed wrapped around her all-encompassing balling ache of loss, the magnitude of which wasn't far from what she'd lived with for most of the past year. Until the events of the night before, she had thought that pain was finally diminishing, or perhaps she'd just become accustomed to it being there. Now it was back as a debilitating physical pain that no amount of twisting, turning or shifting could alleviate. She'd got up earlier to feed the cats, and had done so in an automatic daze before returning to bed. The tears had stopped and left eyes that were red-raw and puffy from tears and lack of sleep. She'd drifted in and out of sleep, like those first nights after The Accident.

Now she smiled weakly when Holly appeared beside her and curled up against her chest. She stroked the cat and then felt the vibrations start up, and relaxed a little at the sweet thrum of her purr. Calmness began to take over. Just two steps back, she told herself. Disappointing, but it was what it was. A part of her said she was over-reacting, another voice told her to be kind to herself.

Hadn't someone said that once the feeling returned you'd feel more intensely? *Who had that been? Joanne? Beth?*

She sat up a little, careful not to dislodge Holly, and reached for her phone to take it off silent. Sam might need her after seeing Rob off again. But just as she did, Squeak and then Lucky launched themselves at her, grabbing for her hair that had caught their attention when she moved. She laughed and hugged them both to her. You couldn't be too sad and wrapped up in self-pity for long when you had these little bundles fighting for attention. She remembered how Pete had said having an animal to take care of had been the key in his recovery. It was so true.

'Okay, okay, I'm up. No more lolling about,' she told the cats, and looked at her phone. She was surprised to find it was almost nine o'clock. There were three texts from Brad, each variations of begging her not to shut him out. There were also three missed calls from him. She skipped the voicemails – deleted them without listening. Hannah wasn't one to hold grudges – well, actually she couldn't remember anyone hurting her badly enough to know – but she needed time to process. Maybe she was over-reacting, but she needed the space, the distance. She'd felt betrayed last night – enough to come close to making a scene in the restaurant as she walked out on Brad – and still felt it now.

The phone in her hand began to ring. Sam's name was on the screen. She swallowed, planted a false smile on her face – an old trick from a course on phone manners she'd done years ago with her previous job – and answered.

'Hey, Sam. How're you doing? Are you okay?'

'Oh, Hann.'

Hannah could tell Sam was in tears.

'Are you at home?'

'Yes.' Well, that's what Hannah thought she said. It was more like a wet gurgle.

'I'll be there soon.'

Hannah threw back the covers, got out of bed, had a quick shower and quickly put on some clothes. Clutching her phone, keys and handbag she told the cats to stay and that she'd be back later, and left the house.

'Oh, Sammy,' Hannah said, and clung onto her friend in the doorway.

'Thanks so much for coming,' Sam said, closing the door behind her.

'Always. I thought you might be hit hard by Rob going again.'

'I am, but it's not just that.'

'Oh god, what's happened? Where are the boys?'

'They're fine, they've gone down the street to play with the Marinetti boys. Couldn't wait to tell the world they might be going to Singapore next school holidays.'

'Sure. That's exciting, and something for the boys to look forward to,' Hannah said. 'So, I take it everything went well with Rob.'

'He's such a beautiful human being, inside and out,' Sam said, the words coming out with a long sigh. 'I think I love him even more now. And that hurts so much.'

'I can imagine.'

'He's so at peace – well, except for being torn up about hurting me and the boys. Not that they're really all that aware yet – it's still a novelty, a bit of an adventure. Thanks so much for making sure he came over.'

'I'm not sure it had much to do with me, Sammy, but I'm glad it worked out.'

'It was wonderful to be all together again,' Sam said wistfully.

'I'm glad. Now you said it wasn't Rob or the boys that made you so upset. What else has happened?'

'This,' Sam said, touching her iPad and bringing it to life and turning it towards Hannah. 'It's awful, Hann, how can someone say such horrible things?' Sam burst into tears.

'Oh,' Hannah said. She skim-read the review that used words like 'twee' and 'at home in a country craft store along-side the knitted beanies in AFL colours' to describe Sam's work and 'amateurish and like a primary school child's art project' to describe Zoe's. She looked for the by-line and name of the publi-cation. 'This is why I didn't want you searching online yourself, Sammy. I set up a Google alert so I'd see anything first. Sorry, I haven't got around to going through my emails yet this morning.'

'It's not your fault. It hurts so much, Hann.'

'Of course it does. It's cruel.'

'I feel like never doing another piece again.'

'That's understandable. But you will. You need to put this into perspective. It's a blog, it's not even in a real newspaper – respectable or otherwise. I've never heard of *Billy with Balls*. Have you? I hope you scrolled down and saw what else he or she has to say – just the arrogant, negative rantings of a complete ass, by the looks. You can't take it seriously. Or personally. This person doesn't know you personally – has never met you. Well, maybe they did at the launch, but they certainly don't *know* you. For all we know they're a failed artist or someone desperately wanting their own exhibition, but who has been rejected. You can't let it affect you.'

'But it is. It has. I feel terrible. I want to comment and say, "Fuck off!"'

'Of course you do. But you can't. You haven't, have you?' Hannah asked, suddenly worried.

'No, I've been too upset to form words.'

'Good. I don't mean good that you're too upset, but you can't engage. The last thing you need is an online spat.'

'I know, but it's so hard to sit back and do nothing.'

'Of course, but you have to. You have to hold your head up high. Your work in the exhibition is great and much loved. Focus on all the good comments you've had. And remember that a lot of the pieces have already sold.'

'I was so excited. I'm not sure I can take the highs and lows of being a professional artist, Hann. Perhaps I should just focus on being a good mum.'

'You *are* a good mum. Sadly, the highs and lows are part of it. You just need time to pick yourself up and dust yourself off. Don't do anything rash. You're vulnerable right now because of everything going on with Rob, don't forget. Sit tight and don't let the likes of this fool get to you. Remember the lovely things Roger and Brad have said – they're the opinions that matter.'

'Thanks, Hann. What would I ever do without you?'

'You never need to wonder that.'

'I'm sorry if I let you down, since you're my agent.'

'As I've said before, you couldn't if you tried.'

They sat in silence for a few moments.

'So, enough about me. What's been going on with you? I'm sorry I've been so out of touch,' Sam said.

'That's okay. I don't really have any news.'

'You seem down yourself, Hann, is something wrong?'

'I'm upset that you're upset. And missing Raelene and Adrian, I guess.'

'How amazing was it of them to come all that way for the opening? I feel terrible I didn't get to spend any more time with them.'

'They understood. It's fine.'

'Hann, what's going on? Something's up, I can tell.'

Hannah stared at a knot in the timber table, biting the inside of her cheek while looking for the right words.

'I know about Pete,' Sam said. 'I had to pick up some stuff for the dogs and saw him. I'm sorry it didn't work out.'

'Thanks, but I'm not upset about it. Really. We clearly weren't suited. And we only went on two proper dates, so it's hardly heartbreak territory.'

'Yet you look like that's exactly how you're feeling, Hann. I haven't seen you this sad for months. What's going on?'

Hannah looked up and across at her best friend, tears filling her eyes.

'I don't know why I'm so upset, really. It's completely ridiculous.'

'What is?'

'Brad.'

'Brad, the journalist guy?'

Hannah nodded.

'What about him?'

'I had dinner with him last night at The Windsor.'

'Right. And …?'

'He's a deceitful, lying arsehole.'

'Wow. Okay. So, I take it dinner wasn't good, then?'

'I left before dessert. I might have made a bit of a spectacle of myself, too.'

'I find that hard to believe, Hannah.'

'I might have stormed out.'

'Jesus. That's unlike you. What did he do? I thought you liked him – not in *that* way, obviously, since he's married.'

'He's not, as it turns out.'

'But wouldn't that be a good thing? No, not if he's a deceitful, lying arsehole, obviously. Hann, I think you'd better start at the beginning and tell me everything.'

★

'I see,' Sam said when Hannah had finished her account of last evening.

'I'm over-reacting, aren't I?'

'You can't help how you feel. If you feel betrayed, disappointed, upset, that's your reality. Beating yourself up isn't going to help.'

'But you think I over-reacted – last night in the restaurant – don't you?'

'You reacted how you were meant to, given how you felt at the time.'

'Stop with the earthy shit, Sam. I want your honest opinion.'

'Do you though?'

'Right. So you think I'm being ridiculous. Great,' Hannah said with a groan.

'You know I love you and would do anything for you ...'

'But ...'

'Well, no but. I don't think you're over-reacting. As I said, you can't help what you feel. I think it would have been confronting, quite shocking to see the photos, especially when you had no idea they were being taken.'

'But ...? I'm still sensing a *but*. Come on, tell me. Give it to me straight.'

'Well, he's a journalist, and the images *did* come from an official source.'

'He knew I wasn't interested in the court case. I made that clear.'

'Hann, that was months ago. He didn't know if you'd changed your mind – which you sort of have.'

'Why didn't he ask me any time within the past six months or so? We didn't exchange details that first night we met, but

I'm listed in the phone book. He could have easily got in contact with me.'

'And you wouldn't have freaked out and accused him of stalking you? Really, Hann?'

'Hmm, good point.'

'Did you ask him when he got the photos and why? Maybe he has been commissioned to do a story and doesn't have a choice. Or maybe seeing you with Henry at the opening made him think you'd changed your mind about doing a piece.'

'So, the *but* is that I didn't give him enough of a chance to explain?'

Sam gave a non-committal shrug.

'I still feel a bit creeped out,' Hannah said.

'That's okay. But don't be upset with him about the wedding ring. At least it wasn't the other way around – him pretending not to be married when he was. I know a few single women who wear a ring on their left ring finger when they travel overseas alone so they don't get harassed. It's actually quite common. You probably don't know because you haven't travelled much and you're still wearing a ring, anyway. I'm sure that would have been one of Jasmine's wonderful pearls of travel wisdom had your finger been bare. So, don't be upset with Brad for that. Be grateful he didn't try to take advantage of you when you were so vulnerable. Plenty would have. From what you told me, he was a true gentleman. Hold onto that and be grateful for him being there that night – it was an important step for you to take. And it could have been so different for you.'

'I *am* grateful. I really liked him, Sam. That's why it hurts so much. I was disappointed about Pete dumping me, but not sad. I'm really sad about Brad. Devastated even. It's irrational.'

'You're fragile, sweetie. Just like you said to me – it makes it hurt so much more than it normally would.'

'Why am I being so ridiculous?'

'Because you like him so much.'

'But why?'

'God, you sound like the boys. This guy's really got under your skin, hasn't he? You're not usually such an over-thinker – that's me.'

'I know, and I don't like it!'

'Hmm. And what do you mean, why, anyway?'

'I thought he was married. Why would I have fallen for a married man? That's not me.'

'You can connect with someone without wanting them in a physical, sexual way. And maybe the fact you couldn't have him made you like him even more – it meant you wouldn't need to be more vulnerable than you already were. Perhaps what this is all about is simply shock and having to rearrange your view of the situation and how you feel about him being available after all.'

'You're so wise.'

'I try. Though only, it seems, when it comes to everyone else's life.'

'So, what do I do?'

'God, I don't know. When in doubt, do nothing?'

'I really don't want to do an interview.'

'You don't have to. But maybe it would give you closure or something. He's right in that it might help other victims. I know,' Sam said, holding her hands up in surrender, 'you're not a victim.'

'And I'm not special.'

'You are. You're very special.'

'You're biased.'

'Hannah, I know you can't see it, but you befriending Louise and Henry like you have is pretty remarkable. It shows a lot of courage. Just meeting with them would, but you've done so much more than that. You know Brad's going to write a story about you regardless, right?'

'I know.'

'So maybe you should get your side across how you want.'

'I don't think so.'

'That's up to you.'

'You think I'm being stubborn, don't you?'

'It doesn't matter what I think, it's what you *feel*. Do what feels right to you, not what you think people might expect you to do.'

'Okay. I need to think about it. Thanks, Sammy.'

'We're sad sacks, both of us! Come on, let's take the dogs and our self-pity for a walk and then pick up the boys.'

Chapter Twenty-nine

Hannah headed out to meet Louise Peace for lunch. She'd been a little surprised to receive a call from her as she was leaving Sam's the other day. She liked Louise and looked forward to getting to know her better so she had agreed to lunch on Monday. She'd also deliberated on sending Brad an apologetic text, but hadn't found the right words. She still didn't want to do an interview and it didn't seem fair to let him think she might. The knot of sadness had loosened, but it was still noticeably present as a slight ache deep within.

Hannah looked for a park near the café and when she found one right out the front she took it as a sign lunch would go well. After locking her car she waved to Louise through the window where she was already seated at a small table.

Louise jumped up and hugged Hannah.

'Thanks so much for coming,' she said, beaming. 'It's so lovely to see you.'

'Thanks for inviting me,' Hannah said. 'It's really nice to see you, too.'

'And thank you again so much for inviting us to the launch. Henry and I both had the most fabulous time.'

'I'm glad you were able to make it – and enjoyed it so much.'

'I'm not sure if you know, but Henry bought me Zoe's piece titled *Hope*. He's paying it off, bless him.'

'No, I didn't know. That's lovely of him.'

'Would you ladies like a few more minutes to decide?' asked a waitress Hannah hadn't noticed was standing beside them.

'Oh. Yes, please. I haven't even looked,' Hannah said, picking up the laminated menu.

'I'm in no rush,' Louise said.

'No, me neither,' Hannah said, studying the offerings.

'I'll get you some water while you decide,' the waitress said.

'Thanks,' Louise and Hannah said in unison.

'I can recommend the chicken salad,' Louise said.

'Okay. Great. Sounds good to me.'

'I think we're ready now, aren't we?' Louise said when the waitress returned a few moments later. She looked at Hannah for confirmation.

'Yes. I'll have the chicken salad,' Hannah said.

'Make that two,' Louise said cheerfully.

Suddenly Hannah was startled to find Louise reaching across the table and gently taking hold of her hands before saying, 'Oh, Hannah, thank you so much.'

'For what?' Hannah asked with a slight laugh. She was feeling a little disconcerted. 'I haven't done anything.'

'Oh, but you have. You've done everything, changed everything – for the better.'

'Sorry?'

'The exhibition opening was the turning point Henry needed. To see you living, really living. And happy, truly happy, amongst your friends, has made all the difference to him. He's let go of the guilt. I could practically see it seep out of him while he watched you that night. He thought you were taking pity on him by having him around to prune, but that evening he saw that you really are okay. Oh, Hannah, you've no idea how much it means. He actually moved home Sunday.'

'Oh, Louise, I'm so happy for you. That's great news.'

'Thanks to you.'

'Well, I'm not sure …'

'You've given him his self-esteem and his confidence back. You've given him a job!'

'A what? No, he only pruned …'

'Your friend Joanne met him at the launch and offered him a trial at the retirement village. He's been there a week. He has a permanent job again thanks to you, Hannah. He's on probation for three months, but he'll be fine. He's a changed man. He has a sense of purpose, of belonging again. I have my family back together, Felix has his father back. It's such a relief.'

'Louise, I'm so pleased for you.' Hannah's eyes filled with tears as Louise's spilled over.

'And …' Louise said, wiping her cheeks with her serviette.

'There's more?' Hannah said with a laugh, trying to regather herself.

'Your friend Brad has put Henry in touch with an industrial relations lawyer to see if he can get anything out of his previous employer. It looks promising.'

'That's great. Brad's great,' Hannah added dully.

At that moment their salads arrived and Hannah was glad of the distraction.

'Has Brad done something to upset you?' Louise asked. 'Or have I, in mentioning him?'

'Oh. No. It's just that he wants to interview me for a story. And I don't want to.'

'He mentioned it. He phoned. Please don't think I asked you to lunch to pressure you into anything one way or another. It's entirely up to you. But, please understand, Hannah, how much you have done for Henry and me and how grateful we are. You don't see it, but you are special. What you did in just talking to Henry that day at the court was special. It doesn't matter if you contribute to Brad's article or not, Hannah, but please know how truly grateful we are. You've been the glue to put us together when we didn't know how. I hope you won't mind if we've told all this to Brad.'

'It's your story to tell, Louise. I think you're being far too generous. I'm a little lost for words, to be honest.'

'You don't need to say anything. Enjoy your salad while it's still warm,' Louise said, smiling at Hannah.

Hannah concentrated on her meal while she gave Louise's words a chance to sink in.

'No matter what you say,' Louise began again and spoke quickly between mouthfuls, 'it *is* a story worth telling. Perhaps if other people affected – from both sides of a tragedy – could come together there might be less pain in the world. Fewer suicides, marriage break-ups. I've been reading about it. The statistics are shocking. And it doesn't just stop with those directly involved – or even their generation. Many kids from broken homes suffer their entire lives. It changes them. Just think how it would be if more people can show forgiveness, a little bit of compassion.

'I'm sorry,' Louise said, suddenly putting her fork down. 'I don't mean to pressure you. And I'm absolutely not. Brad's going to do the story and obviously Henry and I have already given our side.'

'Hmm. So, is Henry going to continue doing his private gardening now he's working?' Hannah asked, desperate to change the subject and give her head a chance to clear. She was starting to feel a little overwhelmed.

'Yes. His job is only during the week and he has a rostered day off each month. So for now he'll continue and see how it works.'

'That's great.'

'Hannah, promise me, if there's anything Henry or I can ever do for you, you'll let us know?'

'There's really no debt here, Louise. Our friendship is enough.'

'Promise me, though.'

'Okay, I promise. I'd like to have a lifetime of friendship.'

'Me too. I know you deny it, Hannah, but you really are a remarkable person.'

'So are you, Louise. You've stuck by Henry, supported him when it must have been excruciating to watch. Most women might have simply walked away, given up.'

'Well, what can I say? I love the silly sod,' Louise said with a shrug. 'I know I'm harping on, but thank you for bringing him back to me and Felix.'

'You're welcome.' They stayed silent while the waitress bustled about collecting their plates.

'So, how about dessert?' Louise said when they were alone again. 'Their lemon cheesecake is just like my mum used to make.'

'Okay. You've twisted my arm,' Hannah said.

'So, how do you know Brad, anyway?' Louise asked after they'd both ordered the cheesecake and pots of tea.

'We met quite by accident last year. I guess you could say he's part of the ripple effect as well.'

'The what?'

'Doesn't matter, I'll explain that another time.'

'Do you realise you light up when you talk about him?' Louise said innocently when their desserts had been delivered.

'Do I?' Hannah said, equally as innocently, feeling her neck heat up.

'You do,' Louise said with a grin. 'He does too, when he talks about you.'

'Really?'

'Yup.'

'It's a pity he's a journalist.'

'*Freelance*. And I think he's using his powers for good,' Louise said.

'I certainly hope so.'

*

Hannah left the café feeling happy, not just because of all the praise and gratitude Louise had heaped on her, but because Louise was such good company. She could see her becoming a treasured friend. Hannah had heard it said that once you hit your thirties you didn't tend to make strong new friendships. But she had become very close to Joanne and Jasmine only quite recently too, and was so grateful she had.

In her car, Hannah dialled Brad's number.

'Hannah! Hi! How's things?' he said, clearly a little shocked to hear from her.

'Can we meet up – say, for a coffee?' Hannah asked.

'Sure. When were you thinking?'

'Could you manage today – um, now-ish? Say, in around half an hour? I'll understand if you can't. It's very short notice.'

'That's okay. I'm in Carlton.'

'I'm just leaving Yarraville and heading towards Hawthorn, so I can meet you in Carlton.'

'Okay. I'm at the Black Pot Café on Johnston Street, but I can meet you somewhere else if you prefer.'

'No, that's okay.'

'It's just next to the 7-Eleven, which is on the corner of Johnston and Brunswick.'

'Great. I'll probably be twenty minutes.'

'No problem. I'll be here.'

'Okay. See you when I see you,' Hannah said.

Chapter Thirty

Hannah pushed the heavy glass door open, stepped into the café and looked around for Brad. Her stomach flipped and her heart soared when she saw him. He was busily tapping away on his laptop, deep in concentration. As she stood, fully aware she was staring but unable to tear her gaze away, she felt as if she were seeing him for the first time. Her heart began to ache, as though it had expanded so far it was squashed up hard against her ribs. She caught herself in time to wave back when he looked up and raised his hand to attract her attention.

He closed his laptop and took it off the table. Then, as she made her way over, he seemed to be deliberating over whether to stand or remain seated. He half-rose and Hannah gave a general sort of wave and pulled out the chair opposite. He sat back down again.

Hannah was suddenly very nervous. She'd never seen Brad looking anything other than friendly – he always had a smile on his face. Not now. He seemed troubled, perhaps a little confused. Could he be angry? As much as she liked how his smile lit up his face, she thought this brooding look suited him too. She imagined he could be quite intimidating when he was angry, but she couldn't picture him like that, despite this slightly stern expression now. She knew he was gentle – soft underneath. She hated that she might be the reason he wasn't smiling. Or perhaps he was just unsure of why she was really here.

'Um,' she said.

'Yes?' he said.

Hannah took a deep breath and tried again. But before any more words had the chance to come out, a waiter appeared with notebook and pen in hand.

'Hi, can I get you anything? Coffee, cake perhaps?' he asked, looking from Hannah to Brad and back again.

'A peppermint tea would be lovely, thanks,' Hannah said, looking up.

'Same for me, please,' Brad said. And then they were alone again. Brad was looking expectantly at Hannah. She had to avert her gaze in case she became entirely lost in his brown eyes and long dark lashes and completely tongue-tied. She fiddled with the jar of packets of sugar before stopping herself.

'I've been an idiot. I over-reacted and I'm really sorry,' she said.

'Oh, Hannah,' he said and let out his breath. 'God, what a relief. I've been going insane.' He rubbed his hands over his face and through his hair. Again Hannah tried not to become mesmerised. She loved the look of his long fingers and smooth, strong hands.

'I'll help with your article,' she said quietly.

'You will?'

'Yes, if you still want me to. I've just come from lunch with Louise Peace, and I think I understand it all a bit better now. And I trust you, Brad.'

'You *can* trust me, Hannah. I promise it's nothing too onerous, just a couple of questions. I've got most of what I need.'

'Okay. Fire away,' Hannah said, linking her hands on the table.

'What, now?'

'If you like.'

'Okay. Let me just get organised,' he said, reaching down and then putting a notepad and pen on the table. 'Do you mind if I record it?' he asked, pointing to his phone still sitting on the table.

'No, that's fine. I don't really know what you want me to say.'

'It's only me. Just talk to me and be yourself. There's nothing to be nervous about.'

'All right for you to say.'

At that moment the waiter delivered their drinks and they both thanked him.

'So, how was Louise?' Brad asked, picking up his cup.

'Great. Henry moved back home, so she's over the moon. I'm really happy for them. I'm glad I met her, I can see her becoming a dear friend. And Henry. When he gets himself fully sorted. I can't help thinking I haven't seen the real Henry yet – just a bit of a shell. You know, my friend Joanne has employed him at the retirement village. It's where my parents lived. I guess that's a little ironic, actually, when you think about it. Of course you know all this because you've been in touch with them.'

'Yes. I'm so pleased for them.'

'Brad, I'm sorry I accused you of stalking. I was just a bit shocked seeing the photos.'

'I'm very sorry about that. I didn't think. I've thought so many times of trying to contact you since we met.'

'So, why didn't you?'

'Timing. You were running away from the media pack, remember? You made it clear the last thing you needed was me asking questions. And it's nearly a year on and look how you reacted,' he added gently, smiling warmly.

'Good point. I guess I got scared. Of what, I'm not entirely sure. Well, no, that's not true. Brad, I like you. I felt a connection to you that evening. And you'll never know how much your kindness and consideration that night meant, and will always mean. Then when I saw you at the launch I felt something I never thought I would again, which was so wrong of me when I knew you were married. And I was seeing someone. That's not me. I don't prey on other women's husbands. Or cheat.'

'Then when I turned out not to be, you felt overwhelmed? And since I'd lied, you felt betrayed? I get it, Hannah, I really do. I am so, so sorry. The last thing I would ever want to do is hurt you. I promise. Please believe that.'

'I do. I really did completely over-react, which isn't like me either. Can you forgive me?'

'Oh, Hannah. What do you think? Of course you're going to be scared and overwhelmed. You've learnt to fend for yourself, go it alone after a terrible tragedy and upheaval to your life. As you told me that night, things had been quite cruisy in your life up until then. Now I'm asking you to essentially open up that partially healed wound again, even if only a little. Of course you're going to want to run away or fight – it's natural. I don't think I quite realised the magnitude of that before. I never want you to feel like that again. Next time, please just talk to me. I'm here for whatever you want or need – not that I don't think you're strong enough on your own.'

'Everyone spent last year telling me I was stronger than I thought I was. I don't think I was at the time, but it helped to hear it. I realised during my grief that as wonderful as my parents had been, they didn't equip me very well to deal with the harsh realities of life. I can see now that they'd kept me protected and I hadn't really lived, not that they mollycoddled me. And then

I was suddenly facing this huge, tragic upheaval. I didn't know
what to do, except that I didn't have much of a choice but to get
on. My parents were ones to just get on with things without a
fuss, not that I remember them dealing with much. Perhaps that
was something else they did a good job of protecting me from.
Anyway, I don't know, somehow you just keep going. I guess I
wasn't raised to sit in a corner and cry, though I did shed plenty
of tears. Sometimes I thought I'd never stop crying. I think I
only got through it because of my wonderful friends. I'm so lucky
there.'

'I love how positive you are. Did you decide to become Sam's
agent to pay her back in some way?'

'Not consciously. That came about a bit by accident. Sam's very
talented, but talented people often struggle to believe in themselves. And if you don't believe in yourself, how can you convince
anyone else to – like, say, a gallery owner? If I can help, why not?'
Hannah said with a shrug.

'Tell me how you felt when you met Henry at the court and
how that came about.'

'Oh, well, that's quite an interesting story. A bit spooky,
actually. One of the lifts at work wasn't working and ...'

'Go on,' Brad urged when Hannah paused.

'Okay, it was lunchtime. He looked hungry. Food can be a
great source of comfort, and who doesn't love a ham, cheese
and mustard sandwich?' she said with a smile. 'But, seriously,
my parents were big on sharing food. Every year we had a huge
Christmas Day lunch where friends dropped in and ate and then
left or stayed on. They were often people who didn't have any
family or friends in Melbourne. It was just the way it was, so it's
part of who I am.'

'I know it meant the absolute world to Henry.'

Hannah shrugged again. 'I love food and I don't mind sharing,' she said with a smile, thinking about the pudding and cheese platter she'd shared with Brad.

'You don't think you're special, do you?'

'I don't see what's special about showing someone some kindness and consideration.'

'Have you *never* felt angry towards Henry?' Brad asked.

'No. I haven't. Honestly. I'm desperately sad it all happened, but there's no point being angry – it's not going to bring my family back. Nothing will. And anger just grows into bitterness.'

'Hannah, not only are you not angry, you've even forgiven Henry Peace, haven't you?'

'There was really nothing to forgive. The poor man was in the wrong place at the wrong time in a truck that has been proven to be badly maintained by a company also proven to have cut corners.'

'Have you ever considered suing the trucking company for compensation, Hannah?'

'No. I'd rather have nothing to do with them. I'm okay financially, and I'd rather keep moving forward and not look back. That's not to say I don't think Henry should be seeking compensation. He and Louise are doing it tough financially because of what's happened and it sounds like Henry's been treated very badly by his former employer. They didn't give him any support. Worse, they tried to use him as a scapegoat. Henry is a good man. I saw it the moment I met him. He was trying to take responsibility for something he wasn't in the least bit responsible for. The guilt was consuming him. Just living with what happened has been hard enough for me. The fact Henry almost let it consume him tells you he has a good heart, too. I just wish I'd met him sooner and he hadn't suffered for so long. But perhaps that was a journey he needed to be on.'

'You're incredibly optimistic and philosophical, Hannah.'

'I hope so. I try. And I'm trying to make the most of my life, appreciate it, because I could have easily been in the car that day too. I still have really sad times and days when I struggle to get out of bed. But I make myself. The danger is becoming too wrapped up in your sadness and guilt for too long and it turning into self-pity, which is especially hard for loved ones to deal with, I think. Someone who is sad and pessimistic all the time is no fun to be around – even if they have reason to be. Thankfully I have some really special people who knew what I needed when I needed it. I'm so lucky. And I'm glad Henry and Louise and their son, Felix, weren't three more victims to that tragic accident and have found a way back to each other.'

'You've become quite close to Henry and his wife Louise, haven't you?'

'Yes, I feel sure we'll be friends for a very long time. We share a unique bond. Of course I wish it hadn't happened, but good things can come out of tragedies if you're only willing to look for them. Oh, like my cats. Did I tell you I became the scary cat lady overnight?'

'No. Tell me.'

'I took in a mother cat and her two tiny kittens when they arrived on my doorstep all wet and dishevelled. I've never been a pet person, never had one growing up, but it was pouring with rain and it was Christmas. I took pity on the poor little things and brought them in. Holly, Lucky and Squeak. I couldn't part with them now. And having them to be responsible for has been so good for keeping me grounded, keeping things in perspective. They cuddle up when you're feeling sad or they demand you feed them. Now the kittens are bouncing around and getting into things they make me laugh. They are hilarious. Just the tonic, my mum and dad would have said. I think they've helped me heal.'

'Do you know you light up like a neon sign when you talk about them?'

'No, but I'm not surprised. They are the light of my life. It's a relationship I thoroughly recommend.'

'You said Christmas was a big deal to you before the accident. Has that changed? How do you feel about it now?'

'Oh. Well, I did run away from it last year – the first anniversary. I went to New York. I just couldn't face the cheer and people feeling the need to tiptoe around me, and being the elephant in the room wherever I was. But I realised what I was really running away from was myself – and that's ultimately impossible to do.'

'Better than drowning yourself in drink or some other demon, which plenty do,' Brad said.

'Hmm. I guess I'm lucky there as well. I've never been a big drinker and don't seem to have an addictive personality. Except when it comes to cats – perhaps they've become my addiction,' she said, smiling.

'They look like they're a good influence on you. So, what about Christmas this year?'

'Brad, it's only the end of April! I haven't given it a thought. But I won't be running away overseas. You know, I just might embrace it again. We were never big on giving expensive presents. It was always more about the coming together to share a meal and companionship. Tristan, my husband, had also really got into doing light displays in the last couple of years. So, actually, maybe I'll make the effort to do something special on the house. I love the colour, sparkle and excitement of Christmas, even if I forgot that for a bit.'

'Completely understandable. Was your ladybug a Christmas gift from Tristan? I notice you touch it a lot,' Brad said.

'Oh,' Hannah looked down at her arm where her charm bracelet sat. *Do I?* 'Yes, it's really special to me,' she said, holding it up for him to see. 'It was his last Christmas gift.' Tears filled Hannah's eyes. 'I opened it after he'd died. So much for it being a symbol of good luck,' she said sadly, and dragged a tissue from her bag and wiped her face.

Brad touched her hand. 'I'm so sorry. I didn't mean to upset you.'

'It's okay. It's not your fault. I'm sorry, I thought I'd be all right. I still really miss him. And, as you can see, sometimes I'm not as strong as people think I am. Or I think I am. I don't get angry, but I do get sad and disappointed.'

'And that, too, is quite understandable. I think you're incredible, Hannah. Just one last thing. Would you mind if I used the photo of you from at the court with Henry?'

'Sorry? Oh,' she said, 'I forgot again you were interviewing me.' She blushed. 'You're clearly very good at putting people at ease. God, I've done a lot of babbling. Please feel free to paraphrase me and tidy up my words so I don't sound too ditsy.'

'You could never be ditsy, Hannah. And you've done very well. About the photo …?'

'Oh. That's okay. I don't mind if you use it.'

'I'll turn this off now,' he said, and touched his phone.

'Have you got enough for your article?'

'I think so. Thanks very much. You were great.'

'I'm not sure about that, but thanks. If you need anything else, let me know.'

'Okay. Great. I'll see how I go.'

Chapter Thirty-one

As Hannah walked up the path to Jasmine's house she hoped Craig was still out and, equally, that Jasmine was home. She so badly needed a friend and she couldn't go to Sam's because the boys would be too distracting in their after-school boisterousness. She rang the doorbell and held her breath, listening for footsteps.

'Hannah! What a wonderful surprise!' Jasmine said, throwing her arms around Hannah who let out her breath and relaxed a little.

'Come in. I'm afraid Craig's still out. He should be back soon, though.'

'No, I came to see you, actually. If that's okay.'

'Of course. Hey, are you okay?' Jasmine asked, pausing to scrutinise Hannah's face more closely. 'What's up?'

Hannah felt her chin wobble and her eyes fill with tears. *Oh god.* 'I'm just being ridiculous.'

'I doubt that. Come through.'

'Thanks. As long as I'm not disturbing you.'

'Not at all. I can do with a break anyway.'

'What are you working on?'

'No you don't, Hannah. We'll talk about me later. Now, peppermint or English breakfast?'

'English breakfast, thanks,' Hannah said, suddenly craving the comfort of the smooth milky richness.

'No, thanks,' Hannah said to the plate of Tim Tams that Jasmine held out towards her. 'I've been out to lunch. With Louise Peace, actually.'

'Oh, how lovely. I thought she was nice when I met her at Sam's launch. And Henry. Has she upset you, though?'

'No. I really like her. She's helping Brad – you know, the journalist ...'

'Yes, I liked him too until he upset you at The Windsor.'

'Anyway, listening to Louise made me realise that refusing to participate in Brad's article was a bit short sighted. I've always thought I'm not much of a story ...'

'You are, Hannah. You could inspire people with how you've ... Sorry, carry on.'

'The thing is, I realised it doesn't matter what I think. Well, not completely. It's bigger than me. I've been selfish by not commenting, adding my side to the story, the article Brad's writing. Thankfully I'm pretty sure it's mainly about Louise and Henry – Henry's going to try to sue the trucking company for some compensation. Brad's helping, and of course anything to help stop an accident like that happening again. Anyway, so I rang Brad and I've just come from speaking to him. You know, *on the record*.'

'Right. Well, good for you. Or are you now having regrets? Is that what's upset you?'

'No. No regrets, except for a ridiculous amount of babbling. I spilled a whole lot of beans – probably far too much information – but what's done is done.'

'Clearly you needed to let it out.'

'Hmm.'

'Okay. You don't look like someone who has unburdened themselves – quite the opposite.'

'Oh, Jas. I like him. I *really* like him.'

'Darling, blind Freddy could see that. And the way he was looking at you at the launch, well ...'

'Right, so why didn't he so much as hug me or peck me on the cheek when I left just now? He was all business. He shook my hand, for Christ's sake!'

'Well, you did walk out on him at dinner and then refused to answer his calls for a week.'

'But, I apologised. I guess all he wanted all along was an interview. And now he's got it ...'

'Not necessarily. He seemed a decent guy to me. I didn't get a hint of him being anything but genuine at all. Craig thought so too, and he can smell a bull-shitter a mile away, as you well know. Maybe he just needs more time to get over being hurt.'

'Hmm.'

'Did you tell him or give him anything to indicate you like him, as in *like* him, as part of your apology?'

'Um. No. I offered to give him his interview.'

'So, you apologised for leaving dinner so abruptly and ...?'

'Well, I did admit to being an idiot.'

'Then you got straight down to business and answered his questions?'

'Well, yes, pretty much.'

'Darling, you put him in the work zone.'

'That's a thing?'

'He's a professional doing an interview. It's not personal in the way you wanted it to be. I'm sure, like in every profession, there's a state he has to enter to get what he needs from his subject – and himself.'

'But what about afterwards?'

'Well, maybe he doesn't snap right out of it. He was probably too distracted.'

'Or he doesn't like me as much as I thought he did – or not in that way.'

'Maybe you left too quickly. Did you give him a chance to leave work mode behind?'

'I don't know. Actually, probably not,' Hannah said, a little sheepishly. 'I sat in my car for a minute or two, though.'

'You could have gone back inside,' Jasmine said gently.

'True. Maybe it's too soon for me to be thinking of going out with anyone. Look how it went with Pete.'

'Ah, that was just a good trial run. You never lit up when discussing Pete the way you do when you talk about Brad. You spent more time talking about the food you ate with Pete rather than the man himself.'

'Really?'

'Yup.'

'God, I thought Beth was bad, but you don't miss much, either do you?'

'I'm not as sharp as Beth, but no, not much,' she said, smiling warmly.

'So, what do I do?'

'I don't know. Whatever you want to. Phone him, arrange to meet again. Or nothing. It's only just happened. Perhaps sleep on it. Maybe Brad will come to you. Maybe he's having the same thoughts.'

'I think I've blown it.'

'If it's that easily blown, then it's not meant to be. For what it's worth, I think you're feeling too much for it to be nothing. You weren't this upset over Pete.'

'Hmm. Thanks so much for this.'

'You're welcome. So, what else has been happening?'

'Well, Sam's freaking out and is never going to create again because of a nasty online review.'

'Oh dear. I think I saw that. I wanted to call her, but didn't want to reveal it if she didn't already know, or rub it in.'

'Yes, it's a delicate situation.'

'I actually wanted to talk to her – professionally. You know how I've got my first major interior design client ...'

'Yes, it's fantastic! How's it going?'

'Great, thanks. I'm so excited with how it's come together. It's a huge house and a client with pretty much an open chequebook – not that I'd ever take advantage. All from a lady who took my card at the market. Incredible! Anyway, there are some magnificent blank walls in the house so I was wondering if Sam might be interested in doing some commission pieces.'

'A few weeks ago she might have leapt at the chance. Now, I'm not so sure. Also, she might think you were asking out of pity – she's in that sort of mindset, I'm afraid.'

They looked up at hearing the front door open and close. Craig appeared in the doorway.

'Hey there, my two favourite women,' he said. 'Your friend Brad is an absolute legend, Hannah. I have five serious leads from the lunch today that he got me an invite to. Awesome! What?' he asked, noticing the women sharing a look. 'Please don't tell me he's pissed you off, Hannah, and I can't be friends with him anymore, because that would be hard. He has the potential to be very useful.'

'It's fine, sweetheart, you can carry on with your little bromance, can't he, Hannah?'

'Yep, go for it,' Hannah said with a smile and a nod.

'Great. This looks like serious women's business, so I'll just leave you to it.'

'You can unwind here if you like, I was just going to show Hannah what I've been working on,' Jasmine said, pushing her chair out.

Hannah stood up and followed her.

'Jasmine, this is incredible,' Hannah said after she'd scrolled through Jasmine's file of ideas and images for the interior design project she was working on.

'I have to admit to being a little chuffed. It's coming together so well. I can't wait to show you when it's done. The owners are staying in another of their properties, so it's empty.'

'Ooh-ah, lucky them,' Hannah said.

'Yes, it certainly makes it easier.'

'I can see what you mean about the blank walls.'

'I just know Sam would have some good ideas. I'm probably too close to it or trying too hard,' Jasmine said.

'If you're going to ask Sam, take her there so she can feel the space, too.'

'Okay. Good idea. Hey, what about us doing a lunch at the house? I'll ask Mary what she thinks – she's the owner. I am sure she won't mind. It would be fabulous to catch up with everyone after all the excitement of the exhibition, and the others might have some ideas too.'

'Sounds great. It'll be the perfect way to remind Sam we're all here for her – through thick and thin, especially now Rob's gone again.'

'What do you think about inviting Louise Peace? I liked her very much.'

'It's your lunch to invite whomever you like – entirely up to you. I'd like to get to know her better, too. Oh, you'll never guess what.'

'What?'

'Joanne has given Henry a job as groundsman at the village.'

'Oh, that's fantastic. Isn't it funny – weird funny – how everything is so connected? Even in a city like Melbourne there seems to be only one or two degrees of separation.'

'Yep, it's crazy all right.'

'When's Beth back? I'm not doing a lunch without her.'

'Sometime this week, I think.'

'How would Sunday week work for you?'

'Fine.'

'Pencil it in and I'll check with Mary and then the others.'

'Great. Oh, I'd better get going,' Hannah said, looking at her watch.

'The traffic will be horrendous now, you're welcome to stay for dinner, if you like.'

'Thanks, but no, I'd better get home. It's been a big day.'

'See you, Craig,' Hannah called as she and Jasmine made their way down the hall past the kitchen.

'Bye, Hannah. And thanks again for introducing me to Brad.'

'No worries. Speak soon.'

'Don't worry about Brad,' Jasmine said. 'It'll work itself out. Just sleep on it and I'm sure it'll be clearer in the morning.'

'Yeah. Thanks so much for listening, Jas,' Hannah said, hugging her friend.

'Always. Call any time. I'll confirm lunch.'

'Can't wait.'

★

At least I've helped with the article. Louise and Henry will appreciate that, Hannah thought, as she waited for the first set of traffic lights to go green. Perhaps she was meant to meet Brad in order to help Louise and Henry Peace. And Craig. Those thoughts only comforted Hannah a little as she continued her slow drive home in the heavy traffic.

*

She felt exhausted – better after catching up with Jasmine, but still drained. She wondered what she wanted for dinner. Something, but something light. Brad was still on her mind – particularly whether she should phone him or not. A part of her thought she probably should, but another part – the part that was currently winning – told her to let it go.

She was pleased to suddenly have the distraction of the doorbell.

'Brad! Hi!' Hannah thought her eyes might pop out of her head.

'Hannah. Firstly, I'm really sorry to intrude. Please don't think I'm stalking you – I found your address in the White Pages.' He looked down at his feet.

'Okay,' Hannah said, unsure of where this was going and trying to wait him out. But he seemed to have lost his words.

'This time I'm the one who has been an idiot – the biggest, most colossal one there is.'

'Would you like to come in?' Hannah asked.

'No, thanks. I need to get this out, Hannah, please.'

'Okay.'

Suddenly the hand she only now realised he'd been hiding behind his back presented her with a large bunch of sunflowers wrapped in brown paper and tied with raffia ribbon.

'Oh. They're lovely. Thank you.'

'Because you are an absolute ray of sunshine, Hannah Ainsley.'

Right. Okay. Where is this going? Before she could comment she was being pulled into a hug – a trademark beautiful, comforting, protective Brad bear hug. Just as she was beginning to hope he'd never let go, despite actually beginning to struggle to breathe, he released her. She stumbled on her jelly legs, but he caught her elbow and steadied her in time. She looked at the flowers. While the paper was a little crumpled, the blooms seemed to have survived the hug.

'There, that's what I should have done earlier – twice. I'm so sorry, Hannah. I had my mind on the article. My work turns me into a robot – and an idiot, too, apparently, when it comes to being a proper human being.'

'It's okay. I understand. You *were* working. You were interviewing me. Really, it's fine, Brad. It's business.'

'Oh, but Hannah, it's so much more than that. No, I mean *you're* so much more than that. To me. I apologise in advance if what I'm about to say puts you under any pressure or makes you feel awkward – that's not my intention at all. I promise. I just need you to know. Hannah, since the night I met you I haven't been able to get you out of my mind. I know it's been an incredibly difficult time for you and you might never want to open your heart fully or share your life with another man again. I bided my time and then … Well, I've been wretchedly sad about upsetting you the other night and then I think I went into a state of shock when you wanted to meet. Then when you agreed to the interview, I wasn't sure if that was as far as it went. Maybe I hid behind the story – work. So, I'm here to ask you – at the risk of sounding like a pathetic geeky teenager – will you, Hannah Ainsley, go out with me?' He stood looking at her with a slightly helpless, pleading expression on his face.

'Yes. *Yes* I will go out with you,' Hannah said, grinning broadly.

'You will? Really? Oh, Hannah!' He gently took her face in his hands and kissed her on the lips before dragging her into another hug.

'You really do give the best hugs, Brad,' she said, when he had released her again.

'As do you,' he said. 'It takes two, you know.'

'So, now would you like to come inside?' Hannah asked, smiling at him.

'No, better not.'

'Oh. Okay, then.'

'I want to do this right, Hannah. I want to woo you, not get too comfortable too quickly. I mean, I want us to be comfortable together, but not ...'

'It's okay, I know what you mean,' she said, her thoughts flashing to Pete.

'I have to head off to Sydney tomorrow for a week, but would you like to accompany me to a movie in the city on the following Saturday afternoon and then dinner afterwards? Perhaps in Chinatown?'

'That sounds really lovely.'

'Are you okay with trusting me to select the movie? I don't do horror or anything remotely scary.'

'Yes, I trust you. And me neither – I don't do scary – so that's something we have in common.'

'Great, we're off to a good start, then,' Brad said, beaming.

'Shall I meet you in the city?'

'Absolutely not. I will pick you up.'

'I'm happy for us to catch a tram – the stop is right at the end of my street.'

'We can decide on the finer details later. Don't think you won't be hearing from me between now and then.' He then clasped both of her hands, which were wrapped around the flowers, and looking intensely into her eyes said, 'Thank you for giving me a second chance, Hannah.'

'Thank you for asking me to, Brad.' She held his gaze for a moment before leaning in and kissing him deeply.

'Okay, I need to go now,' Brad said, letting her hands go and becoming a little flustered.

Hannah grinned as she waved him off from the porch, her heart feeling as if it would explode within her chest.

Chapter Thirty-two

'Goodness gracious, I feel underdressed,' Beth said, gazing up at the stately Georgian style home.

'I think anything less than ball gowns and tiaras would feel underdressed,' Hanna said, staring around in awe. 'Jasmine did say it's casual, so don't worry. Come on, I'm dying to see it.'

'If you two are underdressed, I'm practically a hobo,' Sam said. 'God, it's gorgeous. I'm glad I brought my good camera,' she said, getting out of the car.

'I'm glad the owners won't be here to see us nosing about,' Beth said.

'That really suits you,' Hannah called to Jasmine standing in front of the huge, glossy black front door at the top of sweeping marble steps.

'Isn't it stunning? Aren't we lucky? Welcome,' Jasmine said bounding down to them and gathering Beth, then Hannah, and then Sam into a hug.

'What a wonderful idea this is, thank you so much for including me,' Beth said.

'Of course I'd include you! But don't think it's all going to be fun and lamingtons – I want your help.'

'Ooh, intriguing,' Beth said.

'We're all here now. Joanne and Louise are around the back checking out the garden. No, here they are. Perfect timing, ladies, we can go in now,' Jasmine said.

There was a gaggle of greetings and hugs, which Sam quickly left in order to take some photos.

'Sam, we're going inside,' Jasmine called.

'Be there in a sec. I just want to take some shots of the front when you're all out of the way.'

'Thanks very much,' Hannah said, feigning offence.

'Don't worry, I've already taken a heap of you all while you were standing there gasbagging.'

Hannah smiled. It was good to see her friend a little more cheerful again. She hoped that meant she was back to being creative too, and had put the nasty review behind her.

'Glory be!' Beth said, looking up and turning around to take in the full three-hundred-and-sixty degrees of the large foyer with its parquetry floor and wide staircase leading from it.

'Wow,' Hannah said breathily. 'Do they do weddings here, or at least allow brides to have their photos taken?'

'I'm not sure about weddings, but Mary does …' Jasmine said.

'Oh my,' Louise and Joanne said at the same time and then laughed at their synchronicity.

'You said your date was good, I didn't realise it was quite *that* good,' Beth said, grinning cheekily at Hannah.

'Oh ha-ha. But, yes, it was very nice. Perfect, in fact!'

'I hope your date was with Brad the journalist,' Louise said.

'Yes, with Brad,' Hannah said, fully aware she was looking and sounding a little dreamy. She felt as if she wasn't even walking on the ground.

'Right, this way, people, into a kitchen that is to die for,' Jasmine said.

'Oh my,' Louise said again. 'I have a feeling I'm going to be saying that a lot today.'

'Me too,' Joanne said.

'Something smells good,' Hannah said as she gazed around the cavernous space with its enormous granite bench tops.

'Don't get too excited. When I said casual, I meant it, in every sense of the word.'

The only person not exclaiming or murmuring was Sam. She was busy moving around silently, snapping photo after photo at various angles.

'My whole house would nearly fit inside this kitchen,' Joanne said.

'Why would anyone ever need four ovens?' Louise said. 'They must do huge parties.'

'They do,' Jasmine said. 'Mary runs the Comforting Cats charity, so the house gets used a lot for that, especially black-tie fundraising events. There's one coming up, which is why I'm under the pump to be finished.'

'I like Mary already,' Hannah said.

'You know, I love this spaciousness, but I've never craved living in a big house – I detest cleaning with a passion,' Louise said.

'Well, your home certainly doesn't say that about you,' Hannah said. 'It was immaculate when I turned up unannounced.'

'Smoke and mirrors,' Louise said, smiling, 'smoke and mirrors.'

'Surely if you could afford this you could afford a cleaner,' Beth said.

'Unless every cent has gone into the mortgage and upkeep,' Joanne said. 'This is Toorak, after all.'

'Good point. Though it's certainly not dilapidated.'

'So, did you have a hand in doing up this kitchen, Jas?' Hannah asked.

'Yes, I did play a big part in its design and we used very good cabinetmakers and stonemasons.'

'I can't believe you've done so much without telling us a thing about it. It seems like only last week you were saying you were ready to start thinking about setting up your business,' Beth said.

'Well, I got a lucky break thanks to Sam.'

'Me? What did I do?'

'Mary picked up my card at your market stall and decided to give me a shot.'

'That's fantastic. I'm glad,' Sam said.

'Yes, and you deserve it,' Hannah said.

'Thanks. Mary has been an amazing first client – decisive but open to options and suggestions. And she has a decent budget. I've been very blessed. I had to source the right people and products, and then just order everyone about, really. I've got an album of before and after shots in the dining room that I'll show you later. I started the tour in the kitchen so I could check on the food. We'd better keep moving so it's not ruined.'

They *oohed* and *ahhed* as they made their way up the stairs and through all the six bedrooms, which were similar in style and furnishings but each in a different colour scheme. Over and over the women exclaimed how impressed they were at how much Jasmine had achieved in such a short amount of time. While she brushed off their compliments, Jasmine was clearly pleased with her friends' approval.

'Are you okay?' Hannah asked Sam quietly when they found themselves together and a little behind the others. 'You seem a little frazzled,' she said, linking her arm through Sam's.

'I think it's my permanent state of mind.'

'Has something happened?'

'Yes. No. Not really. Just the usual malaise of creative block.'

'Still nothing?'

'I'm desperately hoping these photos might prove a spark. Yesterday I literally sat staring at a blank canvas for three solid hours.'

'That's not healthy. How many times have you told me it can't be forced?'

'I know. But still I do it, despite being fully aware it's completely ridiculous and fruitless.'

'Why is it any different now from all the other times?'

'Because I'm meant to be a professional. I'm supposed to be making a living. I've had an almost-sell-out exhibition, in a proper gallery. I don't want to be a one-hit wonder, Hann. I'm scared,' she said, with tears in her eyes.

'You're not letting that one negative review get to you still, are you? Because it's really not worth it.'

'I know, but it hasn't helped.'

'Come on you two, keep up,' Jasmine called.

'You'll be fine,' Hannah said, squeezing Sam's arm.

'But how?'

'I don't know, but beating your head against a wall or berating yourself is not likely to help. I bet in a year you'll be complaining that you can't find enough days to deal with all the ideas rushing out of you in a torrent.'

'Well, right now I'd prefer that. Sorry, don't let me drag the tone down. I'm just being a grizzly grumps, as the boys would say,' she said, smiling weakly.

Back downstairs they came to a halt at yet another door.

'This is the library,' Jasmine said, opening the door and turning on the light. She then stood aside for the other women to enter.

'Oh, this is my absolute favourite,' Beth said.

'Oh yes, mine too,' Louise said.

They looked around the huge room, the largest wall of which contained floor-to-ceiling bookshelves full of books and complete with a wooden ladder on a brass rail. On the other walls was oak panelling to chair height. Above that they were painted in the most magnificent rich charcoal–purple. It worked perfectly with the oiled timber windows, door frames and furniture. Hannah found herself gaping.

'That colour is stunning,' Louise said. 'It seems heritage but contemporary at the same time. How can that be?'

'That colour is actually making my mouth water,' Hannah said. 'How is that even possible?'

'What can I say – I have a gift,' Jasmine said, waving a dismissive arm around and laughing.

'You certainly do,' Louise said.

'Yes, it's absolutely incredible. I've loved every room, but this one is something else,' Joanne said.

'Thanks, everyone. Now, see that wall – what should I put there?' Jasmine asked, pointing.

'You could leave it blank. Showcase the gorgeous colour,' Louise suggested.

'Yes, I agree. Though now you've mentioned it I'm starting to feel like something is missing,' Joanne said.

Sam was busily taking pictures, the camera constantly clicking.

'Isn't it that less is more these days? Isn't that what they say?' Beth said.

'They do, often,' Jasmine said. 'But I really feel that it needs something in here – a painting, probably. I just don't know what colour or style. I've trawled every gallery and store I can find. There are gorgeous pieces everywhere, but nothing that shouts *I'm perfect* to me. Sam, any ideas?' she said to Sam who was still moving this way and that looking at the wall from different angles and at different distances – sometimes looking through the camera lens and snapping pictures.

'Please tell me you've whipped up the perfect piece this week,' Jasmine said with a laugh.

'I'm afraid not,' Sam said. 'Let me ponder it.'

'Does Mary like modern as well as classic pieces – you can mix old and new, can't you?' Beth said.

'Yes. Her husband, Bart – Bartholomew – he's the quieter of the two, but he still has his say. They're both pretty open to anything and are more about feeling that a piece works and living with it than what a critic would say.'

'Oh, in that case, how about a larger version of that abstract you had at the market?' Beth said. 'The one that I said was like sunset over the city looking through a wet window. Sorry, my description certainly doesn't do your work justice.'

'It's not the worst description of my work I've ever heard,' Sam said.

'I can just see the shades of orange working beautifully with the purple here,' Beth added.

'Hmm. Maybe,' Sam said.

'Please, Sam, don't feel pressured. We're here for a lovely lunch and catch-up more than anything. It's not your problem.

Something will come to me eventually,' Jasmine said, putting her hand on Sam's arm. 'Now, I've left *my* favourite room until last.' She led them out into the hall and to another door.

Again they were all blown away by the stunning room. Like the other rooms there was lots of oiled timber, but the walls were painted in an incredible green. It was a shade somewhere between emerald and sea green, which again, like Louise had said, managed to look both traditional and contemporary.

'I need advice with those two walls, too, especially that one,' Jasmine said, pointing to the back wall, which was huge – as was everything within the space. Hannah counted twenty-six dark polished timber, curved back chairs pushed in under the table, which was covered with a stunning white damask cloth and set for the six of them around the nearest end.

'Wouldn't a still-life of fruit or something edible be the natural subject for a dining room?' Joanne asked.

'Yes, if I could find one that was big enough. I found something that was not too far off the mark, but it didn't feel quite right. And it was definitely too small.'

'Can you commission the artist to do a bigger one?' Louise asked.

'No, he's dead.'

'Oh. That's a shame.'

'Again, I'm sure the perfect piece will turn up. I just don't like leaving things unfinished. And the event is coming up soon. Take a seat and think about it while I get our lunch.'

There was a chorus of offers of assistance.

'Actually, if someone can come and carry a bottle of bubbly and the jug of water that would be great.'

'I'll do it, I'm closest to the door,' Hannah said.

Sam continued taking photos and gazing around her with a concentrated, appraising expression.

'Now,' Jasmine began when she'd returned, served up slices of steak and mushroom pie and filled everyone's flutes with sparkling wine and their tumblers with chilled water with floating rounds of lemon. 'I want to start by saying it's wonderful to have you all here and how much I appreciate you being so supportive of my new venture and so enthusiastic about what I've done. Your kind words mean a huge amount to me. I never thought I'd meet such a great group of women, to which I'd like to welcome Louise. So,' she said, raising her champagne flute, 'to Louise, welcome …'

Louise raised her glass, smiled and said, 'Thank you.'

'… and to good friends,' Jasmine said, raising her glass higher and then holding it out towards the group.

'To good friends!' they all cheered, clinking glasses.

'I must say,' Louise said when they'd all taken a long sip and put their glasses down, 'I'm relieved you didn't say grace, Jasmine. I'm completely against organised religion. As far as I'm concerned, it's all about fear-based control and the oppression of women. A terrible business all round. In my opinion. Sorry, I tend to get a bit vocal about it. I'll stop now,' she added, blushing slightly.

'Don't worry. I think you'll find we're all of the same view – perhaps just to different degrees,' Beth said.

There were murmurs of agreement.

'Does anyone even say grace anymore?' Sam asked.

'Yes!' Louise said. 'I had an embarrassing incident only last week – hence my comment just now. I was invited to the home of a new colleague for dinner and got quite a shock when not only were we asked to hold hands, but being the guest, I was expected to say grace. It was all I could do to politely decline without giving them a terse lecture on my views.'

'How awful for you being under the spotlight like that,' Joanne said.

'I doubt I could have been so restrained,' Sam said.

'The most surprising thing was that I didn't pick her as being quite so staunch. She's the biggest gossip and most judgemental of everyone in our whole office.'

'I've seen a lot of that sort of hypocrisy in my work over the years,' Joanne said.

'I'm giving her a wide berth now,' Louise said, 'but I suspect she may have set her sights on saving me from my evil heathen ways. Anyway,' she continued, cheerfully, 'thank you so much for not asking me to hold hands and pray or say grace! But seriously, I really appreciate the invitation and you offering the hand of friendship. It's been a truly shitty year that is finally looking up, thanks to Jasmine inviting me here today, Hannah's generosity and Joanne's in offering Henry a full-time job.'

'Oh, really?' Beth said.

'That's fantastic,' Jasmine said.

'He was the right man for the job,' Joanne said, looking a little embarrassed at the attention.

'At the risk of sounding like the head of a sorority, since we're going into the deep and heavy already, there are two things you need to know and remember, Louise,' Hannah said, 'if you're to remain popular.'

'Oh?' Louise said.

'We don't do the Spring Racing Carnival – well, no horse racing for that matter. So, best you don't mention it.'

'Or any events exploiting animals for entertainment,' Sam said.

'Right. Well, I'm glad about that,' Louise said. 'I'm all for the animals. I'm actually quite active on the ban live-export front.'

'Oh, me too! I'm surprised we haven't met at a rally. It's a bloody disgrace,' Sam said.

'Best we don't get started on that, either,' Louise said, laying a hand gently on Sam's arm. 'So, what's the second thing I need to know?'

'No balloons!' they all practically shouted at once.

'Because they're so bad for the environment or does someone have a phobia?' Louise asked, looking around the little group.

'No, just the environmental factor,' Hannah said, 'which is such a pity because I love them – their colours, their symbolism.'

'Right. Got it,' Louise said.

'Okay, quick, tuck in before it goes cold. And save some room for dessert – meringues filled with cream and fruit salad,' Jasmine said, digging her fork into her pastry.

'Oh, yum, one of my all-time favourites,' Louise said. 'I love that you guys eat – enjoy food, too.'

'Can we make that another rule while we're at it?' Sam said. 'No talk of dieting, putting on or losing weight, no holding back on food, which is to be enjoyed.'

'Since when have we ever done any of those things?' Hannah asked.

'I love you guys,' Louise said with complete admiration as she cut into her pie. 'I have to admit, I've struggled to find women I enjoy spending time with more than once – they always seem fixated on how they look, or with competing with each other. I like to look presentable, but what's a bit of muffin top or squidgy thighs between friends? I'd rather focus on what's on the inside. Denial just leads to misery, in my opinion.'

'Hear, hear,' they said, and raised their glasses again.

'Can I ask you a personal question, Sam?' Louise asked when they were well into their meals and there was a lull in the conversation.

'Sure,' Sam said, looking a little nervous.

'Why are you so down on your creative abilities when you're clearly so talented? I've seen your work. I love it.'

'I appreciate you saying that.'

'You're welcome.'

'See, that wasn't so hard, was it?' Hannah said gently.

'What wasn't?' Sam said.

'Accepting a compliment,' Hannah said.

'You're going to have another exhibition, aren't you?' Louise asked.

'Maybe if I'm asked I'll think about it.'

'I guess it's not easy putting yourself out there through your work – that's what you're doing, isn't it?' Louise continued, 'Making yourself vulnerable. I'm sorry. I'm not creative, so I don't know what it must be like. But I'd like to understand.'

'Honestly, it's both the best feeling and the worst feeling in the world – people saying nice things then someone else saying horrible things. All for public viewing. The actual creating is exhilarating and heartbreaking, sometimes both at the same time,' Sam said, clearly try to laugh it off, but only managing to look sad. 'It hurts. And it's true when they say it's not something you choose, it chooses you. Only an insane person would choose to feel like that on a regular basis. I can totally see why so many artists end up completely broken.'

'I'm sorry, I shouldn't have said anything,' Louise said. 'But please don't let one or two comments from people you don't know – people who might have any one of a number of issues or insecurities – stop you doing what you love. Because you couldn't produce work like you do if deep down you didn't truly love it and didn't have a gift.'

'Thanks, Louise. I think I'm still working through it – getting over the bad reviews. Telling myself it's not personal and isn't worth worrying about doesn't seem to help. I loved the feeling of lots of people seeing and enjoying my work – who wouldn't? And of course to earn money from doing what I love … That's always been my dream. But now I think I was kidding myself. Like I've told Hannah, I don't think I'm cut out for the highs and lows of it.'

'You know you don't have to exhibit – put yourself completely out there in public – to earn money, to be a professional artist, don't you?' Jasmine said.

Sam looked up and across at her, frowning.

'I'm sure my clients will happily commission pieces from you.'

'And all the large offices have art on their walls,' Louise said. 'I work for a building management company – we actually have someone whose job it is to source suitable artworks.'

'Really? How extraordinary,' Beth said.

'Maybe that's what I should be doing. I know art,' Sam said.

'With your talent, I bet you'd find *that* as frustrating as all hell,' Louise said.

'Well, whatever talent I might possess is completely useless at the moment. But thank you for your kind words, they mean a lot to me. Really. I'm sure it'll come back, it always seems to,' she added, sounding less than convinced.

'Meanwhile, please think of something for the walls in this fine home,' Jasmine said, with a cheeky grin.

'You're not going to let up, are you?' Sam said.

'No. I'm starting to get a little desperate. Sorry, I didn't mean …'

'It's okay. I know what you meant. I promise I will try and think of something. Now, to completely change the subject and put someone else in the spotlight, I want to hear all about Hannah's date with Brad,' she said, turning and fixing her gaze on her best friend.

'Ooh, yes, me too,' Beth said.

'I told you in the car.'

'You didn't tell me,' Louise said.

'Or me,' Joanne said.

'Do I have a choice?' Hannah said with a resigned sigh, but a big grin.

'No,' they all said.

'I'm happy to hear it again. We elderly have to live vicariously through you young ones, you know,' Beth said.

'Well, it was perfect. He picked me up – well, he drove to my place and we caught the tram into the city. And he put his arm around me – all strong, protective and manly,' Hannah said, sighing again as she relived it in her mind.

'I knew he'd be a gentleman, I just knew it,' Louise said, looking a little dreamy herself.

'We had dinner in Chinatown – crispy skin pork, rice and steamed greens, if you must know. Both our favourite Asian dishes, as it turns out.

'Then we went to a movie. *Sully* – the one with Tom Hanks, about the pilot who landed the plane on the Hudson River in New York. It doesn't sound like the perfect date movie, but it was perfect to me and brought back so many memories of my trip to New York, which seems like both last week and a lifetime ago. It was an interesting story, too. And then we shared a chocolate mud cake and sticky date pudding – both with mountains of cream and ice-cream. As I said, it was just perfect.'

'Look, she's all glazed and dreamy eyed,' Sam said.

'I am and I'm not afraid to admit it,' Hannah said, beaming. 'It was comfortable. Like we'd known each other for years, but not the sort of comfortable like with Pete. I had fluttering in my belly.'

'You didn't tell us *that* in the car! Did she, Beth?' Sam said, feigning shock.

'No, she didn't.'

'How about tingling down a little further?' Sam said.

'Sam!' Hannah blushed.

'Oh, come on, Hannah, you're amongst friends,' Sam said.

'Yes. If you must know,' Hannah said.

'So …' Sam persisted.

'So, what?'

'And …'

'And we caught the tram home, he deposited me at my door, and then we kissed.'

'Kissed, as in …?'

'Yes, Sam. God, you're too much,' Hannah said, laughing, now bright red in the cheeks and down her neck.

'I'd say leave the poor thing alone, but I'm enjoying this a little too much – it's been so long since I went on a date,' Joanne said, laughing.

'Thanks very much. And, yes, before you ask, he's a wonderful kisser. Then like the gentleman that he is, Brad got in his car and left,' Hannah said, refraining from adding, 'So there!'

'Oh,' Sam said, clearly disappointed.

'I know this is the twenty-first century, but we're not rushing into things.'

'Good idea,' Beth said. 'Regardless of what century it is, you want them to pursue you, make sure they work for their, um, rewards.'

'Thanks for that, Auntie Beth. Almost too much information,' Hannah said.

'Oh, Hannah, I might be old, but I'm not completely clueless, dear.'

They all laughed.

'Well, you certainly look happy. Radiant, really, which is lovely,' Jasmine said.

'Speaking of Pete,' Sam said quietly.

Hannah looked at her friend. 'What about Pete?'

'He asked me out. I saw him again when I was getting dog food.'

'Oh. Wow,' Hannah said.

'Would you mind? If you do, I won't.'

'Why would I mind?'

'Well, we're best friends. If it works out we'll all be together. So, would that be awkward?'

'Oh. Right.' Hannah thought about it. She genuinely liked Pete, they just clearly weren't suited as a couple.

'You didn't sleep with him, did you? Because that would be icky,' Sam said.

'No, Sam, I didn't sleep with him. I agree, eew.'

'So, what do you think? I think I might really like him,' Sam said coyly.

'I do too, just not in *that* way. I think you'd make a lovely couple. Much more suited than he and I were. I say go for it.'

'If nothing else, he could be a good distraction from my creative block,' Sam said with a shrug.

'Wow. So, Joanne and Beth, do you have any exciting news to share?' Jasmine said.

'Nothing that measures up to that,' Joanne said.

'No, I'm just busy being servant to Joseph and Jemima – and loving it, I might add,' Beth said, grinning.

'Hey, Jas?' Hannah asked, following Jasmine into the kitchen with the dishes.

'What's up?'

'I love that purple wall colour in the library. Do you think it would work for my bedroom?'

'Of course. It would be gorgeous.'

'You've got me all inspired. I want to re-do my bedroom. I've just thought of it. When the time comes for Brad to, um, stay over, I don't want us to be in the same room Tristan and I had – well, at least not a room that looks or feels the same.'

'I'd love to do you a new bedroom. I thought you'd never ask! I'll come around and have a look this week and bring some ideas.'

'Great. Thanks. Now, what can I carry back out?'

Chapter Thirty-three

'You know, it's not too late to change your mind and get out of this,' Hannah said when she'd finished hugging Brad on the doorstep of his rented apartment.

'Not a chance,' he said. 'Unless you don't want to go.'

'No, of course not. They're my dearest friends.'

'I hope they'll become mine too. If you're worried I'm going to feel uncomfortable because they were Tristan's closest friends, don't be,' he said, gently brushing back a few rogue strands of hair from Hannah's face. 'I am fully aware they might feel awkward seeing you with someone else in the same situation you used to be with Tristan, but I certainly don't feel I'm competing with a ghost. Darling, you will always love Tristan and that love will take up a large piece of your heart. I know that. And I'm fine with it. Better than fine. The fact that you were happy and retain a love for him is a big part of what makes you *you* – who and what you are now. So, please don't feel uneasy on my behalf. I'm a big boy. Anyway, I met most of your friends at Sam's launch, remember?

I know, this is different. They love you, Hannah, and only want you to be happy. When they see us together they'll be fine.'

'Okay. If you're sure.'

'Absolutely. We're going to have to do this eventually, so we may as well rip the sticky plaster off now. Unless of course you were thinking of hiding me away or dumping me to avoid it altogether,' he said with a cheeky grin.

'No. I just don't want you to feel uncomfortable.'

'I know and I appreciate your concern. But it's all good. Anyway, I'm a journalist, remember? I'm used to feeling awkward and under scrutiny.'

'Yes, but you're usually the one doing the scrutinising.'

'Come on, no more stalling. Would you like me to drive?'

'If you want.' The truth was, Hannah liked Brad driving her. She couldn't quite put her finger on why. Perhaps it was because she felt so safe and secure with his burly presence. Like she never had with Tristan, if she were being completely honest. She and Tristan had felt equal, despite their five-year age difference. Brad was a little older too, but seemed even more so than the actual gap in years. Not in looks, but in his outlook on life. Perhaps it was a result of his professional curiosity – all the things he'd seen, the people he'd interviewed.

As much as Hannah wouldn't say this to anyone, he did feel a little fatherly to her. And she liked that. He oozed care, compassion and consideration, and went out of his way to attend to her – not in a patronising or misogynistic way, but different from what she'd experienced with Tristan. He'd treated her wonderfully, but not the same as the way Brad did. Hannah wished she could stop making comparisons between the two. Hopefully she would in time, but she also didn't want to forget Tristan – how he felt, smelt, tasted, sounded. Though she was struggling to remember.

Whenever she realised how much she'd forgotten she had to try hard to not panic. Joanne and Beth had told her it was part of the journey. They'd assured her that forgetting the finer details was a good thing – a sign of progress – and not something to be feared. She'd always hold some strong memories of Tristan in her heart, but it was important to make new ones. And she was blessed to have met Brad.

Oh how you make my heart swell and flutter, she thought, sitting beside Brad as they made their way to Sam's.

'So, is there any reason for today? It's not someone's birthday or anything, is it?' Brad asked.

'Not that I know of. It's all a bit mysterious because the invitation actually came from Pete. Sam's been in a bit of a rut creatively, so maybe it's his way of jolting her out of it by making her think of something else and be sociable.'

'They've just started going out, haven't they?'

'Yup, this could be their first proper date for all I know. As I've said, Sam's been a little distant.'

'Understandable, she's been through quite a lot already this year and we're not even halfway through. Now, just double-checking, the twins are Oliver and Ethan, aren't they? And they're identical? Right?'

'Yes and yes. Their personalities are a little different – you'll see. Oliver is a bit more serious and grown up. Don't worry about getting them muddled – they're used to it. Oh, and the dogs are Oofy and Inky – the boys named them, so don't laugh.'

'Okay. Got it. Anything else I need to remember?'

'No, I don't think so. Just have fun. There's no need to be nervous.'

'Darling, I'm not, but I suspect you are,' he said, laying a hand on her leg.

'I am a bit. I don't know why.'

'Because you're bringing together two very important parts of your life, that's why. Well, I *hope* you consider me an important part of your life.'

'You know I do,' she said, putting her hand over his and gazing at him. She was so close to using the 'L' word. She felt it, but also felt it was too soon to say it. She didn't want to lessen its significance. She told herself that was the reason she was holding back and not because she was waiting for Brad to say it first. Anyway, it was early days. Even though they'd packed a lot in, their first date had only been two weeks ago. Though, to Hannah it felt much longer – in a good way. While they hadn't yet slept together, they'd spent plenty of time enjoying each other's company talking and cuddling.

Last night Hannah had asked Brad to stay – had come close to begging him – but he'd left. Gazing after him, instead of feeling rejected, she'd felt a whole new rush of love and respect for his strength and respect for her and their relationship. He'd said he wanted to get the foundations right – make sure they formed a strong bond based on mutual respect and shared values before complicating and clouding things with sex. While Hannah found the waiting increasingly frustrating, she also really enjoyed it – the exciting anticipation. She'd almost melted when he'd said, 'We have our whole lives to explore the physical side of us.' That was different from her and Tristan – they'd slept together the second weekend after meeting.

'One other thing,' Hannah said, to bring herself back to the present and lighten things, 'cross your fingers that it's Pete cooking. I love Sam dearly, but she's far from being any sort of domestic goddess. It's okay, it's not a secret.'

'Oh well, she is a pretty talented artist – she can't be everything.'

'Exactly. It's that one just up there,' Hannah said, pointing to Sam's house.

'Oh. I expected at least a hint of artiness – maybe a bright orange fence or something,' Brad said.

'Maybe when she actually starts believing she really *is* an artist.'

Pete and Sam both greeted Hannah and Brad at the door, and seeing them standing side by side for the first time Hannah thought they looked great together – actually better than Sam and Rob ever had. They were like perfectly fitting jigsaw pieces standing there, each with an arm around the other, both smiling and so at ease. Hannah felt a surge of warmth flow through her.

'Hi, Pete,' Hannah said, giving him a hug. She was relieved to find nothing awkward about doing so. 'This is Brad, who I think you might have met at Sam's launch.'

'Yes, hi, Brad. Welcome.'

'I was expecting you to be flustered,' Hannah said as she hugged Sam while the men shook hands and Brad handed Pete the bottles of wine they'd brought.

'Nothing to be flustered about – Pete's got everything under control. Even the boys, and the dogs. You've no idea how much calmer this house is now the dogs are obedient. Can you believe they actually lie quietly on their beds in the corner?'

'No. Now this I want to see. So, who's coming?'

'Just you and Brad and Jas and Craig. I'm not entirely sure what it's all about. It's all Pete's doing,' she whispered. 'Seriously, he's a miracle worker, especially with the dogs,' she said at normal volume.

'Food rewards and consistency are what it's all about,' Pete said, coming up to Sam again and wrapping his arms around her waist.

'I'm good with the food rewards part of it,' Sam said, with a laugh.

'Too much of a softy, which is one of the traits that makes you so loveable,' Pete said, nuzzling her neck.

Hannah was a little surprised Sam didn't gently push him away. She'd never been a fan of overt public displays of affection.

'Ah, here they are,' Pete said, looking up. They all turned to see Craig's car pulling up at the kerb. The familiarity was such that Hannah found herself wondering if Pete had met Craig and Jasmine other than at Sam's launch party.

After all the greetings had been made they were ushered into the house.

'Now, before we get settled, I need to show you something – the real reason I've invited you here,' Pete said, leading them towards the door into the garage and her studio.

'Oh, Pete, no,' Sam said, clearly realising where he was going.

'You need to stop with the I'm-not-good-enough. You *are* good enough. You're *brilliant*. Sorry, but I'm not letting you hide your talent away just because of one or two misguided reviewers. These are incredible, even if you refuse to see it,' he said, opening the door.

Hannah held her breath and waited for Sam to start shouting at Pete for interfering, or at least walk off in a huff. But she didn't, she merely shrugged and said, 'Well, don't blame me if they don't share your enthusiasm.'

Pete flicked the light switch on and stepped aside as the overhead fluorescent lights flickered to life and the space was illuminated. There, sitting along the long bench, were four framed works of art – all in black and white; a charcoal sketch still-life of what Hannah recognised as items from the desk in the library at Mary's gorgeous house – blotter, inkwell and nib pen with ostrich feather. Next was a still-life of a pair of highly decorated cups and saucers stacked inside each other, a still-life of a bowl of fruit in white pastel on black paper, and then two sketches of dogs curled up together – one in charcoal on white paper and one in white on black paper. There was a collective intake of breath from Hannah, Brad, Jasmine and Craig.

'See,' Pete said.

'They haven't said anything yet,' Sam said, with arms defiantly crossed.

'Oh, Sammy, they're incredible,' Hannah said shaking her head with wonder.

'Really?'

'Are you seriously asking that?' Craig said. 'Seriously? They really are very good.'

'Yes, they're absolutely stunning,' Brad and Jasmine said at once.

'See, darling, I told you,' Pete said, more gently this time, and hugged Sam to him. Hannah noticed there were tears in her best friend's eyes. Sadness gripped her. She seemed so much more fragile than the Sam from before the exhibition, or perhaps the Sam from before Rob had left and set her world out of kilter. Sam had always been insecure about her work, but she used to have the attitude that if she liked it, it didn't matter what anyone else thought. Hannah yearned to see the old carefree Sam again. Or perhaps she'd disappeared for good. She hoped not.

'Can I send some pics to Mary?' Jasmine said, pulling out her phone.

'Sure,' Sam said.

'That's why I wanted you both here,' Pete explained. 'Hannah, you can help with the pricing if Mary is interested.'

'Oh. Okay. Um, no problem.' Hannah didn't like being put on the spot. Hopefully she and Sam could discuss it in private later.

'God, I'm sorry,' Pete said, clearly sensing Hannah's reluctance. 'I'm completely overstepping the mark, aren't I? I got a bit over-excited. Please accept my apologies.'

'Yeah, sorry, Hann,' Sam said.

'It's fine,' Hannah said, swallowing down her slight frustration. 'Why are those off to the side?' she asked, looking at two large photos on the floor, leaning against the wall – one was of the ornate knocker on the door of the Georgian house and the other of the front porch and door.

'They're just some of the photos I took that day. I blew them up to see how they'd look. There's something I really like about them.'

'That's because they're great. I love the angle and the light,' Brad said.

'Make sure you take photos of them too, Jas,' Hannah said, indicating the images.

'She wouldn't want pictures of bits of her own house,' Sam scoffed.

'Why not when they're such incredible photos?' Hannah said.

'Well, whatever. What would I know?'

'See, this is why I needed you guys here as reinforcements,' Pete said.

'I can't believe how much you've done in just two weeks – you said you were completely blocked,' Hannah said.

'Well, you can thank Pete. He gave me the kick up the backside I needed. And Beth for planting the black and white seed. I'd completely forgotten for a while there how much I love charcoal and white pastel. And sketching, and just silly doodling.'

'Darling, I'd rather you called me supportive, actually,' Pete said, pecking Sam on the forehead.

'Sorry. I wasn't meaning to sound derogatory. Or ungrateful.'

'Mary is going to love these. I just know it. They're perfect for her spaces. Trouble is, all of them could work,' Jasmine said, putting her phone away.

'Great. Now, come on, let's ponder it over food. No major decisions on an empty stomach, that's my motto,' Pete said.

As he led the way back out into the main house, Hannah's phone began to ring.

'Oh,' she said when she'd fished it out of her bag and was looking at the screen. 'Sorry, but I'd better take this.' She'd put all the numbers of the galleries she'd contacted on Sam's behalf into her phone and there, staring at her and brightly lit, was 'Black and White Gallery, Sydney'. She felt herself go a little pale. *Seriously, what a coincidence?*

'Are you okay?' Brad whispered, putting an arm around her.

'Yep. You go, I'll be there in a sec. Hello, Hannah Ainsley speaking.'

'Is that the agent for Samantha Barrow?'

'Yes, speaking.'

'This is Annika from The Black and White Gallery in Sydney. Do you have a moment to speak right now or should I call back?'

'No, now's fine. Go ahead.'

'Firstly, please accept my many apologies for taking so long to respond to your email enquiry. This year has quite got away from me. I'll come straight to the point. In the portfolio of Samantha's you attached you included a few charcoal sketches. As the gallery's name implies, I specialise in exhibitions in black and white – any medium. Really, for no reason other than to draw a line somewhere and differentiate us. And they are colours that work equally well in a contemporary or a traditional setting. Sorry, I'm getting carried away. My question is, is Samantha still doing charcoal sketches – or any other media in black and white, and if so do you think she would be up for a solo exhibition early in the new year? I'm thinking around twenty to two dozen pieces. Or am I too late and she's already been fully booked for next year? I wouldn't be surprised if I've missed the boat – I saw some great reviews of her ceramics. So, what do you think?'

'Well, first of all, thank you so much for the call and for considering Samantha. She is very busy at the moment, but I will certainly discuss it with her and get back to you as soon as possible. Would that be okay?'

'I'm sorry to be pushy, especially considering you emailed me over a month ago, but if I could know one way or the other by Wednesday that would be very helpful.'

'I understand, Annika, I'll get back to you as soon as I can. Thanks again so much for the call.'

'Great, I look forward to hearing from you soon. Thanks very much for your time.'

Hannah hung up feeling a little light-headed. She made her way through to the kitchen where Jasmine, Craig and Brad were seated at the table and Pete and Sam were at the bench with their backs to her.

'Are you okay?' Brad asked, leaping up and coming over to her. 'You look like you've seen a ghost. Have you received some bad news?'

'No. I'm fine. Just a bit of a strange call.' In a daze she sat down on the chair Brad pulled out for her.

'Well, come on, don't keep us in suspense!' Jasmine said.

'Okay, so who's for wine – red or white – or beer?' Pete asked as he turned from the bench. 'I'm on call, so, I'm actually having a glass of ginger beer. Anyone is welcome to join me. Or not. Up to you.'

'Oh, ginger beer, yes please,' Jasmine said. 'I haven't had it for years.'

'Count me in,' Hannah said.

'Actually, and me,' Craig said.

'Ginger beer would be great,' Brad said. 'I tend to want a nap if I drink alcohol in the afternoon these days.'

'Okay, four more ginger beers it is,' Pete said.

'Something does smell very good,' Hannah said.

'Quiche. And, yes, real men eat quiche – so there!' Pete said.

'You'll have no arguments from me,' Brad said, 'I love the stuff.'

'And me,' Craig said. 'Especially when it's got lots of bacon in it.'

'I told you!' Jasmine said suddenly, raising her phone and startling Hannah. 'Mary loves, loves, LOVES them – all of them!' At that moment her phone began to ring. 'That's her. Sorry, but I'm going to be rude and take this,' she said, getting up from the table and walking briskly back up the hall out of earshot.

'Darling, can you please get the boys in?' Sam asked Pete. Hannah felt a tiny surge of disappointment. She was hoping to share her exciting news about Annika before the tornado-like twins arrived.

'Could we just wait a sec? I need to tell you about the phone call,' Hannah said.

'Okay,' Sam said, putting the quiche on the table next to a large bowl of garden salad. Pete brought over a tray of tumblers of ginger beer and then sat down at the head of the table around the corner from Sam and started handing them out. There was an expectant air as they all sat silently and tried to look like they were not eavesdropping on Jasmine's conversation.

'Wow. So do I have some news!' Jasmine announced as she sat back down. 'Mary wants all of the pieces.'

'Even the photos? And without knowing the prices?' Sam asked.

'Yes. She loves the one of the dogs but said she will completely understand if you don't want to sell that one since they're your dogs ...'

'Oh. I hadn't got as far as thinking about selling any of them.'

'But you're a professional artist, darling, that's what professional artists do – they sell their pieces,' Pete said.

'I know, I just didn't think they were ... Oh, well, I guess I don't see why not. I can always do another one.'

'That's the spirit.'

'Actually, about that,' Jasmine said. 'I'm not sure how you'll feel about this, but remember how I said Mary's having her Comforting Cats black-tie fundraiser event next month? She was wondering if you would agree to having one of your paintings as part of an auction or raffle to raise money.'

'As in donate one? Of course. I'd love to help raise money to help the cats.'

'She said she's happy to buy it and donate it herself. But she just wanted to check you didn't mind because she'd also love it if you'd be present on the night.'

'Oh, wow, really? Hannah, what do you think?'

'Now *that* would be great exposure,' Brad said.

'Absolutely,' Craig agreed.

'I agree. Hang on. Since it's the Comforting Cats, how about offering someone the chance of winning a commission piece of their own pet?' Hannah said, the idea just coming to her. 'Only if you're okay with it, Sam.'

'I don't see why not,' Sam said.

'I think it's an absolutely brilliant idea!' Jasmine said.

'See, that's why she's my marketing manager,' Craig said, beaming proudly.

'Yes, I knew she was a lot more than a pretty face the night I met her,' Brad said.

Hannah blushed. 'It's just a thought.'

'So, what was your news, Hannah, anyway? Sorry to take over. I got a little carried away,' Jasmine said.

'Well, you're never going to believe this. But it was The Black and White Gallery in Sydney that rang – right when I've just stood looking at nothing but …'

'Black and white pieces! That's quite the crazy coincidence,' Jasmine said.

'Yes, no wonder you looked like you'd seen a ghost,' Brad said.

'There aren't really any coincidences. It's all the work of the universe,' Sam said quietly.

And there's my friend and her philosophies that I've been missing, Hannah thought, smiling to herself. *Oh yay, she's back.* She felt the overwhelming urge to go over and hug Sam, but stayed put.

'Okay. But it is a bit spooky,' Brad said.

'Yes, I'd agree with that,' Craig said.

'So, the point being,' Hannah said, trying to regain their attention, 'Annika from The Black and White Gallery in Sydney rang to ask if you'd be interested in a solo exhibition of around twenty to two dozen pieces early next year.'

'Oh! Wow!' Sam said. 'Well, um, I'll have to think about it – whether I could get them done in time.'

'Of course you could,' Pete said.

'No pressure, but I need to let her know by Wednesday,' Hannah said.

'Just say yes, dearest, and deal with the details later, I reckon,' Pete said.

'Don't decide right now. Sleep on it for a few nights,' Hannah said.

'Sorry, I didn't mean to sound pushy,' Pete said.

'Oh, I wasn't having a go at you,' Hannah said. 'It's just …'

'No worries. I'm trying to be supportive, but I'm probably coming off a bit strong. Again.'

'I really appreciate it,' Sam said, smiling at him and laying a hand on his arm.

'What a day. I brought you around to look at art and confirm it was as good as I thought it was. And now look where we are,' Pete said. 'Who's for quiche?' He picked up the knife and began cutting into the pie.

'I'll go and get the boys in,' Sam said.

'Ah, yes, good idea,' Pete said.

'I didn't have to go far to find two hungry boys,' Sam said, returning moments later.

'Hello, boys,' Hannah said as the twins appeared either side of her.

'Hello, Auntie Hannah,' Oliver and Ethan said in unison.

'I haven't seen you guys for ages. You've got very big since you've been at school. You're not too grown up for hugs, are you?'

'I'm not,' said Oliver, leaning in close to Hannah.

'We'll never be too grown up for hugs, will we, Mum?' Ethan said.

'That's right,' Sam said.

'Goodie,' Hannah said, enveloping them in her arms. 'You do give very good hugs. Now, this is my friend, Brad,' she said when she'd released them.

'Hello, boys,' Brad said, holding out his hand. 'It's lovely to meet you.'

'It's very nice to meet you, too,' Oliver said, giving Brad's hand a little shake.

'Hello,' Ethan said, copying his brother.

'So, tell me about school. Are you still enjoying it?' Hannah asked when the boys had settled themselves on chairs at the end of the table.

'Yes, but Mrs Smith is a bit crabby sometimes,' Ethan said.

'Yes, quite often,' Oliver said. 'She almost shouted the other day. Not at us, we're very good.'

Hannah heard Sam clear her throat.

'I'm sure you are,' Hannah said, trying to stifle a laugh. They were very cute when they became earnest and serious and sounded so grown-up. She wouldn't mind betting they were at the heart of plenty of naughtiness at school.

'Guess what, Auntie Hannah?' Oliver said.

'What, Ollie?'

'Daddy's coming home.'

'He misses us *far* too much,' Ethan said.

'I bet he does,' Hannah said, looking at Sam.

'Boys, remember, it's going to still be a little while. He's trying to get moved back here by Christmas,' Sam explained to the adults at the table. 'I'll tell you all about it later.'

'That's wonderful. I miss him too,' Hannah said.

'He's bringing Uncle Nick with him,' Oliver said.

'Oh. Great,' Hannah said.

'We've met him on Skype. Loads of times,' Oliver said.

'He's nice,' Ethan said.

'That's wonderful. Then, I'm looking forward to meeting Uncle Nick too,' Hannah said, not sure what else to say. Thankfully a plate of food was handed to her and soon they were all engrossed in eating and talking about Pete's great cooking skills.

Chapter Thirty-four

'Wow, Mr Thomas, you do look handsome in a tux.' *Quite breathtaking in fact.* Hannah kissed Brad on the lips gently, being careful not to smudge her makeup.

'Why, thank you very much, ma'am,' Brad said, stepping inside and taking a bow. 'You're looking very fetching yourself. Absolutely beautiful.'

'Well, you ain't seen nothing yet.' She was in her bathrobe with underwear on underneath. While they hadn't yet slept together and explored each other's naked bodies – maybe tonight would be the night – Hannah didn't feel at all embarrassed or self-conscious.

'I am very keen to see this dress that needs two to get you into,' he said, rubbing his hands together.

'I can get into it okay, just can't tie the corset strings. Come in.'

'Ooh-ah, I'm liking the sound of this more and more,' he said, grinning.

'Not *that* kind of corset.'

She'd found the perfect dress over a week ago. She'd never owned something so elegant, nor quite so revealing up top, but hadn't been able to resist. Especially when it had been marked at over fifty percent off as an end-of-season bargain. She absolutely loved the purple shade, which was similar to what her bedroom walls were now painted.

Hannah couldn't remember the last time she was so excited about getting dressed up and going out. A shot of nerves shot through her belly like lightning at noticing the duffle bag he carried, despite them having discussed him staying over.

'Through here,' she said, leading Brad to her bedroom, which she'd been careful to not let him see on the several times he'd been to visit. Now it was finished, she was keen to show him. She hoped he wouldn't mind the purple. Jasmine had assured her it was a masculine enough colour.

When she'd explained she was having Jasmine re-do the room, and why, Brad had said not to do it on his account. But Hannah had said she wanted a change. And when Jasmine had turned up with her samples and portfolio of ideas, she was past the point of no return. The room hadn't needed much – really just the walls done, new curtains and a few styling touches. Hannah had wanted to keep the lovely timber suite of bedroom furniture that had been her wedding gift from her father's parents.

Behind the bed, which was covered in a pale grey, textured bedspread with embroidered details, was a feature of wallpaper in charcoal floral on white, matching the colours in the silk curtains. Jasmine had found someone to make pleated shades for the bedside lamps in fabric similar to the curtains.

In the few nights Hannah had been sleeping in her newly done room, she'd struggled to decide which parts she loved the most. She was absolutely thrilled with the result and still found herself gazing around with a big grin on her face and warm feeling inside. She really didn't think she could have felt so much emotion about a room, but she did. In here now she felt incredibly happy and content, like she never had before. She knew it had something to do with Brad being in her life, but also thought it was a testament to Jasmine's skills. The only fly in the ointment was having to carefully place the four pillows and six decorative cushions back each morning to complete the look. Hannah secretly wondered how long she'd be bothered doing that.

'Ooh, the bedroom that's always been off limits,' Brad said, as Hannah pushed the door open and stepped inside. 'Wow,' he said, standing with his mouth open and looking around him. 'It's stunning. That purple is amazing.'

'So, not too girly?'

'No, not at all. I really like it – and I'm not just saying that.'

'Thanks. As much as I'd like to take credit, it's pretty much all Jasmine.'

'Well, you had final say. I'm sure she didn't hold a gun to your head. So you're allowed to take some credit.

'Do you guys like your new room?' he said to the three cats curled up against the cushions.

They opened their eyes, looked up and gave Hannah and Brad a cursory glance before returning to their snoozing.

'Thrilled, as you can see,' Hannah said with a laugh.

'Where shall I put this?' Brad asked, lifting up his overnight bag.

'Just there in the corner,' Hannah said, a flutter of butterflies causing a brief commotion in her stomach. She loved how respectful he was. While they both knew it was probably inevitable – well, she did – that they would share a bed for the first time tonight, Brad hadn't mentioned it, let alone put pressure on her. They'd been together for around seven weeks and she felt so much for him her heart swelled to the point she became almost breathless and overwhelmed.

'If you're sure. You can always change your mind,' he said, looking deep into her eyes.

'Yes, I am. And, no I won't.'

'Gotta love a decisive woman,' he said, hugging her to him. It was the closest he'd come to telling her he loved her.

'And I love a man who's always on time.'

They were still both dancing around using the 'L' word seriously. Hannah didn't mind. She really did feel they had their whole lives together ahead of them, however long that might be.

She was very conscious of all the talk about people who had faced death or lost loved ones suddenly rolling out bucket lists and embarking on obsessive journeys to consciously make the most of life. She just wanted to be happy. She was someone who'd never been taught to swim in the pool of life but had been thrown suddenly into the deep end. She figured keeping her head above water for so long and not drowning was adequate proof of making the most of life. Now she felt lucky enough just to have survived.

'Okay, I'm just going to step out while you put your dress on,' Brad said.

'You don't have to. I'm sure you've seen a woman in underwear before,' Hannah said, but he was already out in the hall and the door half-closed behind him.

'Yes, I have. But, I do need to step out. If I don't, we'll be late. *Very* late,' he called from out of sight.

Hannah smiled as she took the strapless dress out of the wardrobe and off its hanger, stepped into it and pulled it up.

'Okay, it's safe to come in now.'

'Oh,' he said breathlessly. 'You look absolutely stunning.' He stood staring at her.

'Thanks, but I think you'll find it'll look much better when it's done up.'

'Right, yes, sorry,' he said, and snapped back to attention. 'The zip and then the strings, right?'

'Yes, please. Nice and tight.'

Hannah couldn't help staring at herself in the mirror. She looked and felt like a princess. And oh how she loved Brad so close to her, touching her ever so gently.

'There you go. How's that? Not too tight? Just check you can breathe okay.'

'Perfect. Thanks.' Hannah could breathe, but she wasn't sure how she'd go with eating and drinking in the firm bodice. Oh, well.

'I would hug you right now, but I don't want to crease that gorgeous dress. You really do look incredible.'

'As do you,' Hannah said, putting a hand to his face. 'Just one last layer of lipstick and final going-over with the lint roller and we're good to go. Fingers crossed they stay right there,' Hannah said, nodding at the cats.

'Okay. Ready?' Hannah asked less than a minute later.

'I certainly am. And here's our cab. Excellent. Right on time,' Brad said as the doorbell rang.

Hannah grabbed her wrap, keys and evening bag from the hall table and did a quick inventory as she opened the front door.

'I hope Sam's excited and not too nervous this time around,' Hannah said once they were settled in the taxi. 'Jasmine said Mary has put her paintings on easels in full view. At least she won't be expected to give a speech tonight.'

'She'll be fine with her support crew gathered around and taking care of her,' Brad said.

'Thank goodness there are no surprises, not like the opening. I can't wait to meet Nick,' Hannah said.

'I love how non-judgemental and welcoming you ladies are and I feel so fortunate to have met you all,' he said, turning towards her and gazing into her eyes.

Hannah beamed and her heart swelled for the umpteenth time that evening.

'You're such a beautiful man,' she said, and squeezed his hand.

They lapsed into easy silence, both seemingly content to watch the evening traffic pass outside the taxi windows.

'The house is even more impressive at night. Look, on the wall, lights in the shape of a sitting cat and kitten,' Hannah said, gazing over at the large display of white fairy lights.

'Now *that* is quite something,' Brad said.

'Ooh, and a red carpet,' Hannah said as the taxi stopped at the foot of the steps, where the carpet ended. 'Goodness me, I feel like royalty,' she said as she tucked her arm through Brad's and they made their way up the red-carpeted steps to the house.

'Or a celebrity,' Brad whispered.

'Perfect. And there's the talent herself. Oh, and that must be Nick because there's Rob,' Hannah said, waving.

'There's Beth, Joanne, Louise and Henry, and Craig,' Brad said, also waving.

'Jasmine must be off helping Mary somewhere,' Hannah said, as they headed over to where their friends stood.

They mingled and had a few drinks and tried the delicious food, and then silence was called for. Hannah was enjoying herself immensely. Jasmine introduced her and Brad to Mary and her husband Bart, and then in turn Hannah met many other people. She took note of how well Mary networked and introduced strangers to each other. She liked that Brad was comfortable to work the room too, though he and Craig seemed to be spending a lot of time talking business – their heads close together and both looking very serious. She loved that Brad fitted in so well with every one of her friends. It was as if he'd been there all along.

Somewhere a bell rang and gradually the rabble of voices died down.

'Don't worry, everyone, there's still plenty of food and drink, thanks to our wonderful sponsors Belly Up Wines and Feast Catering, and I won't keep you for long. I want to thank you all so much for coming, and for your ongoing support. I'm so proud of what Comforting Cats is achieving with our limited resources, which have gained a significant boost thanks to you all tonight and your generous donations. I'm particularly thrilled to have been given a cheque for fifteen thousand dollars from a donor who wishes to remain anonymous. Thank you, and bless you.

'You can rest assured all your donations will be put to good use as we strive to rid this city of its unloved homeless cat population and educate the public about the importance of responsible pet ownership and loving care and the wonderful benefits cats provide in return. For those of you who'd like to help at a practical level, we're always on the lookout for more dedicated foster carers, and of course assistance all the way around. My dream is to not have any cats in a kennel situation.

'Please remember to check out the silent auction list and put in a bid – there's a wonderful array of goods on offer this year. Truly something for everyone. Huge thanks to those who have donated items. There are too many contributors for me to name now, but I've included a list in your gift bags. Please support these very kind and generous businesses as much as you can.

'And, last but not least, I'd like to tell you about these gorgeous paintings,' she said, indicating the artworks displayed on easels standing on either side of her. 'Hannah and Sam, please come up here for a moment – it's okay, you're amongst friends and I promise I won't make you give a speech,' she said, smiling warmly and holding out her hand in a welcoming gesture. Hannah grabbed Sam's hand and urged her forward.

'This is Sam Barrow, the artist responsible for these exquisite works of art.' Hannah gave Sam the gentlest of nudges and Sam stepped forward and raised her hand and gave a little self-conscious wave. Applause erupted. 'And her agent, Hannah Ainsley.'

'I was lucky enough to meet these lovely ladies through my interior designer – oh, what the heck, come on up here too, Jasmine. You should be celebrated as well for your amazing talent and getting the house together in time.'

Jasmine made her way to the front and also raised her hand in acknowledgement. Again there was enthusiastic clapping. When the noise had died down for the second time, Mary continued. 'Jasmine is responsible for the transformation of the interior of this entire house, which was tired and very much in need of tender loving care, as those of you who've been here before will be all too aware. So, for anyone needing a superstar of an interior designer, Jasmine Pearson is your girl,' she said. 'Now, sorry, I got side tracked. Where was I? Ah, yes, the magnificent art – donated by the very lovely Samantha. Some lucky person will soon own the painting on my left – the incredible still-life in white pastel on black – and another lucky person will win a commissioned portrait of their pet – or pets. This example on my right is of Sam's lovely dogs.'

'Sam's more a dog person, but we won't hold that against her,' Mary said, putting her arm around Sam.

'So, please, fill your glasses and get your arms limbered up ready for the art auction while my wonderful husband Bart finishes warming up his voice. We won't be long. Again, thank you all for coming, for your support, and – in advance – for digging deep. That's all from me for now, folks.' Mary bowed as loud cheering and clapping ensued.

'Thanks for coming up and joining me. I hope that wasn't too traumatic,' Mary said to Hannah, Sam and Jasmine.

'Not at all,' Sam said.

'Thank you so much for the plug, Mary – I really appreciate it,' Jasmine said.

'Well deserved and my absolute pleasure,' Mary said, hugging her.

Chapter Thirty-five

'Good morning again, gorgeous,' Brad said, rolling towards Hannah and then kissing her.

'Good morning, handsome man,' Hannah said, wrapping an arm and a leg around him. Her body hummed and glowed in the aftermath of wonderful lovemaking. After arriving home late, Brad had carefully peeled Hannah's dress off and then her underwear. He'd proceeded to massage her sore feet, which were unaccustomed to being in high heels. He'd then worked his way slowly and gently along her body until she'd practically begged him to make love to her. While the first time had been beautiful, the second and the third time had both exceeded all expectations. That was a few hours ago, then they'd drifted off to sleep again. *What a perfect way to wake on a Saturday morning*, Hannah thought.

'How lovely was last night?' Brad said. 'I don't think I've ever enjoyed an event so much.'

'I loved it. It helped that everyone could be there.'

Just as Hannah was about to say something more, Brad put a finger to her lips and said, 'Don't you dare say how lucky you are to have such good friends in your life. Because I don't think luck has anything to do with it. You deserve them and they're just as fortunate to have you. As am I. And to show my appreciation ...'

'I think you already have, Mr Thomas, several times in fact,' Hannah said, seductively. She began frowning quizzically as she watched him get up and go to the gift bags they'd left on the upholstered chair in the corner.

'And I will again, later. But first, I have something for you,' he said, riffling through. 'Close your eyes.'

Hannah did as she was told and listened while Brad came back to the bed.

'Okay, you can open them now.'

Hannah looked up. Brad was sitting on the bed with something hidden in his hand.

'When I saw this I thought of you and wanted to get it for you. You're the epitome of community, you bring people together. You're the kindest, most generous person I've ever met – always thinking of others, putting their needs before your own. Anyway, I wanted you to have this,' he said. 'Open your hand and hold it out flat.'

Hannah gasped. 'Oh, Brad, it's beautiful,' she said, staring at the exquisite piece of marcasite and yellow and black enamel jewellery in the shape of a bee. She bit her lip to stop the gathering tears from flowing.

'It's been said that one of the most remarkable things about the bee is the fact that it can fly when aerodynamically speaking it really shouldn't be able to,' Brad continued. 'And that's you, Hannah, you haven't let what happened to you dull your spirit. Despite your grief, you've soared.'

'Oh, Brad. I love it and I'll treasure it always.'

'I know it's a brooch, and you probably don't even wear them, but I so badly wanted you to have it.'

'It's perfect. And when I'm not wearing it, I'm going to keep it on my desk or beside the bed to remind me of you and the wonderful event we had together. I love that you bought it as part of the silent auction to raise money for the cats – that means so much too.'

'Speaking of silent. It was you who gave the anonymous fifteen-thousand dollar donation, wasn't it?'

'Yes. Do you mind?'

'Why would I mind? Your money is yours to do with as you wish, and always will be, regardless of me.'

'I also think I'd like to volunteer a day a week to work with Mary, perhaps in admin. Maybe that's the reason for my job with Craig only being part-time.'

'Maybe it is. I think she would really appreciate the help,' Brad said.

'What do you think? Honestly,' Hannah said.

'I think you do whatever makes you feel whole and happy.'

'*You* make me feel whole and happy.'

'As you do me, but I'm not sure we could live permanently in this bubble and not eventually go mad. We both need stimulation. Er, of a different sort to earlier,' Brad said.

Hannah leaned over and gave him a firm, lingering kiss.

'You really are the most exquisite creature,' Brad said, pushing back the hair framing her face and tucking it behind her ear. 'I just can't get enough of you or close enough to you. I want to climb inside your heart and soul and never leave.'

'You're already there,' Hannah said, and pressed her lips to him again. She groaned with pleasure as he began kissing her back passionately.

'You're yummy. You even smell nice in the morning,' she whispered when they paused for breath. He looked intently into her eyes for a moment before easing away.

'I'm a little weary,' he said with a laugh.

'Me too. How about some breakfast? There's bacon and eggs in the fridge. Or fruit bread for toasting and plenty of cereal, if you prefer.'

'Allow me, my princess,' he said. 'If you don't mind me taking over your kitchen.'

'Not at all. I would love you to make me breakfast. But be warned, I might get used to being taken care of and become high maintenance.'

'That would never happen. It would be my pleasure to cook for you,' he said, leaning back to kiss her again. 'I have a warning of my own. A bit of sustenance and I might just want to make love to you all over again.'

'You'll hear no complaints from me.'

'A big breakfast it is, then! Would you like poached, boiled or fried eggs, my darling? Bacon soft or crispy? And toast or no toast? And please say you have a tin of baked beans lurking about.'

'Yes, there's a tin in the pantry. A big breakfast is not complete without baked beans. I'm so impressed you even take orders.'

'Of course. And I can cook, you know.'

'Okay, two soft poached eggs, please, on toast with plenty of butter. Bacon – however it comes – and, yes, a generous helping of baked beans, please. Are you sure you don't want some help?'

'Absolutely not. You are to stay here and look beautiful.'

'Could I trouble you for coffee, too? Or am I pushing my luck?'

'Not at all. Coffee is a need, not a want, so consider it already on order. Now, is there anything I can do for my lady before I leave?'

'I'd love the papers to read, they should be on the lawn,' Hannah said a little sheepishly. 'Am I stretching the friendship now? Because I can at least go and do that.'

'No, I'll get them. Great. I love the idea of reading the actual physical papers in bed. It's ages since I've done that. I've got so used to reading online. Okay, be back soon,' he said, tying the belt of the plush charcoal coloured robe he'd pulled on and then blowing Hannah a kiss as he left the room.

She leaned back on the headboard. What a perfect time she was having – the evening before and now all this.

She brought her hands to her swelling heart and as she did her gold wedding ring caught her eye. She looked at it, turned it around, and then slowly eased the plain band from her finger. She opened the drawer in the cupboard beside her, took out the small jewellery box and opened it. *Tris, I'll always love you and remember you.* She picked up the larger ring already there and kissed it. A few tears gathered in her eyes. *But it's time.*

'I'm very impressed you get both of the good ones,' Brad cried as he strode into the room. 'It's like Christmas!' he said, tossing the rolled-up, plastic-wrapped newspapers onto the bed. He stopped short at noticing Hannah's expression. And then he saw what she was holding – the two wedding bands in the open box. He came around to her side of the bed, sat close and put his arm around her.

'You don't have to do that. I don't want you to do anything that will upset you,' he said, drawing her to him.

'I'm fine. Really. I want to. It feels right. I'm just having a moment,' she said, turning and kissing him.

'I know how much you loved him, and still love him. Tristan was a truly fortunate man and I'm going to do all I can to have you feel that way about me.'

Hannah closed the box, gave it a kiss, placed it out of sight and closed the drawer.

'Weren't you cooking breakfast so you can rebuild your stamina, Mr Thomas,' she said seductively.

'Yes, ma'am,' he said, gave a mock salute, and made a show of turning on his heels.

Hannah smiled as she unwrapped the newspapers and laid them out. She'd only just started reading them again fully since meeting Henry. Before then she hadn't been able to bear looking at them in case they contained something about the accident or the subsequent court cases.

She'd considered cancelling the subscriptions not long after Tristan and her parents' deaths, but she hadn't wanted to make that change. Newspapers had been delivered to her family at this address for nearly forty years. It had seemed disloyal to end the tradition. Also, she still preferred the hard copy to reading online. And she'd discovered newspaper was very useful to cat owners for bundling up the bits taken out of litter trays, and general clean-up.

At that moment Holly sauntered in, followed by Lucky and Squeak. She loved how they wiggled their fluffy little butts and looked about as if they owned the place, which of course they pretty much did. Hannah knew her place. She'd been smart enough to feed them when they'd come in late last night in the hope she and Brad would get a couple of hours of time alone.

'Good morning. Did you have a little sleep in?' she said, patting their heads and stroking them when they presented themselves on her lap. 'Nice of you to respect our privacy. Thank you.' As she hugged each of them to her in turn, the glow in Hannah's heart went up a notch. *I'm like a cat having landed on my feet after falling from a great height*, she thought, as she enjoyed the drone of their purring. After a few moments they wriggled free and began looking for somewhere to get comfy. Hannah was pleased to see them curl up together at the end of the bed near her toes rather than the warm spot Brad had left.

'Good kitties,' she told them.

Hannah balled up the plastic wrapping and tossed it on the floor. She then separated the main papers from the magazines and glossy advertising supplements, which she liked to save until last. She'd just started flicking through the financial paper, which was her least favourite, when her phone let out a series of beeps in quick succession. No doubt everyone was texting to ask how her first night with Brad had gone. *Perfect. Just perfect*, she'd say. *And I'm not about to elaborate on just how perfect*, she thought, smiling, as she picked up the phone. The first message was from Sam and wasn't what she was expecting at all.

OMG!! Have you seen the magazine in the paper? Read it now!! Xxx

Hannah quickly scrolled through the other messages, which were similar. She frowned, put her phone down and looked at the covers of the two glossy magazines. And there it was. *Making Peace – the story of one woman's extraordinary capacity to forgive. By Brad Thomas.*

She hoped the title of the article – a clever play on words – was his doing. She knew having his by-line on the cover of this particular magazine was something he'd been working towards for a long time. She was really excited for him. Why hadn't he said anything?

She opened up to the article. There, taking up the top half of the first page, was the photo of her and Henry embracing – her face with her eyes closed resting on his shoulder. She turned over to the next page where there were three smaller photos. Up the top of the page was the group shot of them at Sam's launch party, and was captioned *Firm new friends*. It was a good photo, but Hannah found her eyes being drawn to the two images at the bottom of the page of Henry alone, which were captioned *Henry Peace before* ... under the first and then ... *And after meeting Hannah Ainsley* underneath the second.

If he wasn't wearing the same distinctive pinstriped suit in both she'd have sworn the images were of a different person entirely. The change was remarkable. So much of the tension seemed to have gone from his face in the time between the shots were taken. Hannah still felt discombobulated about that being her doing – that something that came so naturally to her could make such a profound difference to someone. Actually, more than just one person. Louise had said over and over that Hannah had saved her family, made the Peace family whole again.

Hannah turned back to the beginning of the article and started to read.

I met Hannah Ainsley quite by accident almost a year ago. She'd re-treated to a city hotel to escape media interest after the tragic accidental death of her husband and both parents one Christmas Day. She told me she didn't have a story to tell and wasn't a victim. Of course she's a victim in the true meaning of the word, but from the moment I met her I thought her one of the strongest, bravest women I'd ever met ...

Hannah paused. Her eyes were filling with tears and she was having trouble keeping track of the print in front of her.

On Christmas Day before last, Hannah Ainsley's world collided with Henry and Louise Peace's when the truck Henry was driving failed to stop at the intersection of Victoria Parade and Hoddle Street, killing Hannah's husband, Tristan, and parents Daniel and Daphne White. Henry has been absolved of any wrongdoing and the trucking company he worked for as a driver has been held culpable.

Henry and Louise Peace were victims of this catastrophe as well, though not to the same tragic extent as Hannah. 'Henry took it really hard,' Louise Peace said. 'He's a very good driver and had never even had so much as a scrape in the more than twenty years he'd been driving professionally.' But to be responsible for the deaths of three people saw Henry fall apart mentally and emotionally. 'He withdrew,' Louise said, 'he left me and our son, Felix. It was the shame, the guilt ... The company wasn't at all supportive. They essentially wiped their hands of him, pushed him out into the cold.'

For over twelve months the now unemployed Henry followed the court proceedings, sitting there day after day, week after week. 'I think he saw it as his penance,' Louise explained. 'He wanted to go to jail, be made to pay for what he saw as his fault. It didn't matter to Henry that the brakes were faulty because the truck had been poorly maintained – none of which was in his control. He was behind the wheel that day. Henry's a responsible, decent man, so he found it really hard. The only thing that has helped him has been meeting Hannah. I just wish it had happened sooner.'

While Henry spent his days in the court and his nights in a dingy bedsit, Hannah Ainsley was doing her best to piece her life back together. She refuses to see herself as strong or brave and instead credits others with getting her through – her close-knit group of friends. 'Sometimes I thought I'd never stop crying. And I think I only got through it because of my wonderful friends. Thankfully I have some really special people who knew what I needed when I needed it. I'm so lucky there,' she said.

Rather than feeling sorry for herself or wallowing in her grief, Hannah says she is trying to make the most of her life and appreciate it. 'I could have easily been in that car that day too,' she said. While she admits there are still some days she is so sad she struggles to get out of bed, she pushes herself on.

Not only is Hannah optimistic, she seems to genuinely have one of the biggest, most forgiving hearts of anyone I've ever met.

Hannah was leaving her office for lunch one day early this year when the lift was broken. While waiting she found herself watching the news and upon seeing the court case was on felt compelled to attend. She can't explain why after not being interested in the proceedings at all from the beginning, except to say, 'I was clearly meant to be at court that day and to meet Henry.'

Hannah paused to let her words soak in. She was a little embarrassed at what she'd said, but there was no misquoting, no twisting of words. And her thoughts were her own, and hadn't changed.

When Hannah arrived, the court had been emptied and was on a lunchbreak. She found herself sitting down beside Henry on a bench – a further coincidence. They got talking and that's when Hannah changed the course of Henry's life, which was spiralling out of control.

'I'd decided I was going to kill myself that night,' Henry said.

'Oh no,' Hannah said aloud, and brought her hands to her face. She took a deep breath and forced herself to read on. It really was a gripping read, even if she did know almost all of what the article contained.

'I had bought some tape and hose and was going to gas myself with the car. I just couldn't bear my life. I'd killed three people. I'd ruined Hannah Ainsley's life. How do you live with that? I couldn't look my wife and child in the eye, I didn't have a job and despite applying for dozens couldn't get a look-in because my name was known. I was a marked man. I got a couple of interviews but all they asked

was about the accident – just being nosey – not interested in employing me at all. I was a mess and couldn't support my family financially. I'm not sure if I could have really gone through with it or not, but Hannah definitely saved me that day. I know that.'

Tears dripped from Hannah's nose and landed with little plops on the print. She pulled a tissue from the box nearby and tried to wipe them away. *Poor, poor Henry.* She blinked her sight clear and forced her attention back to the story.

'She told me she forgave me. She hugged me. She even shared her lunch with me. I don't know how she made peace with it all, but I will be forever grateful to her. She's an extraordinary woman – so brave, so kind. Seeing that she was okay – well, as much as she could be after all that – really helped me start to get my act together.'

And what does Hannah say to that?

'I don't see what's special about showing someone some kindness and consideration,' says Hannah Ainsley, who seems genuinely perplexed that I would suggest such a thing. It's almost incomprehensible, but Hannah said, "There was really nothing to forgive. The poor man was in the wrong place at the wrong time ...' As Henry said, Hannah went several steps further. 'The man was in need of a hug, so I gave him one. Sometimes a hug can make a lot of pain go away – I know that all too well.' But Hannah Ainsley went a step further, sharing her lunch with Henry. Again, she seemed genuinely surprised that I thought that act extraordinary. 'Food can also be a great source of comfort. My parents were big on sharing food. It was just the way it was, so it's part of who I am.'

'Not only did Hannah save me,' Henry Peace said, 'but she's opened up her heart to me and my wife, Louise, and son, Felix. We've actually become quite close friends. And that's all thanks to

Hannah's truly generous nature. She's a really beautiful person inside and out. She's shown us that good things can come out of a terrible tragedy. We can't thank her enough. And, you know, it's also thanks to Hannah that I now have a full-time job. I only wish I could somehow repay her.'

And what does Hannah think of all this?

'I'm just glad Henry and Louise and their son, Felix, weren't three more victims to that tragic accident that day, and have found a way back to each other.'

Hannah insists she's not special, but Henry and Louise and I disagree. Very few in this world today would have been so gracious. It's heartening to see and something society needs a lot more of. I would have liked to have met Daphne and Daniel White, the parents who raised such an incredible young woman, a woman who has endured so much yet is still able to say, 'Good things can come out of tragedies if you're only willing to look for them.'

It was very clear to me when interviewing Hannah that she's not just survived, but she's thrived. She has two exciting new part-time jobs, a renewed zest for life, and a love of cats, which she never had before the accident. But that's a story I look forward to bringing you another day ...

Hannah sat with the magazine in her lap. She felt a little shocked as the words soaked in. She wasn't entirely comfortable with it being so much about her, but couldn't deny Brad had done a good job. She let the tears she'd been holding in flow.

'Hey, it wasn't meant to make you cry,' Brad said, putting a tray of food down on the tallboy and going to her.

'It's beautiful, Brad, just beautiful. *You're* just beautiful,' she said, looking up at him.

'I'm so relieved you like it,' he said, gently wiping away her tears with his thumb and kissing her on each cheek.

'I love you, Brad,' she said, gazing deeply into his eyes, 'so, so much.'

'I love you. I've loved you since that first night we met. I feel like I've been holding my breath since then and now I can breathe. Oh, darling,' he said, holding her tight.

Epilogue

Christmas Day

Hannah stood at the glass door leading to the backyard. She'd come to call Felix, Oliver and Ethan in for Christmas lunch, which was on the table ready to be devoured. They were racing around the garden, stopping at various plants and then examining their leaves with the microscope Felix had received for Christmas.

'Leave them be,' Louise said, appearing beside Hannah and reading her mind. 'They'll come looking for food when they're hungry. Or a drink when they're thirsty. They know where we are.'

'I feel like I could stand here and watch them forever. It's lovely to see them playing so happily together,' Hannah said.

'It is. So, let's enjoy the peace before they get over-tired and someone starts a fight!'

'Ha-ha, yes, good idea,' she said, turning away and linking arms with Louise.

'Sorry about the delay, folks,' Hannah announced and took her seat with everyone else. 'Now, please, help yourselves before it gets cold.'

The table erupted into a melody of clinking of silverware on crockery, murmurs of delight, and requests to pass this or that. Before too long each person had a piled-up plate of food in front of them – stuffed roast turkey, lamb, pork and four different types of baked vegetables and four steamed. Large jugs of gravy and pots of various condiments were strategically placed around the table.

Hannah tapped her glass gently to get everyone's attention.

'I'll make this quick. Thank you all for being here. It's wonderful to have old friends and new friends come together to celebrate what's been and the good things we have ahead of us. I for one feel very blessed to be surrounded by a group of such wonderful, caring people. Thank you for being my dear friends and for all the support. And, to absent friends and family,' she said, raising her glass and swallowing hard, 'know you are in our hearts and thought of every day. So, please raise your glasses. To friends, old, new, and absent,' she said.

There was a rumble of agreement, the words being repeated around the table and the clinking of glasses.

'That was just beautiful, sweetheart,' Brad said, leaning close, putting his hand on her leg and kissing her on the cheek.

There was another round of agreement.

'Thanks, everyone. Now, tuck in. And while we do and the children are out of hearing, I want everyone to share their latest news since life seems to be getting busier by the day and it's getting harder and harder to catch up. I have no idea where the last six months disappeared to.'

'Well, at the risk of talking with my mouth full, because I can't hold this in any longer,' Craig said, 'I'd like to announce that Jas and I are nearly four months pregnant. Please don't anyone be offended, but we've kept it to ourselves because of the trouble we've had previously. So far all is well – fingers crossed it stays that way.'

Everyone cheered.

'Oh, my god. That's wonderful. Congratulations,' Hannah said. 'As if we'd be offended. I'm just surprised you could keep a secret that long when you and I speak or email every day! Oh, I'm so excited for you both.' Glasses were raised and clinked again.

'I knew it!' Sam said. 'Well, I didn't *know* – I guessed. Ages ago.'

'Okay, well, we'll be next cab off the rank,' Rob said. 'After a trial run these past few months, Nick and I are staying permanently with Sam. This gorgeous, incredibly generous girl has agreed to us being an unconventional family – as in, all living under the same roof.'

'It's going to be tight, because I'm moving in in the New Year too,' Pete said cheerfully.

'I'm not sure there is any such thing as conventional anymore,' Beth said. 'I say, good for you for being yourselves and putting your boys first. You'll make it work. Of that I have no doubt. Cheers,' she said, raising her glass. 'I actually have a little news of my own, too. I've struck up a friendship with a very nice man at Comforting Cats while volunteering. So, after several decades of being alone, and at the ripe old age of seventy-five, I might just have myself a boyfriend,' she said with a laugh, blushing slightly.

Hannah smiled and patted Beth's hand. She'd met Geoff several times and had enjoyed watching their acquaintance blossom into full-blown romance.

'I'm just disappointed he couldn't be here with us,' Hannah said.

'Maybe next year,' Beth said.

'Speaking of next year,' Raelene said. 'We'd like to know what you think about coming to the farm for Christmas – all of you. Adrian and I have decided to set down roots again, at least for the year.'

'Ooh, yes. How about we start a new tradition and rotate every year?' Sam said.

'Great idea. We'd love to have you all sometime, too,' Louise said, 'wouldn't we, Henry? Not that we have to wait until Christmas Day, of course.'

'Exactly. And we have a bit of news, too. No, we're not pregnant – we're happy just the three of us,' Henry said with a laugh. 'But we've finally settled with my former employer. The terms are confidential, but let's just say we're *very* happy with how it's all turned out. And we have Hannah and Brad to thank – for turning everything around for us.'

'What about your other announcement?' Joanne prompted. 'Henry has been promoted to head groundsman and not just for our village, but he's also going to be consulting to the rest of the group.'

'Oh, wow,' Hannah said, 'that's fantastic. I'm so happy for you.'

'Yes, I'm really excited,' Henry said, looking a little bashful.

'See why we have to all get together – there's so much news everyone is holding onto,' Hannah said. 'What a day!'

'I hope you've all got your tickets booked for Sydney,' Sam said. 'I'm going to need my whole cheer squad at my opening on Friday February second.'

'You don't *need* us, but we will all be there, won't we, gang?' Hannah said. Unbeknown to Sam, she'd been planning their interstate trip for months.

'Certainly will. The accommodation is booked,' Brad said, 'all within walking distance to the event. It's going to be a wonderful weekend.'

'I can't wait!' Beth said. Everyone agreed.

'Thanks guys,' Sam said, beaming. 'I really appreciate the support. So, so much.'

'While we're all here, and before we're all drunk and disorderly, I have something I'd like to say ...' Brad began.

'I don't know, I think I've already had three champagnes,' Sam interrupted. 'Sorry, carry on.'

'Normally I wouldn't do this in such a public manner, but well, I think this gathering is different. I feel like we're a family who has chosen each other or been chosen by powers beyond us to be together ...'

Hannah looked at Brad and nodded with agreement. Her brain was a little fuzzy from the wine, too, and she wondered where he was going with his speech. She looked at Sam who was smiling, and then at Raelene who was too. And Adrian. Looking around the table there seemed to be something going on that everyone was in on, except her. She frowned slightly as she tried to focus on Brad as he continued speaking.

What's going on?

'I'm particularly grateful for everyone giving me their blessing, especially Raelene and Adrian.'

Blessing? For what?

'Hannah,' he said, turning towards her, 'it took me nearly a year to find you again. We've been together a little over six months now and from my point of view it's been perfect. I hope you feel the same ...'

Oh! Are you ...?

'If so, would you do me the honour of becoming my wife?' *Oh my god, you are!* He held out an open jewellery box with the largest, most beautiful sparkling round diamond solitaire ring she'd ever seen. *Oh my, that's gorgeous. Yes, yes, YES! Oh, Brad, of course I will.*

'Hann?' he prompted.

Didn't you hear me shout yes, several times?

'Please say something – preferably yes,' he said with a nervous laugh.

'Shit. Sorry. Here I am sitting here with my mouth gaping like a fish. I'm a little stunned. I wasn't expecting this.'

'And ...?'

'Yes! Yes, yes, YES! Of course, Brad, I can't wait to be your wife. I love you so much,' she said, throwing her arms around his neck.

'Well, thank goodness for that!' he said with obvious relief. 'Can I put the ring on your finger, then?' he added as he gently extracted himself from her clutches.

Hannah held out her hand and watched as Brad took the ring out of the box and then slid it on to her finger.

'It's perfect, absolutely stunning. Thank you,' she said.

'Thank *you*,' he said, looking deep into her eyes, cupping her face with his large gentle hands, and kissing her passionately.

Applause, cheering and whistling erupted around the table followed by congratulations. Hannah felt she was glowing with happiness.

A few moments later the excited chatter and *oohing* and *ahhing* over the news and ring was suddenly shattered by the thunder of small feet and chorus of voices as Oliver, Ethan and Felix ran into the dining room and up to their mothers, crying in unison, 'Muuum, I'm *hungry!*'

Acknowledgements

Many thanks to:

James Kellow, Sue Brockhoff, Annabel Blay, Adam van Rooijen and everyone at Harlequin Australia and HarperCollins Australia for turning my manuscripts into beautiful books and for continuing to make my dreams come true.

Editor Bernadette Foley for her kindness, valuable insights and guiding hand to bring out the best in my writing and Hannah's story.

Amy Milne at AM Publicity for getting the word out, and the media outlets, bloggers, reviewers, librarians, booksellers and readers for all the amazing support. It really does mean so much to me to hear of people enjoying my stories and connecting with my characters.

And, finally, to my dear friends who provide so much love, support, and encouragement – especially Mel Sabeeney, NEL and WTC. I am truly blessed to have you in my life.

Turn over for a sneak peek.

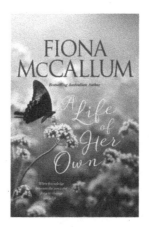

A Life
of
Her
Own

by

FIONA
McCALLUM

Available April 2019

Chapter One

Alice heard David's key in the front door. She raced up the hall and waited until he'd put his bags down and closed the door behind him before throwing her arms around his neck.

'Welcome home – to your new home!' she cried, determined to treat it as a celebration. He travelled so much she usually didn't bother to make a fuss on his return – for David, coming back from Europe or Asia was pretty much the same as coming in from the Melbourne office half an hour away – but as it was the first time he'd come home to their new abode, she thought it warranted a bit of extra fuss.

'Thanks,' he said, grinning. 'Hooray, all the boxes have gone. Well done, you.' He pecked her on the lips before easing her away from him.

Alice didn't feel as if she'd been dismissed – they weren't a very touchy-feely couple. She'd been a little disappointed in the beginning, nearly four years ago, but she had become accustomed to his lack of romance and displays of affection. David had plenty of other fine qualities.

'I'm a bit manky,' he said. 'I didn't get to have a shower in Singapore.' He left his bags where they were and strode down the hall, into their spacious open-plan living and dining area. 'Oh, wow, how much better does this place look with everything unpacked?' He folded his arms across his chest and slowly did a three-sixty degree turn, taking in the space, a smug, satisfied expression plastered across his face. 'Yum, something smells good.'

'I've got a lasagne in the oven. I thought you might be craving something home cooked.'

'Sounds perfect,' he said with a contented sigh. 'Do I have time for a quick shower?'

'Yep. No problem.'

★

Alice was just putting their plates heaped with lasagne and green salad on the table when David walked back in. She smiled at seeing his tousled dark hair and casual attire – loose track pants and t-shirt. She loved him in a suit too, but to Alice this was more her man, and a side no one at his work ever saw. David Green was the epitome of cool, calm, collected, controlled, and driven – and he dressed accordingly. Sometimes it seemed to Alice as if by putting on his suit David was putting on a costume and getting into character. She had always kept this thought to herself. David didn't like being made fun of, no matter how innocuous. Not that he didn't have a sense of humour. He did. But he was very ambitious and took his career, money and success very seriously. He'd worked hard to be able to afford this house – well, for the deposit, anyway.

They were staring down the barrel of thirty years of being tethered to the bank. Of course Alice had helped a little with the hefty deposit. She would have been happy with a small fixer-upper, but that didn't suit the image David was keen to project. Anyway, with him travelling all the time, when would it ever get done up? No, this place might not exactly be to her taste, but it was a sensible plan for their future. And oh how she loved no longer having to traipse from property to property all weekend, every weekend, and stand around at auctions being beaten by wealthy, cashed-up investors who were simply adding to their portfolios.

A little over a month ago, she'd been stunned when she realised they were the successful bidders for this place, so much so she'd stood there in silence for a moment wondering what had happened after the hammer had gone down. And then, instead of jumping up and down, Alice and David had stared at each other with their mouths open and eyes wide until real estate agents flanked them and clasped them each by an elbow and urged them towards the house to sign the papers.

Now, here they were, in for just over a week and boxes and all signs of moving out of sight. They were now able to properly breathe and settle into their new home. Alice was sure she'd grow to love it, find character in its new construction and clean, sharp lines, and bright white walls.

'So, tell me about your trip,' Alice said after they'd clinked glasses of wine and each taken a long, satisfied sip.

'Same old. Planes, meetings, hotel rooms, lunches, dinners, and not much else. How was your week? Hopefully more interesting than mine, though unpacking probably isn't so much fun. I hope you managed to rake up some hours for Todd.'

'I have some news on that front, actually. Look what Todd gave me today,' she said, taking a large envelope from the chair beside her and handing it to David. Todd was a friend of David's from uni – a few months ago he had given her a casual job doing some market research and cold-calling for the packaging firm where he was business development manager.

'What's this?' David asked, opening it up.

Alice didn't say a word while he extracted two A4 pages and slowly read them. After she and Todd had talked about the offer, Alice had left the CEO's office feeling as if she'd been given the opportunity of a lifetime, even if she wasn't all that excited about it. She'd felt flattered, which was a pleasant change after all the fruitless job hunting she'd done. But the more she thought about it, the less excited she became. Marketing for packaging? She'd rolled it around on her tongue several times, trying to muster some enthusiasm, and failed. If it were not for the fact Todd was a friend and would mention it to David in due course, if he hadn't already, she might have torn the offer up and pretended it had never existed. Anyway, what successful company took a risk on an unknown like Alice with such an important position as marketing?

'Oh wow. A permanent job. That's great,' David said, leaning over and kissing her. 'Phew, well, we certainly need this,' he added.

'Yeah,' Alice said, digging her fork into her meal.

'So why haven't you signed it yet? Or is this a copy?'

'No, that's the one I have to sign.'

David looked up at her over the document, clearly waiting for an explanation. She hated the way he could reduce her to feeling inadequate, even child-like with just that one look.

'Sorry, David, but I don't want to do it. I'm just not excited about it.' She shrugged.

'It's an amazing opportunity. Look at this, they're going to train you up in marketing and you could be national marketing manager in a year. Wow, Alice, that's huge!'

Yes, I have actually read it, Alice thought.

Why wasn't he getting it, hearing her? She wanted to scream with frustration. Instead she tried a different tack. 'It is a bit strange. I mean, I don't even have any marketing qualifications. That's a whole degree right there.' She really didn't want to disappoint him, but ...

'So? If they didn't think you were capable they wouldn't be making the offer. And we really do need the extra money. How do you know you won't grow to love it if you don't give it a chance?'

How else do I say it just doesn't float my boat?

'A challenge is a good thing,' he said, misreading her silence. 'Look how well you did at uni when to start with you didn't think you could do it. You've got to believe in yourself, Alice.'

'It's not that I don't think I could do it – with the appropriate training ...'

'So, what, then?'

'I've told you, it just doesn't interest me.' She hated how petty and ungrateful she sounded. But it was the truth. And why shouldn't she be honest with her partner, the man she loved?

'You can't keep waiting for a museum job, or whatever, to come up. It might never happen.'

He was right about that. And that it was an opportunity when she hadn't found anything else promising.

'And you can't stay at uni. We've discussed this,' he said, reading her mind, and let out a tired, exasperated sigh. He was right – again. What Alice really wanted to do was stay at university and do honours in History, despite not having settled on an area she really wanted to delve into in depth. She'd just loved university life, full stop. Being surrounded by books and knowledge and people passionate about learning, being encouraged to think for herself, and be analytical had really stretched Alice intellectually for the first time in her life. She'd realised she had an insatiable thirst for knowledge. She hadn't always found her studies easy, but she'd enjoyed being challenged and had discovered an energy and sense of determination she never knew she had. The three years at uni had been filled with moments of joy and excitement as well as hard work. Now it was over, and she was scared – well, terrified, actually. She really didn't want to disappoint David. But if she had to get a full-time job, she wanted one she was truly excited about – otherwise she figured she might as well go back to admin temping. Her eyes had been opened, her soul fired up, now she wanted more, to keep moving forward. In that sense, university had proven to be a double-edged sword.

David should understand that – after all, it was because of him that she'd embarked on her studies in the first place. He'd seen her change, watched as her wings had unfurled, all the time telling her how proud he was of her progress and achievements. Gradually Alice had begun to believe she could be more than a wife and mother in a small town in country South Australia, contrary to her mother's indoctrination.

Alice had met David in Adelaide, at a party held by a friend of a friend. Only a few weeks before, her marriage to farmer Rick had imploded. She'd fled Hope Springs, Rick, and her unsupportive mother, Dawn, and her sister, Olivia. Without her dear friend Ruth she might never have had the courage to leave the district. Ruth was a warm, loving mother figure to her, the opposite to Alice's own mother. She had organised for Alice to stay with her daughter Tracy in Adelaide while Alice tried to pull herself together and deal with two-fold heartbreak – the end of her marriage and losing her best friend of twenty-five years, Shannon, who'd let slip she'd slept with Alice's husband. Only the once, mind! And it really didn't mean anything – according to both Shannon and Rick. As if that made a difference!

In the days and weeks after finding out about the betrayal, Alice struggled with her anger and disappointment. She didn't know who had hurt her the most, then concluded that Shannon's actions were the more painful and their friendship was actually the bigger loss. Shannon and Alice had been best friends since meeting on their first day at kindergarten and were the last of their school group still living in the district. One by one their friends had left for a job, a relationship, to study or travel, or just to have a better or different life. Once a close group, these days their interactions were mainly confined to Facebook, email, or the odd text message.

After the experience with Shannon and Rick, Alice vowed never to let anyone get so close again. Ruth told her the pain would ease and to not let it change her generosity of spirit. Unfortunately Alice thought it probably already had. She came to understand first-hand the meaning of the saying 'Once bitten, twice shy'.

Alice hadn't planned to stay in Adelaide permanently – Hope Springs and its surrounds were all she'd ever known and thought she wanted.

The last thing on her mind when she met the alluring, friendly, confident and sophisticated David had been finding a new love interest, so instead of being coy or mysterious or flirty, she'd confided in him about what a mess her life had become.

When David suggested that going to university might be the answer, Alice had been taken aback. She'd never considered it before – she had only been an average student at school and had no burning career desires. She'd always thought she'd work alongside her dad in the family's corner shop and, being the elder sibling, eventually take over when the time was right. But soon after her father died, her mother had dropped a bombshell – the shop would go to the younger daughter. Olivia was always the golden child, and the chosen one now too. Alice had sought solace in an admin job at the largest business in town – an insurance brokerage. She loved her job, but was shocked when four years in she was let go in favour of the boss's teenage daughter, who had just returned from secretarial school in Adelaide.

David pointed out that a few years at university would give Alice time to sort herself out while having a focus, and she could see it made sense. When he added that she could afford to live in the city by working part-time in admin or temping, it became possible, and exciting. Over the weeks and months Alice slowly began to believe him and, more importantly, to believe in herself.

They were meant to just be friends, but it soon became physical, and gradually they seemed to form a stronger bond. When David announced he was moving to Melbourne, Alice was devastated. He'd become her rock. But then he suggested she could come too, if she wanted to. It wasn't a marriage proposal or declaration of together forever, or even love. He wasn't gushy or very emotive, but Alice didn't mind. David was dependable and supportive and was offering something completely different from her old life, and that was what mattered and appealed. She wasn't even sure she believed in true love anymore, certainly not happily ever after. Maybe she just needed time.

Alice made the big move to Melbourne with not much more than a few suitcases and a ten-year-old hatchback car, which she'd sold soon after. Now, nearly four years on, she felt so much bigger than Hope Springs – not better, but that she'd outgrown it – and only went back for significant events such as Christmas, weddings, funerals and milestone birthdays.

Having found her feet and discovering that she really loved to study, Alice had well and truly left behind her average student status and excelled academically. Being realistic, she knew she had to find a full-time job, and she wasn't sure she wanted to become an academic, but the extra year of study would surely help her prospects. Four months on from uni – not to mention just turning thirty – she still hadn't sorted out a proper career. She'd volunteered for a day a week at the National Trust head office in various departments and enjoyed every minute of it, but unfortunately there weren't any paid jobs going, especially for someone who didn't have a specialist area of expertise or post-graduate qualifications. She'd love to be in archiving, doing research, helping others with their research, or involved in writing policy, but she hadn't found any vacancies for jobs that came even remotely close to what interested her.

At her graduation a few weeks ago she'd felt quite sad when she realised that her university days were behind her and it was unlikely she'd ever be able to go back to study. She was almost on the verge of tears – not at all triumphant and excited like everyone else. It hadn't helped that none of her family had been prepared to make the trip from South Australia, especially as she was the first in her entire family – cousins included – to go to university, let alone graduate. Alice suspected her mother and sister's disinterest had more to do with jealousy or tall poppy syndrome than the inconvenience of travelling to Melbourne. It wasn't a secret that they thought Alice saw herself as high and mighty for leaving Hope Springs, and completely above herself for daring to study at university.

'Alice?' David prompted, his eyebrows raised.

'I know,' she said, her thoughts turning back to the offer letter on the table in front of her. Yes, she was being picky. But why shouldn't she want to do something she was at least a little excited about? *And what sort of a name for a business is Outercover? Even if it is packaging.*

'Well, you've got the weekend to think about it. But we can't afford for you to be too choosy. The salary is good. It's a good job.'

Alice stared down at her plate of food, her appetite having left her. David was right. He usually was. She needed to forget uni, and start being a proper adult and an active contributor to society, and their bank balance. Not that she hadn't been, but she thought she'd never have an income that would equal David's – even this 'good' salary was only around a third what he earned.

Okay, so come on, get excited about it. It's a great job. Be grateful, she told herself as she forcibly chewed a mouthful of pasta.

'Todd's nice and you said everyone else there seems nice too,' David added.

'Yes, they are.' And wasn't that a good enough reason on its own?

'Half of any job is the people,' David pointed out.

'You're right. I'll accept it on Monday,' she said, smiling as she stood up and started to load the dishwasher.

David smiled. 'All change is scary. You'll be right. You just have to push through it,' he said, drawing her to him and kissing her.

'I know,' she said quietly.

'I've got an idea. We should celebrate – the new job and the house – and I know exactly how.'

'How?' Alice said, brightening and looking up at him.

'Let's go to the pet store and get a dog. Now we don't have a landlord who doesn't like pets. And it'll be good training for us ...'

'Oh, wow. Really? You mean it?' Alice nearly skipped in excitement, but restrained herself.

'I don't say things I don't mean, Alice.'

Well, you do, actually. Quite often, Alice thought, but let it go.

'Can we go to one of the shelters instead?'

'Sure. Whatever you want,' he said, yawning. 'I'm knackered. I'm just going to check my emails and then have an early night.'

'Okay, I'll be in soon.' Alice smiled, properly this time. She was going to get her tablet out and look at what dogs were available for adoption. Something small but not one of the shrill, yappy breeds. They didn't want to bother their new neighbours with a barking dog when they were both at work all day. They didn't have much of a backyard but thankfully the park was only a few streets away.

LET'S TALK ABOUT BOOKS!

JOIN THE CONVERSATION

HARLEQUIN
AUSTRALIA

@HARLEQUINAUS

@HARLEQUINAUS

HQSTORIES

@HQSTORIES